THE SONG
OF THE
JADE LILY

THE SONG
OF THE
JADE LILY

A Novel

KIRSTY MANNING

WILLIAM MORROW
An Imprint of HarperCollinsPublishers

P.S.™ is a trademark of HarperCollins Publishers.

THE SONG OF THE JADE LILY. Copyright © 2019 by Osetra Pty Ltd. All rights reserved. Printed in the United States of America. No part of this book may be used or reproduced in any manner whatsoever without written permission except in the case of brief quotations embodied in critical articles and reviews. For information, address HarperCollins Publishers, 195 Broadway, New York, NY 10007.

HarperCollins books may be purchased for educational, business, or sales promotional use. For information, please email the Special Markets Department at SPsales@harpercollins.com.

Originally published as *The Jade Lily* in Australia in 2018 by Allen & Unwin.

FIRST U.S. EDITION.

Library of Congress Cataloging-in-Publication Data has been applied for.

ISBN 978-0-06-288201-1 (paperback)
ISBN 978-0-06-293865-7 (hardcover library edition)

20 21 22 23   10 9 8 7 6 5 4 3 2

To my parents, Richard and Carolyn,
who showed me that family is always home

Yes, the past is in the present, but the future is still in our hands.

Elie Wiesel, "Bearing Witness, 60 Years On,"
speech to the United Nations General Assembly, January 24, 2005

◇

Wheresoever you go, go with all your heart.

Confucius, 551–479 BCE

Prologue

This was the first time she had broken Papa's rules. Romy's throat tightened as she fingered the refugee pass in her jacket pocket and stepped closer to the ghetto's checkpoint. Her pass was to study at the university in Frenchtown, yet it was well past suppertime. She intended to make an infectious diseases evening class as an excuse and her textbook hung heavy in her satchel, the strap digging into her shoulder.

Romy held her breath as she stood before an expressionless Japanese soldier. She started to pull the textbook from her bag, but the young soldier sighed as he swatted a mosquito and nodded her through—he looked every bit as sweaty, tired, and bony as she did.

"Back before curfew," he barked. "Otherwise . . ." He sliced his finger across his neck.

Romy nodded, not trusting herself to speak.

Too scared to look back and too penniless to hail one of the pedicabs or rickshaws weaving between trolleybuses, she raced toward the Garden Bridge. The bag with the textbook thudded against her thigh. Romy wiped the sweat from her brow with the sleeve of her mother's jacket and tried to push all thoughts of her parents aside. They would have forbidden her from leaving the ghetto. The risk of being caught was too great, and after everything . . .

As she stepped onto the iron framework of Garden Bridge, smells from the sampans crowding Soochow Creek floated up. The warm air was thick with the scent of sewage and frying fish mingled with cardamom, cinnamon, and star anise. Families on tiny boats shouted and giggled. Rows of washing strung across beams flapped in the evening breeze and the clang of spoons hitting woks and pots rang deep into the evening.

As Romy reached the far end of the bridge, a hawker pulling dough into noodles gave her a toothless smile and asked, "You buy, missee?"

She shook her head. Romy's stomach ached—she'd had nothing except a watery bowl of congee that morning.

To avoid all thoughts of food, she spent the ten-minute walk trying to work out how to sneak into Shanghai's grandest hotel. Soon enough, she turned a corner and the Bund shimmered beside the black Whangpoo River. Romanesque-style banks and Renaissance-inspired office buildings leered over the pavement with Rising Sun flags dotted on their rooftops. She walked toward the art deco hotel lit up with an apple-green pyramid on the roof: the Cathay. Outside the revolving doors, Japanese soldiers laughed and lit cigarettes for lanky Russian whores with translucent skin, red lips, and silk dresses.

Romy inched past with her head down, careful not to make eye contact. She was thankful for her mother's dowdy brown suit. She was so close now . . .

Romy walked nervously into the Cathay's soaring atrium, making sure her heels didn't clatter on the mosaic tiles. The lobby was filled with staff in white pressed linen carrying magnums of champagne and silver trays of whisky. Japanese soldiers mingled with German, French, and Chinese couples, the men in white dinner jackets and the women with pastel feather boas threaded over their arms, diamond necklaces at their throats. These couples chatted with elegant Chinese ladies buttoned into cheongsams and low-backed lamé ball gowns. The women preened and smoothed their dresses as Romy overheard a waiter say in English, "Ladies and gentlemen, if you'll follow me, the show is about to start. I'll escort you to your tables."

Romy's eyes watered a little from the sting of smoke and cloying perfumes as she gazed at the roomful of silky decadence. She felt dizzy and frightened. But she was too close to back out now. The person she was so desperate to find—had risked her life for—was in that bar.

Romy was only a few steps away. A band started to play the opening chords of George Gershwin's "Summertime." Romy took a deep breath to calm her racing heart and followed the scent of smoke and whisky through the wooden door into the jazz bar.

No one must ever find out. They would *both* be killed.

Chapter 1

VIENNA, NOVEMBER 10, 1938

It was against Papa's newest rules to look up, but when Romy stared along Wipplingerstrasse, shards of glass dangled like broken teeth from heavy wooden frames. Pretty shop windows had turned into scary *Tatzelwurm* monsters overnight. The wide, grand street was a sea of dark coats—black, brown, navy, and gray—weaving desperately between ornate stone buildings.

None of the adults knew where to go.

Some were trying to sweep up glass. Crowds gathered and swirled, chattering, crying, and screaming. Black cars honked in the teeming street. Instead of waiting for their path to clear, some cars plowed into crowds without slowing, forcing people to leap out of the way.

With her father grasping one of her wrists and her mother the other, Romy was dragged through the chaos like a small child, though she was twelve. Still, she made no noise except for the glass crunching under her boots. She tried following Papa's rules, avoiding eye contact with any of the heads above the coats. Instead, she concentrated on the feet of her older brothers, Benjamin and Daniel, who walked an arm's length in front.

Romy glanced sideways from under her navy beret. The smashed and battered doors had scraps of paper pinned to them, flapping in the breeze.

WEHRT EUCH! KAUFT NICHT BEI JUDEN!

DEFEND YOURSELVES! DO NOT BUY FROM JEWS!

KEINE JUDEN!

NO JEWS!

There were twice as many signs as yesterday. "Why do they keep putting up these signs?"

Papa looked at her with tears in his eyes and shook his head without breaking his stride. "Herr Hitler hates Jews. I fear nothing will be the same while the Nazis are in charge of Austria."

"But I don't understand why the Führer hates us. Why—"

"This is not the place to talk," Papa said, cutting her off. "The streets aren't safe . . . Hurry. Remember the rules, Romy." Papa usually had an answer for everything, but today he looked as lost as Romy felt.

She stumbled on an overturned chair as Mutti tugged at her arm. The Bernfelds just needed to get home.

Three blocks behind them, all that remained of their synagogue were charred bricks, gray tiles, and still-burning wooden planks collapsed beneath the debris. The synagogue's library of rare books and manuscripts lay in a pile of smoldering cinders on the footpath.

They weaved between piles of rubbish. Romy coughed—her throat burned and her eyes stung. The air was heavy with the smell of smoke and gasoline and it hurt to breathe. She wished her parents would slow down. She had a nasty blister on her heel from her new patent leather boots, and her thick, double-breasted peacoat with the shiny gold buttons—such a treat last week—scratched her arms and rubbed the back of her neck.

From the corner of her eye Romy saw Papa pat the inside top pocket of his own coat, which bulged with their passports. They had walked miles to the British consulate to plead for visas.

"I studied at Oxford for my doctorate. I taught surgery in their hospital for a year. We all speak English. Does this mean nothing?" Papa had demanded.

The consular official with the mousy hair and gold pocket watch was apologetic. "We have our orders, I'm afraid, Dr. Bernfeld. Britain has strict immigration policies. There is a waiting list for visas. No exceptions. Not even for specialist skills." He swallowed and looked at his shoes as his ears turned pink. "America has the same rules. Even Palestine won't take any more boatloads at this moment, I hear. I'm terribly sorry . . ." He shrugged and raised his palms helplessly.

Papa nodded, put the passports back in his coat pocket, and turned away to grab his brown felt hat off the desk.

The official coughed. "You know," he said, "there is somewhere you don't *need* a visa." His voice dropped to a whisper as he leaned toward the family. "Shanghai. You . . ." He hesitated.

Mutti blanched and shook her head.

"It might be worth . . ." His voice faded.

Papa shook his head and muttered, "*Danke.*"

Romy thought Mutti was going to crush her hand as she whipped her out of the office, heels clip-clopping across the parquetry.

Mutti had barely slowed down since they had left the consulate, but as they approached Romy's favorite café she hoped they might stop for afternoon tea. She opened her mouth to ask, then remembered Papa's rules: *No speaking.*

As they marched past the café Romy peered in at the dark wooden bar and saw gentlemen in dark suits sipping their coffee and reading newspapers, ignoring the mess and chaos outside. She pictured herself and Mutti sitting at one of the small marble tables, a dainty coffee cup in front of Mutti and, for Romy, a dark hot chocolate piled high with cream. It was their ritual after her Saturday afternoon piano lessons. Romy suspected Herr Bloch tolerated half an hour every week out of loyalty to her brothers. Daniel played in a jazz band at his university and Benjamin had applied to study at the prestigious Wiener Staatsoper—the state opera—before the new government said he wasn't allowed. Last week her stumpy fingers had stretched themselves to a D-major arpeggio without stopping, plus passable opening bars of Mahler. Herr Bloch had applauded and said, "Bravo!"

As the Bernfelds approached Herr Bloch's piano shop through the bitter smoky haze, Romy strained to see the gleaming black baby grand perched in the window. Instead, twisted ebony piano legs dangled through broken glass.

"Look!" said Romy, pointing with alarm. Herr Bloch was being dragged out by his hair to join a handful of middle-aged men on their hands and knees, picking up the glass and scrubbing the street clean. A pair of blond soldiers threw Herr Bloch onto the ground, but as he righted himself the smaller of the two soldiers swung his military boot into his stomach and sent him sprawling onto his back.

"*Halt! Bitte hören Sie auf!*" Stop. Please stop!

Romy's head swiveled as Benjamin stepped off the footpath and reached out to help Herr Bloch sit up. Papa cursed as Daniel followed his older brother. Romy held her breath as Mutti squeezed her hand. The boys were going to be in big, big trouble when they got home.

One of the soldiers walked over to Benjamin and Romy stiffened, then relaxed as she recognized him; it was Franz, a baritone from

Benjamin's choir. There was obviously a misunderstanding with the music teacher and Benjamin would be able to sort it out with his friend. But when Franz looked across at Benjamin the smile didn't reach his eyes. Nor did he greet him with a handshake. Instead, the soldier flipped his long rifle upside down and whacked Benjamin in the head with the butt.

Years later—when she was an old woman—Romy would still be trying to forget what happened next, but the memory was seared into her brain.

Benjamin and Herr Bloch were knocked sideways onto the cobblestones. Blood dripped from their ears, down their chins. Mutti let out a high-pitched scream and all around them the crowd fell silent. Romy's breaths were shallow, filled with the smell of sweat, smoke, piss, and fear, as the soldier lifted his rifle to his shoulder.

A shot.

"Benjamin!" Romy's skin turned cold and clammy as part of Benjamin's forehead and ear exploded. Warm blood splattered her face. She moaned.

Another shot.

Herr Bloch's limp body fell onto the cobblestones.

Beside her, Mutti collapsed to the ground. Daniel lunged forward to run to Benjamin but was grabbed around the neck by Franz.

Romy stood frozen. Her brother—was he—?

Benjamin was dead.

Papa was howling like a wolf as he tried to claw his way through the crowd to reach his sons, but he was held back by a wall of shoulders. There was a crack in the air, more rifles fired, and this time everyone crashed to the footpath. Romy felt her knee grind into a shard of glass and let out a cry.

A hand pulled her out from under the person sprawled half on top of her, and she crawled across to a freezing stone wall between shopfronts and leaned against it.

Papa was on his haunches, cradling his head in his hands. Mutti was trying to sit up but was having trouble breathing. Romy remained still. Empty and in shock.

She held her breath as the soldiers lined up all the young men in the middle of the street.

Romy began to cry. Surely they weren't going to shoot Daniel too?

The leader waved his arm, and three covered trucks pulled forward and all the young men—including Daniel—were instructed to climb in. As Daniel clambered onto the truck, he looked over his shoulder at Mutti and Papa, his eyes full of fear.

"Daniel!" Mutti screamed.

Papa reached for Daniel, but all at once their neighbor Herr Gruber was charging through the crowd toward them. His face was drawn and pale as he put both his hands on Papa's shoulders.

"You must go, Oskar. Now! For Romy and Marta. They will kill you too. Leave Vienna. Austria has lost her mind."

Papa shook his head. "I—Benjamin. Daniel. My boys . . ." His voice was cracked and broken. "I won't leave them," he croaked. "I—I can't." He bowed his head and began to sob as, around them, people started to help each other up. Some avoided looking at Papa, as if his misfortune might infect them, while others shared teary glances filled with sympathy.

Mutti crawled toward Papa and they huddled together, sobbing and rocking back and forth.

Herr Gruber bent down. "Let me help you," he whispered. "You *must* get over the border. We should leave at once."

Romy's skin was clammy and her heart was beating too fast. Her knees throbbed where they had been cut. She felt faint. Then darkness . . .

◇

When Romy awoke, her face was buried in Papa's neck as he carried her along Wipplingerstrasse. Her mother—ashen-faced—walked close behind them, a protective hand on Romy's shoulder. Her head throbbed with each of Papa's steps. *Crunch, crunch, crunch.* Were they going home or leaving?

Romy peered over her father's shoulder. It was evening now, and a flickering yellow horseshoe was lit up by one of the few unbroken lights in the street. A faded picture of a chimney sweep dangled over the awning. Beneath it—in cheery green and red letters—*Geh nicht am glück vorbei.*

Don't let luck pass you by.

Chapter 2

MELBOURNE, APRIL 9, 2016

Alexandra smiled and nodded at the palliative care nurse Sally—who was busy writing on charts—as she tiptoed into Oma and Opa's grand sitting room. She caught a whiff of something woody; it was vaguely familiar but she couldn't quite place the smell.

Opa was propped up in a hospital bed. When she'd arrived home last night Alexandra hadn't recognized this withered man with the sallow face. The rhythmic whistle of the oxygen machine and the tiny beep of the heart monitor screen filled every corner of the room, nearly drowning out the tick of the mahogany grandfather clock.

Alexandra stared at walls of screens all day, watching for the faintest nudge in the graph—a variation—that told her to swoop on gold in Shanghai at breakfast and trade it in London by lunch. She spent eighteen-hour days under fluorescent lights searching for volatility. Hunting numbers. Alexandra didn't need to study the beeping screen to know her beloved *opa*'s number was up. She'd been home for twelve hours but she was yet to see him conscious.

She shuddered. Perhaps she was too late?

Alexandra sank into the cushions of the old peacock-blue armchair by the fireplace and traced the curve of the arms, circling the rough patches. Burlap stuffing poked through threadbare velvet and the springs had gone in the base. She shivered and sneezed—so typical of her to pick up a bug in transit. She rubbed her cheek on a cushion. So many hours spent in this very chair snuggled onto Oma or Opa's lap for Aesop's fables and Grimm's fairy tales and—as a teenager—curled up with a textbook, practicing endless algebra and algorithms with a lead pencil.

The house—Puyuan—was a redbrick Edwardian nestled behind a picket fence weighed down with pale pink climbing roses. Wisteria scrambled up the veranda posts and dangled from the iron lace trim, its blue flowers spent. Oma's sitting room, with the bay window overlooking her precious garden, had lost none of its grandeur with age, though paint peeled from the deep gray-blue walls and wide baseboards, and the large cream plaster ceiling rose could do with patching. The floor-to-ceiling bookshelves on the far wall were spilling over with books on herbs, Chinese medicine, history, and photography. Crammed between books at every angle were political memoirs, British thrillers—le Carré, Forsyth—and five decades of French *Vogue*.

Alexandra gulped back tears as she replayed her hurried departure from London. She'd left her Sloane Street apartment for Heathrow and was on a flight to Melbourne within hours of Oma calling to say the tumors had come back and spread into Opa's organs, bones, and bloodstream. Her grandmother's voice had lost its customary calm. Instead Alexandra could hear the deep, low tones of sadness and resignation.

When she'd finally emerged from customs in Melbourne twenty-four hours later, Oma and her friend Nina were standing with their shoulders pressed together in the arrivals hall, one dark and wiry, the other broad and soft. Alexandra allowed herself to be swallowed by their hugs, closing her eyes and breathing in traces of gardenia from her *oma*'s neat bun and the smell of fried garlic and smoked paprika that always accompanied Nina's kisses.

"*Danke* for coming so quickly. I know with the move . . ." Oma's voice had a new quiver.

"Oh!" Alexandra leaned down to press her cheek against her grandmother's as she stumbled over her suitcase. "Opa—is he still . . . ?"

Her grandmother lifted a tissue and dabbed her eyes as she nodded. "He's waiting."

Nina laid a gentle hand on Alexandra's shoulder. "Your *opa*'s still conscious. Just. He's been asking for you. Come. I'll take your bags." Nina wrenched the cart from Alexandra's grip with surprising force for a nonagenarian, insisting on pushing her bags.

Alexandra threaded her arm through her grandmother's and asked quietly, "And you, Oma? How're you? It must be hard."

"I'm fine, *Liebling*. All the better for seeing you," said Oma.

◇

Alexandra shifted in the old chair as her Samsung vibrated in her back pocket and she pulled it out. Another text from Hugo: *Call me back. I'm sorry A.*

She deleted the message, resisting the urge to put a permanent block on her ex's number. She wasn't prepared to forgive him, but there was a tiny part of her that didn't want to say goodbye. She was an expert in analyzing risk, predicting outcomes, but she had failed to see how exposed her own heart was.

Never again.

She slid the phone back into her pocket without so much as a glance at spot prices on Bloomberg. The market could wait.

She stood and threaded her fingers through Opa's and squeezed gently, as if she could send some of her own energy surging through their joined hands. Oma would say she was channeling her *qi*. Alexandra grinned; perhaps the apple didn't fall so far from the tree after all.

"Li . . . Sophia?" Opa rasped as Alexandra crouched beside him. He reached up and tried to touch her jade pendant. She shivered and cleared her throat.

She glanced over at the photo of her parents on the marble mantelpiece above the fireplace. Once she'd been a smiling, clapping toddler with glossy hair, dressed in crimson overalls and a stripy turtleneck as she sat on her mother's knee. Her father, Joseph, tall, broad, and fair, stood to the side with a hand resting on Sophia's shoulder. Her mother was wearing a blue denim sundress with a strap falling from a tanned shoulder, the jade pendant nestled at the top of her cleavage, and she was laughing with Joseph, gazing into his blue eyes. Alexandra's stomach clenched as she stared at the photo, trying to remember this fierce love. It was her sole memory of her parents.

Opa barely mentioned Sophia to Alexandra by name. Oma merely shook her head and smiled when she spoke of "her gift." Their clever child adopted from China. Cherished. Like Alexandra.

Opa strained forward, peering to get a closer look at her face.

"Li?" he repeated.

"Opa, it's Alexandra," she said, stroking his cool hand with her thumb, noticing how spindly it had become. His muscles had wasted away, and with them his strength and his memory. Alexandra had never heard either of her grandparents mention a Li.

"Oh." His head dropped to the pillow with a weak smile. Then, confusion. "Your job in Shanghai?" he asked faintly.

She paused. Was he lucid? "Shanghai can wait," replied Alexandra as she adjusted the drip line so she could perch on the edge of the bed. She could hardly tell him she'd delayed her transfer to Shanghai to spend as much time with him before—

She blinked away tears.

"Shanghai waits for no one, my dear child." He patted her hand and pushed out a deep belly chuckle, followed by a coughing fit. Between coughs he said, "You should—" More coughing. "Li. You won't find her . . . You look so like her, you know."

Like who? Alexandra wondered. Did he mean her mother? Her heart sank. Her grandmother had warned her Opa was not making any sense. He'd forgotten her parents were long dead, killed in a car accident just weeks after the photo on the mantelpiece was taken. Alexandra was pulled from the wreckage by a paramedic, the back of her head sliced open like a peach. She traced the smooth scar at the nape of her neck, hidden by long hair. Some days it burned and puckered when she touched it, but most days she felt nothing. It was a grafted void.

As her eyes clouded with tears, she looked up at the blurry crystal chandelier and watched the rainbow of light swim across the ceiling and wall. This gray-blue room was home. Her grandparents were her anchor. And now she was losing her *opa*. She squeezed his hand again and rubbed his other arm, trying to warm his skin and ease his pain.

Opa spluttered and wheezed. "The spitting image. Your grandmother . . ."

"Shhh," said Alexandra as she looked to the nurse for help.

"Your grandmother—Romy." Cough. "She was the strongest of us all. The three of us—"

More coughs. Opa's shoulders shook so hard Alexandra thought he might burst a lung.

The nurse jumped up and came over to rub Opa's back as he continued hacking. Alexandra stepped aside to give Sally room. "Can we give him something?" she asked helplessly. "Water, medicine?"

The nurse ignored her, focusing on her patient. "There, there, Mr. Cohen—Wilhelm. Nice deep breaths . . ."

"I'll fetch Oma," said Alexandra, glancing out the window to where her grandmother was gardening.

"No need, love. It will pass in a sec. Besides, she'll only get her smoke going, or stick some more needles in his ankles. None of it helps much. Not at this stage."

Alexandra's head thudded as she realized what the smell lingering in the room was: moxa. Alexandra pictured Oma waving dried sticks of Chinese mugwort over Opa's head, under his nose, then lighting the ends for an instant before blowing the smoke softly and pressing it straight onto pressure points on his ankles, wrists, and neck. She giggled just a little—no wonder Sally was bewildered.

Sally raised an eyebrow at her and bustled over to the other side of the bed to tap the drip. "Hydration and morphine. Your grandfather's on the good gear—aren't you, Wilhelm?" The nurse articulated her words slowly and clearly as if Opa were in nursery school.

"Opa . . . will he?" Alexandra hesitated. "This coughing—do the drugs actually stop the pain?"

"They certainly do. We're doing everything we can to make sure he's comfortable."

"Is there any possibility . . . I mean, this cancer . . ." She looked at Opa, who had lapsed into unconsciousness once more.

Sally shook her head. "I'm sorry, love. But he knows you're here. Apple of his eye, you are. Talks about you nonstop."

The nurse rolled Opa gently onto his side without waking him. She looked back over at Alexandra: "So you just arrived from

London? You must be jet-lagged. I hear it's shocking this way, coming home." The nurse was friendly and businesslike—rubbing Wilhelm's back as she spoke to Alexandra.

Alexandra nodded. Her legs ached and her body felt like she'd been run over by a truck. Last night she'd stepped off the kangaroo-hop flight clammy with a cold and a barking cough despite using the nasal saline spray with a hint of eucalyptus she'd picked up from the pharmacy in departures. The smell made her homesick. But it turned out a whole ocean up her nose couldn't stem this cold. No sooner had the taxi pulled into the driveway than Oma rushed Alexandra straight into a deep warm bath sprinkled with cinnamon. The steamy bathroom smelled like Christmas. Alexandra smiled to herself as she absentmindedly rubbed her jade pendant. Opa might be dying, but Oma still fussed over Alexandra. Some things never changed.

"Your grandmother tells me you're some kind of financial bigwig over there in London." Sally eyed Alexandra's navy Stella McCartney yoga pants and gold-trimmed hoodie. "Sounds very flash." She grinned.

Alexandra shrugged. "Not really. I trade commodities. Precious metals. Copper, gold, zinc, nickel, aluminum . . . but mostly I just trade paper," she joked.

"I see," said Sally, looking momentarily confused before breaking into a shy smile. "I guess you'll never have to worry about topping up your retirement pension."

Alexandra was too embarrassed to respond—her job seemed pointless today. As she watched Sally soothe her *opa*, rearranging the white sheets around his legs and up under his arms so he wasn't irritated by the scratchy hems, it seemed to her that Sally was the gold in this room.

"There you go, Wilhelm. Just have a little rest for a minute or two and then you can have a catch-up with your granddaughter. Gorgeous creature, she is." The nurse winked and picked up a thriller sitting on a chair in the far corner.

Alexandra sat back down in her comfy chair and pulled a woolen throw over her legs, wishing she could roll back the years. She didn't want Opa to go. Not yet. Not ever. But she hated seeing him like this.

She picked up the soup Oma had made her before ducking out into the garden. It was still warm. She held the cup in her hands for a heartbeat before taking a sip and savoring the familiar rush down her throat, heating her stomach. It was the taste of her childhood colds: dried black bean paste with crushed garlic, ginger, and chives.

Alexandra shifted her gaze back to the window and watched as Oma wandered around her vegetable garden chomping on a green bean. Along the back fence was a thick bay hedge. In the middle of a blanket of thyme stood a row of trees. A gnarly Meyer lemon, limes, and a tiny gingko. These were underplanted with waves of lilies, budding peony stems, and purple clouds of flowering garlic and chives floating among blue monkshood.

Alexandra had missed the chaotic color and whimsical combinations of Puyuan's garden. When was the last time she'd had her fingers in soil? She stretched out her manicured hands. They were so smooth—as if they belonged to someone else. As a child, Alexandra had loved to work alongside Oma and Opa in the garden and the kitchen, climbing the old oak tree, shelling peas, staking tomatoes and cramming her mouth with the tiny ones before they popped and sprayed down the front of her T-shirt.

She took another sip of soup and felt the ginger warm her throat.

Oma's silver hair bobbed among the long rows of tomatoes. The staked rows were about the same height as her grandmother. Oma plucked the leftover red-and-green tiger tomatoes from the vines, not stopping until she'd filled the wicker basket slung over her forearm. Then she picked handfuls of the purple and deep green basil huddled under the tomatoes. Alexandra's stomach rumbled as she realized Oma was out picking lunch.

Alexandra closed her eyes and listened to the rhythm of the oxygen machine, beeping monitor, and grandfather clock. Then she prayed.

Chapter 3

When she'd finished in the garden, Romy walked into the kitchen, dropped her basket onto the wooden bench. She popped two tiny red tomatoes into her mouth; they were still warm from the autumn sun, and the sweet juice and seeds exploded, filling her cheeks.

She had mountains of coriander, so she put the leaves and stems into the blender with a glug of olive oil, a handful of almonds, three cloves of garlic, and the juice of half a lemon to make pesto for today's lunch. Alexandra certainly looked like she could do with a good feed, and the coriander would be a bit of a wake-up call for her system—helping to fight any bugs still lurking from the flight. Any leftover paste could go in the freezer.

Romy found she was eating less and less these days, so she pulled the curly green leaves of bok choy out of the basket and gave them a rinse, leaving them in the colander to dry. Just before it was time to eat, she'd steam the leaves and make a dressing of basil oil, chili, Sichuan pepper, and a dash of maple syrup. She'd have a small bowl of greens, instead of the pumpkin and water chestnut risotto left over from the night before.

Nina had joined them for dinner after they'd arrived home from the airport, helping herself to a second serving of the risotto. Some things never changed.

"Is this pumpkin from your garden, Oma?" Alexandra had asked, clearly trying to be bright and cheery as she divided her meal into neat piles on her plate.

"Yes. It'll strengthen your spleen and rebuild your *qi*. The thyme is good for your lungs."

Nina rolled her eyes at Alexandra in solidarity.

"Well," Nina exclaimed in her cutting Austrian accent, "you're fortunate you missed the sautéed lamb kidneys your grandmother forced on me last week. Dished up with orchid stems and shiitake mushrooms." She winked.

"It's good for your lower back and knee pains," Romy protested. "Good for longevity. Look at you—strong as an ox." She marveled at her friend's golden skin, full blond bob, and one of her endless parade of sequined kaftans.

"*Ach*," said Nina, "perhaps it gave me more energy. It certainly gave me more"—she paused as she hunted for the right word—"vigor? Ardor? Old Mr. Thompson from my book club certainly appreciated it. I gave him my best Anaïs Nina."

Nina shimmied her broad shoulders and chuckled as Romy narrowed her eyes and shook her head, exasperated.

Alexandra choked on a piece of pumpkin.

"They're going to throw you out of your apartment in the retirement village if you keep up that sort of carrying on," Romy said sternly. "What about the warning letter last week?"

"Psscht. We're old. Not dead."

The women fell silent. For some minutes, the only sound was the clatter of forks against blue china bowls.

Then Nina reached out and took a hand of each of the other women. She lifted them both to her mouth and kissed first Romy's, then Alexandra's. "Sorry. It was thoughtless of me to make such a joke. I'm here. Lean on me, okay?"

She sighed and looked at Romy, her serious brown eyes pleading. "It's my turn."

Romy ran her hands over the fresh mint leaves and raised them to her face to take the scent deep into her lungs. She'd brew up some to help with her granddaughter's sore throat.

She was worried about Alexandra. The minute she set eyes on her in the arrivals hall—the dark rings under her eyes, gaunt cheeks, hunched shoulders—Romy thought of her own mother standing at Brenner station, icy winds stinging her cheeks. Fleeing Austria to begin a new life in Shanghai.

Bereft.

What was Alexandra fleeing? There was the breakup, of course. She'd always felt Hugo and Alexandra were two lonely souls who had lashed themselves together like a hastily constructed life raft. Romy always wondered if Alexandra chose Hugo not so much for his mathematical wizardry and companionship, but because she was simply tired of being alone.

Nina, bless her, had noticed too, raising her eyebrows behind the girl's back as they'd loaded her bags into the taxi the night before.

There was pressure, of course, being the only child. Romy's time in Shanghai weighed heavily on her. The need to be *enough* for both parents. It was a burden Romy had always tried to hide.

But here she was—their only grandchild—home in time to watch her cherished grandfather die. Wilhelm and Alexandra had always been quite the twosome over the years, playing tennis, poring over spreadsheets, swapping stock market tips.

Romy had made a point of loosening the ties of their circle of three and was accepting when Alexandra chose to pursue study, career, and then love overseas. Yet it was hard to watch her move so far away.

But time had a way of pulling back the past. The family—the life Romy and Wilhelm had created in this vast, baking, lucky country—was about to end.

Romy wiped the tears from her eyes, raised her arms, and stretched her back, taking in the smell of herbs filling the kitchen.

What was going on with Alexandra? Her usually glossy hair was limp, dull, and there was a tinny optimism, a false bravado, to her smile. Her brown eyes flickered to one side when she spoke, and there was a constant twitch to her legs. She had a cold, yes, but this was something else. A dangerous energy was flooding her robust body.

A lifetime of burying her own uncertainties had taught Romy to recognize the signs.

Chapter 4

Romy tugged the collar of her blue coat so it sat high at the nape of her neck. She was too frightened to take it off. Not until they were out of Austria. Beside her, Mutti and Papa shifted in their second-class seats as their narrow carriage rolled on its tracks through the tight turns of the Brenner Pass. When they had reached the Brenner *Bahnhof*, Papa had instructed Romy to pull her hat low, hold his hand, and not make a peep as they quickly changed trains for Italy. *She must follow the rules.*

Mutti laid a reassuring gloved hand on her daughter's leg to stop her swinging it and kicking the seat in front. Romy was frustrated and fidgety after sitting for six hours with nothing but a slice of beef sausage, a bread roll, and half a hard-boiled egg passed back by the kindly old lady with the eye patch from the seat in front. She leaned against the glass to look out the window and catch a better view of the mountains.

She'd never been this far south and Romy wanted to remember every second. The gray sky was filled with swirling snowflakes and the mountains were covered with pine forests. They shot up so steeply Romy couldn't see the peaks, not even when she pressed her cheek to the icy window and tilted her head to look up. She'd always dreamed this narrow pass would be magical—like something out of her fairy-tale books. With each click of the track, black shadows appeared and disappeared. Her numb ear pressed hard against the window and the jagged mountains seemed to hiss, *You can't come in here.* The countryside of her dreams was cold and forbidding. She felt lost.

The engine bellowed and huffed as it pulled the carriages along the tracks, through the snow. Forests gave way to hamlets dotted with small stone houses as they crept closer to the Italian border. The carriage, which had been full of nervous chatter for the past few hours, fell silent as the brakes started to squeal on the wet tracks.

When Romy was pretending to sleep with her cheek on her mother's soft brown woolen suit, she had heard the adults' desperate whispers, as fluttery as the snowflakes. *Would they be allowed to cross into Italy?*

The night after Benjamin was killed and Daniel was taken away, Herr Gruber had forced himself through the queues and chaotic crowds to the gates of the Chinese consulate. The gates were guarded by half a dozen Wehrmacht soldiers, but their friend heard a rumor that the Chinese diplomat Feng Shan Ho was issuing visas under the bistro table at a café next door as he took his afternoon coffee. Alas, the café was closed for the evening, but as he was leaving Herr Gruber saw a black consular vehicle approaching the gates. Taking a risk, he thrust the Bernfelds' passports through the open window of the car. Feng Shan Ho stopped the car and took the papers with a tip of his hat. No words were exchanged lest the soldiers overhear. The next day at noon, as he took his black tea, Feng Shan Ho slipped a yellow diplomatic envelope under the bistro table to Herr Gruber.

Three days after Kristallnacht—the night of the broken glass—
Mutti had told Romy they were going to Italy to catch a boat to the
other side of the world. To China. Though it was rumored you didn't
need a visa to enter Shanghai, Herr Gruber insisted the Bernfelds
get visas—just in case there were problems crossing borders. They'd
sail back just as soon as the Führer no longer governed Austria. Or,
when Daniel joined them, they would apply to move to America.
Because who wanted to return to a country that had told them they
were less than nothing?

"It will be soon," Papa promised. "Now that the world knows
about Kristallnacht, they will put a stop to this madness." But Papa's
voice had lifted with uncertainty.

The night Herr Gruber brought the Chinese visas, he had
instructed them to pack two small suitcases of practical clothes.
Thick shoes. Best coats.

"Take ten Reichsmarks only in your wallet," he'd instructed Papa.

"Ten?" Papa objected. "That will not even buy the coffee and
some plum jam *Liwanzen* at the station." He tickled Romy under
the chin but his smile was forced. "They will have us leave Austria
like beggars? After all we have done? Why—"

"Hitler is a fool," Herr Gruber interrupted. "No one will take
Reichsmarks. They're worthless. Take my camera and sell it in
Shanghai."

Papa shook his head. "You could be shot for helping Jews. You
should come with us."

"My place is here. I need to keep the school running. The children
didn't start this war."

"You're a good man." Mutti paused in her sewing and turned a
tearstained face to their neighbor. "Herr Gruber, why would you
risk yourself to help us?"

"We all bleed the same color, Frau Bernfeld." The teacher blushed as if he realized too late the memories his words might summon. Benjamin . . .

Romy watched Mutti concentrate fiercely on each stitch as she sewed her grandmother's pearl necklace and her own diamond engagement ring into the lining of the collar of Romy's coat.

Herr Gruber turned and patted Romy on the head. "Your daughter has always been a good student. Like her brothers." He paused. "You need a valid ticket to leave Germany—proof of a destination. I'll go purchase your first-class tickets for the next boat from Genoa."

"That's too extravagant . . ." Papa raised his hands in the air, then dropped them, exhausted.

Herr Gruber reached over and gently squeezed Papa's hand. "Trust me. It's the only way. You can convert your tickets at the port in Italy, cash them in for second or third class before you board. You can't get money out of Austria. You'll get caught and it will be confiscated. You'll be punished . . ."

Mutti touched a gold button on Romy's coat and whispered a prayer.

Daniel had been transported to a concentration camp at Dachau, Herr Gruber had discovered. Herr Gruber wasn't entirely sure what work Daniel had been assigned, but said he would do his best to find out. He had contacts in Germany, and it might be possible to get some release papers using the Chinese visa once the Bernfelds had reached Shanghai.

Mutti's eyes had flickered with hope, before dimming like a broken lamp.

The train's steam whistle blew and the train shuddered, and Romy rocked against her parents as they pulled into Brenner station. The carriage doors were flung open and several Wehrmacht guards with guns invaded the cabin and stood in the aisle, ordering all the passengers off. Papa reached for their suitcases and, petrified, Romy tugged at her collar.

Mutti shot her a quick reassuring look and narrowed her eyes as if to say, *Don't touch*. A guard shoved Papa in the back with a gun as he stumbled onto the platform, following the crowd to the next platform where the smaller train for Italy sat with the engine running.

A guard yelled, "*Juden. Emigranten. Da drüben.*" Jews. Emigrants. Over there.

Papa ushered Romy and Mutti away from the queues for customs to where a nervous circle of weary passengers stood shivering, despite their fur coats and leather gloves. They all had their felt hats pulled low, as if trying to make themselves inconspicuous.

The rest of the train's passengers had their passports inspected and stamped, but the circle of Jewish passengers were surrounded by more guards with guns and ushered away from the train.

The remaining passengers—those without a large red *J* stamped on their passport—clambered onto the waiting train with their luggage, casting furtive looks over their shoulders. Some appeared cold and defiant, others apologetic. The engine blew three deep whistles before chugging away from the platform and into Italy.

A man with a gray beard and a narrow face yelled out to one of the soldiers: "Stop! What about our tickets?"

He was answered with a swift knock in the back of his head with the butt of a rifle. He fell to the ground, unconscious. The guard who had hit him took the man's suitcase and threw it to another guard, who took it inside the station.

"Anyone else have questions?" The guard smirked. "Line up your suitcases on the platform and open them—*now!*" he barked.

Papa placed their two small leather suitcases on the platform and flicked open the lids, baring Mutti's silk petticoat and three pastel cashmere sweaters. Mutti tucked Romy under her arm, like a hen with her chick, and Romy could feel the individual pearls pressing into her neck. The guards rummaged through each suitcase, tossing out silver candlesticks, jewelry, cutlery, and any other valuable that could be sold or melted down. The bitter wind roared up the valley pass, stinging their cheeks.

Shivering, Romy looked through the white lace curtains into the platform café where a fire burned in a neat black hearth, making the apricot walls glow with warmth. There were round marble tables just like in the café on Wipplingerstrasse. She longed for a hot chocolate. Would they be allowed to go inside to get out of the icy wind when the inspection was over? She groaned as she spotted the sign on the door.

JUDEN VERBOTEN. Jews forbidden.

Her stomach gurgled and her mother tugged her closer.

They were poking through Papa's suitcase. A watch, a stethoscope, and Papa's gold-and-black fountain pen—a gift from the medicine department in Oxford—were extracted. His medical textbooks were ignored. Papa pursed his lips but said nothing. Romy swayed on her feet. Why weren't they allowed to sit on the wooden benches under the station signs? It was so unfair. The next gust of icy wind threatened to knock her over.

"Close them." The guards pointed at the suitcases and everyone rushed over to reclaim their own.

"Place your suitcase in front of you and stand up straight until the next train." The guard raised his voice as he pointed his index finger at the straggly line of weary travelers. "Do not move. Do not sit down."

Romy crossed her legs; now she needed to pee.

The guard looked at his watch. "The next train to Genoa will be in exactly three hours and fourteen minutes. If you Jews"—he paused to spit before continuing—"so much as blink in the wrong direction, then you will not board that train. Have I made myself clear?"

"Yes, sir."

Papa spoke clearly and looked the guard in the eye.

The man raised his arm and shouted, "*Heil* Hitler!"

"*Heil* Hitler!" the other guards repeated with a stomp of their black boots as they saluted in return. Then they swiveled on their heels and marched down the platform in neat pairs into the café.

As the door to the coffee shop swung open, the scent of baked apple, cinnamon, and coffee wafted across to the passengers before being whipped away by the wind.

Romy tried to stand perfectly still by focusing on a single spot. It was a trick she'd learned at ski school when they were learning to balance on one leg. She stared hard at a sodden brown leaf being lifted and tossed against the iron track. As she concentrated, she felt a warm trickle slide down the inside of her stockings. But she didn't even flinch.

Chapter 5

SHANGHAI, FEBRUARY 5, 1939

Romy stood gripping the dark handrail of the SS *Conte Verde* as they entered the Yangtze River; the choppy brown river would lead them to their new home in Shanghai. Mutti stood beside Romy, pale-faced and lost inside her elegant camel coat. Underneath the coat, the waist of Mutti's pleated brown skirt sagged on her hips. She turned and forced a smile at Romy. Pressed against her left shoulder, Papa stood grim-faced, hunched over the rail in his double-breasted herringbone coat, felt hat pulled low over patches of hair that had turned white in the month they had been at sea.

Papa reached out and squeezed Romy's shoulder, leaning down close to whisper in her ear: "Be brave, my *Liebling*. We'll write to Daniel and he will join us soon enough."

That morning, the luxurious ocean liner *Conte Verde* had left the endless expanse of blue sea after four weeks. For the most part, the passage had felt like a holiday cruise, and Romy and her new friend Nina spent hours exploring every corner of the ship: card games in the women's parlors, watercolor classes and book salons in the palm-cushioned tearooms, beauty lounges where women read magazines and had their hair set high and lips painted red for formal dinners, a dark-paneled whisky lounge for the gentlemen after dinner. When the ship reached the equator and the almost unbearable thick treacly heat of the ports of Bombay, Colombo, and Singapore, the children spent the days on board swimming and splashing in the pools, shrieking and whooping as their mothers sipped sodas or cocktails, served with mint and lemon on silver trays by friendly Italian waiters in white gloves.

Now, the *Conte Verde*'s bow was slowly nudging its way along a murky river with the texture of goulash. There were more than five hundred passengers aboard and it seemed most were crowded onto the trio of top decks. Necks straining, mouths open in disbelief.

Sharp salty air had been replaced with smoke, filth, and the unfamiliar cooking smells of fish and meat. Some passengers held handkerchiefs over their mouths, others wiped tears from their eyes. With each chug of the engine, Romy felt a pang in her stomach. As the unfamiliar smells settled in her hair and over her collar, she gulped down her losses, her fear and uncertainty, to concentrate on her new surroundings.

All along the shoreline were flat fields, with terraces carved into distant hills. The countryside was so unlike the neatly fenced slopes of Austria that Romy didn't know what to make of it. Every now and again the layers of lurid green were interrupted by a cluster of factories coughing dirty smoke into the sky. Surrounded by these larger industrial buildings were funny little brown houses with dark roof tiles that curled up like waves at the edges. Mutti put her arm around Romy, pulling her close with a long sigh. Romy had to agree: this countryside was the strangest sight.

"Rice paddies," said Papa as he pointed to the shore. He turned and gave Romy an encouraging smile. "I have a feeling we'll be eating quite a bit of rice while we're here."

Romy bent over the rail to get a closer look as the ocean liner forged its way up the river. Every spare patch of water was filled with tiny wooden boats, red and cream wing-shaped sails flapping as they crisscrossed the river. Some boats just managed to skim in front of the *Conte Verde*'s bow, causing the captain to lean on the foghorn in frustration. One boat that sailed past was so loaded up with barrels it looked like it might sink at any moment. Another had its open deck piled with green melons, the next had rolls of fabric lined up as if it were a tailor's shop. Other boats carried brown burlap sacks of glossy rice, tiny pearls that winked and caught the light.

Romy heard crying and looked down at a little wooden sailboat with a crimson sail skimming the waves at the bow. A squawking toddler with red cheeks was strapped to his mother's chest. The child grabbed a handful of navy fabric and pulled it aside to expose her breast. Romy couldn't help but stare; she'd never seen a bare breast before. The toddler opened his mouth wide as if he were going to bite the nipple right off, before using a hand to nudge the dark purple circle into his mouth. He tucked his head under his mother's chin, and she rested her head on top of his, stroking his back and wrapping her arms around him to protect the child from the bitter breeze. Between both sails was a line of washing, rags hanging from a line.

"Orientals. No better than animals."

Romy jumped with fright. The German first mate stood behind her in his freshly pressed white uniform, chiseled jaw clenched with disgust. Mutti gripped the handrail, saying nothing. Papa tipped his hat and nodded at the sailor, his mouth taut, face expressionless.

"They live on the river on these filthy sampans," he said in disgust. "Look at them." The sailor waved his arm at the buildings onshore. "Cotton. Silk from those filthy mills over there." He pointed at the sheds dotted along the shoreline spewing gray smoke and filling the winter air with smog. "They load up and come out here onto the water to trade. It's damn chaos."

The smell of frying fish and some unfamiliar spices, warming scents that were cinnamon-like, drifted up to their deck. Romy tried to draw the scent deep into her lungs to drive out the cold. For her, unlike the other passengers retching over the railing, these strange sweet and spicy smells were a comfort.

"And their food . . . ugh." The sailor wrinkled his nose and spat into the water, just missing the little boat. "They are like animals," he repeated. He turned to face Romy and her parents. "You belong here," he said before he turned on his heel, almost crushing little Nina, who was tiptoeing through the crowd to join the Bernfelds.

"Out of my way!" he boomed as the crowd shuddered in sympathy for the little girl.

Nina weaved quietly between the passengers to join Romy at the railing.

"Ah, Nina," Papa said kindly. "Come join us." And he proceeded to point out the rice fields and cottages along the shore as if it were a giant adventure. As if Shanghai were just another port where they were docking to refuel on this endless crazy holiday.

Nina, with her pretty blue ribbons and smocked frock, had shared a cabin with Romy since the Suez Canal. Her pregnant mother had suffered preeclampsia and died in labor. Papa delivered the stillborn baby just before the mother died, but without proper medication he was at a loss to stop the seizures and the bleeding out. The captain had refused to help, saying, "There are supply shortages, do I need to remind you, Herr Doktor? I'm not at liberty to waste valuable drugs."

Romy hardly thought saving a dying woman was wasting drugs. The captain wanted to throw both bodies overboard immediately, but Mutti begged him to allow them to deliver a mitzvah with a makeshift sea burial. The bottom deck was full as passengers joined Mutti and Papa in reciting the Kaddish with low, breaking voices. Mutti and another lady a few cabins down had managed to find some spare cotton sheets to swaddle the bodies. Nina sobbed and held Romy's hand as her mother and her tiny baby sister who never took a breath were dropped into the ocean. The shrouded bodies slowly sank to the endless blue depths, swallowed by the waves.

Today, as the boat tipped and lurched through the filthy chop, Romy bent her knees to keep her balance, swaying as she reached out to clasp her friend's hand. She smiled to reassure Nina. Any nerves Romy had about what her life with Mutti and Papa would be like in Shanghai were overshadowed by Nina's loss. How would Nina adjust and survive when she set foot in this strange land? Nina's papa had been killed in a pogrom, like Benjamin. Who would love and care for her orphaned friend?

As they sailed into Shanghai, thin wooden jetties and pontoons jutted out from every available space along the riverbank, and people with jet-black hair, identically dressed in navy shirts with small round collars and matching pants, swarmed across every surface. Jumping on and off motorboats, sailboats, and fishing vessels, and filling the air with loud chatter as they formed lines and unpacked barrels, crates, and fishing nets, often carrying cargo on poles across their shoulders. The shouts and clanging were overshadowed by the vile undercurrent of gasoline, sewage, sweat, and rotten fish mingling with the intriguing scent of spices, smoked meat, and strange fruits and flowers.

As the *Conte Verde* slowed and released two deep blasts of its foghorn, they cruised beside a promenade in front of the grandest European buildings Romy had ever seen. Halfway along the promenade was the peak of a roof that soared upward, an apple-green pyramid that pierced the soft gray winter sky.

Romy blinked three times to check she wasn't just tired and imagining it. Nina stood with her mouth agape and even Mutti managed to raise an eyebrow. These buildings were nothing like the shanty huts and factories along the muddy Yangtze. These buildings were grand yet modern, with soaring clock towers, shimmering domes, marble columns, and wide balconies. But where Romy was used to marble statues of famous musicians, politicians, and the occasional Greek or Roman god, in front of these buildings were polished bronze lions and shiny oversized brass nameplates.

A giant billboard boasted the head of a glamorous blond with bare shoulders in a ball gown, advertising Castile Toilet Soap for Sensitive Skin with Chinese characters running down the left-hand side. Another offered gold diamond watches and a third had a smiling Shirley Temple in puffy blue satin sleeves holding a white birthday cake with pink trimming, with THE LITTLE PRINCESS over her head. Romy nudged Nina and they giggled with excitement and surprise. They certainly hadn't expected the latest American movies to be shown here. Perhaps Mutti and Papa would take them to see it?

What was this city, Shanghai? Papa had called it "the Paris of the East," but Romy had never been to France. The grand stone buildings looked like they might be from Europe, but the glitzy billboards? They seemed straight out of Hollywood.

Between the row of buildings and the swampy riverbank were four lanes of traffic filled with bumper-to-bumper black, blue, and dark green cars and sleek electric trolleybuses. Weaving among the traffic were wheelbarrows, or small carts that were pulled by men instead of horses. Some were filled with flowers, melons, or bamboo baskets, others with people in fine suits, fur coats, and felt hats with colorful plumes.

Romy's little suitcase knocked between her knees as the *Conte Verde* nudged its nose into the dock. Mutti stood perfectly still, her neat brown suit nipped in at the waist, hat tilted, camel coat wrapped tight around a face so pale Romy feared her mother would fade into the paintwork. While the other mothers had laughed and played cards, smoking in the drawing rooms after supper while the men drank whisky or walked the decks, Mutti would stay in her cabin penning long letters to Daniel, promising him they would be reunited in Shanghai just as soon as she could manage it. She arranged for one of the cabin boys to post the letters when they went ashore for supplies at each port.

Sailors in starched white uniforms they must have been saving for Shanghai shore leave yelled at each other as they unfurled coils of rope, to be hoisted around the huge iron bollards sticking up from the jetty. There were dozens of angry gray warships bobbing around them, and Romy and Nina competed to see how many flags they could recognize: small gunboats from Britain and America, large British and American cruise liners anchored midstream, plus merchant ships from Holland and Italy . . .

Romy squinted at a white flag with a large red dot in the middle on a nearby warship. "Papa"—she tugged on her father's sleeve—"tell us, which one is that?" She pointed to a larger version on a pole over a lean-to room. It had capital letters in English she could just make out.

"*Iz . . . Izumo.*"

"Japanese. They control some parts of Shanghai." Papa's voice sounded resigned.

Romy hesitated. What if it was like the Italian border?

But she didn't get to ask Papa, as the steel gangplanks were wheeled out from the ship, screeching as they slid across the bottom deck to shore. The first mate gave a whistle with his thumb and forefinger, and the crowd obediently poured down the stairwells, men hitching their suitcases in front of them and women clasping their fur coats at the neck as if they might be ripped from their backs. No sooner had they stepped ashore than Romy and Nina were shunted with Romy's parents into a small tender smelling of rotten fish and gas fumes, luggage piled around their feet, to make the short, choppy journey to what the deckhands called the Bund.

The tender pulled up at a rickety wooden dock and their luggage was tossed onto it as they clambered from the boat. Papa went ahead to clear their paperwork as Nina, Romy, and Mutti gathered their suitcases and walked down the jetty.

As they stood on firm land for the first time in weeks, legs still swaying with the rhythm of the sea, they linked hands and waited for Papa to return and their new life in Shanghai to begin.

Chapter 6

Romy left Alexandra in the old blue chair reading *Faust* to Wilhelm. She didn't have the heart to tell her granddaughter her *opa* had never much cared for Goethe. Rather, he had read it with the child in her middle school years to help her perfect her German, only because it was on the curriculum at the Goethe Institute.

So many tiny mistruths she'd never corrected.

Romy had been curious about Goethe when she was a schoolgirl in Shanghai. Her papa said Goethe hated Jews, but her French education in China taught Romy nothing was so clear cut. She'd received an A-plus for an essay during her matriculation year, arguing Mephistopheles was a victim of circumstance. Now, perhaps, she'd make the case that Mephistopheles was a survivor.

Lately, when Romy drifted off to sleep, she heard voices calling out to her from the past. She'd smell gasoline and blood, feel glass cut her feet as she fought her way through a crowd clawing at her clothes.

Benjamin would step forward from the mist and crowds, face covered in blood, begging, "Please . . ." Her mother, her father, and Daniel stood behind her, arms linked, with their eyes closed, revealing nothing. There was also a Chinese family. Two parents, an older boy, and a girl. Over all this swirling noise, a baby was squalling.

Desperate.

The Chinese family refused to look at Romy. Disappointment radiated out through the mist, melting the figures until she awoke . . .

Romy had long ago made her own Faustian pact.

The trouble was that she was no longer the only person suffering the consequences.

Romy crept outside to the garden, through the oak Moon Gate Wilhelm had made for their fiftieth wedding anniversary, and felt her heart swell and hammer with love and guilt.

She was heading to her home clinic to fix some herbs for Alexandra. After a week back in Melbourne, the girl still had a dry cough, a mottled tongue, and dull eyes, and Romy wanted to make up a proper tincture for her. She stepped gingerly across square pavers set into soft grass and bent for the key hidden under a terra-cotta pot planted with jade. As she opened the door to her clinic, swirling dust specks and the faint trace of incense greeted her. She flicked on a light and swiped more dust off the frame surrounding her diploma for traditional Chinese medicine, then ran her foot over the few speckles of off-white paint that had escaped the drop sheet and stained the floor forever.

She could never bring herself to scrape them away. Her heart ached.

Wilhelm had built this studio for Romy to celebrate her graduation. Late one summer afternoon, when the painting was done, Nina and Wilhelm had sat in ripped shirts and pants, sipping champagne and toasting their good luck.

Sophia had been seven at the time, hair in neat pigtails, and eager to help. Wilhelm, always the soft touch, couldn't deny her. An old shirt was found and pulled over her little green jumpsuit, and she was given instructions to paint the back of the door, despite Romy's protestations.

"She'll make a mess of it."

"Then we'll clean it up," Wilhelm said gently, ruffling his daughter's black hair.

Sophia had thrown her head back with glee and scuttled off to find the biggest brush, then dipped it in the pot and dribbled it in a long line back to the door, singing to herself, ignoring Romy shaking her head.

"You spoil that girl," she'd said, voice softening.

"Ex-actly!" declared Wilhelm with a glint in his eye, and that was that.

Sophia had been buried more than thirty years ago, but the paint speckles reminded Romy of her giggles, which had filled the room. She cherished the spattered imperfections on the floorboards.

Romy braced herself against the worktable, overcome by loss and perhaps too much dust. She needed to open the window, let the fresh air blow these memories away before they suffocated her.

Romy would never forget the moment she had opened her front door with a smile—expecting to see Sophia, Joseph, and Alexandra arriving for lunch to celebrate Sophia's forty-first birthday—and found instead a pair of freshly minted police officers in crisp uniforms shifting uncomfortably on the doormat.

"Mrs. Cohen? Is your husband here too? I'm afraid we have some bad news."

The scent of the chocolate cake baking in the oven filled the hall as they stepped inside.

Romy's knees buckled and the young policewoman—a slip of a girl, really—caught Romy by the shoulders in a surprisingly firm grip, while her hapless partner blanched and stared at his shoes as he tried to compose himself. They'd shuffled inside and deposited Romy in the blue chair by the bay window, while the young man went to find Wilhelm and make some weak tea with far too much sugar. Meanwhile, the young woman, who introduced herself as Constable Mary Fisher, held Romy's hand as she explained that Sophia's car had been knocked by a truck from behind into the path of an oncoming semitrailer. Sophia and Joseph were killed on impact, but their daughter was currently in surgery, doctors working to stem the bleeding from a nasty cut on her head.

Alexandra had been discharged from the hospital into the care of her grandparents the following week and had lived with them ever since.

Wilhelm and Romy had experienced so much loss in their lives, but nothing had prepared them for the loss of Sophia. Her husband had always held his faith close, even in the Shanghai ghetto. The rituals brought him comfort. Wilhelm spent hours praying with the rabbi after Sophia's accident, always holding out his hand for Romy to join them. But how could she?

Romy sniffed the musty air and looked at her hanging bunches of dried mugwort tied with brown string along the wall. She always harvested the new growth at the end of summer, plucking as many of the silky gray branches as she could store in her room. Some years ago she'd started making her own moxa sticks—shaped a little like cigars—to be lit and held to smolder a few centimeters above a pressure point, heating cold or painful areas where *qi* had weakened or become stuck.

She didn't take patients anymore, not since Wilhelm's turn for the worse. His time was near and easing Wilhelm's way to a painless death—and preparing Alexandra—occupied her every thought.

The room itself was only a few meters wide—more a corridor, really—with windows down one side overlooking the garden. Patients always commented they felt calmer just sitting there. She had arranged the treatment bed to face the window so those having acupuncture would have something lovely to contemplate.

Along the opposite wall was a line of bookshelves filled with glass jars topped with airtight silver lids. Romy stood in front of her wall of jars, leaning in to read the labels.

She wanted to make a *tang* to soothe Alexandra's cough and strengthen the *qi* in her lungs so she didn't develop bronchitis. Her granddaughter had never been one for crying—more was the pity. The deep breaths and exhalations that accompanied a good weeping often churned up all the negative energy and expelled it from the body. Alexandra tended to cling to her sadness, clench it deep inside where it couldn't be touched.

Romy knew all too well what happened when grief and sadness lingered for too long.

She brushed her hair back and reached for her *Compendium of Materia Medica* wedged beside a mottled leather diary. She used both arms to hoist the hardback volume off the shelf and onto her tabletop, flipping open the pages smeared with ground star anise and pink flecks of tree peony bark. A crushed gardenia pod was stuck in the gutter between the pages. She ran her fingers over the black-and-white illustrations of ginseng, lotuses, lilies, peppermint, and magnolias until she found the page she was looking for. If Alexandra were beside her, she'd ask why her grandmother hadn't moved on to an online database with something stored in a cloud, but Romy couldn't bear to part with her book.

She pulled some jars down onto her old wooden worktable to make a *Sang Ju Yin* formula, weighing all the ingredients on her old silver scales before dropping them into a copper bowl. First, she added the dark green anti-inflammatory strands of dried mulberry leaf with a golden chrysanthemum flower to clear the wind and heat. Then she added some crushed bitter apricot kernels to calm the coughing, plus a few dried roots of the magnificent blue balloon flower, mint, forsythia, reed rhizome, and licorice root.

She bent to sniff the dried herbs—the spicy notes of the licorice, zing of the mint, and sweet woodiness of the chrysanthemum—then placed the jars back on the shelf. She glanced at her watch, checking it wasn't yet time to relieve Sally and Alexandra. She'd need to take the herbs into the kitchen and boil them in a terra-cotta pot for a few minutes until the mixture resembled a thin, bitter broth. The pungent smell would fill the kitchen.

Before she picked up her bowl, she flipped to the back of the compendium and slipped out a piece of bamboo scroll with perfect calligraphy running down the left-hand side. On the right was a series of botanical drawings, all annotated. The first was a chrysanthemum. It was so vivid, from the peach tips of the petals, to the veins on the green leaves—including the holes where they had been nibbled by an insect—to the scraps of grass behind. She ran her fingers down the lines, translating as she went until she found notes and annotations for *Sang Ju Yin*. She held the bamboo parchment alongside the compendium's recipe for comparison and made adjustments to the formula and ingredients.

Same trunk, different branch.

Romy gently circled the flower illustration with her index finger, pressing the soft page to her cheek and enjoying the faintest whiff of mint—such a cooling herb—even after all these years. Then she turned to the back of the compendium once more and slid the sheet with the chrysanthemum under the pocket created by the back cover flap so it lay flat with the others. She didn't dare leaf through the other illustrations and letters, nor glance at the red envelope that lay tucked away and hidden at the bottom.

These ancient pages were remnants of another life, another time. One day soon they would be passed to Alexandra.

With the scents and the delicate script came the memories she'd worked so hard to repress. Romy pushed the book back onto the shelf, switched off the light, and hurried from her little clinic, locking the door behind her. As she passed through the Moon Gate Wilhelm had made, the faded timber turned silver in the last of the afternoon light.

Wilhelm—the man who gave her a new life. A family. Her heart swelled and plunged as she picked her way over the piles of red and yellowing leaves and a cool gust of wind caused yet more leaves to swirl down around her. Wilhelm . . .

Sweet, kind Wilhelm was about to leave Romy with her ghosts.

Chapter 7

Opa's rabbi had announced on the final night of sitting shiva that Alexandra and Romy must resume normal life. Alexandra wasn't sure how to go about normality, or work, when she felt so bereft. But Romy had insisted they host an afternoon tea for Opa's friends and colleagues. Today, the living areas, courtyard garden, and terrace at Puyuan were buzzing with people who had come to pay their respects.

For the last week of Opa's life, the only noise in the house had been the ticking of the old clock and the beeps of the heart monitors. Alexandra had kept vigil beside her grandfather in the dim sitting room day in, day out, holding his hand and recounting tales from her childhood, reading to him in German and helping the nurse with his daily sponge bath. Anything to keep herself busy and fend off her tears.

Opa hadn't stirred since that fateful coughing fit on her first morning back from London, and Sally had warned that his vitals were fading. "He's in no pain. I see it a lot. Patients hang in just long enough to see their loved ones, to say goodbye," the nurse said. "He knows you're here."

Sometimes, Romy would wander in from the garden and sit with Alexandra, clutching both her hand and Opa's before sending her granddaughter out for bread and milk or to pay an urgent bill at the post office.

"Get some air, *Liebling*," she'd urge softly. "Take your time." Romy would look across at Opa, unconscious beneath his oxygen mask. "He's determined." She gave Alexandra a mischievous look. "He won't do something until he's damn well ready. A trait you share."

On Opa's last day Sally had prepared Alexandra for what was to come. Shaking her head, the nurse said, "I've never seen a passing like this. So beautiful." She glanced around the room, which was full of flowers and candles. "Your grandmother, she goes about her business without a fuss, doesn't she?" The nurse smiled. "She's a quiet force, that Romy. And so proud of you, love."

◇

Today the old house felt more itself, ready for a celebration. The hospital bed and equipment had been removed from the sitting room and along with it the pervasive smell of antiseptic and death. Cut crystal vases were filled with loose white, red, and pink roses, along with a forest of curling white lilies and the more aromatic pink belladonnas. Roses for love. Lilies for pure, unconditional love.

Alexandra could picture her flamboyant grandfather standing in the doorway and adjusting his emerald silk cravat with a smile, ready for the party. Cocking his arm for Romy to slip her hand through, forever linked. One handsome, tall, and gallant, and the other small and unassuming.

Alexandra was touched by Romy's unfiltered love for her husband. Her grandmother had always worn her heart on her sleeve and loved quietly but fiercely. Romy was the earthy yin to her grandfather's larger-than-life yang.

When her grandparents had given Alexandra the jade pendant inscribed with a lily for her twenty-first birthday, the night before she'd boarded her flight for London, Romy had treated Alexandra to more Chinese herb lore: "To give a lily, my *Liebling*, is to show pure, unfiltered love."

Alexandra had blushed as Romy continued: "In friendship, for a child." Another meaningful look. "For a partner." At the time, Alexandra had never had a serious boyfriend, just the usual university flings: a fellow math honors student; a German tutor whom she met fighting for the last salad roll in the cafeteria one lunchtime; and a disastrous few months with a particularly needy pianist with an insipid voice and soft fingers. Bach would forever sound wet and whiny now.

She'd shivered as Romy brushed her overgrown fringe from her eyes. Alexandra had assumed, in that selfish way of all privileged twenty-one-year-olds moving to the other side of the world, that her grandmother was crying because she was leaving for London. Who'd cry over a jade lily?

In the few days since Opa had passed, Oma's behavior was just as perplexing. Her grandmother's last moments with Opa just didn't make any sense.

Alexandra had been sitting in her favorite sunny corner at the kitchen table making *Semmelknödel* dumplings to go with their roast chicken for dinner when Sally came in to let them know Wilhelm was slipping away.

Sally's voice was low and clear as she ran through the checklist they'd drawn up, phone calls that needed to be made. Alexandra had sat there, swimming in grief and stirring the dumpling mixture with her right hand as the fingers of her left hand found the lopsided *W* she'd proudly scratched into the knotted table with a skewer as a five-year-old. She remembered Oma's scolding and the twinkle in Opa's eyes as he declared it the finest piece of engraving he'd ever seen. "You'll make your mark on this world, *Liebling*." He was always the softer of her two grandparents.

Romy had set to work with her own checklist of sorts. Romy was determined "to give Wilhelm the peace and strength to die." The heavy velvet curtains in the dining room were partially drawn, a row of thick vanilla-scented candles lined up on the marble mantelpiece. Sticks of incense burned in every corner.

When Alexandra finished lighting the candles, she walked over and sat beside Romy before leaning over her grandfather's bed. "I love you, Opa—so much," she managed to blurt out before she started crying.

The heart monitor beeps slowed and Opa didn't move.

He looked gray and sallow, his eye sockets sunken. This still man bore no resemblance to the vivacious and outspoken man who pottered around his garden on weekends in faded work shorts and boots and went to work at five each weekday morning in a tailored three-piece suit with a gold pocket watch.

Romy sat beside Opa's shoulder and squeezed his hand, gently stroking a lock of hair from his forehead. Alexandra felt like an intruder. The tenderness in the stroke, the squeeze, the glistening eyes as the rhythm of Opa's heart slowed and stalled.

"We've had a good life, Wilhelm, you and I. Such blessings." Romy's words were so tender, so filled with love and adoration. The hole in Alexandra's stomach widened as she realized that, apart from Opa and Romy, there would be no one who loved her so deeply. Hugo never had.

Alexandra stood to leave the room and give them privacy, but Romy reached over and clasped her hand. "Stay. We both need you." Her hand was warm, her grip strong.

"*Danke*," said Romy as she lightly kissed Opa's lips, before twisting her head and pressing her cheek to his. "You've made me so happy."

Alexandra could make out tears sliding down Romy's face and dripping onto the crisp white sheet, leaving a wet stain that enlarged with each drop. She whispered softly in Wilhelm's ear, rubbing her cheek gently against his.

Not wanting to eavesdrop, but unable to move because Romy was still clutching her hand, Alexandra turned her head to watch Sally. The nurse was hovering in the background, discreetly on the phone to her supervisor. Murmuring numbers and medication amounts.

"Any time now," she said under her breath. She looked up and met Alexandra's eye with kindness. "No, there's nothing more we need, thank you. I'll call you when—"

Alexandra looked at the ceiling as the nurse ended the call.

The rabbi had come that morning to sit with Wilhelm. "*I lift my eyes to the mountains—from where will my help come?*" he recited.

Alexandra turned back to see Romy still murmuring in Wilhelm's ear and her heart sank. She couldn't hear the words, but she could lip-read—a skill perfected by years of working on the trading desks. Her eyes narrowed and she repeated Romy's words over and over to herself. Perhaps her German wasn't up to speed? For Alexandra could have sworn Romy said, "*Vergib mir.*" Forgive me.

But why? What could her grandmother need forgiveness for?

The irregular beeps of the heart-rate monitor stopped. Romy let out an almighty sob and Alexandra's tears flowed unchecked. Her grandparents were her only family. Now one of them had drifted away.

Sally stepped over and pressed her fingers against Opa's neck, checking for a pulse before saying out loud, almost to herself, "Time of death: three forty-two P.M."

"*Baruch dayan ha'emet*," whispered Romy. Blessed is the true judge.

"Amen," replied Alexandra automatically as she closed her eyes, inhaled the cinnamon, and let the grief seep deep into her bones.

◇

Forgive me . . . Had Oma really said it? And if so, what had she meant by it? Forgive her for what? It was like trying to solve an equation with too many unknown factors and it kept Alexandra awake at night, fidgeting and tugging at the pillow until sleep finally came. There hadn't been an appropriate moment to discuss what she had heard with her grandmother. Now there was the mourning to attend to. Besides, grief behaved in mysterious ways—yesterday Alexandra had dissolved into tears after tripping on Opa's garden fork when she walked in the garden with her espresso.

Alexandra rubbed her eyes. She was so tired the sockets ached. Slipping her hand under the collar of her shirt, she touched her pendant as she moved into the hallway to greet the guests. As she traced the sharp curve of the lily's stem, Alexandra's heart yearned for her grandfather and their tight circle of three. She frowned as she tried to remember her *opa*'s last words—something about *the three of us*. Was that what he meant? Now her only blood tie, her only family, was Romy. Nothing before and—she sighed—nothing in the future. Unless you counted work.

She leaned her cheek against the faded blue silk wallpaper as guests streamed in the front door in pairs as if they were entering the ark.

"Vat iz zis? A flower show?" muttered a hunched lady with mauve hair in a thick Russian accent as she ran over Alexandra's left foot with her walker frame. "And my hands stink of toothpaste." Clearly she didn't approve of Romy adding a few drops of peppermint oil to the basin placed by the front door so the mourners could wash their hands. Her stocky aide shot Alexandra an apologetic smile as he dashed past her, trying to regain control of the steering.

The thick curtains of the sitting room were tied back with a pretty velvet bow and the French doors were thrown open as an invitation for guests to wander out into the walled garden and enjoy the last traces of autumn sun. It was a still, clear day and outside on the gravel a handful of round tables were draped with damask tablecloths that billowed at the bottom.

The tall row of lipstick maples was dazzling against the old brick fence. Alexandra smiled to herself as she remembered planting them with Opa, gently removing them from their pots and unfurling their roots before placing them deep into the soil with fertilizer.

"Gently," he'd said as she brushed the pot soil from the roots. "It's easy to move a plant. But for a successful transplant we need to pay attention, nourish the roots. Let them spread and find their own way. You watch, Alexandra. It will still be the same tree—it just needs to find a new way to live."

Even at seven years old, Alexandra had understood that Opa wasn't just talking about plants.

The branches of the espaliered lemon trees were thicker than her arm and wove their way up the dark lattice. Pockets of blue catmint and lavender tickled the trunks and released a sweet scent as guests meandered through the backyard sipping sherry, vodka, homemade lemonade, and ginger beer.

Alexandra went to the kitchen to fetch some more food and in a daze wandered into the dining room with a plate of warm rolls straight from the oven. At each step she was greeted with a peck on the cheek, a pat on the shoulder as condolences coupled with unwanted marriage advice were offered. Some had heard about The Breakup and wanted to talk about Hugo. Others poked or gestured at her slim hips and wondered aloud when her belly would swell with child. She mustn't wait. Not at *her* age.

Her empty belly ached, but not as much as her heart. Her pulse thrummed in her ears at the mention of a baby. Children hadn't been part of Alexandra's plan—until she moved in with Hugo. But when she turned thirty-five last year she'd started nudging around the subject, treading lightly to gauge his response. But Hugo had carelessly waved the topic of children away, joking about how they would forever chain him to his desk in London—or, worse, the family's country estate, Crossington. How could he be at a work dinner in St. Petersburg and meet her for a weekend in Ibiza if they had kids to consider? School. Sports. Plenty of time for all that, wasn't there? "Life's so good, babe, why ruin a sweet thing?" he'd say with his head tilted before planting a deep, tender kiss on her lips that made her forget everything else. The ghost of his older brother still rattled around his family home and he was scared to go home and fill his role. Alexandra understood. But it meant she lived with a troubled Peter Pan.

Her best friend, Kate, had warned her about him every time she returned home to Melbourne. "Al, he doesn't want kids. Are you okay with that? Because, trust me, the bloke is not going to change. They never do. You can pick the ones that don't really want them in the maternity ward. And if you force it, then you'll get a partner who's on autopilot."

How could she confess to Kate they'd already switched into that mode some time ago?

She stood near a table arranged with three different pots of tea and grabbed a bun and chewed on it as more guests greeted her, eyeing her as if she were a prize lamb. Many local grandsons were enthusiastically offered as a suitable match, if only she was prepared to come home to Australia: *Jacob's a physician now*, or *Todd has just accepted a partnership.* There was talk of London: *This Brexit madness won't last long.* Queries about whether she had an investment property or two in Melbourne: *How much did you pay?* And the inevitable requests for investment advice: *Cash or commodities? Onshore or offshore? Interest rates up or down?* She didn't mind. Anything to avoid talking about Hugo.

Instead she focused on remembering Opa and helping Romy. Until she spotted Eugene Johns—her grandparents' longtime lawyer.

"Hello, Mr. Johns." She kissed him on both smooth-shaven cheeks and stepped back as he adjusted his gray double-breasted jacket.

"Alexandra." He took both her hands in his. "I'm so sorry I couldn't stay longer yesterday when I dropped off the probate paperwork. But let's make a time that suits you tomorrow?"

"Okay."

"He was so proud of you, my girl," the lawyer said in his broad Yorkshire accent. "Your grandmother too. When you went off to Oxford . . ." He poured himself a cup of tea and raised his eyebrows to ask if Alexandra would like one.

She shook her head. "No, thank you. Oma has almost drowned me in mint and jasmine tea this last week."

The lawyer gave a deep chuckle and lifted his teacup to take a sip. "Can't beat Yorkshire black."

"I haven't had a chance to go through the papers yet," Alexandra confessed. "But I did have a couple of questions. Not so much about probate, but about my mother's documents. I was going through *her* probate documents, and there was her death certificate, and some adoption papers, but no birth certificate. Obviously, we know my mother was Chinese—Oma brought her out on the boat—but the paper trail just doesn't make any sense."

Mr. Johns's hand shook and the teacup clattered on the edge of the saucer.

She leaned in so she was close to his ear. "I'm going to try to find my mother's birth family when I'm in China. I don't want Oma to know—I don't want to upset her."

Mr. Johns cleared his throat, but his hand was shaking so much she worried he was going to spill his tea and burn his wrist.

"It's an upsetting time, Alexandra. Losing your parents when you were so young, and now the man who raised you . . . It's *always* a shock to lose a loved one." He coughed again, this time with force. "But I'm not sure if looking to China will help with your grief. Don't take for granted what's right in front of you."

Alexandra flushed with embarrassment. "That's not what I meant; it's just that my mother's paperwork is incomplete. If I could just find out who her birth parents were—"

"My dear, there was a war on. Children were abandoned. People died." His voice was kind but firm. "I'm not sure those documents even exist."

"But I've looked up some organizations in Shanghai who help track—"

"I wouldn't want you to get your hopes up, Alexandra," he interrupted. "It was a time of chaos."

Alexandra half nodded, keeping her frustration to herself.

"I'm just not sure what can possibly be gained." The lawyer's light blue eyes locked on hers as he took a giant swig of tea. "Your grandparents gave your mother a wonderful life. You too."

Her shoulders dropped. Did Mr. Johns think she was ungrateful? How could she explain that the death of her grandfather had torn a hole in her chest, opening up a deep well of loss and longing that she sensed had always been there?

"I'm very lucky, I *know*. I'm sure my mother was *very* grateful. But I've been looking through some of her old stuff since I've been home, and I know she definitely had questions about her origins. Her identity. It just seemed her birth certificate would be a good place to start."

Mr. Johns sighed, finished his tea, and slid the cup and saucer back onto the table. "I'm sure it would, Alexandra. But"—he shook his head—"I'm sorry, I just can't help you." He fished about in his pocket for his phone, pulled it out, and checked the time. "I'll see you tomorrow. Say, two o'clock?"

"Yes. And thanks for coming today, Mr. Johns. It means a lot to us. To Oma."

"Of course," he said as he stepped into the hallway and reached for his hat. "Tomorrow then."

When the lawyer had left, Alexandra weaved among the crowd carrying plates of food. The living room was filled with synagogue members, former colleagues, and friends from the local Austrian and Polish clubs, some of whom had started to wander out through the French doors into the garden.

"Och," said a bearded Scot with a Friends of the Royal Botanic Gardens pin on his lapel, "so this here is the wee garden Wilhelm created. Very nice."

Alexandra fixed a smile on her face. It would have been churlish to point out that much of the magnificent garden was actually her grandmother's handiwork.

Still, Alexandra was touched by the guests' proffered condolences. *Very strong, your* opa. And, *A fine head for business—you must have got that from him.* Or, *Such a generous benefactor. Are you involved in*

any charities yourself? So many old friends of her grandparents' . . .
So many questions.

But Alexandra's mind was humming with questions of a
different sort.

◇

Alexandra made her way back to the dining room and the guests,
carrying a blackwood platter made by her grandfather. She'd helped
him shape it across the saw bench in the back shed and then spent
weeks sanding it until it was smooth. Opa had helped her write her
name with a soldering iron underneath and then dated it—1994.
Through the window, she could see his little weatherboard work shed
tucked in the corner, covered with the crimson leaves of Boston ivy.

Her arms felt so heavy with loss she almost dropped the tray.
She was so lost in her own thoughts she didn't look where she was
going and knocked the edge of the doorframe with her shoulder.
Wilhelm had always been her north. How was she going to cope?

Alexandra had moved to London to try to make him proud.
Won awards. Built a successful career. Failed in her relationship.
She had missed her grandparents so much. Why hadn't she come
home earlier to these people who loved her?

Last week's graveside ceremony had been brief, the coffin a
simple pine box tucked into the earth, high on a hill in the far
corner of the Jewish cemetery. Alexandra and Romy had each
thrown in handfuls of wet soil and at the last minute Romy had
tossed in a bouquet of white lilies she'd smuggled in under her
navy cashmere shawl.

Flowers were not the norm at Jewish burials, but Wilhelm had
hardly led his life by the book.

As the rabbi spoke, Alexandra scrolled through Wilhelm's life, checking off the facts.

Smuggled out of Austria. A war spent baking Austrian rye bread and Vienna rolls and other European delights at a corner store in Shanghai. He had known Romy a little in Shanghai, but they had become reacquainted in Melbourne and married there. Then he had been a simple refugee baker who started with a Monday and Thursday round, delivering fresh rye bread to the Jewish and European delis in Melbourne's inner suburbs, desperate for something other than tasteless white sandwich loaves that went stale on a dry afternoon. Wilhelm's magic blend of *Brotgewürz* spice mix using ground caraway, fennel, anise, and coriander seed was improved by Romy's addition of Chinese allspice, celery seed, and cardamom. After a couple of years, along with an interest in olive oil, coffee, charcuterie, and cheese of the nonplastic variety, Australians started begging for better-quality bread. Wilhelm's Bakehouse ended up supplying major grocery stores nationwide.

One precious child: an adopted Chinese daughter. Wilhelm and Romy's history was a patchwork of countries and cultures threaded through the blood of so many. Alexandra didn't think she could detect any clear patterns if she tried. Her maternal grandparents were Austrian but had migrated to Australia from China. Her father's parents, dead decades before she was born, were fifth-generation Australians of English and Scottish stock who farmed sheep and crops out in western Victoria. When her father, also an only child, decided he was going to become an academic, they sold the farm to an investment company that filled the slopes with blue gums. Her mother's history was less certain. Alexandra had asked many times where Sophia actually came from, but Oma and Opa always deflected the question, instead telling dazzling tales of discovering star anise, ginseng, and cardamom at a Chinese medicine dispensary, describing the smell of peach blossoms in spring and visits to markets where everything still wriggled, rickshaws raced, and beautiful ladies wore silk dresses finer than any in Paris. China had given Oma and Opa their freedom, their vocations, and the gift of a daughter. By the time Alexandra hit her teens, that was all the information they were prepared to divulge. Oma's brow would crease with pain every time Alexandra asked. So she stopped. Why keep pushing when the topic was taboo?

As the wind whipped their hair at the graveside, Alexandra reached for Romy's hand and turned it over. The nubby fingers and the nails cut short. These were honest, hardworking hands. Romy's hands belonged in the soil and had made this land her own. Hands that traced the meridians of people's bodies, decoding their yin and yang. Encouraging people to find balance. Harmony. Make adjustments.

Her grandmother was good, clear, and true.

So what did Romy need Wilhelm's forgiveness for? It was bugging Alexandra and she traced a circle in the dirt with her foot. Maybe she should just ask? But the hurt in Romy's eyes told her everything . . . Whatever it was, it was buried deep. Her grandmother had suffered so much loss. Her brothers in Austria, her parents, the car accident that killed her only child. Alexandra ran her fingers through her hair until she found the scar running like a fault line down the back of her skull to the nape of her neck. What did Alexandra know about burying a child and now a husband? Perhaps it was better to let some things go.

Alexandra shook her head and reminded herself that her duty right now was to focus on the guests. With all this daydreaming she'd tipped the platter and the warm rolls threatened to tumble onto the floor. Clusters of Wilhelm's employees from the factory lingered shyly in the corners of the room, politely making way for some of the older, more outspoken guests as they sipped water and Romy's ginger beer. Alexandra smiled and nodded as she passed. They spoke quietly in their own languages—Vietnamese mostly. She quickly made her way to the center of the room where a heavy sixteen-seat dining table with legs like Greek columns stood. It was an old Bank of Australia boardroom table Wilhelm had picked up at an auction.

The table was laden with all things round, to represent the circle of life. Boiled eggs, a salad of chickpeas, and her bread rolls. As Alexandra examined the plates brought by the guests she realized this spread told the story of her grandparents' lives. Anh and the team from the factory had brought Vietnamese spring rolls—so many that there was hardly any need for the mushroom dumplings and *xiao long bao* she'd ordered from the Red Dragon up the road because she'd been in a panic about making sure there was enough food for everyone—and a vinegary dipping sauce. Romy said, "To be sad is one thing—but to be hungry is cruel." Her shoulders had slumped and her grandmother had looked as frail as puff pastry.

Alexandra reached over and picked up a steamed vegetable bun, breaking it in half and allowing the vapor to swirl from the center as Nina brushed past and plonked a plate of Puy lentils on the table.

"Are you okay, my *schatz*?" asked Nina as she placed a gentle hand on Alexandra's wrist and another on her shoulder. Alexandra felt buoyed by her kindness.

"You look empty," Nina continued as she patted Alexandra on the chest right near her heart. "It's tough, of course. Losing a grandfather. A father he was to you, really." She shook her head. "So much loss for you, my child." She tutted. "Can I get you a drink, Alexandra?"

Nina's rich German accent had not softened or flattened despite seventy-odd years in Australia.

"No thanks, Nina," she replied with a weak smile as she stuffed the other half of the bun into her mouth.

"You eaten enough? You must keep eating. So thin!" She pinched Alexandra's waist.

"I'm okay. I'm more worried about Oma."

"*Ach.* It's natural." She nodded. "But your grandmother is strong. More than you realize." Nina started to rearrange some dumplings on a plate.

"I don't think I should go to Shanghai, Nina," Alexandra said quietly. "I can't—" She shook her head as her eyes welled with tears. "I've been away far too long." Her back stiffened with guilt. "I can't leave Romy here by herself. Not when . . ."

Nina raised an eyebrow and the edge of her lip curled into a cheeky grin. "Not when she is so old, you mean. Careful. I'm the same age. A real ger-i-at-ric." She pronounced the crisp vowels with care. "Look, you heard the rabbi at the final minyan—he said to move on with normal life, to go back to work. It's part of the healing. You *must* go to Shanghai. I insist . . . Your grandmother will too."

Alexandra turned slightly so Nina couldn't see the heat and embarrassment creeping across her face. She eyed the cakes at the far end of the table. A carrot cake with lashings of cream cheese icing, Black Forest cake, and an assortment of apricot and apple strudels. The upside of owning a bakery was that people had gone to the effort of putting on a decent spread.

The Scot with the Botanic Gardens pin brushed past and helped himself to a couple of oversized scones, adding a spoonful of raspberry jam and another of double cream. He dipped his finger in the cream and tasted it, grinning and nodding with pleasure before giving Alexandra a guilty smile as he scuttled back outside.

Alexandra couldn't help but exchange a smile with Nina. She adored people who enjoyed their food.

Nina was the shape of a dumpling. Little sausage fingers, short hair, and dimples. She wore an exquisite silk beaded aqua kaftan. A patch of black cloth was pinned to her chest, for Opa. She was still pretty and girlish in her early nineties. When Alexandra was thirteen, Nina had proudly held up a personal ad she'd placed in the local newspaper.

Looking for an intelligent gentleman over 70 with a sense of humour. Must like laughing, going to the pictures, hiking, skiing, tango, salami and garlic.

Alexandra had been shocked at the time, but now she envied Nina. She never hid behind masks.

"Nina—" She stopped herself. What should she ask her grandmother's best friend?

Nina took a step back, looked Alexandra in the eye, and inhaled through her nose. "I'm sorry to hear about Hugo. But you're better off without that rascal, so I hear."

Alexandra blushed and changed the subject. "Was it love at first sight for Oma and Opa?"

Nina let out a whistle and wiped her forehead with a lavender-scented handkerchief. "Well"—she paused for just a beat too long—"you'd have to ask your *oma* that. But what I *can* tell you is their love was deep and true." Another beat. "There are so many ways the heart can love, Alexandra."

It was an odd answer. Alexandra opened her mouth to speak but she wasn't sure how to respond, so instead she said nothing. Nina was an orphan, like her.

Nina reached up and tucked a lock of hair behind Alexandra's ear. It was a gentle, intimate gesture that reminded Alexandra of all the times Nina had babysat her as a child. With no family of her own, she was always happy to take Alexandra to tennis lessons, swimming competitions, and math extension club when Romy was working or studying and Wilhelm was at the factory. There was a ferocity to her love coupled with a sense of irreverence, and Alexandra had always adored her and her bag of forbidden gummy frogs and snakes.

Alex felt a pang of nostalgia and rested her chin on Nina's shoulder as she leaned in for a hug. She missed Nina's softness.

"*Ach*, Alexandra, you are so much like your grandmother when she was young," the older woman whispered.

Alexandra closed her eyes, warmed by the compliment even as she wished Nina had been talking about a blood grandmother— someone from whom she'd have inherited more than mannerisms. Had her mother leaned on this same pudgy shoulder, smothered in love, and wondered, *Who am I?*

"Oh, Nina, are you pining for your youth again?" said Romy with a slight edge as she bustled past them with another tray of barbecued mushroom and shrimp buns.

Alexandra inhaled the smoky caramel flavor of the buns and her stomach grumbled. But this time, it wasn't the food that set it churning.

Nina reached over and squeezed Alexandra's hand, her eyes darting between Romy and Alexandra, as if she had more to say but didn't want to upset her oldest friend.

Nina was right, she needed to go to Shanghai. Alexandra bit into a dumpling, savoring the allspice, chili, and chives as she wondered how to learn more about her history in Shanghai without unleashing more pain.

Chapter 8

Romy and Nina sat slumped on their suitcases with Mutti, who held a pink silk handkerchief to her nose, and waited. They were on the lip of the promenade overlooking the crowded docks and river beyond, while behind them was a congested road with the grand buildings of the Bund forming a backdrop. In front of them were rows of wooden barrels and bales of cotton beside a man with wrinkled brown skin. He wore a faded blue tunic and a conical straw hat. Over his shoulders was a stick, long and straight like a broomstick, a bamboo basket dangling from each end. On one side he had a basket of faded green leaves, on the other a handful of glossy orange fruit. Romy's mouth watered as the man yelled "Per-simm-on!" at them in English and smiled to reveal a black void of missing teeth.

"You buy, missee?"

Mutti shook her head as she quietly reassured the girls, "Your father won't be long. Then we can get something." She eyed the fruit suspiciously and sighed as she took in the alternative food choices around them.

The persimmon man chuckled and shook his head at the foreigners, then cried out in an unfamiliar tongue as another seller in identical garb stepped forward and banged his half barrels with a stick. The second seller tilted a barrel toward the girls, who flinched as a dozen black eels slithered and turned on themselves like snakes. In the next tub, hundreds of lumpy black bullfrogs croaked and climbed over one another. The man picked up one between his thumb and forefinger, then, cupping it between his scarred hands, waved it in Nina's face. Mutti stood up and shooed him away with her long black umbrella.

Romy's appetite had disappeared.

Now laughing and determined to make a sale, the frog-and-eel man dipped his head into the next barrel and proudly held a squirming silver fish with both hands, kissing it on the mouth before proffering it to Mutti to make amends.

The two girls stood mesmerized as its scales glinted with each flap of its tail. What would they do with a live fish?

Papa emerged from the crowd of refugees and smiled as he walked toward them. "Ah, there you are," he said as he turned to take in the fish seller. "Buy anything?" he joked as he kissed Mutti's colorless cheek and squeezed her hand. He tucked their passports into the inside pocket of his long cashmere coat.

"Did our visas get stamped?" asked Mutti. "And did you ask how we can get paperwork for Daniel?"

Papa reddened as he said, "There's no one checking visas. I couldn't find anyone to ask . . ."

Romy touched Mutti's arm to reassure her.

Mutti shook her head, uncomprehending, but said nothing. Her eyes were bright with tears and her thin shoulders hunched a fraction more, as if she were withdrawing further into herself.

Papa lifted his hand to Mutti's cheek and stroked it with the utmost tenderness with his thumb. He said, "Come, my dear. Right now we must help Nina. She needs us. We must help her find her uncle and ensure she's going to be looked after. Then we can sort ourselves out."

As if to reinforce his point, Papa looked back at the line of refugees standing in the cold, damp air, wondering what to do. A cavalcade of khaki trucks with open backs—like cattle trucks— pulled up alongside the queue.

Romy's breath froze in her lungs.

The driver's door swung open, and out jumped a curvy lady in a two-piece pantsuit. She wore bright red lipstick and her hair was tied back with a fuchsia headscarf. She looked every bit as glamorous as one of the billboards yet she took big, firm strides, almost like a man.

She smiled at the Bernfelds and Nina. "Welcome. I'm Eva Schwartz from the International Committee—the IC. But around here we call it the Komor Committee." Her accent was American.

Miss Schwartz shook Papa's hand and then reached for Mutti's. This strapping American woman might crush her mother's fine fingers in a handshake if she wasn't careful.

"I'm Dr. Oskar Bernfeld and this is my wife, Marta." Mutti nodded and smiled weakly at this unusual woman. "This is my daughter, Romy. And this here"—he rested his hand on Nina's shoulder and smiled down at her encouragingly—"is Nina Milch."

Miss Schwartz's brows came together in a slight frown as she glanced at her clipboard.

Papa took a deep breath and cleared his throat before continuing. "I understand you were expecting Nina to arrive with her mother, Gerda. Unfortunately, Frau Milch passed away on the voyage. Her father was killed in Vienna."

Nina's head dropped and she started to sob with her eyes closed and her hands balled into fists.

Romy's heart broke for her friend. This was exactly the moment you needed a hug from your mother. Romy stepped closer and put her arm around her friend's shoulders.

Miss Schwartz squatted down so her head was level with Nina's. She looked the little girl in the eye. "I'm very sorry for your loss." She fished in her pocket. "Here's a tissue, sweetheart. Now you just sit on your bag here for a moment while I talk to the doctor." Her voice was low but steady. "We're going to look after you, you hear?"

Romy sat beside Nina on the suitcase and busied herself with retying her friend's hair ribbon.

Miss Schwartz was busy whispering to Papa and Mutti. Romy strained to hear snippets while consoling the still-sobbing Nina.

"Her mother—"

"—preeclampsia—"

"I understand she has an uncle here . . ."

Miss Schwartz flicked through the pages on her clipboard. She stopped and nodded. "Ah yes, I know who you mean. David Damrosch has been living at the *Heime* in Hongkew while he waits for his sister and niece." She turned to look at Nina. "Do you know what the *Heime* are, Nina?" asked Miss Schwartz.

Nina shook her head.

"They're the boardinghouses the IC has set up for the Jewish refugees. Funded by local businessmen, like Komor. You'll be in a female *Heime*."

Mutti frowned. "She won't be staying with her uncle?"

Miss Schwartz shook her head. "Separate, I'm afraid." She touched Nina on the shoulder. "You'll be able to go to the school we've set up, and we cook all your meals. I'll look after you, I promise. You'll be safe there."

Nina asked softly, "Will I be able to see Romy?"

Miss Schwartz looked at Romy's parents, who both nodded and said, "Of course."

Papa leaned forward and murmured to Miss Schwartz, "Perhaps the child could stay with us—"

"I'm afraid not. It's important to reunite her with her family." She hesitated. "But I can ask . . ."

"Where will you be?" asked Nina.

Papa said, "We're not exactly sure where our apartment will be yet, but I've been led to believe it is in the French Concession—whatever that means."

Miss Schwartz smiled. "It's a bit confusing. Shanghai is unusual . . . an open port.

"Shanghai is divided into three parts, or concessions—the International Settlement, the French Concession, and the Chinese areas. Totally separate, with four different governments. That's why no one checks for visas at the moment—it's just too hard to control."

Miss Schwartz picked up a discarded length of bamboo from the ground and began to sketch a map in the dirt.

"This large area in the middle of Shanghai, including the Bund"—she waved her hand at the street behind them with its fancy buildings—"and Nanking Road, is the International Settlement. It started out as British, but extended to include other nations like Italy, Germany, and America."

She turned her attention back to the map she was sketching and drew a deep line. "This is the Whangpoo River and this area across the Garden Bridge on Soochow Creek—*within* the International

Settlement—is carved off and controlled by the Japanese. The Japanese have some tobacco, mechanical, and munitions factories in Hongkew—it has good access to the river."

"But didn't you say the *Heime* are in Hongkew?" asked Romy, puzzled.

"Yes. That's where some of the European Jewish refugees have been settling these past few months—thousands of new arrivals. There's some big old American charity buildings there. It's not a very wealthy area; most people have nothing but their bags when they arrive."

"Is it safe?" asked Mutti, putting a protective arm around Nina's shoulders.

"For Jews, absolutely." Miss Schwartz nodded. "But relations between the Chinese and Japanese are . . . strained."

Romy looked from her parents to Nina as she shivered. Shanghai was meant to be safe.

"Why?" she asked.

"Japan and China are at war. They have been since the Imperial Japanese Army invaded Manchuria up in the northeast of China in 1931. Then, in 1937, Japanese troops used their base in Hongkew to spearhead an invasion into the Chinese areas of Shanghai and beyond. The other governments did little to intervene."

"They wanted to keep their concessions," said Papa, his voice low. "Stay neutral."

"Exactly," said Miss Schwartz. "During the battle, the Chinese bombed the Japanese area, including Hongkew, to drive out the Japanese. It didn't work. Instead, it was Chiang Kai-shek's Nationalist government and forces who were eventually driven from Shanghai."

Romy huddled close to Nina, confused.

Miss Schwartz looked at Romy and quickly reassured her. "But Shanghai has steadied herself, for now. Our committee organizes teams of Jewish carpenters, builders, and engineers to rebuild Hongkew alongside the Japanese troops. New schools. There are plenty of young people arriving here with skills who need to be kept busy.

"I'm feeding over a thousand people every day at the *Heime* and there are more coming every week. Plus, we have to find homes for thousands of displaced Chinese *and* the European refugees. The Japanese have taken the best apartments, so Chinese and Jewish families have to squeeze in together."

Miss Schwartz started scratching in the mud again with her stick, drawing a circle. "And this huge area running behind the International Settlement is the French Concession—Frenchtown, we call it. *Parlez-vous français?*"

"Enough to get by," Papa responded.

"How about Russian?"

Mutti and Papa looked at each other, confused.

"There are a lot of wealthy Russians in Frenchtown," Miss Schwartz explained. "They came here in 1918 after the revolution. Some of them have even built their own synagogues."

Romy watched the fish man pull another two fish out of his barrel and knock them on the head with a hammer. He wrapped them in newspaper for a lady being pushed along in a cart.

"What about the Chinese zone?" Romy asked.

"Another good question," said Miss Schwartz with a smile. "There's an old part of the city governed by Chinese anti-Nationalist collaborators. Most of the areas outside the French Concession and International Settlement are controlled by the Japanese using a puppet government."

"You mean the Chinese don't even control their own city?" Romy turned to her parents. "I don't understand. It's just as bad as the Anschluss!"

Nina was holding her breath, eyes wide and terrified.

"Not quite," said Miss Schwartz in a soothing voice. "You'll be safe here. Trust me."

There was a pause as Romy's parents exchanged a meaningful glance.

"You're lucky to be here," Miss Schwartz assured her.

Romy flushed with guilt as she closed her eyes. That word again. *Lucky.* Just like the chimney sweep sign on Wipplingerstrasse. She tried to ignore the memory of the click of the rifle and then a blast. The warm splatter of blood . . .

No one spoke for a minute and then Miss Schwartz threw her bamboo stick onto a pile of rubbish.

"Very well then. Let's get you into the truck, Nina. Dr. Bernfeld, if you wouldn't mind giving her a hand onto the back there. I just need to check with these other people on my list . . ." Miss Schwartz smiled at Nina. "We won't be too long, honey."

The IC representative carried her clipboard to a line of more than a hundred people, most of them in furs and carrying two suitcases each. Along with their thick coats and felt hats, the refugees wore the same two expressions: shock, resignation.

Romy felt weary. As if Kristallnacht had been only last night. Would she ever forget the smell of burning rubber, the sound of smashing glass? The smell of Benjamin's dried blood on Mutti's face . . .

What had all these other refugees in the queue lost? Who had they left behind?

Beyond the line of refugees, an elegant Chinese woman, her graying hair curled and styled into a bun like a Hollywood movie star, was sitting in a red cart with her knees and feet tucked beneath her. She wore a silk dress with a high collar in magnificent peacock blue and carried a silk fan she pointed with increasing urgency at the open barrels and baskets of produce as she was pushed past. Two long strings of pearls were draped around her neck and a bright red silk rose was fastened at her throat. Every now and again she would direct the wiry man who pushed the cart to stop at a stall and, after serious bargaining and a flourish of hands, she would add to the cart green melons, brown burlap bags of rice, a bag with two writhing eels.

Several other women with creamy skin, far younger than her mother, were being pushed in carts too, all of them in these beautiful blue silk dresses and wearing red roses. They weren't old, so why couldn't they walk? Romy wondered.

She inhaled the exotic cooking smells wafting through the cool air. Her stomach started to rumble as all of a sudden people rushed past to line up in front of a small flatiron stove propped on rickety wooden legs.

An old lady with silver hair was pouring a white batter as if to make a thin circular crepe. In the center of the crepe, she cracked an egg, then scattered a handful of sliced leek, some herbs, and a deep-fried sheath of pastry for crunch before rolling it up and passing it to the person at the front of the queue in exchange for a small brown coin. Romy was so hungry she thought she'd happily swap her coat and all the jewels for one of the crepes. They had no Chinese money.

Beside the old woman was a large pot of boiling stock. Romy sniffed. Chicken. The smell reminded her of *Griessnockerlsuppe*, Mutti's special semolina dumpling soup. Except this soup carried all the new smells of Shanghai: spicy and other sweet and bitter traces she had never encountered before. She wanted to take a sip just to try . . .

Instead Romy watched, transfixed, as a parade of barefoot men parked their rickshaws by the footpath, then brought over small ceramic bowls to be filled with broth. A grinning boy with three missing front teeth, smaller than Romy, carefully ladled soup into each bowl and threw in a handful of green herbs, chopped vegetables, and some tiny sliced red chilies.

Some of the men stank of urine, their hair fluffy at the back as if it had never been brushed. Their bare heels were cracked and bleeding. How could they not wear shoes in this wintery place where the roads and gutters were filled with fetid icy brown mush? Wearing faded blue rags, filthy and torn at the cuffs, these men looked to Romy like ghostly skeletons. Their eyes reminded her of those of the dead fish in the barrels.

Romy's stomach turned over and she wasn't sure whether it was curiosity, hunger, or revulsion. Her mother held her pretty silk handkerchief over her mouth.

Papa returned from helping Nina into the truck. Miss Schwartz approached them with her clipboard and broad smile. "Is someone coming to greet you? Where are you off to from here?" she asked Papa.

"The Cathay Hotel." He tapped his pocket for reassurance.

"You mean Sassoon House?" Her brown eyes widened. "Lucky you." She scanned the Bund, then pointed. "It's that one. With the green copper pyramid on the roof. Fanciest building in Shanghai."

They all gazed at the bizarre apple-green roof.

"Someone's taking care of you."

Romy saw Mutti and Papa exchange glances.

Papa had explained on the train before they left Austria that a wealthy Baghdadi merchant and property developer he'd met at Oxford—Sir Ellice Victor Sassoon—was now living in Shanghai. Papa had once operated on a distant cousin of Mr. Sassoon's and saved his life. Papa had sent him a telegram before they boarded the ship in Italy, and the ship's captain had received a message with instructions for the Bernfelds when they landed in Shanghai. The German first mate couldn't suppress his surprise and disgust as he delivered the message, muttering under his breath, ". . . wasted on Jews. *I* never stay at the Cathay."

Papa had read the telegram, then handed it to Mutti, who read it aloud.

WHEN YOU ARRIVE AT DOCK CHECK INTO CATHAY HOTEL AS MY GUEST STOP WE WILL ARRANGE A HOUSE FOR YOUR FAMILY STOP THERE IS A JOB AT THE JEWISH HOSPITAL IN FRENCH CONCESSION STOP MORE ON ARRIVAL STOP SASSOON

"But we have nothing, Oskar," Mutti said, folding the paper and handing it back to him before she stared at the horizon. "How will we pay him back?"

Her father replied, "We'll work something out."

Standing on the Bund's foreshore as her parents gaped at the green pyramid, Romy looked back at Nina, who was now sitting squashed between other refugees on the wooden bench seat in the back of the IC truck. Her brown suitcase was clenched between her knees and she was gazing around with wide eyes.

Romy didn't want her friend Nina to go. Not alone. She started to cry.

"Well," said Miss Schwartz with attempted brightness as she glanced at Nina. "We're off, then. We must get to the *Heime* for dinner." Seeing Romy's tears, she added consolingly, "Nina's uncle will be back by then, and we can make some plans for her family." She smiled. "I promise I'll look after Nina."

"It's better for Nina if she is with her family, *Liebling*," said Papa, though his voice betrayed his uncertainty. "We will contact Nina through the IC."

"I'm there every day," said Miss Schwartz as she handed Papa an address card from her top left pocket. She gave him and Mutti one last intense stare, as if trying to decide what to make of them. "Once you are settled, Dr. Bernfeld, I think perhaps we should have a little chat. We are always looking for help"—she gestured to the trucks—"and it sounds like you might have some important friends."

She walked over to the truck where Nina sat waiting, swung open the driver's-side door, and got in. As she started the engine and drove away, Romy stood waving until her friend was out of sight. She wondered how long it would be until she could visit Nina, and what their new lives in Shanghai would be like.

Chapter 9

Alexandra unwound her cashmere scarf as she strode into the discreet suburban wine bar Kate had chosen. She felt like she'd stepped into the middle of Milan. Outside it looked like an Edwardian terrace, but inside was all curved hardwood, black-and-white mosaic floor tiles, dim lights, and elegant brass fittings.

"There you are," said Kate as she wrapped Alexandra in a bear hug, then stepped back to give her friend the once-over. She wolf-whistled. "Look at you. How is it possible you get more glam each time I see you? If I hadn't known you since you insisted on pinafores, long white socks, and sandals, I'd hate you. Seriously." Kate took a swig of her white wine and laughed. Her shoulder-length blond hair needed a trim and, though her broad face was tanned, she had dark rings under her eyes.

"It's great to see you too, Kip."

"I am so sorry about missing your *oma*'s gathering. We had a hemorrhage right on changeover so I didn't feel I could walk out on the team." Kate was a midwife at one of the biggest maternity hospitals in Melbourne. With three kids under five and a builder for a husband, it was a miracle she managed a night off.

Alexandra waved it away with her hand. "How are my god-children? I'm looking forward to seeing them on Sunday."

"Monsters! Appalling, the lot of them. They tear the house apart from five every morning. I'm pretty much parked out the front of the child care center before it even opens at seven thirty, I'm so desperate to get to work for a rest!" Kate picked up her glass, slugged down her wine. "Anyway, they're all yours on Sunday. I'll just lock you in the basement with a bottle of chardonnay for two hours until Brad has burned the butterflied lamb." Another sip. "Enough about me. Nothing's changed. Kids, work, renovations. Repeat."

"How's Brad?"

"Busy! I'm still cooking on the camp stove four months later—since you were here last."

Alexandra rolled her eyes in sympathy.

"I'm hoping he can get a break between jobs so the kitchen can at least go in! He didn't even do the cupboards. I got sick of waiting and got the lot from IKEA." Her tone was mock scolding, but at the mention of Brad, Kate's eyes sparkled and her face softened.

Alexandra chuckled as she signaled to the barman to bring her a glass of whatever Kate was having. She took a handful of spiced almonds from the bowl in front of them. What exactly did true love feel like? she wondered. Sure, Kate looked exhausted and there was a stain on the cuff of her white shirt, but the woman sitting in front of Alexandra was unmistakably happy. She knew Kate wouldn't swap her chaotic life for anything.

Kate hopped off her stool and hugged Alexandra, who was blinking back tears.

"I'm so, so sorry about Wilhelm. He was a good man. A great father to you."

"Yes, he was," said Alexandra, wiping her eyes with a tissue she'd pulled from her sleeve.

"And how's Romy? I'll call in and see her on my next day off."

"Thanks," said Alexandra, flashing her a grateful smile. "Romy's amazing. Devastated. But noodling on, caring for everyone else as usual. Nina's having a few issues with her legs so she's over there tonight and Romy is doing some massage and acupuncture."

"Same old Romy," said Kate with affection. "Will she stay in the house, do you think?"

"I'm not sure. She wants to, and she's as fit as a fiddle. She's more mobile than half the people who have come by the house, most of whom are young enough to be her children." Alexandra shook her head. "But I'm not sure about this Shanghai posting now. Romy insists I still go, she doesn't want me to put my life on hold. Yet I can't help feeling I should probably come home."

"Romy's right, of course," said Kate. "But I know what you mean about Shanghai. At least it's closer than England. Anyway, you're here for a few more weeks. Just enjoy your time with her and then see how she feels. The last thing Romy would want is to make you feel guilty or for you to stay here out of a sense of duty."

Alexandra tucked her tissue back up her sleeve. "That's good advice. Hey, I've started sorting out my old room. I found this." She reached into her bag and pulled out a crinkled photo of two girls in white standing at the edge of a tennis court, each with an arm draped around the other's shoulders. Messy hair was falling out of their ponytails and they were hoisting a gold cup between them.

"The state doubles final, right?"

"Yep. I found the trophy too. Reckon it's time I gave it to you. Remember we said we'd share it? I never gave you a turn."

"Plenty of time," said Kate, giggling. "What's the rush?"

It felt good to laugh, Alexandra thought. "Might be time for a rematch. You up for it?"

"Just name the date, babe. A bash of the tennis ball would be great—it's been too long between games. I remember one of the girls on the opposition was a real pill."

"Nasty. You smashed her, though," Alexandra recalled. Kate had always looked after her.

"What did she call you? 'Chink'?"

"I've heard worse."

Kate reached over and grabbed Alexandra's hand. "Bugger 'em!"

Alexandra smiled. Her childhood friend was as constant as the waves.

"So. Hugo."

And there it was. The topic she'd been avoiding. Alexandra couldn't pretend, not with her oldest friend. Her bottom lip trembled and Kate shifted her stool across so she could drape her arm around Alexandra.

"Yes, quite," said Alexandra. When had she started sounding so British?

"I'm so sorry, Al. What a tool."

"Mmm," agreed Alexandra as she nibbled on another almond. "Turns out the young soon-to-be Lord Crossington was a walking cliché." She bit the nut in two with force. "I mean, *his secretary*? C'mon." She'd never forget the triumphant look on Victoria's face when Alexandra had burst into Hugo's office late on a Thursday night on her way to the National Theatre. She'd had champagne downstairs with Cath and Rashida, her girlfriends on the trading desk, before realizing she'd forgotten their tickets. So back upstairs to their office she went . . .

Hugo was one of the top commodity traders. He'd recruited her straight from university. In a multitude of ways. She'd opened the door to see him sitting on the desk with Victoria's endless legs wrapped around his waist. They weren't dancing.

"So? Good riddance!" Kate declared. "The guy was a tosser anyway."

"Now you tell me." Alexandra raised her eyebrows. "I was about to marry the guy." Her bones ached with a grief she was too afraid to admit. She gulped it down with her wine. "I just didn't see it coming." But had she *really* loved him?

"Oh, Al." Kate leaned over and hugged her and Alexandra blinked the tears away.

Witnessing the way her grandmother had selflessly tended to her *opa* had reminded her of the unbreakable bond her grandparents shared. They would never have deceived each other like that. Her grandmother's moral compass was as strong as the meridians circling the globe.

But lately Alexandra had begun to wonder if she wasn't as big a cheat as Hugo. Miners and governments in third-world countries benefited from her quick-fire speculation dollars. Everyone made a profit. But what was the real cost? She'd always told herself that her job was to neutralize risk, but with the global markets being so jittery, margins were tightening. Alexandra made sure companies and governments still operated inside the rules, but perhaps the benefits were not flowing to the wider population as she'd projected when she was a newly minted mathematician.

Kate shot her a sympathetic look. "All that *I rowed at Henley. I ski in Zermatt. I went to Oxford.* Blah, blah, blah." Kate mimed sticking a finger in her mouth.

"Hey, *I* went to Oxford."

"You were on a scholarship, freak. That's different."

Was it? She got the university medal in mathematics. Princeton, MIT, and Caltech all offered her a postgrad place. Alexandra could have chosen any university in the world, so why did she choose the one her mother went to? It was as if by following in her mother's footsteps—schools, majors—she had a template for how to become an adult. At Oxford Sophia had met Joseph, an Australian Ph.D. physics student with a lopsided smile and appalling taste in terry cloth tracksuits, and together they'd come home to Melbourne to teach at Melbourne University. Then along came Alexandra and life was perfect. Until—

Alexandra allowed her hand to travel to the tote bag she'd discreetly hung on a hook under the bar. She stroked the soft Italian leather. Inside, swaddled in a French linen tea towel, was her mother's childhood diary. She'd found it in a box of her mother's old schoolbooks and university folders stored under her bed, tucked away in the differential equations folder with a peeling, faded sticker of the Rolling Stones on the front. Oma had said many times over the years that it hurt too much to look at Sophia's scrawled handwriting and lecture notes—all that youthful energy on the page needled her heart. So she had left the boxes untouched for Alexandra to do with as she wished. She was a mathematician herself, after all.

As Kate ordered two fresh glasses of wine and a charcuterie board, Alexandra took the diary from her bag and unwrapped it carefully before passing it over.

"Look what I found when I was sorting through some of Mum's old stuff today."

Kate took the diary and opened it to the first entry, before hesitating and asking, "Are you sure you want me to read this?"

Alexandra nodded. "You have to! Please?"

15 July 1959

Mutti and Papa have given me this diary for my birthday, but I can't imagine I'll be writing much. I'm 14 in two days, too old for baby secrets and "what I did today" stories.

Here's some basic information:

Height: 160 cm (same as my mother but I plan to grow taller).

Hair color: Black. Really black.

Eyes: Brown.

School: St Margaret's Ladies College. I'm on a scholarship.

Parents: Romy and Wilhelm Cohen.

Favorite subjects: Math, physics, chemistry, biology and German (because I can already speak it—that's what we speak at home).

Worst subject: Music (even though Mutti says I'm a really good singer, I don't believe her. I sounded like a pigeon in my solo at the last school recital. NEVER AGAIN!!!).

Best friend: Tie between Jane Piper and Audrey Frisk.

Worst enemy: Fiona Hamilton (she's so dumb, anyway I'm not in any classes with her).

Favorite foods: Apple strudel. Mangoes. Chocolate.

Hobbies: Bike riding, athletics, calisthenics.

Other significant fact: I'm adopted from China (which explains why I look so different to everyone at my school). Mutti says it doesn't matter because I'm smarter than all of them put together. But the other day when Audrey and I rode our bikes down along the foreshore in our coats and beanies to fetch some cocoa for hot chocolate, she said her mother used to ride along the same track as a child. It was as if her mother had carved a path for her along the edge of the city.

Mutti is my mother, but somewhere in China I have another mother and father. We never talk about it. There are lots of adopted

children like me in Australia (even if I've never seen any others).
I know I'm lucky and I should be thankful. I am.

But lately, I've been wondering if my new body shape, if my eyes,
if my math skills, come from my real mother and father. Wherever
they are. I'm too scared to ask Mutti and Papa about why I was
adopted. What if my real parents are horrible? Or dead? But mostly
I wonder: Did they love me?

Because if they did, then why did they give me away?

Kate scanned the diary entry and chuckled as she said, "It sounds like this could be you at the same age."

"You think?" asked Alexandra, pleased.

"Explains where your big math brain comes from, doesn't it?"

"Well, my dad was a professor too, remember!"

"Of course," said Kate as she turned the page.

The waiter placed the platter on the bar and Alexandra helped herself to a slice of prosciutto.

Kate started flipping through the diary. "I don't understand— why's there only one entry? Other than that it's just math stuff."

"I bet I know—remember when we had to keep a diary for a whole term in year eight English? Such a pain!"

"Way too many words for you," Kate agreed, before continuing. "But what she said, Alex, about being adopted, wondering about her parents . . . I mean, don't you ever wonder about your other family?"

Her blue eyes were wide and sympathetic, and not for the first time Alexandra thought that this love, this bond with someone who knows what to say when you can't speak, was real love. Kate was the sister she'd never had.

"Have you shown this to Romy?"

Alexandra shook her head. "I can't. She's being strong, but she's so frail. She's just lost the love of her life. They were together for seventy years. Can you imagine?"

Kate looked dreamy. "Only sixty to go with the builder. Hopefully I'll have a kitchen by then."

"You'll have ten!"

"I'm happy to start with one. But seriously, why don't you ask her? You guys have always been close."

"That's the problem. It feels like a betrayal. I get why my mum didn't talk about it with Oma; in those days you didn't really talk about that stuff. And her parents had been through the war. Leave the past in the past. But now, when Oma is grieving . . . It just seems cruel to add to her grief."

"Fair enough. So what are you going to do—just leave it? It's a pretty big thing to ignore, Al."

"I've tried asking the family lawyer, but he's got no information. Seemed to think any search would be fruitless given the paper trails lost during the war." Alexandra closed her eyes for a second before she opened them and started to speak. "It's been thirty-five years. Another few months won't hurt. Maybe I'll do it when Oma's just a bit stronger. When the grief . . ." She slumped back in her chair, as empty as her wineglass.

Kate leaned over the bar and ordered two more glasses, before adding, "I should've ordered the bottle."

"Next time."

Alexandra decided to keep the old black-and-white photos she'd found tucked inside the back cover of the diary to herself.

"So you're just going to slip this diary back under your bed and pretend you never found it until your next visit?"

"Maybe." Alexandra picked up the diary and flipped to where the pages of notes and formulas started. "But see this?" She tapped a page. "These notes are dated 1980. Mum would have been pregnant with me."

Kate leaned over and had a closer look at a page filled with numbers scrawled in fierce black ballpoint pen.

"That's some pretty mean formulas and notes. Like Ph.D. stuff."

"Exactly. It could be she rediscovered the diary when she was home for a visit but then got sidetracked when she was doing some workings for her methodology."

"Happens to the best of us," Kate said dryly as she rolled up a piece of salami and popped it in her mouth.

"Hmm." Alexandra smiled as she closed the diary.

What she didn't mention was that her mother's dissertation was on mathematical genetics. Perhaps, among these random workings, was some hint or clue as to exactly what Sophia was looking for. These threads of numbers connected her far more closely to her mother than the awkward diary entry hastily scratched across two pages.

Alexandra had always found mathematical theory and facts far better tools than emotional ones for providing answers. She was going to look for an agency in China that could provide her with facts. This time, she'd tuck her unreliable heart away and lead with her head.

Chapter 10

The truck bearing Nina had disappeared and it was starting to drizzle. With the rain had come a discontented wind, rushing under Romy's coat, stinging her wet cheeks, and causing the chickens and roosters in the lines of cages to cluck and crow, as if begging for mercy from this bitter cold. Mutti gathered her fur tighter around her neck with one hand while Romy allowed herself to be pulled along by her mother, jumping over puddles and out of the way of rickshaws appearing from nowhere as the runners in blue rags shouted, "*Aya!*" She turned her head every which way as she took in these dark Shanghainese people and the lingering scents of stock and spices before the wind whipped them away. Romy had never seen so much business and bustle or so many animals and fish in a street before, and she was enthralled. What a filthy, strange, and fascinating place Shanghai was.

How could this new place become home? She wondered what Nina's *Heime* was like and how soon Papa could arrange a visit.

Papa, Mutti, and Romy ran quickly in single file, luggage banging against their knees as they dodged more rickshaws and a steady line of flashy cars across the boulevard of the Bund. Romy's coat chafed the back of her neck as they at last arrived at the opulent entrance to the hotel.

A brown-skinned doorman wearing a white turban, a smart button-up white suit with polished gold buttons, and white gloves greeted them with a gleaming white-toothed smile.

"Good evening," he said in the same round English accent as the unhelpful official in Vienna's British consulate as he clasped the gold handle of the door and swung it wide.

Inside, three more men in white silk turbans rushed to greet them and take the bags from Mutti and Papa. Mutti was too busy gaping and wouldn't let go of her suitcase handle, and the man looked at her in kindly confusion.

He bowed. "Madam. May I?"

"Darling," said Papa as he touched Mutti's arm gently, prizing open her fingers and passing the suitcase to the man.

Romy swiveled on her heels, almost falling sideways as a jazz tune was pounded out on the black grand piano in the far corner of the lobby. She recognized the melody; it was "I've Got a Pocketful of Dreams," a song Daniel used to play for her, shoulders loose and relaxed, as she sat on the stool beside him, avoiding her own practice. Romy drew a sharp breath when she caught sight of the pianist. He was as dark as the baby grand.

Never had Romy seen so many people with different skin colors. Certainly not at home. What would the Führer make of this strange new land where people came in every hue? She had an uneasy feeling these people would be as unwelcome as she was in Vienna. What no one could explain was why.

She must remember to tell Daniel about this strange city. She would write to him as soon as she had the chance. Her brother would be just as fascinated as Romy. Perhaps when he arrived, he could get a job playing piano. Go back to studying. Mutti was going to write a letter and organize official paperwork to get him released from that horrible-sounding camp in Dachau. Romy couldn't wait for him to join them so the family would be together again . . . what was left of their family.

While Romy had been taking in the people and listening to the music, her mother was standing in the middle of the soaring two-story atrium, staring up at the ceiling. Following her gaze, Romy saw that at the apex of the ceiling was a dazzling modern jigsaw of yellow- and gold-stained glass. They had stepped from a slum straight into a golden jewel box. In the middle of all this geometry sat a giant bronze flower.

Mutti turned to Papa with a frown. "But, Oskar, how can we possibly afford—"

Romy froze, her collar tight at her neck.

"It's only for two weeks, Marta," Papa assured her. "Mr. Sassoon insisted we recover from our journey." He tapped his pocket. "Then one of his staff will come and take us to our new apartment."

"But—"

"Marta, please." He wrapped his arm around her waist. "I will start at the hospital and we will pay him back. Every penny."

"Herr Sassoon is a good man."

"He is."

"Will we meet him?" asked Mutti.

"He's traveling for business. But I'll certainly be in touch on his return."

Mutti rested her head on Papa's shoulder with the beginnings of a smile. The late-afternoon sun streamed through the patchwork of stained glass, making the striped marble floors and walls look like liquid gold. In the center of the room stood a dark wooden table with straight modern legs topped by an octagonal slab of marble as thick as a mattress. Mutti's eyes were wide, as if she couldn't quite believe what she was seeing. It was such a contrast to the chaos outside.

Taking Romy's hand, Mutti led her over to the decadent floral centerpiece on the table and drew a deep breath, inhaling the scent of white lilies bunched in vases of every height.

Romy was reminded of their Wednesday visits to her mother's favorite *Blumenhändler* on Wipplingerstrasse, filled with buckets of tight red and pink roses smelling every bit as sweet as they looked. Or the delicate white buds of edelweiss from the Alps with which Mutti filled the house in the late summer and autumn.

As mother and daughter purged the filth, salt, and smog from their lungs, the doorman approached and plucked a lily from one of the vases. A few of the petals were dusted with yellow pollen and he gave it a shake before he presented it to Romy with a deep bow.

"Welcome to Shanghai, miss," he said, beaming. "Will you be staying long?"

Chapter 11

Cathay Hotel
20 February 1939

Dear Daniel,
We have arrived in Shanghai and you wouldn't believe the sights that greeted us on the docks. Oh, Daniel, I cannot wait to share Shanghai with you. Papa says I must keep busy and my eyes open for new things, to treat our stay like an adventure, because when I think of you and Benjamin I am so, so sad I can barely breathe.

I understand why Mutti feels so heavy she stays in bed (although I am forbidden from telling you so).

I worry about you having enough food and I know Mutti and Papa do too. They talk about it a lot. Mutti has sent a parcel to you with some salted crackers, a sack of rice, tinned beef, and Papa's best sweater. I hope you get it with this letter soon.

I made a friend on the boat, Nina, who ended up sharing my cabin and we played skat, Doppelkopf, and Schnapsen just as we three used to. She's thirteen. I hate to tell you but Nina is much better at Schnapsen than you. When you come we can have a challenge.

I miss you so much and hope you can join us soon. Everybody here is talking of the laws passed last month by the Führer to rid Europe of Jews. This surely means you will be delivered your travel papers soon now that you have a permit to take up residence in China.

I think of you and Benjamin every day. Every minute. You are in my heart.

Your loving sister,
Romy

Chapter 12

MELBOURNE, MAY 17, 2016

The flourish of autumn hues in the garden had dimmed in the weeks since Opa's death. The maples stood huddled together with spindly yellow branches and the giant chestnut trees soared like mottled gray sculptures over the fence. Most of the trees in her grandparents' garden had shed their dried-out leaves, and Alexandra's neat piles of rakings stood sodden in every corner. The bright golden dahlias were drooping, waiting to be cut to the ground. Romy insisted she was too old to be digging up the bulbs every year; the dahlias would just have to stick it out as long as she did.

Only the purple lips of the crocus pushing through the soil under the maples reminded Alexandra there was a new season and far more color to come. In early winter, when the crocus petals bloomed, Romy would pluck the orange stamens with tweezers and lay them like threads of gold on tissue paper beside the fireplace until they dried out and could be used as saffron. As a child Alexandra had loved their winter ritual conducted over hot chocolate. Romy placed threads as thin as cotton into tiny airtight jars, while Alexandra knotted fat bulbs of dusty pink French garlic into plaits and hung them proudly with the copper pots above the stove. Wilhelm weighed clumps of ginger and stowed them in neatly labeled bags in the freezer.

How many years was it since she had been home for this winter family ritual? Ten at least. Perhaps eleven.

It seemed cruel to leave Romy to do all this on her own. She'd tried years ago to hire a gardener to help her grandparents out with the bigger jobs, but they insisted on doing it themselves. It kept them young, they said.

She hadn't realized until Opa was gone how much she missed these seasonal rituals.

During the "saffron harvest" Alexandra always imagined that she was somehow plugging the gap in the circle where her mother had once sat. A replacement link. Her grandparents never made her feel that way. She was loved. First by her own parents, then by Oma and Opa. No question. *She* was the center of this circle. And yet she was part of a chain linking to somewhere else too.

Alexandra stopped weeding and sat back on her haunches and braced herself with both hands as grief flooded her veins. This had been happening for weeks now, a sudden sadness ebbing and flowing when she least expected it. She tilted her face to the waning sun like a sunflower, closed her eyes, and waited for the moment to pass.

Romy was on the other side of the path, on her blue cushioned kneepads, concentrating on weeding. Alexandra stopped and watched her grandmother nimbly reaching across the flower bed. Her movements were precise as she plucked errant weeds and tufts of grass from clods of soil, tossing them over her shoulder into the faded red wheelbarrow. Her grandmother was right; it felt lovely to be doing some physical work. She'd sleep well tonight.

The phone in Alexandra's pocket beeped. She took off her gardening gloves, pulled it out, and checked the message.

A series of numbers with a country code popped up on her screen. She sighed. She needed to call the office and talk them through the best trades. Alexandra had already spoken to London at 2 A.M. and 5 A.M. as well as Shanghai twice this morning. What part of annual leave didn't her company get? She had made it very clear to human resources she was delaying her Shanghai posting to take some personal leave to be with Opa in his last days and then spend some time with Oma. Six weeks.

But still her Shanghai team kept calling. It wasn't lost on her that the cargo ships of copper, gold, and iron ore snaking their way around the world were far slower than the electronic deals oiling the desks of her company. Two or three taps of a keyboard and the deal was done. She'd been the top spot trader in London.

Alexandra looked at her grandmother pulling weeds from the soil, making room for new plants and new life. Her white hair was tucked under her yellow bandanna and she hummed to herself as she worked. Alexandra considered their different lives. Romy was dedicated to nourishing the soil and her garden, and nurturing and healing people. Romy made everything beautiful, people better. She was always so dignified. Alexandra made some people richer. She pulled things from the ground without giving a second thought as to what was left behind. Beside her grandmother, Alexandra had as much dignity as a pub brawler.

Romy took a sip from her water bottle and raised an eyebrow at Alexandra, who was still staring at her beeping phone.

"Go, take the call," said Romy.

"I'll just send this one text."

56 and not a penny more.

A reply beep.

Done. Profit 306K. Nice.

Alexandra smiled and slipped her phone back into her pocket. Three million pounds. Over 10 percent profit. Not a bad outcome from hands deep in straw and pig shit. Romy met her eyes and Alexandra's smile dropped. With her grandmother watching, her glee over the sale felt vulgar. Greedy even.

Romy held her gaze and said, "You need to go back to work, *Liebling*." It was a simple statement, not the reprimand she was expecting.

"I've got another week, Oma. But"—she hesitated—"I'm not sure I should leave you."

"Rubbish," said Romy. "I may be old, but I'm not an invalid." Indeed, Alexandra had noticed a little more color in Romy's cheeks the last few days and she seemed to be regaining her energy. Alexandra had underestimated the pain and grief and fatigue of caring for Opa. It was like her grandmother had lost five years in age overnight since they'd started work back in the garden.

"But I don't want to leave you alone," she argued. "It doesn't feel right." Who knew how long her grandmother had left? She pictured Opa on the hospital bed with the ventilator.

"Your *opa* wouldn't have wanted you to stay, nor do I. You can't put your life on hold for me. The *right* kind of work is one of the things that gives your life meaning. I would be lost without my herbs and my clinic." Romy gave her a reassuring smile. "It's okay to go, *Liebling*," she said softly. "You go with my blessings. I insist . . ."

Alexandra's phone beeped again and she pulled it out and read the message, scrolling through prices, as her grandmother said, "See, you have important work."

Her stomach churned, because her work didn't seem that important lately. She didn't use her math skills like her parents had. For genetics, for research. The trouble was she couldn't quite put her finger on what *was* the right kind of work for her.

She'd never forget the look on her probability lecturer's face at Oxford when she'd told him she'd taken a job as a commodities trader in the City. He had inhaled sharply through his nose and then said, "Right. Well, best of luck with your new job. I hope you find it interesting." He'd paused then, holding his notebook to his chest as he gazed at the ceiling, as if searching for the right words, before he said very slowly, "I hope, Alexandra, you find the job *fulfilling*." She'd thought it a strange and particularly pompous statement at the time.

Alexandra glanced from the phone to her grandmother, scanning her *oma's* face for any traces of disappointment. As usual, there were none. Romy's eyes were full of love and hope. Her grandmother was the eternal optimist.

So why did phrases like "important work" seem to mock her? Her big wins feel hollow? She'd just bought her third apartment in one of Melbourne's best suburbs, paid for in full with this year's bonus. She should be feeling proud. She'd worked so hard and achieved so much. She was living the dream.

On paper.

Because Alexandra was already feeling sad, she started making a mental list of all that was wrong with her life. She thought of Hugo. He'd stopped messaging her at least. His last one was just before the burial: *I'm sorry. Forgive me.*

As his words ricocheted around her stomach, Alexandra felt so drained she couldn't even cry. She yanked out some parsley and coriander that had gone to seed in a single fistful and hoisted it into the wheelbarrow. It wasn't just losing Opa, although that made her saddest.

"Alexandra?" Romy had put her trowel down and come to rest her hand on her granddaughter's shoulder. "This broken heart,

I wish I could give you some herbs. But trust me when I tell you it will heal. With time."

How was it that her grandmother could always read her mind?

Hugo didn't deserve the headspace she spent analyzing how it all went awry. But when she thought back to that moment eight years ago when he popped in at the back end of her final recruitment interview in the city boardroom, pink pin-striped shirt, blue eyes holding her gaze without blinking . . . well, there was no other word for it: she'd been smitten. He'd glanced at her CV and said, "I'm sure Pete has explained that you'll be deep-diving into options and derivatives." He shook his blond fringe away from his face, smiled, and said, "I just have one question: You won't be leaving me for Wall Street any time soon, will you?"

Alexandra swallowed to stop herself from blushing.

"I want my big gun staying in London," he continued smoothly. "We've got plenty to do here."

Alexandra flicked some tomato leaves into the wheelbarrow with both hands while she wondered just who she was trying to impress by smashing through the spot trades.

She looked at Romy, who had her head tilted to the side, tanned wrinkled face creased with concern.

"I'm sorry, Oma. You're the one who has had so much heartbreak. So much loss . . . I just feel silly. It's just a bad breakup with a boyfriend." She fiddled with her trowel, knocking it against the border of the garden bed three times and watching the clods of soil tumble from the pointed tip. Anything to avoid making eye contact with her grandmother. Even though Oma could read her like a book and they were close, she hadn't talked about Hugo these past few months.

Romy raised her eyebrows. "A bit more than that, surely. You lived with him for three years."

Alexandra opened her mouth to speak but then closed it. How to explain that they'd really lived out of suitcases, and in the last six months she'd probably exchanged more words with their apartment building's concierge than Hugo? One of them was always on the way to or from Heathrow. Alexandra paused, realizing these enforced breaks had been a relief for her. She was used to being alone.

Romy spoke firmly. "What nonsense. Grief is not a competition. It can't be measured, Alexandra."

She smiled wryly. Her grandparents had always kept the European tradition of using her full name, while the rest of Australia lopped it off to make it as short as possible. Alex, Al, A . . . she answered to them all.

"Maybe a change will do me good. I can start afresh in Shanghai."

Romy rubbed her back, then twisted a few times to loosen it up. "Shanghai. It's the perfect city for reinvention." She closed her eyes.

"You never went back. Nor did Nina or Opa. To Shanghai, I mean." She thought she'd bring it up. For way too long Shanghai had almost felt like a taboo subject.

"I have Shanghai here, in my heart." Romy thumped her chest. "Besides, you need to go there, my *Liebling*. It's in your blood." Romy gave a resigned sigh but offered no new information.

Alexandra's heart skipped a beat. Had she left her laptop open last night when she was googling *Agencies for Finding Chinese Birth Parents*?

It was a strange thing for Romy to say.

Alexandra's face flushed and she looked Romy in the eye. She had already packed her mother's diary and she planned to use her free time, if she had any, to research her Chinese heritage.

Perhaps Shanghai could be Alexandra's city of reinvention too.

Chapter 13

SHANGHAI, MARCH 4, 1939

A month after their arrival in Shanghai, it was time for the Bernfelds to leave the Cathay and start life in their new apartment in Frenchtown. The porter knocked on the heavy oak door to their suite to fetch their suitcases, which he conveyed down the marble staircase to one of the shiny black Daimlers lining the circular driveway outside.

Romy stood in the lobby, watching the stained-glass ceiling glint yellow and gold in the morning light and enjoying the faint traces of vanilla and cloves that seemed to be coming from the new flower display. Today's flowers were like delicate creamy butterflies sitting on long gray twigs. The tips of the petals looked like they had been given the faintest splatter of purple and yellow paint. She turned to her parents, eyes wide with wonder, but her father was hastily whispering something into her mother's ear. Perhaps it was one of his jokes, because the edges of Mutti's lips twitched in the beginnings of a smile.

It was a start.

Mutti had spent most of the boat trip in bed, drinking valerian tea and taking some sleeping tablets Papa said might help. Since they'd arrived at the Cathay, Romy had brushed her mother's dark silky hair out every night and tucked her into bed with a kiss on her clammy forehead. Romy shared her mother's pain, although she tried to hide it. Romy didn't want Papa to worry his daughter was feeling sad too. His skin looked gray, and deep charcoal rings had appeared under both his eyes—rings that no amount of sleep seemed to erase.

So Romy kept moving, exploring every corner of the Cathay, sampling every pastry in the tearooms and reporting back her discoveries to her listless mother. Perhaps one of these delicacies—the pastel-colored French macarons or the Chinese *basi pingguo*, delicious chunks of apple deep-fried and coated in caramel and sesame seeds—could coax Mutti out of the dim room.

Romy had always loved a sweet treat, and as she sat on her own in the salon, with its palm-tree wallpaper and white wicker and marble, it was hard not to fall in love with the tidbits of dessert the waiters smuggled to her table along with the vanilla milkshake or soda she had ordered. She giggled at the translations of the Chinese names. Dishes that came from every corner of China. The soft bean-paste fudge coated in crispy fried soybeans—*lü dagun*—became Rolling Donkeys; pillows of dough with a crunchy skin of dark sugar and sesame seeds were Laughing Doughnut Holes. But her favorite, served with a silver pot of steaming tangy black tea, was the sticky red dates stuffed with a sweetened dough made with a flower blossom syrup: Too Soft a Heart.

Romy tried to explain to her mother how the dates in Too Soft a Heart had so many textures, sticky and crunchy and squishy all at once, in the hope of luring Mutti downstairs to sit among the other women in the Cathay tearooms. The ones speaking Yiddish, Italian,

French, German, and Dutch, as well as the impeccably dressed Shanghainese women, who looked like movie stars with curled hair, fitted silk cheongsams, and pearl and jade necklaces around their necks or woven into a headpiece, diamonds dripping from their ears.

It felt good to laugh with the waiters during the day; it helped her to forget. And then, when night fell, Romy tried to keep her eyes open as long as possible, because when she closed them, all she saw was a line of bloody droplets. The dark hole in Benjamin's head. When she awoke, her pillow stuck to her cheek with salty tears. But Romy thought if she could *try* to be happy, if she could make the best of Shanghai like Papa said, treat it like an adventure, then when she'd had enough rest, Mutti would join them. It was as if her vibrant, glamorous Mutti had been lost in Vienna with her brothers. She didn't seem to notice her daughter at all.

So Romy started asking Papa if Nina could come and join them at the hotel.

Finally, Papa called Miss Schwartz to ask if Nina's uncle would permit her to visit Romy for afternoon tea.

A few days later, accompanied by Eva Schwartz, Nina walked into the gold lobby, mouth agape, her skinny white legs poking out from the blue-checked smock of Romy's that Mutti had given her on the *Conte Verde*, socks sagging around her ankles. As Papa made his apologies for Mutti, Nina and Romy hugged. Nina smelled of soap and something harsh—like the chemicals Mutti used to clean their apartment in Vienna.

"Come, you won't believe your eyes," said Romy as she tucked Nina's arm through hers and hurried across the lobby to the Jasmine Lounge. Lined with dark wood, the lounge was filled with clusters of wicker chairs with bright green cushions. Potted palm trees stood in gold pots in every corner.

They sat at a corner table where they could survey the room, Nina clearly dazzled by the sight of all the elegant women, hair coiffed, necks adorned with pearls, diamonds, or emeralds. Though it was well before lunchtime, some were sipping champagne.

A pianist played soft melodies and tears started to well in Romy's eyes. Music always made her think of her brothers.

Nina reached over and squeezed Romy's hand under the table.

"Order anything you like the look of," said Papa as Nina eyed a silver tray with croissants and jam being carried to the table beside them.

After they'd had their fill of croissants, Black Forest cake, and honeyed sesame seed cake, Papa said to Romy, "Why don't you take Nina for a tour of the hotel while I have a chat with Miss Schwartz?"

The two girls ran back out to the lobby and peered inside the jazz bar, trying not to gag from the smell of cigars and whisky. The room was hazy and a band played "Sing, Sing, Sing." Inside were Chinese faces, Japanese uniforms, and English, French, German, and Dutch accents. But it was mostly men in the hotel's English-style pub; the only women present were dressed for a ball, wearing fitted satin dresses that showed off a daring amount at the front and fanned out behind them like the gowns of movie stars.

"You know, Charlie Chaplin stays here," boasted Romy. "The doorman, Mr. Khaira, told me."

While the men conversed loudly in their deep voices, the ladies with them didn't talk; they just sat demurely, sipping cocktails and occasionally pulling compacts from their bags to powder their already perfect noses.

"They're beautiful," Nina said wistfully.

A rotund man in a three-piece checked suit, who was talking to a Japanese soldier, turned to look at the girls. He had an angry red scar down his left cheek. His eyes narrowed as he looked the girls slowly up and down before smiling to reveal a gold front tooth.

Romy grabbed her friend's hand and started to inch away from the doorway and the cruel gaze of this ugly man.

"This is not the place for little girls!"

Romy and Nina jumped as the doorman, Mr. Khaira, spoke quietly but firmly behind them. He moved forward to usher them away.

Romy bit her lip, hoping he wouldn't send them back to the Jasmine Room. She was reluctant to interrupt Miss Schwartz and Papa. They had been talking about making a list of hospital equipment and drugs—Romy was hoping it would prove to be a long list so she had more time with Nina.

To her relief, she saw Mr. Khaira's eyes were twinkling. "Follow me," he said. He led them across the lobby, heels clicking on the marble, until they reached the beginning of the corridor, where he pulled a lever to one side of the wooden paneling. The wood slid open to reveal a dark tunnel.

"Step inside, Miss Bernfeld. And you are . . . ?" He looked at Nina questioningly.

"Miss Milch," answered Romy for her friend, who was peering around nervously. She pulled Nina into the tunnel and Mr. Khaira flicked a switch.

Romy saw a dim corridor leading up to a set of stairs.

"Perhaps we should go back," said Nina, her hands scrunching the hem of her dress.

"No, let's see where this goes!" Romy whispered over her shoulder as she raced after the pressed white pants disappearing up the stairs.

They walked past a row of unmarked cedar doors.

"This is the service entrance in and out of the building," the doorman explained. "These doors lead to the kitchen. And up here . . ." Without finishing the sentence he bounded up another flight of stairs and the girls followed him into a dressing room with a teak-lined sitting room attached. The club chairs and lounge were upholstered in gold velvet, twin chandeliers sparkled over marble coffee tables, and the Persian carpet was plush underfoot. Romy wanted to take her shoes off and curl up and read a book, but she wouldn't dare.

A peacock-blue feather boa was draped over a chair and Nina reached out and stroked it as if it were a cat.

"This is a special room," said Mr. Khaira. "Secret. Writers such as Mickey Hahn like to stay here. Charlie Chaplin too. Sometimes their dressing rooms get too busy and the singers like to warm up here." He smiled. "This is the perfect place for curious little girls. But you mustn't tell anyone I brought you here, Miss Bernfeld, or I'll lose my job."

Romy and Nina spent the next hour in the dressing room, taking turns wearing the boa and swinging and tapping like Ginger Rogers to the other's Fred Astaire. When they thought it must be nearing Nina's time to leave they hugged each other tight—both trying not to cry—before hurrying back to rejoin the adults.

Romy had returned to the secret dressing room every afternoon since, sometimes with a plate of dates or slices of jackfruit. She would stretch out on the sofa and write to Daniel. On her last day, she carved her initials on the outside doorframe in the hallway with the nib of her pen: *RB 1939.*

As they waited to check out of the Cathay, the lobby echoed and filled with words of every language as women in fur coats, their servants pulling trunks big enough to fit a bathtub, clicked across the marble in their high heels. Men greeted each other with firm handshakes before retiring to the cigar lounge. Inside the entrance to this grand hotel, buzzing with joy and possibility, it was easy for Romy to forget about the pogroms and the growing control of Hitler in Europe, to forget that she and her family were not welcome in their own home. She leaned into the flowers, made giddy by the spicy pollen. She lifted a finger and tapped one of the petals, a butterfly wing.

Mr. Khaira walked toward her, seemingly delighted by the interest in his prized centerpiece.

"Orchids. Grown specially." He plucked one of the smaller butterflies and placed it behind Romy's ear, causing her to blush. "Ah, this flower, it suits you. Orchids are a most noble flower, Miss Romy." He leaned in and said in a low voice, *"An orchid in a deep forest sends out its fragrance even if no one is around."*

Romy blinked at him twice, uncertain how to respond.

"Confucius." He grinned, as if that explained everything.

Romy traced her finger along the orchid behind her ear. It felt like silk and smelled a little like cinnamon.

"You remember: noble." He pointed at the flower in her hair with a nod. "Enjoy Shanghai, miss," he said as he opened the door with a flourish and walked her to one of Sassoon's waiting cars. As she stepped outside into the freezing winter air, she was momentarily shocked by the biting chill, the strange smells and sounds on the breeze. She slipped into the back seat of the car beside Papa and rolled down the window even though the cool air stung her cheeks.

Romy was finally on her way to her new home, and she didn't want to miss a second.

Chapter 14

Alexandra let the driver take her bags and place them in the back of the black town car as she sent a quick text to Romy.

Arrived safely. Muggy. Will call tomorrow. A x

The heat made the minimalist lines of Pudong Airport shimmer as she flopped into the back seat of the car and sipped on a bottle of cool water. They sped away from the airport into the hazy pink dusk, past kilometers of identical high-rise apartments that fanned out from the freeway in every direction. Alexandra was used to the urban sprawl around Heathrow, but this was a whole other level.

She reached over and pulled her mother's diary out of her handbag and flipped it open to the back cover. There was a tiny pocket where the decorative paper overlapped with the cardboard, and secreted inside were two old photographs. The first was a faded black-and-white picture of Romy at thirteen, wearing a checked school uniform with box pleats and a white Peter Pan collar. She was standing beside a Chinese girl in front of some type of fruit tree loaded with cream blossoms. The light behind the trees made the petals luminous, almost translucent. The girls looked relaxed; their heads were tilted back, and they were laughing at whoever was behind the camera. It must have been hilarious because Romy was letting her leather satchel drop on the ground and the other girl in uniform was reaching for Romy's hand.

Alexandra flipped over the photo. On the back was scrawled the year: *1939.*

Alexandra pulled out the other photograph, taking care to hold it by the corner between her thumb and forefinger as its back was still sticky from where she'd ripped it out of Romy's photo album. This one was a school photo of her mother in a pinafore, crisp white shirt, and tie. Her black hair was pulled back in a ponytail and fastened with a ribbon. She had a strong square jaw and dark eyes, but it was the dimple in each cheek that had made Alexandra sit up and snatch this image from the album when she was curled up on the old blue chair in the living room last night.

She'd seen those dimples before, and as she held the two photos side by side in the back of the taxi, she smiled. Forget chasing orphanages and paperwork; all Alexandra needed to do was find out who the other girl in the photo was. Alexandra dismissed her excitement as soon as it surfaced. She could have asked Romy, of course. But if Romy did know Sophia's mother, there must be a reason she was keeping it a secret . . . Oma was happy to talk of trips with the amah to the markets to get fresh bamboo for braising, herbs and spices to make into decoctions for her *mutti*, fish to smoke, or buds of dried chrysanthemum to boil into tea. To point out that, apart from dim sum, the sweet-and-sour pork with lurid pink sauce and other Chinese restaurant staples in suburban Melbourne bore no resemblance to the rich provincial cuisines found in China. Alexandra understood. No, if she wanted to get to the bottom of her mother's history, then she would have to do it alone.

◇

After forty minutes of an endless parade of high-rises, the driver pulled into an area of low-rise art deco buildings, wide streets, and magnificent avenues of plane trees. It was just as described in the welcome pack prepared for her by Barbara at the relocation company.

The car pulled up outside a pair of wrought-iron gates. The driver jumped out and opened the door for her, then moved around to the trunk to fetch her luggage as she was greeted by an elegant woman in her midthirties with glossy black hair blow-dried to perfection.

"Welcome to Shanghai, Alexandra."

She strode over, shook Alexandra's hand, and gave her a thick cream card with her name embossed in an elegant gold script.

Barbara Chen
Relocation Consultant

Barbara held the gate open and ushered Alexandra through. "We were lucky to find this apartment for you. Lots of expats like to come to the French Concession area—it's the trees, I think." She gestured to the canopy of plane trees overhead.

It was charming, like a Left Bank arrondissement, Alexandra thought; not what she was expecting at all.

"I'm sorry for your loss." She looked at Alexandra somberly. "Your office explained the delay with your move."

Alexandra nodded. "Thank you."

Staring at the trees, she felt a gap in her chest where her grandfather used to be. Gnawing at her. It felt as if pieces of the jigsaw of her life were slowly being removed. She and Romy were the only ones left.

"Shall we go inside?" Barbara suggested as she hugged her clipboard to her chest and led the way into a smart art deco building with a curved facade.

"There are just ten apartments here and you're at the front overlooking the street on the ground floor. Yours is one of only three with a garden." Barbara smiled. "Lucky you."

They stepped across mottled gold mosaic tiles that flowed through the lobby and front door and into a reception room that was a modern take on a Parisian Haussmann-style apartment. The soaring ceilings had exposed wooden beams, the floors were dark parquetry, and the walls were painted dove gray. The oversized lounges were in darker shades of gray. The galley kitchen featured glossy white cabinetry with a black marble island.

Alexandra hadn't cooked in London for months, but the minute she'd arrived home to Romy, she found herself baking chewy *Brötchen*, rolls smothered with toasted sesame seeds, to dip into soup filled with garlic, broccoli, and spring onion from Romy's garden. One night Nina had joined them for a bowl and then insisted on plonking down between them on the couch and watching the final episode of *The Bachelor* through her fingers, screaming for the broad all-American *Lustmolch* with the square jaw and oversized teeth to choose the chatty blond *Labertasche* over the scrawny *Spargeltarzan*. It was a master class in German insults. Nina always said she left her *Heime* with a suitcase full of harsh words. And Oma always looked sad when she said it, even though it was supposed to be a joke.

Alexandra smiled at the sight of the well-equipped kitchen, then pointed to a black vase filled with a large bunch of sunny yellow chrysanthemums. "These are lovely, thanks, Barbara." She moved forward to breathe in their peppery scent. The symbolism wasn't lost on her as Romy used to fill the house with assortments of pink and yellow chrysanthemums to attract good luck into their home. When Opa died, Romy had replaced the colorful blooms with white, as if the flowers shared her grief.

Alexandra closed her eyes and took the good wishes deep into her lungs, then opened her eyes to gaze around her new home. It was a beautiful place to make a fresh start. If only she didn't feel so hollow.

Beside the floral arrangement was a glass teapot filled with steaming water and a golden dried flower bud unfurling, so the petals filled the pot. "*Juhua*," said Alexandra.

Barbara looked surprised as she glanced at her clipboard. "I'm sorry. It says on this form you don't speak any Chinese—"

"I don't," said Alexandra with a chuckle. "My grandmother speaks a few Chinese dialects. She lived here during the Second World War. She still practices traditional medicine on her friends. And me, when I let her." She reached for the teapot and poured a cup for each of them.

"Well," said Barbara, "a cup of this tea is just what you need after a long-haul flight. Kill all those plane bugs. Freshen you up a bit."

Alexandra sipped the hot tea and hoped it would ease the knots in her belly. Romy used to brew pots of the buds to reduce a fever or move a flu along. It was good for the liver too, although Alexandra had been fairly tame in the booze department since her catch-ups with Kate.

"Thank you. It was very thoughtful of you."

"My pleasure," said Barbara. Cup in hand, she spun on her heel. "But I haven't even shown you the best part yet." She strode past exposed firebrick walls and threw open the oversized black industrial doors that opened onto a courtyard. She waved her hand for Alexandra to join her. "The garden."

Alexandra smiled. It was hard not to be impressed. Still sipping their tea, the women stepped outside into one of the most striking courtyards Alexandra had ever seen. Paved with large granite tiles, it had a river of crushed white stone on either side that acted as a kind of ground cover for the wall of bamboo on one side and the row of maple trees on the other.

"There's a fishpond over here," Barbara said, leading her to it. In the other corner was a large dark stone that must have been craned over the wall, for it was way too big to carry. It stood on the gravel with a layer of moss at its base. A few tussocks of dark grass swayed beside it. Nearby was a pair of wicker chairs with lime-green cushions so thick and plush they would have looked at home at the Peninsula Hotel. In front of the chairs was a low rusted-steel fireplace holding an elegant line of river stones, each the size of Alexandra's fist. "Watch this," said Barbara as she leaned down and touched a button on the side, bringing a fire to life.

"The developer who owns this building, Mr. Chang, is based in Hong Kong. One of our best landlords, in fact. He takes pride in restoring all these art deco buildings in the French Concession. The ones everyone else wants to tear down for a high-rise. Anyway, that's beside the point. His nephew, Zhang, a landscape architect, is staying in an upstairs apartment. He built this garden. He's working on some big projects over in Pudong, as well as some private commissions."

Barbara looked at Alexandra and the corners of her lips twitched in a smile. "He's about your age—I could introduce you, if you like?"

Alexandra blushed and thought of all the business cards of doctors, accountants, lawyers, and owners of tech start-ups that well-meaning friends of Romy's had pressed into her hands in the past few weeks. But surely Barbara wasn't trying to matchmake. No doubt she just thought it would be nice for Alexandra to have an acquaintance in the new city. Someone to fix a pipe if it broke. He was the landlord's nephew, after all.

It was probably a good idea to know her neighbor. "Certainly," Alexandra replied. "Maybe in the next few days, once I've settled in."

"Shall we?" said Barbara. Placing her tea on an antique wooden coffee table, she sat in one of the green wicker chairs, gesturing for Alexandra to take the other. She opened her leather clipboard and started to go through a series of forms and lists with her client.

As Alexandra half listened to Barbara talk, she looked at the smooth tiles, the river stones, the exposed teak around the pond, and the feathery wall of bamboo.

Barbara ran through her driver's details, how to use the subway (surely she could work that out herself?), and the numbers to call for any emergencies. She paid more attention when Barbara started to go through a list of restaurants in the neighborhood. "Lost Heaven. Mostly expats. Good cocktails downstairs, Yunnan folk food upstairs. Don't miss the tofu and eggplant salad. Or the *jin bo* ghost chicken. Then there's Shintori, Sichuan Citizen, Tapas . . . Do you like food? This is a great city for eating."

Alexandra nodded. There was no point in telling Barbara she'd probably be at the office fifteen hours a day while she sifted through her new projects and organized her team.

Barbara continued with her list. "Cuivre, if you like French. Better than Paris. Or there's Café Montmartre for something more casual. There's a mall . . ."

Alexandra allowed herself to relax back into the cushions and enjoy the greenery around her. In this strange garden she felt calm. She took another sip of her chrysanthemum tea and smiled to herself. Perhaps it was a good sign. But Alexandra didn't believe in luck. Or destiny. A decade studying numbers and patterns had seen to that.

Barbara must have noticed her client starting to doze off, as she closed the folder and touched Alexandra's knee. "Sorry. I get a bit excited when I meet someone who's never been here before. I'll leave you with this to help you settle in." She held up the folder. "There's information on how to use all the services inside. And you have my card, so anything you need just let me know. The driver will be here to take you to the office on Monday morning."

She stood up and smoothed her skirt. "Don't get up, I'll show myself out. Enjoy exploring your new home this weekend." Barbara smiled and headed for the front door.

Alexandra repeated the word *home* to herself. She'd lived in so many homes this past decade, her heart had been strapped together across two continents. The only home that gave her real comfort was Puyuan. But it would never be the same again without Opa.

She twirled her jade pendant with her right hand. Maybe there was comfort to be found here, she thought, in her mother's birthplace. She had searched Puyuan for her mother's birth certificate before leaving Melbourne, even looking in the attic, but there had been no sign of it. But birth certificate or not, she was determined to find her mother's family—*her* family—in Shanghai.

Chapter 15

SHANGHAI, MARCH 18, 1939

Since moving to Grosvenor House two weeks earlier, Romy had tried her best to explore every piece of Shanghai so she could record it in her letters to Daniel. Their elegant art deco building was straight out of a Hollywood movie set, with a central brown-brick tower flanked by two curved wings in the middle of a French garden. Grosvenor House stood opposite a popular sports and social club, Le Cercle Sportif Français, and the Lyceum Theater was on the next block—they'd landed in the very heart of Frenchtown. Papa had started work at the Shanghai Jewish Hospital and Romy was to start at the French school next week. Papa had also promised to speak to Miss Schwartz to arrange a visit with Nina.

In the meantime, she spent her days trailing their new amah with the laughing eyes across the endless parquet of their apartment, learning to speak in a rapid-fire dialect of their own invention that incorporated English, German, and Shanghainese.

Romy had taken to rising at dawn, dressing quickly in her pinafore, and tiptoeing down the curved marble staircase with her shoes in one hand so she didn't wake Mutti and Papa. She'd slip through the servants' entrance to the kitchen and perch herself at the worktable, waiting for her amah, Mei Yao, to hand over a little blue porcelain bowl of steaming chicken broth with slivers of shallots, ginger, and chili floating above a handful of soft rice noodles. Every other day Mei would crack an egg into her boiling soup and Romy would have to stir like crazy with her chopsticks until the egg set and drifted like ghostly noodles around the broth.

It had taken a few days to master eating with the strange wooden sticks. Noodles slipped back into the bowl, splashing soup all over the wooden table and her pinafore. She'd eat breakfast wearing one of Mei's starched white aprons over her tunics, so stained was her clothing after her first attempts at fishing for noodles and then lifting the bowl to her lips to swallow the soup. Mutti would have been mortified if she'd walked into the kitchen to see her daughter slurping soup straight from the bowl.

But, of course, Mutti was always asleep.

Most mornings, after the daily trip to the markets, Romy spent the day in the kitchen helping Mei to prepare food. The kitchen always smelled of steaming chicken broth or a clear soup made from fish heads.

Romy stood with her feet in ballet's third position and her back straight, balancing her heavy cleaver between her thumb and forefinger while she diced green onions, garlic, and ginger for the master stock constantly simmering on the cooktop. Her efforts always looked mushy, whereas Mei could julienne carrots into matchsticks, slice potatoes as thin as paper, and dissect a lily bulb in seconds. Romy was mesmerized by the way the cucumber could be cut down to a frilly spiral resembling a dragon, or slices of bean curd could be cut and arranged to look like orchids.

None of this food ever made it upstairs to her mother's bedroom. It was for Romy and Papa to try in the evenings. Instead, they would prepare Mutti's favorites—Papa had written a list—and tiptoe upstairs each lunchtime and evening, Mei with a silver tray set with a candle, fresh flowers, schnitzel or spätzle with potato salad, and a sliver of strudel with clotted cream for dessert, Romy carrying the tea. Mutti preferred coffee, but Mei insisted she try the different brews she made each day, determined to find one her mistress might actually enjoy. So far they had tried the long green needles of *lucha*—green tea—from tiny cups with no handles, the olive *wulong*, and the bitter black tea preferred by Mei.

Today they had placed a dried golden bud in a porcelain teacup. Romy hoped her mother would enjoy watching the chrysanthemum petals unfurl and become a flower when the boiling water was added. Mei had taken her to a tiny store on the way home from the markets, its shingle sign swinging overhead with some Chinese characters and then the English translation: CHINESE DOCTOR.

She'd leaned against the heavy cedar door and led Romy out of the chill into a dark, wood-lined room that was redolent of fresh flowers like lilies, bitter dried teas, and some of the sweet, warming spices she'd smelled at the street stalls and on the docks. The far wall was lined with glass jars filled with dried herbs, mushrooms, seeds, flowers, and even some flat dried frogs and grasshoppers. A cedar cabinet with more than a hundred tiny drawers and looped brass handles ran down the length of the shop, which was little wider than a corridor. Each drawer was neatly labeled with a set of Chinese characters. In front of the wall of jars was a teak cabinet with a chrome countertop and a set of brass scales.

The bell on the door had jingled as they walked in and a middle-aged man with flecks of gray hair at his temples stepped out to greet them. He wore a white coat similar to the one her father wore at the hospital, and his smile was broad and his eyes warm as he welcomed them.

"*Nong hao,*" said Romy and Mei in unison as her amah launched into a conversation in her native language, pointing at some jars filled with apricot kernels, tiny brown stars she used in her soups, and golden petals. The man set about pulling jars from the shelves and scooping powders, leaves, and seeds into silver bowls, then weighing them on the scales before pouring them into paper bags.

Mei and the man seemed to be debating something rather vigorously, as Mei's tone rose when she pointed at some of the drawers in the cabinet. The man stepped from behind the counter to open and close various drawers, pointing, smelling, and discussing as they went.

Mei was convinced she could make Mutti feel better if only they had the right blend of herbs and spices. At one stage she placed her hand on Romy's shoulder and fingered her brown curls, as if proving something to the man, who looked at Romy with a mix of curiosity and kindness. As more drawers slammed closed and the weighing continued, Romy wandered over to the counter and glanced into a tiny room next door.

A boy—perhaps a little younger than Daniel—was sitting at a round cedar table with scrolls of parchment unwound in front of him. To one side were a small pile of creamy cockleshells and some green stems of leaves with tufts of a purplish flower. She could smell the fresh mint. The boy was drawing the mint stem, making some kind of annotation as he went. Then he did the same with a shell, turning it over in his hands and tracing a long finger across the corrugations along the back. After he had finished with his ink drawing, he reached quickly into the bag at his feet and drew out a camera. Working with speed, he rearranged the cockles so their curved backs caught the light of the window, then he stood up to take the picture. The flash blinded her for a second. Stunned, she knocked the lid of a jar near her wrist. As the steel lid clattered onto the counter, the boy lowered his camera and turned to face her. His black eyes glittered, then looked down, and she was struck by the length of his eyelashes.

Her cheeks started to burn.

The shop owner stepped behind the counter and spoke quietly but firmly to the boy—who put his camera back into his satchel—and waved at the parchment. The boy nodded, sneaking a sheepish sideways glance at Romy before resuming his seat and picking up his pen.

Mei gently tugged at Romy's wrist—"Come, come"—and she was led from the shop holding a bag of chrysanthemum buds and some dried herbs for Mutti.

Romy carried the teacup, chrysanthemum buds, and silver bowl with sugar cubes upstairs to her mother as Mei walked ahead with the breakfast tray of croissants, butter, jam, and hot water.

Mutti would sit up in bed in her silk housedress, surrounded by dark oak-paneled walls lined with padded silk panels featuring stylized peacock tails, the floral chandeliers and wall sconces dimmed, matching blue silk curtains drawn. Afterward, she would step into her marble-lined bathroom and relax in the deep claw-foot bath sprinkled with a mix of dried herbs ground in the brass mortar and pestle—the cinnamon or ginger and dandelion stirred into the steaming water by Mei were designed to make Mutti feel better.

The bath salts must have worked, because Mutti spent most afternoons at the large French oak desk in the sitting room, shuffling reams of paper and writing letters to try to secure Daniel's release.

Mutti was uncomfortable having an amah living in quarters at the back of their apartment—their maid in Vienna always went home before supper—but Romy was grateful to have made a friend. Today, she was worried their little ritual was about to end, though, as the night before she'd eavesdropped on her parents as they took a cognac together in the library.

Her mother had said again that she didn't think it was necessary to have live-in servants, and her father had replied, "Please, darling. The Sassoons have been so kind, I don't want to appear ungracious. Besides, the amah was nursemaid for the family who lived here before us, but she is happy to stay on as housekeeper and cook. It will be good for Romy to have a companion."

"But there is just the three of us now—until Daniel arrives."

Peering around the corner, Romy saw her mother gazing at the strange room, with the oversized cedar dresser, plush velvet sofas, and gold-patterned carpet commissioned by their benefactor. On the dresser sat their only adornment from Austria: twin silver candlesticks that had been hidden under the false bottom of Papa's suitcase—thanks to the clever Herr Gruber. A wedding gift from Mutti's parents, they had been crafted by the most famous silversmith in Vienna.

Papa had taken Mutti into his arms and hugged her tight. But Romy had seen Papa raise his eyes to the ceiling in a silent prayer. She knew what he must be hoping for. *Please let Daniel join us soon.*

Chapter 16

SHANGHAI, MARCH 19, 1939

It was a fine spring morning so Romy had begged Mei to take her to the markets. She fancied some of the pulled noodles with chili and shallot oil, and she loved walking past the vendors, marveling at the different-colored eggs, ranging from blue to cream, and the various noodles and piles of leafy green vegetables.

As Romy stepped onto the landing with Mei, their neighbors who lived opposite came out of their door. Romy had heard there was a Shanghainese family living there, but she was surprised to see the man from the Chinese medicine shop emerge with a woman who must be his wife. Behind the two smiling adults came a girl about Romy's age wearing a green velvet dress with a white Peter Pan collar and black patent leather shoes.

"Hello." The girl had jet-black hair braided into two long plaits and her smile produced a dimple in each cheek. She stepped toward Romy and offered her hand. Stunned, Romy obliged and the girl closed her slim fingers around Romy's, nearly crushing her knuckles with her enthusiastic squeeze. "I'm Li. And these are my parents, Wilma and Dr. Ho. What's your name?" Her words were like a river, endless and smooth.

"Romy." She felt herself blush. "Romy Bernfeld. I'm Austrian." Her stomach churned as she remembered the horrible red *J* stamp on the front of her passport. Was she still Austrian? Mutti and Papa said they didn't belong to any country since they'd left Vienna. They were *stateless*.

Li spoke English with ease and appeared every bit as glamorous as her mother, who wore a blue silk cheongsam, a cream fur stole across her shoulders, and triple strands of pearls around her neck. Her skin was as pale as milk.

Wilma noticed Romy staring and put her hand to her collar with a conspiratorial smile. She had the same deep dimples as her daughter and her eyes twinkled.

Romy smiled shyly at her, wishing her mother were here to meet this intriguing neighbor. Mutti's eyes used to sparkle like this, just as her skin used to glow.

Wilma stretched out her hand and said in perfect English, "It's lovely to meet you, Romy. I trust you've settled in well? We must have you over for tea."

Abruptly the door opposite opened again, and Romy's mouth rounded into an astounded "Oh" as the boy from the medicine shop charged out of the front door with his camera swinging around his neck, a violin case tucked under one arm, and two books and some papers slipping out from under the other. He started to mutter something in Chinese before looking up and spotting Romy standing with his parents, sister, and the amah on the landing.

He started as his dark eyes met Romy's, and the books he'd been holding slipped to the floor. They landed with a thud and slid across the marble.

"Here, let me," said Romy as she kneeled to pick them up. She tried to suppress her surprise as the first was a hardback of Marx translated into English. The second looked like the pages of a script, although as it was written in Chinese characters Romy couldn't be sure.

"Mama's directing a play," Li announced proudly. *"Zhe Buguo Shi Chuntian. It's Only Spring.* We're on our way to the dress rehearsal. Jian's playing in the orchestra for the introduction and intermission." She leaned over to Romy and whispered in a voice fit for any stage. "I wanted to be in it, of course. A lead. It's about love and revolution," she emphasized in clipped English. "But Mama wouldn't cast me." She paused. Her eyes narrowed and she glanced from side to side to make sure she'd captured everyone's attention. Satisfied she had the floor, Li raised her eyebrows and took the script and book from Romy's hands. "I'm not old enough, apparently."

Mei stifled a giggle under a cough, and Dr. Ho stepped forward and took the books with one hand and ruffled his daughter's hair with the other as he chuckled. "Plenty of time for you, Li. I have a feeling that in a few years, the stage of the local theater won't be big enough for you. If you keep up your voice lessons . . ."

Jian looked at the floor as he swapped his violin to the other arm. His unbrushed hair was swept to one side and the buttons of his shirt must have been done up in a hurry, as the top one had been missed, revealing a glimpse of a smooth brown chest. Romy shivered. As he moved past her down the stairs, she caught a slight trace of mint.

Li looked bemused as her brother brushed past, then turned her attention back to Romy.

"Well, Romy, I'm honored to meet you at last." Li smiled as she linked her arm through Romy's as if they were already dear friends and continued to walk down the stairs after Jian. "We've been waiting for the new family to arrive. And besides"—she looked sideways at her parents and dropped her voice to a whisper—"I always wanted a sister. Is it horrible being an only child?"

Li cautiously checked to see her mother wasn't listening. "My oldest brother, Zhou, came down in a plane at Harbin."

"I'm so sorry," said Romy, seeing in her mind's eye pieces of Benjamin's brain scattered over the footpath in Vienna. She blinked away tears. "I'm not an only child," she whispered to Li. "My brother—"

But she was interrupted by Mei, telling her to hurry along and moving her hands as if to sweep Romy down the stairs with her basket. They had to get to the markets.

Li reached out to take Romy's hands in her own, staring deep into her eyes.

Unsettled, Romy closed her eyes and opened them again to see if this charming Chinese girl with two sweet dimples and multiple languages was an apparition. Encouraged, Li threaded her arm through Romy's once more and tugged her to start walking.

"Well, Romy Bernfeld from Austria," Li sang as they stepped down the stairs like a couple heading out to a ball, "I can tell already you are going to be my best friend."

The slip of a girl shrugged on the black mink coat her mother was holding for her and ran outside into the sunshine.

Chapter 17

Grosvenor House
30 March 1939

Dear Daniel,
Today we took a trolleybus to the Bund to organize the last of your
travel papers to send to Dachau. Herr Gruber sent word that your
passport and visa are not enough for your release, we must provide
a valid ticket to Shanghai. We went to the Hong Kong and Shanghai
Banking Corporation to withdraw some money for your ticket.

The bank is easy to spot as it has a huge dome. Mutti insisted
it is the grandest building this side of the Suez. The facade is stone,
with Greek-style columns and windows that are several stories high.
Inside the walls are paneled with dark wood, like on the Conte Verde.
What I liked most about this place was the ceiling. I have no idea
why every grand building in Shanghai has a fancy ceiling! This one
has bright frescoes painted with the zodiac, sun, and moon.

When we finally got to the Italian shipping office we were in the queue forever! Most ships from Italy to Shanghai are full for several months, but Mutti begged for a single economy berth and paid a little extra. The good news is the manager seemed to think we could get the paperwork for you to exit Dachau and sail from Italy just like we did.

The man had a promising smile and three gold teeth, which I took to be good luck. He said he would be able to confirm the berth and date within four weeks—Mutti says Dachau should be receiving the paperwork from the shipping line in three months.

Mutti was so happy she actually did a waltz with Papa when she got home.

There's so much to tell you about Shanghai. We live in Frenchtown and all the street names are in French, like Rue de la Tour, Rue Lafayette, and the main street, Avenue Joffre.

It is a strange mix. Trolleybuses run down the middle of the road, with electric wires spun like webs between the buildings. Then there are the cars, plus rickshaws weaving between everything. I always expect a crash as no one makes room for anyone. But I've not seen one. Yet!

The buildings are tall and remind me of Vienna, with many cafés and bakeries. Papa says the bread here is better than any he has sampled at home. Lots of the signs are in Russian, and others are in Polish. There are tailors galore where men get three-piece suits made and ladies go for the most beautiful ball gowns, like the ones on the covers of French Vogue. *The department stores stock the latest in furs, gloves, woolen hats, silk stockings, and scarves. People seem to be richer here than in Vienna. You can eat at any kind of restaurant—French, Italian, American, or Russian. Nobody much likes the British ones.*

Forgive me if this information is too much. I just want to prepare you for when you join us.

The most important fact is that I have a new friend, Li. She has a dimple in each cheek when she smiles, is quick with a joke, and is the most popular girl in our class. Possibly in the whole middle school. Li's much smarter than annoying Haughty Helena from my class last year. Remember her, the one with the lisp? I wonder what my old class is learning now. Even though I wasn't allowed to go to school before we left, I still miss Rachel and Lola. And Papa has promised he will take me to see my friend Nina more often.

Li lives in the apartment opposite and has one older brother, Jian, who seems very shy. Her father is a traditional Chinese medicine doctor. Li's mother, Wilma, knows where to find the best dumplings, ones with the sweetest pleats twisted into the top called baozi. *On our way to school each morning we often join the line to buy them from a hunched old man with white hair and no teeth. His shop is a hole-in-the-wall, no bigger than my cupboard. He hands it to you on a napkin, and you have to bite a tiny hole in it to slurp the soup before you stuff the rest into your mouth. My favorite is the mushroom, Li's is the pork and shrimp* xiao long bao.

Li speaks Chinese, English, and French. She also speaks Japanese because there are more and more Japanese soldiers in Shanghai. They are trying to take over the city, and the locals are quite afraid of them. Don't worry, though, we are fine and it is much safer than Vienna. I'm teaching Li German and she is teaching me to speak the local Shanghai dialect. I am also learning pidgin English. Here's a list of the words you will use the most:

Chop-chop: *quickly*

Chow: *food*

Catchee: *have, bring*

Maskee: *never mind*

Kumshaw: *a tip (very important for the rickshaw drivers!)*

It is very pretty here and we live in an apartment as nice as the one at home. Papa is working hard at the Jewish Hospital and I have started at the French middle school.

I have to finish now, as Mutti says I must work at conjugating my verbs. Lucky me. I was hoping I might get to miss a bit of school, but they have every kind of school here in Shanghai.

Mutti has promised to send this letter with hers. I hope I hear from you soon. Herr Gruber had written to Papa and said he had no news of you but was still trying through his German Red Cross contact.

It will be okay, Daniel, because not all Germans and Austrians support Hitler. You will be in Shanghai soon enough.

Your loving sister,
Romy

Chapter 18

SHANGHAI, MAY 28, 2016

Alexandra slowed down to take a sip from her water bottle. She'd overslept that morning and had decided to make up for it with a welcome run through the leafy streets of the former French Concession and Fuxing Park. The morning was crisp, and the air considerably thinner than in the evening. Still, when she looked at the sky, it was a faded blue gray—not dull like in London, or variable like in Melbourne, but murky, as if it needed a good wipe.

Similar to the streets of the old French Concession, Fuxing Park had a French feel to it. There were clipped hedges and topiary, large swaths of lawn. Alexandra walked past a European rose garden toward a paved area with pergolas and wisteria. Under the thick green canopy of an enormous tree to her right Alexandra could see people doing tai chi, and beyond them, under the pergola, a crowd of elderly men and women were smoking, chatting, laughing, and playing mah-jongg and checkers. Their faces were dark and lean, with eyes that disappeared when they laughed. Like hers.

Pudgy little children—grandchildren, she supposed—wove between tables, receiving tickles, presenting bouquets of blades of grass and stolen roses, and copping a ruffle of their hair in return.

This mix of old and young charmed Alexandra and made her recall tagging along to Opa and Oma's mah-jongg tournaments.

A grandmother turned and grabbed a little girl wearing sneakers that flashed colored lights from the heel every time she took a step. The old lady blew a raspberry on the girl's chubby cheek and the child wriggled and squealed with delight before she was released to play hide-and-seek with the other children in the rose garden.

Two elderly men in matching faded brown Adidas tracksuits, engrossed in a game of checkers, sat on an octagonal bench seat built around the mottled trunk of a plane tree. The older of the two scratched his head and made a move as the other man laughed and threw his hands in the air, yelling. At their feet they each had a small thermos, presumably containing tea. Both wore socks and slide sandals with their tracksuits. Two men of a similar age hovered nearby, shorts pulled high at the waist and arms folded behind their backs as they watched the game, nodding in approval or offering advice by pointing furiously as they waited for their turn to play.

On the bench beside the raucous old men was a young man with headphones snaking from his ears to his smartphone. Also sharing the bench was a couple, probably in their twenties, deep in conversation. It looked personal; the woman appeared upset and kept shaking her head and pressing her hands to her eye sockets as dirty brown pigeons danced at her feet.

Alexandra looked down the boulevard of plane trees that ran the length of the park. Every seat and garden wall was occupied.

Runners weaved between the walkers, toddlers fell about in giggles. Fuxing Park was heaving with people. The energy was exhilarating.

In the southwest corner, she wandered past a sign with a waterfall symbol: JARDIN DU STYLE CHINOIS. Alexandra paused, chiding herself for expecting Shanghai to be, well, more Chinese. What had she expected, men in robes instead of tracksuits, lion and dragon statues where there was tight green topiary?

She strolled through the gates, past a rock garden where grasses spilled onto a lovely terrace paved with river stones in alternate hexagons and squares. In the middle stood the mandatory plane tree, and underneath were round concrete tables filled with people playing board games and their spectators. The terrace overlooked a pond covered with lily pads and lotus flowers, and there was a sweet arched wooden bridge. The far side of the garden was bordered with a forest of dark green bamboo, and she thought of Romy's wall of bamboo at home. Relaxing, Alexandra took a photo of the lake and sat on the only vacant bench seat to send a text to Romy.

Fuxing Park. Loving the Chinese garden. Wish you were here. A x

She chuckled to herself, knowing Romy would be pleased. She'd always sent pictures to surprise her grandmother, whether it was the over-the-top window dressings of Sloane Street during the Chelsea Flower Show, or frost on a blade of long grass beside the Serpentine on a misty morning.

As Alexandra texted Romy, a man about her age slowed his jog to a walk, yanked his earbuds out, and sat at the other end of the bench. She bristled, yet it was crazy to think she could have this space to herself. Twelve hours in Shanghai had taught her that much.

The man stretched his arms out along the bench, running his fingers along the lines of the wood and dropping his head back to enjoy the sun hitting his face. Black tights covered his long muscular legs and a sweaty green tank top stuck to his chest, revealing broad, well-defined shoulders. Since his eyes were closed, Alexandra took a second to admire his strong jawline and messy shoulder-length hair with the slightest wave. He was handsome, in a raffish, nonchalant way. Like Hugo . . .

No, Alexandra chided herself. No more rakes. In fact, no more men. She was here for work, and to find out where her mother came from. That was quite enough.

She glanced back at the jogger, who looked even more relaxed as he continued to breathe deeply with his eyes closed.

Alexandra was still staring at him when he suddenly opened his eyes. He blinked twice, adjusting to the light, and then smiled at her—a broad, lopsided smile that reached his eyes. She felt her cheeks burn; nobody liked to be caught staring. He ran his hands through his hair, and Alexandra admired the chiseled lines of his face. He looked tanned and healthy.

"Good morning," he said, sounding a tad British.

Her stomach lurched as she realized the last man she'd seen with such a radiant smile, who seemed so relaxed and comfortable in his own skin, was her *opa*.

She breathed in, trying to stay calm.

Alexandra spent most of her time with men on the trading desks, who walked around the office with their jaws clenched, veins pulsing at their temples. They smelled of adrenaline, expensive aftershave, and fear.

Though this man was sweaty, he had a sweet earthy smell about him that Alexandra couldn't place. She couldn't resist saying, "I thought you'd fallen asleep."

He threw his head back and laughed as he ran his fingers through his hair again.

"Ha!" His eyes sparkled. "I try not to make a habit of sleeping on park benches." His accent was hard to place. Transatlantic, she supposed. "Actually, I was meditating." He tilted his head to the side and narrowed his eyes a fraction, as if watching for her response.

Alexandra looked at him and tried to guess what he did. Trader? No, too calm. He had fine hands. Strong, like a pianist or cellist, but mottled and calloused. He caught her staring at his hands and he offered one to her.

"Zhang."

She shook it. A warm, firm handshake. A confident man.

"I'm Alexandra. You're the first person I've met in Shanghai. Well, other than Barbara, my relocation realtor." She laughed.

"Wait. You mean Barbara Chen? You must be Alexandra Laird, my new neighbor from London. Except you don't sound British." He wrinkled his nose in confusion.

Of all the people she could run into in this city of twenty-four million!

"Yes, that's me. I've been living in London for work but I'm Australian." She waited for him to ask where she was originally from, or where her parents *really* came from. But there was nothing except a broad smile and quiet acceptance. She stared at him.

"So what do you think?" His eyes were dark and clear.

She looked at him, puzzled.

He nodded at their surroundings. "Of the garden."

"Oh, it's pretty. I like the little lake—the water's peaceful." She recalled her long walks along the Thames and the beaches at home, where she felt most calm.

"I'm heading back—can I walk you? I don't suppose you've had a chance to see much of Shanghai since you only arrived yesterday." He paused, as if deciding whether to ask her a question. "I'm meeting a couple of my cousins for dinner next week. Very casual. I have to warn you, though, Peta and Petra talk nonstop, like true teens, but you're welcome to join us."

"Sounds great," she lied; the last thing she felt like was a cheery family dinner. "But I'll probably be working, I'm afraid."

"At dinnertime?" Zhang raised his eyebrows.

Probably. "I, uh . . ." She paused, reluctant to tell him she was a trader. It seemed so trite given he had designed her magical courtyard. She didn't want to see disappointment in those eyes. Not yet. "Okay, sure. Dinner would be great, thanks." Why not? It would have to be better than skulking at home.

"Great." He beamed. "Give me your mobile number and I'll text you the details. Shall we walk?"

They meandered back out into the shady streets of the former French Concession, past the hawkers selling balls of wool, plastic toys, and newspapers on gray tarpaulins, laid out on the footpath outside elegant boutiques with restored art deco facades. They wove through a number of birdcages dangling from the low bough of a plane tree, parrots squawking within, and by food stalls where people were lining up for dumplings, soups, and fluffy white rice buns.

Alexandra asked, "How do you know which are the good stalls? I'm always a bit nervous . . ." She tried to avoid street food as much as possible. When she was away on research trips she'd hold on to her hunger until she was back in the safe confines of her plush hotel room, and then call down for a BLT, a Caesar salad, or her post-flight staple of chicken wonton soup and a glass of decent pinot.

Zhang stopped walking and turned to face her. "You don't eat street food?"

"Well . . ." She felt her ears start to burn. Now was not the time to tell him she'd once had the runs so badly after a satay on a Kuala Lumpur stopover that she'd been hospitalized for twelve hours and put on fluids.

Zhang said gently, "It's okay. Look how many people need to be fed every day in Shanghai."

Alexandra eyed the teeming footpath.

"Most people here have tiny apartments. Little more than shoeboxes. Many still share with their extended families. It's just cheaper, and easier, to eat out." He shrugged. "Get away from Grandma and Grandpa," he joked.

Alexandra half laughed, but was aware of a pang of grief. She felt for her pendant. Was that what she had been doing all those years ago when she moved to London to do her Ph.D.? She'd thought she was following in her mother's footsteps, trying to make her grandparents proud. But had there been a piece of her that was trying to escape?

Sensing her unease, Zhang touched her arm and said softly, "Look, I'm only here for a few more months before I head to Singapore briefly, then back to Hong Kong. I've got a few gardens to finish and some planning for new projects to do. I'll be working long hours." His eyes were open and kind, and his eyelashes the longest she'd ever seen. "But I'd love to show you around. Shanghai's a crazy town. So much history."

Alexandra swallowed her nerves and guilt and let herself enjoy the smell of ginger, garlic, and herby chicken broth wafting from a food cart with only two massive silver pots and a ladle. Just beyond the footpath, lines of black four-wheel drives clogged all four lanes of the road, while an endless stream of scooters and bicycles poured from gaps in the stationary traffic, ignoring the honking cars and scooting through red lights. Surrounded by gas fumes, smog, and tantalizing spices, Alexandra looked up at the soaring canopy of the plane tree above them. The bright green leaves shimmered with the breeze, allowing slivers of sunshine to slip through to the streets below.

It was a lovely gesture. What was the harm in taking up Zhang's offer? Just for a second she imagined running her finger down his jaw, touching those full lips. He was leaving soon, and she'd never see him again.

Alexandra smiled. "I'd like that. Thanks."

Zhang grinned back. "Okay. But I warn you, I take my role as tour guide very seriously."

Chapter 19

SHANGHAI, APRIL 16, 1939

After four weeks, Romy was starting to feel like a local in Frenchtown. Papa had persuaded Eva Schwartz to bring Nina over the previous Sunday because Mutti and Papa wanted to discuss the possibility of Nina coming to live with them rather than staying by herself in her female *Heime*. Miss Schwartz had said there was no chance Nina's uncle would allow it. Papa had even sent a letter of introduction and requested several meetings with David Damrosch, but each request had been turned down. Mr. Damrosch was too proud to admit he couldn't support his sister's child, so the Bernfelds would have to make do with visits until Miss Schwartz could convince him it would be in Nina's best interests to move.

While the adults sat in the drawing room sipping coffee and nibbling at shortbread, Romy and Mei had taken Nina to the grand Cathay Theater to see Errol Flynn in *The Adventures of Robin Hood*. Afterward they had wandered down Avenue Joffre for a hot chocolate. The girls pressed their noses against the windows of the Russian coffee shops and bakeries, swooned over the lengths of colored silks and rotating French *Vogue* posters in the windows of the tailors, and mimicked the *cheep-cheep* of the exotic birds in the ornate black cages hanging from a gnarled plane tree.

On the way home, Nina had blushed as she described the thin soups and stale bread in the *Heime*. When it was time for her to leave, Mei had gone into the kitchen and filled a blue-checked tea towel with fresh brown rolls, three salamis, some Swiss cheese, and an entire block of cooking chocolate. Miss Schwartz thanked Mei and said she would be in touch with Papa next week about "more supplies" and to arrange a time for them to visit the following Sunday. Romy swallowed and tried to ignore the tightness in her throat when they left. She missed Nina. Also, she worried when Papa went out alone in a rickshaw at night to buy medical supplies like aspirin, charcoal pills, and insulin from pharmacies and, occasionally, on the black market in dark alleys. Drugs were becoming more expensive by the month, and Papa tried to help Miss Schwartz and the hospitals in Hongkew maintain a consistent supply for refugees who could not afford to pay for their own treatment. Romy worried about the police catching her papa doing something illegal. Look what had happened to Benjamin and Daniel. It wasn't like Papa to bend his own rules.

Today, Li had managed to persuade Mei to let them both walk to school with Jian, who studied nearby. Li was a gifted singer and could trill just like the exotic caged birds, even an octave higher. She would do her voice exercises while skipping along the footpath, always taking care not to jump on the cracks. Li managed to be both girlish and coquettish at once, and passersby often turned to catch another glimpse of this beautiful dimpled girl with the magical voice who would give them a cheeky nod and a wave as she sang louder and louder.

"One day you should sing outside the coffee shops and I'll put down my school hat," said Romy. She'd heard about people doing that on one of the New York radio shows she listened to.

"Don't be silly, we'd never be allowed to perform," said Li, laughing as she skipped ahead and launched into a sassy version of Ella Fitzgerald's "A-Tisket, A-Tasket." "Besides"—she linked her arm through Romy's—"I like to sing just for you." She looked over her shoulder at her brother, who was walking several paces behind, carrying her satchel as well as his own. "And for Jian, of course." Romy turned and gave Jian a shy smile.

"Mutti says we shouldn't do anything to attract the attention of the Japanese soldiers or the gangs. Miss Schwartz says they are setting up secret patrols in this area."

"We'll be fine. You're always so worried about our safety. C'mon. Let's choose a snack."

Li bolted to their favorite food cart, run by a man with laughing eyes and a shaved head under his round cap. The girls would use their trolleybus money to buy a newspaper cone of toasted melon, pumpkin, and sunflower seeds, or peanuts. Occasionally there would be some jars of pickled mangoes, Romy's favorite. This sticky orange delicacy—sweet, sour, and salty with just a hint of cardamom—was more expensive, so they had to pool their money with Jian's for a single serving to share.

That afternoon, as the school bells chimed for the end of lessons, Romy and Li dashed through the high black security gates of the former convent, laughing and swinging their bags, disheveled plaits and white ribbons trailing down their backs. In the month since Romy had started school, the pair had become inseparable, convincing their teacher Mademoiselle Dupont they simply must sit next to each other in class. Romy was surprised and a little pleased that the mathematics they were studying was more advanced than in Vienna, and they were soon to start units in chemistry and physics. Shanghai was constantly surprising her.

Dr. Ho, in a gray cashmere coat and felt hat, stood with Jian outside the gates. Li bolted to her older brother and skipped on the spot with delight. Usually in the afternoons they would greet their amahs and catch the trolleybus home for milk, cookies, and pastries. Sometimes Mutti, dressed in her gloves and hat, would take them out for a proper afternoon tea of cream cakes topped with raspberry jam on Avenue Joffre.

Romy smiled at Jian and the apples of his cheeks flushed pink as he flicked his shoes to cover a stone with dirt. When he lifted his head and met her gaze again, it was she who felt whispers of something strange and tingly inside.

Dr. Ho stepped forward and greeted them with open arms. "Well, hello there, girls. All my appointments were canceled this afternoon and I thought why not spend the afternoon with two of my favorite little ladies?"

Romy's heart sank. Dr. Ho was being upbeat but she knew this outing meant her mother was having one of her spells. They had been occurring more often lately; a smell or a noise would bring on a migraine so thick and fast that Mutti became dizzy and had to lie in her darkened bedroom, sometimes for days. Papa had brought numerous specialists home from his hospital to meet Mutti—a neurologist, an anesthesiologist, and two cardiologists—but none seemed to be able to help.

Only Dr. Ho could. He had called in for tea one day when Mutti was in the middle of a migraine. Papa, whose colleagues had mocked Dr. Ho for not being a *proper* doctor, had thought it wouldn't hurt to see what the famous Chinese doctor said.

He made his diagnosis: Mutti's liver *qi* had been disturbed and the energy of her heart was blocked. Mutti's grief and sadness were making her ill. Dr. Ho had spoken in low tones and coaxed Mutti into the sitting room, before he gently squeezed between her thumb and forefinger, asking if it alleviated the pain. It had something to do with a pressure point, he'd said. He'd returned later with some needles that he'd stuck into her thumbs and ankles before rubbing peppermint oil into her temples. Then he gave Mei some jars of dried spices to be boiled up in a pot on the stove, filling the kitchen with a bitter scent.

Mutti was ill again because the window of opportunity in which to rescue Daniel from Dachau was closing. The camp required evidence that Daniel had a valid shipping ticket before they would release him, with a strict deadline for leaving Germany. Romy had accompanied Mutti to the shipping office last Saturday morning to collect Daniel's promised ticket. After posting it they were going to stop at the Astor House tearooms to celebrate with lunch and a glass of champagne. But when they reached the shipping office, the pale-faced manager was most apologetic.

"It would appear the paperwork was left for a certain time on the wrong desk. We are doing our very best to rectify this matter. But I'm afraid this means that no ticket has been issued for your son. We are looking for another berth . . . but we are fully booked so it may take some months—"

Mutti winced. "Months?"

"There are far more . . . passengers than we have boats." His voice dropped. "I'm sorry."

Romy closed her eyes to stem the flow of tears, trying to remember the pitch of Daniel's laugh. When she opened them, her head was so full of Daniel she was almost shocked to see Li, Jian, and Dr. Ho standing on the footpath with her.

Li beamed and clapped her hands together. "Can we go to French Park with you, Papa?" she begged.

"Why not? I have instructions to deliver this one home before dark." He placed a hand on Romy's shoulder. "Until then, the afternoon is ours, ladies, Jian." He smiled.

Jian took Li's satchel and walked behind the girls with his father. The streets smelled of springtime; every newspaper stand had metal buckets of fuchsia and cream peonies for sale and the plane trees were unfurling their green canopies overhead.

"People assume these trees came from Paris," Dr. Ho remarked, "but actually, they were imported from Britain."

Romy considered this for a moment. You couldn't be certain of the origin of anything, or anyone, in Shanghai.

A street sweeper clad in navy rags shuffled past them, sweeping the gutters and placing the leaf litter into burlap bags. A cyclist on a bike loaded with newspapers went past, wobbling between the cars and trolleybuses.

"Can we play mah-jongg with you, Papa?" asked Li.

"It'll cost you a song," he joked, before stopping at a stall to order bowls of freshly pulled fried green noodles for each of them. They sat on small wooden stools and watched as a man pulled a ball of dough from a tray. He folded, twirled, and pulled the dough until he had enough thin noodles to drop into a wok. Romy closed her eyes to breathe in the savory smell of fried shallots and peanut oil.

As the wok sizzled and the noodles were tossed, Li chatted with Jian and her father about their dreadful calculus assignment and how she was lucky to be paired with Romy because at least then she'd have a chance of getting an A-plus.

"I could help you both," offered Jian.

"No need. Romy's the smartest in the class. In the school, most likely."

"Aren't you lucky?" Dr. Ho said as he winked over Li's head at Romy.

The cook came over with their bowls of noodles, and they all busied themselves pouring in droplets of vinegar and a salty black soy sauce that went with everything. All three Hos ladled spoonfuls of chili paste with a few nuts on top and stirred it in with their chopsticks. Romy knew her limits with this new food. She'd tried the wet chili last week with Mei and cried—first from the stinging and burning on her lips, then from embarrassment as Mei had lifted her top lip and shoved a soft square of green melon into her mouth. Today, she decided to settle for a light sprinkle of the dried red chili flakes the cook kept in a chipped white bowl. She stirred the chili and soy sauce with her chopsticks like a local and lifted the noodles to her lips as if she'd always lived here. It felt good to have a belly full of food before they joined the games at French Park.

◇

At French Park the delicate honey-and-almond scent of peach blossoms filled the air. Rows of peach trees stood proud and squat, offering branches covered with tight pink blossoms up to the spring sunshine; the park was a haze of pink. Romy and Li each pulled a twig down and picked a blossom, tucking it behind their ears as Dr. Ho explained to Romy, "The honey nectar peach is the prize of Shanghai. In a few weeks, every corner in Shanghai will have a peach stall."

Li twirled and said, "We'll show you where to get the best ones, won't we, Jian?"

Jian nodded and said to Romy, "The blossom suits you."

"Ah, quite the compliment, Miss Romy." Dr. Ho plucked a blossom and sniffed it before he revealed the deep magenta center. "The peach blossom brings you luck; it's the fruit of the gods." Dr. Ho smiled at her and said, "Enjoy these moments, Romy. This pollen will be gone in a few days and the leaves will unfurl. Everything has a cycle, a time to bloom and a time to rest." He paused and then continued. "Your mother, she needs to rest. You shouldn't feel guilty. Give her time, enjoy the blossoms and then the rich sweet juice of the fruit."

As she met Dr. Ho's gaze, Romy felt tears well in her eyes.

"Things will get better soon," the doctor assured her. "You will see. There is nothing more devastating than to lose a loved one." He patted her arm. "It's natural, essential, to be sad and grieve for loss. It goes deep into our lungs. But we must breathe the new in, the yin, and expel the old, the yang.

"In Chinese medicine, if we hold the grief deep inside us—if we cannot express it and make peace with it—it can disturb the work of our lungs and intestines. Grief poisons our body if we don't find a way to process it."

Romy looked up at Dr. Ho for a sign he was going to fix her mother.

"We are all helping your mother to find a way to be well. In the meantime, you just have to love her. Do the breathing for her until she can breathe with you."

Romy nodded and took the blossom from his outstretched hand, touched by his kindness. She thought of the flickering yellow horseshoe on Wipplingerstrasse, and why Benjamin was killed and Daniel taken away, leaving her the only child. She didn't feel lucky—not by any stretch. Her stomach cramped and her breath shortened as she sniffed the fragile blossom. She felt like crushing the soft petals in her palm, leaving a pink pulp. Her guilt was overwhelming.

"Do you believe in luck, Dr. Ho?" asked Romy.

He paused, glancing at a far corner of the garden before looking Romy in the eye. "Yes. Good luck and bad luck. Terrible things can happen to good people, Romy. China is at war with Japan. Who knows—"

He was cut off as Li ran back toward them, having looped her way around the orchard. She swayed as if she were drunk on pollen. She had a garland of blossoms in her hair. "Look, Aba." She turned to Romy. "Did he tell you peach blossoms are the flower of love?" Her eyes sparkled, and she pressed her fingers to her lips. The girl had been giddy with the prospect of romance ever since their amahs took them to see a rerun of *Top Hat* at the Cathay Theater last week. Li had been swooning, dancing, and singing just like Ginger Rogers.

Romy's eyes flickered across to Jian and met his own as his cheeks started turning the color of a blossom. He'd taken his camera from his satchel and was peering up into a tree, taking close-up photos of the flowers and branches and trying to ignore his sister.

"Romy . . ." Li linked her arm through Romy's, as had become her custom, and dragged her toward the mah-jongg tables. "We must ask Papa to buy us each a bunch to give to our mothers."

Romy agreed as she looked back over her shoulder at the orchard.

"Here." Li stopped in front of a laden peach tree. The air smelled thick, like honey. "Jian, take our photo, please."

He sighed and dropped his shoulders as he walked toward them. Romy loved the way he indulged his little sister—it reminded her of how Daniel and Benjamin had indulged her.

"I want one in front of the beautiful tree with my *beautiful* friend Romy." She swept a curl from Romy's face and watched it spring back straightaway. "I'd do anything for your ringlets."

Romy stared at her friend's flawless skin, the color of cream, her narrow nose, and her almond eyes, and compared them with her own square jaw, snub nose, and face covered with freckles. She felt anything but beautiful. But she was grateful to have this rare bird as her friend.

Jian directed them to stand in front of a low-hanging bough as a bemused Dr. Ho shook his head, chuckling.

Li pulled Romy close, hugged her tight, and as she gave her a peck on the cheek she whispered, "You're the smartest and the best friend I've ever had. Promise me we'll always be friends?"

"Of course, silly," said Romy as she gave Li a playful nudge with her shoulder and dropped her satchel. Both girls pulled a face and laughed.

The camera clicked.

"Take it again, we want a proper photo," insisted Li.

They straightened their uniforms, linked hands, looked at the camera, and smiled.

◇

When they arrived at Dr. Ho's favorite corner of French Park, a paved area under the grandest plane tree, Li ran from table to table, greeting the elders glued to their mah-jongg. Some people wore fine cashmere coats and polished shoes like Dr. Ho, others had basic canvas shoes, and one man, clad in the blue cloth of a worker, wore no shoes at all. Each of the players had a thermos of tea at their feet. Dr. Ho greeted his friends warmly and gestured for the younger ones to squeeze around a far table set under a pergola heaving with wisteria.

Dr. Ho started to deal, and the game began with the Prevailing Wind of East. At first Romy had been flummoxed by mah-jongg, but in the past weeks she had quickly picked up on the three different sets of tiles and had set herself the task of learning the characters. Her favorite tiles were the flowers: plum, orchid, chrysanthemum, and bamboo, one for each season. It was fast becoming her favorite game. A million times better than chess.

The Hos had kindly lent the Bernfelds a mah-jongg set, and Romy would sit with Mutti and Papa, listening to Bach and trying to ignore the gaping hole where Daniel should be.

As Dr. Ho started to throw the dice, Li slid her hand under the white collar of her school dress and touched her jade pendant for luck, as she did every time.

"Can I look?" Romy asked.

Li reached under her collar and pulled out a pendant on a long gold chain. Etched into the jade was an exquisite lily, just like the one she'd seen in the lobby of the Cathay Hotel.

Romy ran her finger over the relief. "It's beautiful," she told her friend.

Li's eyes brimmed as her father said, "It comes from Li's maternal grandmother, in Soochow." He looked at his daughter sadly and patted her hand. Jian stared at his tiles. "We have no contact with them now. Not since 1937."

Romy looked back at Li, whose blossoms had slipped and were now tangled in her hair. Her friend always danced and pranced like she was on a stage, but Romy saw the frightened girl she really was. Li looked fragile sitting beside her brother.

As Li took off her necklace and passed it to Romy so she could have a closer look, she said, "Jade is magic—both yin and yang."

Romy must have looked puzzled.

Dr. Ho came to the rescue once again. "It's the energy in everything. At its most basic, good and evil. We all have both these energies in us. We just get to choose which one we use more."

Romy immediately thought of Franz, the soldier who killed Benjamin. Until it was forbidden, Franz sang as the lead baritone in Benjamin's choir. They were colleagues and, she had supposed, friends. And yet Franz shot him, as if her brother were an animal.

She looked across at the Hos, who seemed equally shaken by the massive change in their lives. They might come from different countries, the Hos and the Bernfelds, but they shared this loss.

Jian shifted uncomfortably beside her, accidentally knocking his knee against hers.

"It's a lovely lily," said Romy, continuing to hold the pendant.

Dr. Ho said, "The necklace is supposed to be a gift for Li's wedding trousseau. But her grandmother wanted it to be used as a talisman. It carries her blessing and connects each generation to the next."

"It's my lucky pendant," said Li as she tucked it back under her uniform and picked up a tile.

Chapter 20

SHANGHAI, JUNE 1, 2016

Alexandra looked beyond her bank of computer screens to the floor-to-ceiling windows on the far side of her new office. Outside was a forest of skyscrapers in hues of gray, silver, and gold, piercing the clear blue sky. Suspicious, she wondered what foreign dignitary was visiting: it was rumored that many of the factories upwind of Shanghai were closed when a VIP came to town. It could be true. Most days the view from her office on the fiftieth floor was tinged with a layer of pink-gray smog that hovered just above the city.

The section of the Huangpu River her office overlooked was a working waterway. Always busy. Supply boats and tourist vessels sailed back and forth at all hours on a river as thick as molasses. The main port was a purpose-built island a few kilometers from Shanghai but, watching these dark, squat boats come in and out, it was easy to feel like the whole world was being assembled in China. An ocean liner had carried her grandparents up this same river all those years ago. What had they thought when they first caught a glimpse of the Bund?

What would Romy make of it now?

Alexandra took a sip of water and eyed the green pyramid atop the Fairmont Peace Hotel. Her grandmother called it the Cathay. The grand facades of the old bank buildings remained, but inside were designer clothing stores, chic nightclubs, restaurants, and rooftop bars.

Alexandra flicked her gaze back to her screen and examined the latest report from an analyst as alerts for gold and silver out of the Shanghai Futures Exchange floated across the screen. She'd been tracking the spot prices all morning out of SHFE and cross-checking them against London, Dubai, Nepal, India, and Pakistan. When her hands were flying over keys like this, buying and selling and smashing the price, her heart usually beat with the intensity of a track sprinter. Not today.

Perhaps it was just the market. The upcoming U.S. election was making everyone a bit shaky and most wanted to play it safe with gold. She'd been calling it for a while now, and the boys on her team were just starting to catch up. She'd beaten Hugo's London crew on a deal twice last week and he'd sent a text.

Nice, A. x

Alexandra watched figures dance and float across her screen. Not great. The numbers weren't working today. She'd already traded two hundred million. She sipped the green tea and lemon juice (no sugar) she'd had delivered from Happy Lemon and leaned back in her chair, twiddling a pen in her free hand.

At their team breakfast at the Mandarin Oriental that morning, they'd decided over coffee and crumpets that they wouldn't move more than two hundred today. They wanted to tease out the market. It was eleven o'clock in the morning and her job was pretty much done. She sifted through a pile of research material one of her analysts had sent over with a list of new mines being proposed in central Africa, Mexico, Canada, China, and Australia. She liked to know about any new developments in case she needed to alter her long-term price projections.

Bert Engles, the gruff Dutch CEO, strode past her desk with a thumbs-up and a grin. "Very nice, Alexandra. Top week again. Keep it up." He adjusted his monogrammed gold cuff links. "I won't let them send you back to London at the end of next year. *We* are smashing everyone, young lady."

Alexandra didn't bother to point out she wasn't solely responsible for the day's successful trades. Usually these comments made her bristle, but today she just didn't care.

Bert was like every other boss she'd had. Hugo. Jerry. When Jerry had told her about the *unbelievable* opportunity in Shanghai for eighteen months, he couldn't help flicking his eyes across to Hugo's corner, where his partner reigned over the City. The pair probably arranged her transfer over a bottle of Montrachet and the foie gras tortellini at the Ivy. Little did they know that Alexandra had been deliberately focusing on deals with the Shanghai office and building her contact list since she'd broken up with Hugo. She needed to get out of London, Shanghai was booming, and China was far closer to her grandparents than Europe. Alexandra hoped to visit Australia every month. A Shanghai posting also meant she could explore her mother Sophia's homeland—her history—without dredging up painful war memories for her grandparents. Shanghai had ticked a lot of boxes.

As she'd left Jerry's office he'd said, "We thought it would be a good fit since Shanghai's the center of precious metals. Besides, your language skills will really help you."

She closed the door of his office on the way out, wondering how French and German would help her in the Shanghai markets. He'd asked her some vague questions about her "Asian heritage" a while back. Perhaps he thought some Chinese blood made her a native speaker.

She scanned the fluorescent river of numbers flowing uninterrupted across her screens. All numbers to stockpile gold. To fill a vault, or make some fine jewelry.

What would her parents make of her job if they were still alive? Would they be proud?

Alexandra reached down and rummaged through her handbag for her mother's diary. Opening it, she ran her fingers over the scrawl as if it were braille. As if she could bring her mother back to life.

She was pretty sure the numbers in the diary were some kind of genetics probability formula. She'd hoped to figure it out herself, like she always did. But it was tricky and, if she were honest, she'd need to ask for help to solve it—something that always made her uneasy. What was her mother trying to solve?

She couldn't answer that. But today she was going somewhere to find answers of a different sort. She picked up her handbag, made her way to the elevator, and was in the vast marble lobby of her building in under a minute. Her driver was waiting outside, and she climbed into the back seat and pulled her research folders from her bag. Today was a day for answers.

◇

She stepped into the smart Population and Family Planning Department office, took a ticket, and sat between a red-faced woman trying to give a bottle to a screaming newborn and a downcast old couple quietly holding hands. The elderly woman was clutching a piece of faded blue-checked cloth in her free hand.

Alexandra checked her watch—she'd promised the team she would be back in under an hour—and tried not to notice how slowly the red digital numbers were ticking over on the screen at the counter. Instead, she flipped her folder open again and started flicking through all her documents. Her mother's adoption certificate (and three copies), passport (another three copies), and marriage certificate were all there. She closed her eyes, willing the numbers to move faster.

Her pocket started to vibrate and she pulled out her phone. It was a message from Zhang.

Still up for hot pot tonight?

She started to type a lengthy excuse and then deleted it. Instead she replied: *Great. Thanks. Text address and time and I'll meet you there after work.*

The baby had almost finished the bottle when at last Alexandra's number pinged on the screen. She gathered her handbag and took her folder to the counter.

"*Nong hao.* Do you speak English?"

"Of course," said the middle-aged woman with a smile.

"Great. I have the passport of my mother here, Sophia Shu Cohen. Obviously that's not her birth name. But I was hoping that you would be able to find her birth certificate. I'm looking for her birth parents, my maternal grandparents." Her words rushed together.

The woman took the documents out of Alexandra's hands and started riffling through. She looked at the passport, cross-checking it with the name on the adoption and marriage certificates. Her mouth tightened as she read the faded *1946* on the adoption certificate.

She took a deep breath and started tapping away on the keyboard. Alexandra wished she could crane her neck through the gap in the glass divider to see what was being typed. The control freak in her wanted to own that keyboard. Mine that deep database.

The woman started shaking her head and then started nodding, before shaking her head again.

Alexandra's stomach was churning. She hadn't *really* expected the birth certificate today. But surely this lady could tell her what forms she needed to apply for one?

"Very sorry," said the woman.

Alexandra held her breath.

"Even if we did have a certificate, I could not give it to you straightaway. There's paperwork."

"I understand. Of course."

"But there is no birth certificate. Sorry."

"I understand my mother might have a different Chinese name. But surely that would be connected somehow to this . . ." She gestured to the adoption certificate.

"There's nothing. I'm sorry. During the war, our records . . ." She grimaced. "There are years where we have some administrative gaps."

"Nothing?" Alexandra echoed, feeling tears spring to her eyes. She reached into her handbag for a tissue.

"We are finding more every week." She nodded at the chairs behind Alexandra and she turned to look at the elderly couple, the woman now resting her head on the man's shoulder. "These two come every second Wednesday, three hours on a train from Jiangxi. They gave up a child for adoption. They are still hoping . . ." She shrugged. "During the war many people didn't register births. Or deaths. It was just too hard; there were different governments."

Alexandra wiped her eyes with a tissue. "It's silly, of course. I just hoped there might be a little bit of information. Just a lead. Anything."

"I would say come back in a few weeks, but this adoption certificate was issued in Australia, not China." She tapped it. "How did your mother get to Australia?"

Alexandra suddenly felt uneasy. Had her grandparents been caught up in something illicit? What if she'd unwittingly exposed her grandmother to the Chinese authorities?

She started to gather her documents quickly, glancing at the cameras, half expecting guards in black to appear.

But the woman behind the counter smiled patiently, as if she were reassuring a child. "Do you know *anything* about where your mother was adopted?" she asked.

"I know my grandparents lived in Hongkou during the war—though my grandmother refers to it as Hongkew. They weren't married then." She was nervous. What if she'd already said too much?

The administrator nodded as if that made sense. "You should have mentioned that to begin with. Hongkew Ghetto. Your adoptive grandparents were Jewish, perhaps?"

"Yes."

The woman handed the document folder back to Alexandra. "My department has nothing to help you. But fill out this form with your contact details and I'll see what I can do. I'll need a copy of the adoption certificate too, please. Just sign the bottom."

"Thanks so much. *Anything* would help. This is all I have."

"Then you need to go to the Jewish Refugees Museum. They have many records. Tell them Min Wang sent you." She handed Alexandra a card with her name on it. "Good luck."

Chapter 21

SHANGHAI, APRIL 23, 1939

23 April 1939

Papa gave me this diary for my birthday. Actually, I chose it from the stationer on Avenue Joffre, when I told him I hadn't been sleeping because of Daniel. We've still had no word, but I'm sure we will soon. We can't send so many letters with no reply forever.

I will confide here my stories of Shanghai so I can remember them for Daniel when he comes.

We went to the home of Sephardic Jews for Passover and Mutti said I was welcome to bring Li for company. Of course, I wanted Nina as well but she had to spend the holy day with her uncle.

You would not believe the houses here. This one was a grand Spanish-style villa (according to Papa) with terra-cotta tiles and archways and columns over porticoes that looked like whipped cream. The black wrought-iron balconies were very modern with tiny diamond patterns and a treble clef. It made me think of Daniel and Benjamin. Either side of the main entrance were two trees clipped into giant round balls, and there were miles of flat open lawn where the adults play croquet, a British game where you hit balls around with wooden mallets. The lawn was the perfect green for lying on (Mutti wouldn't let us) with random clumps of grasses and giant rocks in the corner. It's a bizarre arrangement that I am noticing in many of the Shanghai parks. A row of fancy black cars lined the driveway. They were so clean and shiny we could see our reflections in them.

The estate was protected from the street by a high brick wall, and along the fence were lines of feathery trees propped up with special bamboo tripods. Clusters of tiny white flowers filled the garden with a tangy sweetness, a bit like an orange. Li's papa makes a strong tea from the dried leaves, and her amah makes a sticky rice cake cut into diamonds from the black fruits that look a little like olives.

The mansion had over twenty bedrooms. (Li and I ran around and counted upstairs before joining everyone downstairs to listen to a little boy sing "Ma Nishtana.")

Now back to the feast. It was different from all the other Seder meals I've eaten. We had bowls of fluffy white rice, dried beans and lentils, as well as red, yellow, and green peppers stuffed with rice.

My favorite food was a dip called baba ghanoush, which is soft-cooked eggplant with lemon and pepper. There was also a dip made from chickpeas called hummus and a chopped salad with tomatoes, cucumbers, and mint and parsley. The chicken soup had lemon, and you could add some strange pickled lemon on the side. It still had the matzo balls, though. Li hadn't tried them before and she had two servings. And these were just the appetizers!

On the table with the main dishes were baked fish covered with lemon slices and parsley, and a bright yellow grain they called couscous, which was both crunchy and soft at the same time. No gefilte fish! There was also a beef brisket that Mutti said had been *cooking for two days and it was so soft you served it with a spoon. It tasted a bit lemony too.*

I had a sip of Mutti's coffee and it tasted like dirt to me. It's thick, like honey, and they drink it from a tiny cup with no whipped cream or cinnamon. Instead they used cardamom. Papa loved it, Mutti hated it.

But the dessert table! I have never seen one like it. I wish I could post some to Daniel.

Instead of the haroseth being made from apples and cinnamon, they make it with dates and it is much thicker. There were sticky baklava squares made with pastry and pistachios, which oozed with honey, and lemon macaroons shaped like crescents and dusted with sugar. Li and I filled our plates and ran out to the garden and ate dessert next to the large pond, throwing the crumbs onto the glassy surface to watch giant goldfish jump.

Mutti says food is getting more expensive here so we mustn't waste it. (I didn't tell her about feeding the fish.) The Japanese are stopping rice and other food deliveries coming in from the farmlands around Shanghai.

Now that I am home and tucked in my bed, it seems strange to me we went out for the meal. When there was a war in Egypt in ancient times, they passed over the houses of Jews to make sure they were not killed. But now the opposite is happening.

I can't help but overhear the adults discussing the Führer and the Wehrmacht's march into Czechoslovakia and Italy's takeover of Albania, and I know how lucky we are to be away from Europe. But what does it mean to be lucky when one brother is dead and we have no news of the other? Poor Nina has no one, as her uncle has to work all the time to earn enough to feed them and they will need new boots this winter.

How is it possible to be fortunate and not feel the deep guilt that accompanies such luck? I am very sorry to say I snuck ten of Mutti's valerian drops last night as I brushed my teeth. I can't tell if it helped me to sleep.

Until tomorrow,

Romy

P.S. On the radio last night the news broadcaster suggested Hitler may have ordered his generals to prepare for a war. I'm not sure if that means we can go and get Daniel, or if he will be released to come to us. What happens to our family if there is a war?

Chapter 22

SHANGHAI, JUNE 1, 2016

Alexandra stood at the entrance to an anonymous brown skyscraper in Hongkou, looking at about an acre of immaculate white tiles lining the floor to the elevators on the other side of the lobby. It was such a bland space it could be the entrance to a hospital. As ten lanes of traffic continued to snake past them in the street, she raised an eyebrow at Zhang. It wasn't what she'd expected of the best hot pot place in town.

As if reading her disappointment, Zhang grinned at her and gently touched her elbow to steer her toward the elevator. A couple of teenagers, one with a shaved head, the other with a purple Mohawk and multiple nose rings, followed. Earbuds in, the teenagers' eyes were glued to their oversized phones. Perhaps they were texting each other? From what she'd seen so far on the subway, in the streets, and in the park, no one went anywhere in Shanghai without earphones.

She looked up at Zhang. He gave her an easy smile and she felt pleased she'd decided to come.

"How was your first couple of days? Make any new friends?" Zhang asked.

"Some," Alexandra replied. "About fifty! My team's pretty big in this office, so it'll take me a while to get to know them. But they're all super sharp, and they know what they're doing. Although"—she hesitated, not sure how to put it—"I mean, they're all so young. With degrees from everywhere: Beijing, Singapore, London, Amsterdam, Boston, Munich, Sydney. It's an office full of smart pups—the most diverse desk I've come across."

"What were you expecting?" he asked, looking a little bemused.

Alexandra flushed. "Well, I knew they'd be good. I just wasn't expecting my team would be equally comfortable running a NASA program!" She smiled. "Maybe I'll do that next."

"Next? Would you change careers?" Zhang raised his eyebrows. She'd sensed that he was curious about her choice of work when they'd talked on the way home from the park the previous Saturday. "What exactly does a commodities trader *do*?" he'd asked.

Make money seemed too glib, so instead she told him about risk analysis, flexible mathematical formulas, and derivatives.

"Hmm, good question," she said now in answer to his query. "I've been doing this for a decade so I don't really know what else I'd do." She didn't quite like to say that she wasn't sure what other job could give her such a rush. Though, lately, the adrenaline highs had not come so easily.

The elevator doors opened to deafening Chinese pop music and an explosion of color. A girl with a lime-green earpiece and a clipboard and dressed in an incredible silver-sequined miniskirt strode over to them in three-inch wedges. Beside her, Alexandra felt like a dowdy spinster aunt in her tailored pale blue Armani jacket and navy pencil skirt. Clearly this was no ordinary bar.

The hostess waved them to a waiting area with a huge smile.

To one side of the waiting area was a nail bar, where they found two girls barely out of their teens laughing and chatting as they each had a manicure and a complicated set of fruit-salad stickers embossed onto their fluorescent nails. They looked over at Zhang and waved as he walked toward them. "My cousins, Peta and Petra," he said, pointing to a pair of cheeky round faces.

"Hi, Zhang!" they chorused, waggling their fingers at him for approval. They obviously adored their older cousin.

"Very nice, ladies. A step up from—what was it last week? *Star Wars*?"

The girls giggled.

"This is my new neighbor, Alexandra."

"Hi," Alexandra said. "I love your nails."

They beamed at her.

"Right, well, let's get a drink." Zhang ushered her across to the general seating area. "When I'm in Shanghai, I try to bring the girls here every few weeks; they love it." They perched on crimson velvet cubes at a white table, and seconds later a woman appeared carrying a small wooden box filled with squares of watermelon and pawpaw and spicy rice snacks. Alexandra and Zhang sipped on watermelon juice, and Zhang handed his phone and sunglasses to the waitress to be cleaned at the special station.

Alexandra had the feeling she was Alice entering a twenty-first-century Wonderland.

A group of young men in matching college T-shirts sipped Tsingtao beer as they played checkers, while the group at the table beside them played cards.

"What *is* this place?" Alexandra asked. She looked over at a buffet with bowls of every type of condiment. Six different chilies, shallots, shredded greens, lotus root, and tofu. "Is this where all the cool kids hang out?" she teased.

Zhang grinned. "Pretty much. It's cheap, so you get lots of students."

"And families," she said, eyeing a row of kids playing games at a station of iPads.

Two tables away, people were fashioning bright squares of paper into origami cranes.

Alexandra must have looked confused about what they were doing, because Zhang explained, "You get a discount for every crane you make." He nodded toward his cousins. "They loved it for years—until they grew old enough for the nail bar."

Alexandra laughed. "Naturally."

With the loud music, fluorescent lights, and raucous laughter, this was about as far from first-date territory as you could get—not that this was a date, she reminded herself; she was merely having dinner with her friendly new neighbor.

Hugo would hate it here, Alexandra thought as she sipped her watermelon juice from a yellow plastic cup. Their first date in London had been at the Ivy: crisp white tablecloths, waiters so pompous they winced at her accent, and hundred-pound bottles of wine that Hugo had ordered like soda water. Alexandra hated to admit it, but she'd been impressed.

As the music changed and a waiter did a twirl on the way to get some menus, Alexandra found herself smiling. And she considered something else: Did she want this to be a date?

"Your table's ready," said the cute girl in the sequined skirt, smiling and batting her eyelash extensions at Zhang. Clearly Alexandra wasn't the only one who found him charming.

They followed the waitress to a table with a giant stainless steel plate with a hole cut in the middle.

"It's for the hot pots. You can choose from four different types of base broth."

The cousins wandered over and, after confirming Alexandra had no food allergies, started ordering from a menu delivered on the iPad.

"We'll get our favorites, and you can tell us what you think," said Petra.

Minutes later two men rushed over carrying square silver tureens filled with broth. Petra pointed at one: "Sichuan—very hot." She giggled.

"That's okay," Alexandra assured her. "I'm used to chili. My grandmother uses it a lot. Good for a fever, keeps the blood flowing, right?"

"Is your grandmother Asian?" Petra glanced at Peta. "We were trying to work out your background. You look a bit Chinese." She frowned. "Sorry, is that a rude thing to ask? I didn't mean to be . . ." She looked from Alexandra to Zhang.

Alexandra paused before answering. Oma was her true grandmother; to say otherwise felt like a betrayal.

"My grandmother's Austrian; she moved to Australia as a refugee. From China, actually." She hesitated. "So did my grandfather. But he died recently." Her voice cracked as grief flooded her body.

The girls murmured their apologies and Zhang nodded slowly as he looked into her eyes, as if it explained something deeper about Alexandra.

"But to answer your question. I'm not really sure whether my"— she didn't want to use the word *real*—"who my blood grandmother is. My mother was adopted from China."

"Have you met her?" asked Petra innocently before Peta whacked her on the thigh and shushed her.

"I don't know who they are. I was hoping while I was working here I could find out." She ran her hand up through her hair at the back of the scalp and traced the line of her scar.

Zhang nodded, as if that explained why someone would be a commodities trader in China.

"I went to a government department today but it was a dead end. They had no record of my mother. The administrator didn't seem to think that was unusual." She was blushing now; she didn't want to make out her grandparents as having done something illegal.

Zhang gave her a reassuring smile.

Petra said, "It's common for people to come to China searching for their birth families. Our *baba* is a journalist at the *Shanghai Daily*, and he worked on a story once where an anonymous policeman told him that so many 'lost children' turned up at his station that staff didn't record all the cases."

Alexandra flinched and took a sip of her beer.

"The government is working hard to reconcile families, but—"

Zhang softly but firmly interrupted his cousin. "Did they give you any tips on where to try next?"

Alexandra gave him a grateful smile. "The Jewish Refugees Museum."

"I've heard that place is amazing," said Peta.

"I'll go on Friday afternoon. I won't have any time before then."

"I'm sure the staff at the museum will be able to help. You'll find something," said Petra.

Waiters in white smocks bustled over with two more steaming hot pots.

"Mushroom and chicken." Zhang pointed from the dark to the lighter broth, but Alexandra could have told them apart from the pungent smells wafting up from the center of the table. Plates of raw squid, sliced beef, and clams arrived alongside blocks of silky tofu, circles of white lotus root, and a slimy salty green that must have been seaweed. There were five different types of mushrooms she didn't recognize, from gold fans to tiny brown buttons to delicate silver threads. There were plates piled with leafy vegetables and a bowl of tiny pale blue eggs. Petra went off to grab a bamboo box full of toppings like chili, nuts, sliced shallots, and dried tofu skins, as cuts of meat Alexandra couldn't identify piled up around her.

Zhang lifted his chopsticks and started plucking some meat, mushrooms, leafy greens, and tofu, dropping a little of each in the broths and giving them a stir.

A waiter put a plate of sliced watermelon beside Alexandra. She thought it was an unusual choice, more a dessert really, so why would they be serving it now?

The broths boiled and bubbled, making Alexandra hungry. Another waiter appeared—they were everywhere—with a ball of white dough and started tossing it with flicks of his arm; it was far more dramatic than spinning pizza dough. He kept pulling and throwing the white dough, making it longer and longer and folding it over and over on itself.

Alexandra laughed, mesmerized, when she realized what he was making. The dough had become narrow strings of rice noodles. The waiter stopped, pulled some scissors from his apron pocket, held his creation over the broths, and chopped the ends off, dropping equal amounts of long noodles into each of the broths. Zhang gave them a poke so they were submerged for a second.

"You want the noodles to absorb the flavors," he explained. "Can you pass me your bowl, please, Alexandra? You're the guest of honor, so you get served first." He held a giant spoon over the broths. "Which one would you like to try first?"

Alexandra didn't hesitate. "The Sichuan, please."

Peta and Petra looked at each other with raised eyebrows and tried to suppress their giggles behind their hands.

Zhang didn't miss a beat. "Okay." He ladled the clear pink-hued broth and some of each of the ingredients into her bowl, and Alexandra topped it with the crunchy dried tofu, shallots, and crushed peanuts. She was about to sprinkle some chili on top when Zhang warned, "Careful. It's very hot. You might want to try it before you add more chili."

"Okay," replied Alexandra. "But I love a spicy soup." She took a sip of the broth and felt the fluid warm her lips and throat, then quickly used her chopsticks to fish out a noodle. She sucked down the noodle, soft and salty, before the roof of her mouth started to burn.

Her lips were stinging. Her tongue was tingling. Her throat contracted and beads of sweat appeared on her forehead. Everything felt like it was on fire. Gasping, she reached for her Tsingtao but Zhang pointed to the triangles of watermelon. Alexandra shoved one into her mouth, with only the green skin sticking out between her lips. She didn't care what it looked like.

The relief!

She wiggled her tongue against the watermelon, then pulled it in and out of her mouth until the burning, tingling sensation subsided a little. She picked up a white paper napkin to wipe the droplets of sweat running from her temples.

"Like it?" Zhang asked.

"S'great," Alexandra said, her mouth still stuffed with the watermelon. She gave him the thumbs-up sign, even though she had started to wheeze.

"It's super hot, even for me," said Petra kindly.

Zhang ladled out a bowl of the mushroom broth with meat, noodles, and pickled vegetables and placed it in front of Alexandra. "Maybe mix up the two until you get used to it," he suggested.

Alexandra nodded gratefully as she put the green rind on the plate before her, took a swig of her beer, and then shoved another triangle of watermelon in her mouth.

Zhang held his beer up and winked at her. "*Ganbei.*"

"Cheers," toasted Alexandra as she whipped the watermelon rind from her mouth again.

She inhaled fragrant broths deep into her lungs and looked around the restaurant, seeing people get their shoes shined or have shoulder massages as they waited, rap music blaring and the noodle thrower doing his magic tricks and twirls at the next table. Then she turned and watched Zhang serving broth and making jokes with his cousins, admiring the gentle way he had with them, and she felt something shift. Alexandra was surrounded by irreverence and joy. Hundreds of people were having a great time here. Not just existing, but living.

And here she was, with a burning mouth, sitting on a fluffy purple stool in a hot pot chain having a ball with new friends in a strange city that shimmered and sprawled as far as the eye could see. Alexandra had loved being home and sharing meals with Romy and Nina, and making fresh salads for Kate, Brad, and their tribe of young children, who nonchalantly tossed the corn and carrots around the room instead of eating them. Food was best shared with family and friends. Not for show, as it had become with Hugo, juggling caterers and high-end restaurants.

Romy was right, as usual. It was time for Alexandra to let a little joy in.

Chapter 23

SHANGHAI, SEPTEMBER 17, 1939

After school most days, Jian met Romy and Li at the school gate and walked them to Dr. Ho's shop. They'd push through the door, making the bell jangle like crazy, while Dr. Ho would cover his ears and pretend they'd made him forget whatever he was measuring on the giant brass scales. Romy thought she could stay in this tiny corridor of a shop forever, opening and closing the mysterious spice drawers labeled with gold calligraphy, intoxicated by the scent of steaming ginger, an abrasive camphor liniment, or her favorite, licorice root.

She sat at the large oak table, scrambling to finish the algebra and French homework for both girls, while Li braided her hair and practiced her vocal scales.

Jian would pick his way through glass jars, plucking out creamy flakes of *mu li*—oyster shells—and describing how they could be used to help dizziness or headaches, or sketching the rough leathery lines of ginseng root—*ren shen*—onto a dark scroll. Romy would close her eyes as Li waved sweet brown gardenia buds, handfuls of star anise, or shards of tree peony bark under her nose and try to guess each spice.

"You're so much better at this than me," Li conceded.

Romy said nothing, but she committed every smell to memory and placed her books next to Jian. She was starting to read Chinese characters and learn calligraphy—but not fast enough. Instead, Jian would take the time to show her how the tea from mulberry leaf could be used to remove heat from the lungs and clear a cold, but you could also use duckweed or the bitter ground seeds of burdock. Sometimes, if there were no customers, she would tiptoe out to the shop to watch Dr. Ho carefully prepare the parcel of dried herbs and spices she delivered to Mei, who would blend them up and boil them for Mutti.

Color was returning to her mother's lips and cheeks, and she was suffering fewer migraines. Romy was certain Dr. Ho's treatments were partly responsible.

France and Britain had declared war on the Führer and his expanding Third Reich a fortnight ago, so Mutti spent her afternoons glued to the radio, hoping for news of Vienna and southern Germany, praying for Daniel. Instead of retreating to her room at the news of war, Mutti had asked Papa to inquire whether there was a job at the hospital for her. She wanted to go back to nursing. Stay busy.

Mutti was ready to fill her lungs and breathe fully again—just like Dr. Ho had predicted. Romy was intrigued by his decoctions and the needles he used. She wanted to know about these heady scents, the sweet and bitter spices that could not only heal the body but also strengthen the mind.

Li would feign interest in Dr. Ho's lessons for a few minutes before collapsing back in her chair and singing Ella Fitzgerald songs to herself.

Sometimes Dr. Ho would make them a pot of rose hip tea and fill the study with sweet steam. When Dr. Ho was busy in his treatment room, Jian would push his homework, quill, and scrolls aside and sneak his camera out of his satchel. He'd arrange three abalone shells so their silver ridges glistened with all the hues of the rainbow. Yesterday, he'd grabbed knuckles of fresh ginger and white starry clouds of angelica flowers and arranged them in the square of light falling through the high window onto the table, when Dr. Ho walked in.

The doctor's smile faded when he noticed Jian's camera.

"Jian, what have I told you?" He sighed. "Only when your homework is done. Then your classifications. Yang. Yin. Up. Down." Dr. Ho's hands moved up and down as he spoke.

Li jumped up from the table, winding an unfinished braid around her middle finger, head slightly tilted. She smiled at her father and said, "It's my fault. I noticed these beautiful flowers on your counter and thought perhaps they might look like silver clouds in a photo. I insisted, Aba."

Romy glanced at Jian, whose neck was reddening as he studied his hands, spread flat on the table.

"Very well," said Dr. Ho, giving Li's left dimple an affectionate poke. "But no more interruptions. I need Jian to learn these herbal tinctures. Your grandfather's notes. My notes. Soon Jian will have his own notes to add to our scrolls," he continued with pride. "Today you have to transcribe my recipes for Mrs. Bernfeld. Romy can give them to Mei."

Jian blinked, long eyelashes quivering.

"But what if he doesn't want to be a doctor like you?" said Li, squaring her shoulders. "What if he wants to be a pianist, or . . . or a photographer?"

"Li, that's enough," said Jian softly as he passed the stems of angelica to Romy. "You take these. Give them to your mother."

"Thank you. She does love the fresh flowers your family sends each week." Romy took in the musk from the blossoms. "You're all so kind."

Two red apples appeared in Jian's cheeks.

"It is our pleasure." Dr. Ho smiled. "Now remember, Jian: *The father who does not teach his son his duties is equally guilty with the son who neglects them.*"

Dr. Ho winked at Jian, grinned at the girls, and went back into his shop. Before he closed the door, he poked his head back through.

"Oh, and, Romy?"

"Yes, Dr. Ho?"

"Let Li do her own homework."

"I don't—"

"I know how close you are. But she has to learn to stand on her own two feet."

"But, Aba—" Li protested.

"Back to work. Finish your homework, otherwise no dumplings and sticky mango."

All three groaned as they flipped open their textbooks.

Romy glanced over at Jian and whispered, "If you teach me the recipes and how to blend them, I can help you with your notes. It might give you time for—" She waved her hand at the camera in case Dr. Ho was listening on the other side of the door.

Li paused in her algebra and studied her brother's face before turning to Romy. She opened her mouth to say something, but thought better of it as she turned back to her textbook with a dramatic sigh. The corners of her lips twitched as she tried not to smile.

Romy reached over and grabbed a blank piece of parchment from Jian's pile and dipped the nib of her fountain pen in the ink as she asked, "Where do I start?"

Chapter 24

SHANGHAI, JUNE 3, 2016

Alexandra paid her entrance fee at the security checkpoint to the Shanghai Jewish Refugees Museum and stepped through the gate into a concrete courtyard. Immediately she was struck by a life-sized bas-relief sculpture in bronze, so fluid it looked like it had been carved from mud. A bearded old man sat on a suitcase, reading a book, while beside him a tired woman clasped her headscarf to her chest. Standing on the other side was a young couple, the man solemnly holding an ornate set of Shabbat candlesticks and the woman standing behind him, a satchel over her arm and one hand gently touching the nape of her husband's neck. In the lead was a man, tall, broad, and proud, gazing directly ahead. On his shoulder was a young boy—no more than six or seven—staring forward, his arms spread wide.

Goose bumps rose on Alexandra's arms as she studied these anxious, weary refugees.

Behind these six figures was a sea of faces merging into one another, as if the sculptor had kneaded them together from clay.

These were the faces of the Holocaust. Fleeing. Seeking.

She gulped down smoggy air as tears started to prick her eyes. Somewhere in that sea of bodies belonged her *oma* and *opa*.

She'd come to Shanghai chasing people she didn't even know existed, and yet here she was, face-to-face with the people who had loved and raised her.

The immensity of her grandparents' journey immobilized her and she wished she'd agreed to let Zhang come with her. He'd offered to as he walked her to her apartment door last night, but she'd insisted this was a private matter and she needed to do it alone.

All the figures in the sculpture touched. Heads bent together, reassuring hands on shoulders, the gentle clasp of a child's hand. None of them stood alone. Their strength was in their unity. Love.

Alexandra slid her hand beneath her coat to clasp her pendant, running her forefinger over the line of the lily, taking a deep breath to calm herself.

"Can I help you?"

A woman with a smart pageboy bob and purple glasses stood beside her, eyebrows raised. Her name tag read: AL CHENG, MANAGER.

Alexandra started. "Oh, sorry, I just—"

"It's very moving, isn't it?" said the woman, nodding at the sculpture. "Very real."

"It is," Alexandra agreed. "Actually, maybe you can help me." She pulled her folder from her bag. "I'm trying to trace my mother." She told Ms. Cheng the little she knew about her grandparents' lives in Shanghai during the war and handed over her mother's faded Australian adoption certificate, along with the crisp name card the woman at the Population and Family Planning Department had given her. "Ms. Min Wang said to let you know I have already spoken with her."

"The first place to start would be this wall," Ms. Cheng suggested. "We have over thirteen thousand refugees listed here. You say your grandmother's maiden name was Bernfeld?" She walked along a giant copper wall engraved with thousands of names until she reached *B*.

MARTA BERNFELD • OSKAR BERNFELD • ROMY BERNFELD

Alexandra's goose bumps returned. This was her family, their names inscribed on a monument halfway between the city they'd left behind and the country they'd made their own. Shanghai remembered . . .

She reached out and traced the letters of her grandmother's name, then took a photo with her phone. Ms. Cheng moved briskly down the wall, searching for her *opa*'s name. Alexandra leaned in quickly and kissed ROMY BERNFELD. "I miss you, Oma," she whispered.

Ms. Cheng returned. "I'm sorry, we have no Wilhelm Cohen on this wall. But our records are being updated all the time. I'll just leave you to look through the museum if you like, while I do some searches. I'll take this certificate too, if that's okay?" She bowed her head as she stepped backward and then turned and walked into a nearby office.

◇

Alexandra spent the next hour wandering from room to room, studying photos of refugees disembarking from European ocean liners onto docks filled with barrels. Rows of beds in *Heime* dormitories, ambulance trucks, and soup kitchens. On and on the photos stretched: girls with sewing machines, handsome young men in soccer uniforms, Jewish identification cards, passports stamped with ugly red *J*'s, wedding photos with a Chinese groom and a Jewish bride, or vice versa. There were tiny leather suitcases, woolen hats, and—the most precious commodities in Hongkew—leather shoes and oilcloth umbrellas.

Contracts to purchase tickets from the Lloyd Triestino shipping line *Italien–Shanghai* were mounted on the wall. The label underneath read: *Documents like this were often used as proof of emigration to secure the release of Jews imprisoned after Kristallnacht.*

Oma's brother had been in Dachau. Had they tried to secure his release? Instead of questions being answered, each step revealed how little she knew of her grandparents' past.

On the next wall was a photo of a nurse dressed in white, standing in front of an enormous window in a roomful of empty hospital beds. Ms. Cheng came to stand beside Alexandra.

"This is Ward Road Hospital—you said Marta and Oskar worked there, but you didn't mention that your grandmother also worked there as a trainee doctor."

Alexandra stared at the woman, too stunned to speak.

"I have these printouts for you. It's a list of staff who worked at the hospital on Ward Road. The Imperial Japanese Army kept strict census forms in the ghetto. We also have a copy of your grandmother's pass to leave the ghetto to attend her classes in medicine at Aurora University."

Alexandra's head was reeling as she studied the square pass stamped with Chinese or Japanese characters and the word *Frenchtown* in faded letters, a scrawled signature at the bottom.

"Thank you. That's—I had no idea."

"Your grandmother sounds like an incredible woman."

"She is." Alexandra sighed, berating herself for knowing so little about the woman who'd raised her.

"This shock, this sadness you are feeling, I see it often. People do things in war for two reasons: either out of duty and loyalty, or to survive. One is not better than the other. Both have equal merit. But often they are unable to talk about their experiences afterward."

Alexandra looked at the printouts in her hands and was too overcome with emotion to speak.

"You are from Australia, you say? You are lucky. Your grandmother is lucky. But I think already she knows this. It is you who needs to understand."

"Did you find anything about my *opa*—Wilhelm?" said Alexandra, swallowing her sadness. Why wasn't her *opa* on the wall?

"Only that he worked as a baker. But there is no record of his exit from Shanghai. Also, no death certificate. He's not on the wall because we didn't have his records at the time. New information about refugees is still being uncovered, though."

"I see. But what about the adoption certificate? My grandmother said my mother came with her from China."

"That may be so. But I'm sorry to tell you that *this* Australian adoption certification"—she held up the certificate Alexandra had given her—"has no matching documents in China. But what I can tell you is that when Romy Bernfeld left Shanghai, she sailed to Hong Kong."

Chapter 25

Meine Anschrift
Name: Daniel Bernfeld
Dachau, 3K
2 März 1940

Dearest Romy,
I received your letter of March and it brought me great happiness.

At night, I always tuck the letters from you, Papa, and Mutti under the sheet. I reread your letter and then I fall asleep peacefully.

I thank God, dear Romy, that I am healthy and hope you all are the same. The weather here is very nice, and every day it is very warm.

I am glad you are enjoying school and have made a new friend. I am looking forward to meeting Li and would very much like to sing with her, thank you. I noticed you did not mention your own practice. Are you still playing piano? There is no choir here, but sometimes when we are working ███████████████████ ███████

The trees in Frenchtown sound very beautiful, the food exotic. Please tell me more about all you are seeing on the other side of the world.

How is Mutti? You must tell her not to fret. I have never felt so healthy.

Still, I would like to hope that I can soon be with you all. The paperwork should not take long now. My yearning for you all is indescribable.

The future is on our shoulders, Romy.

Behave, be kind, and show that people from Austria are not all awful. We both have to try to make something of ourselves.

Many kisses to our dear parents. (Please take special care of Mutti, I know this separation must be troubling her so.)

A thousand kisses to you,

Daniel

Chapter 26

SHANGHAI, JUNE 17, 1940

Romy took a sip of her tea and tucked the letter from Daniel back in her pocket. The living room of their apartment in Grosvenor House was spotless, and pale pink chrysanthemums spilled over the lip of a large blue-and-white ginger jar. Outside the tall window, the sky was smoggy and the trees dotted with copper leaves that glinted at the hint of sunshine.

She'd shown Li her letter from Daniel on their way home from school and Li had held her tight as Romy sobbed onto her collar. "Now that Italy has sided with Germany, Mutti says it will be im-impossible to finalize Daniel's ticket from Italy. We don't know—"

"Aba says it's best to let the tears run." Li brushed away the curls stuck to Romy's face, then put both hands on her friend's shoulders. "It's okay to be scared."

Romy's skin prickled with shame as she sipped tea and nibbled on a date. She had every comfort at her fingertips, yet she could do nothing for Daniel. Or Nina. Despite Papa's formal written request that Nina come to live with the Bernfelds full-time, Mr. Damrosch had flatly refused. Her place was in her *Heime* and he suggested it was cruel for the Bernfelds to kindle hope that her life could be otherwise. Papa had stopped asking, afraid if he persisted then Nina would no longer be permitted to visit them.

The streets below were full of shiny new Buicks and Rolls-Royces driven by wealthy Russians, Chinese, and French. Patrons of the coffee shops along Avenue Joffre spilled out onto the footpaths every afternoon, chatting and reading newspapers, anxiously scanning the columns for news of home and debating the ramifications of the Führer's latest decree. The Netherlands and Belgium had surrendered in May, and rumors were swirling that France was about to concede. France and Germany were now allies, so what did that mean for Frenchtown?

What did that mean for Daniel? Mutti was determined to find him a new passage from Dachau—possibly via train through Russia like some of the recently arrived refugees.

Romy sighed as she put down her teacup and wiped away her tears with the back of her wrist.

Everyone seemed to think that life in Shanghai would continue as normal. The shops were full of the latest silks from Europe and hats straight from Schiaparelli in Paris.

Romy's own life was continuing as normal too. When they arrived at Dr. Ho's each afternoon after school, Romy would do her homework—and a good portion of Li's. Then she would slide a little nearer to Jian, take a scrap of parchment, and start to copy the herbal blends and remedies he was carefully transcribing.

Yesterday, Jian had a page prepared for her. It was the bald head of a man onto which he drew lines to show how the *qi* moved from the top of the scalp to the neck. Then he placed tiny dots to identify the acupuncture points. They sat side by side, breathing in sync, arms almost touching. Romy hoped Jian hadn't been able to hear her heart thudding.

"The next step will be for you to learn acupuncture. I'll speak to Aba and see if he can teach you."

"I'm not sure my parents would—" Romy stopped herself just in time from saying "approve."

Li put down her pen and cocked an eyebrow.

Jian blinked but said nothing, just waited politely for her to finish.

"But then again, Mutti has been feeling much more herself lately. Papa says it is all because of Dr. Ho. So maybe . . ." Romy shrugged hopefully.

Li leaned over and studied the dissected head. "Hmmm, your lines are wobbly. You won't be practicing on my face." She giggled and Jian and Romy joined in.

Perhaps she would record in her diary for Daniel the long afternoons she spent at Dr. Ho's shop now that Mutti and Papa worked long days at the Shanghai Jewish Hospital.

For three evenings each week her parents also volunteered at the St. Jean Isolation Hospital, treating the mostly homeless Chinese patients struck down by smallpox. Occasionally they went to Hongkew at the request of Miss Schwartz, and they would take a letter from Romy and a huge parcel of clothes and fresh fruit, salamis, and cheese for Nina.

Recently, Papa had started making after-hours house calls to help Chinese families and refugees suffering from dysentery, cholera, dengue fever. He'd take a rickshaw from house to house, loaded up with charcoal pills and syringes of fluids he'd paid for himself, treating anyone who could not afford the consultation fees to see doctors in their rooms at the hospital.

Papa had forbidden Mei from buying oranges and watermelons, as desperate merchants injected the produce with river water—most likely contaminated—to make them appear plump and weigh more.

Today Papa had the afternoon off, so Romy poured a cup of tea for her father, tucked a couple of dates on the saucer, and wandered down the hallway to his study hoping to coax him into a game of mah-jongg. He'd been working such long hours, she missed time with him, playing games and going over her English essays, French verb conjugations, and algebra.

"For you." She placed the cup on his desk in his study and launched herself into a leather chesterfield.

"*Danke*," he said, looking up and smiling.

"What are you working on?" Romy strained forward to read the list he was writing. Her chest tightened. "Is that a list of medicine, Papa? I—" She glanced at her hands gripping the edge of the sofa. "I worry about you going out to buy these drugs all alone. The dark alleys, visiting the homes of strangers . . ." she said softly.

Papa looked up from his paperwork and put down his pen. "You know, *Liebling*, more and more refugees are arriving in Shanghai every week. The Chinese have been displaced too. They have been injured. The people they love are unwell. There are babies who need to be delivered safely. Children will die without treatment. What would you have me do?"

He took off his spectacles and rubbed his eyes before taking a sip of tea. She'd never seen her father look so weary.

"Don't forget where we came from, Romy. This is my *tzedakah*."

"Your duty," said Romy, thinking of Dr. Ho leaning over Jian, a star anise in his outstretched hand. What was her duty?

Romy straightened her back and stared at her father, her cheeks warm with a dawning realization. One brother was dead, another in a concentration camp. There was a war going on between the Japanese and Chinese all around them, yet her life was uninterrupted. How, after all her good fortune, could she be so selfish?

"Sorry, Papa," she said softly, tucking her new black Mary Janes under her legs.

Papa sighed. "I understand it is not easy for you." His voice dropped a fraction. "We all miss Daniel. And school in a different language. You've been forced to grow up way too fast. But"—he waved his arms around to take in the luxuriously appointed room—"we are the lucky ones, Romy. We must never forget that. And now times are tough for many in Shanghai."

"Is Shanghai going to become like Vienna?" Romy asked. "We're not forbidden from anything, are we? I'm allowed to go to school, and you and Mutti went to the French consul general's ball last week." Romy was confused.

"We're safe in Frenchtown. *We're* not forbidden," said Papa, looking at her and holding her gaze.

Romy straightened her back. Mei had taken her to the public gardens last week for a tennis lesson followed by chicken sandwiches and fresh lemonade with some girls in her class.

As they entered the park, Mei had told her that the Chinese were not allowed in ten years ago. Some foreigners still insisted that no dogs and no Chinese be allowed in.

She tugged at the branch of a climbing rose at the entrance to reveal an old bronze sign.

PUBLIC AND RESERVE GARDENS
REGULATIONS
THE GARDENS ARE RESERVED FOR THE FOREIGN COMMUNITY.

Romy scanned the list of rules, shocked to see:

AMAHS IN CHARGE OF CHILDREN ARE NOT PERMITTED TO
OCCUPY THE SEATS AND CHAIRS DURING BAND PERFORMANCES.
CHILDREN UNACCOMPANIED BY FOREIGNERS ARE NOT ALLOWED
IN RESERVE GARDEN.
THE POLICE HAVE INSTRUCTIONS TO ENFORCE THESE REGULATIONS.

Romy had slipped her hand into Mei's and given it a squeeze. She knew what it was like. Before leaving Vienna she had seen a similar sign posted by the entrance of her favorite park: KEINE JUDEN! KEINE HUNDE! No Jews! No dogs! She knew it would haunt her forever.

Romy wriggled in her chair as she tried to understand why some people were given so much freedom, and others none at all. The rules seemed to change all the time. In Austria they were considered no better than dogs, while here in Shanghai it was the locals who were the *Hunde*.

She decided now was the time to bring up Papa's disregard for local Shanghai laws. "What about the drugs you buy every week on the black market? That's not your job."

Papa shrugged. "No."

"Then why break the rules, Papa?"

"Sometimes it is necessary to step outside the rules because they are cruel. There are too many sick people and not enough drugs. Everybody deserves access to quality treatment. Not just the Japanese or the wealthy."

"But you are *breaking the law* by not buying drugs from pharmacies." She hesitated. "You're putting us all in danger. If you go to prison, or—"

"It's worth the risk."

Romy felt like she'd been slapped. Her hands were clammy and she wiped them on her skirt. After all they'd lost, she couldn't bear the thought that Papa would risk their security. Why do anything that could tear their fragile family apart?

Papa shook his head and reached across the desk for her hand. "Life's hard for so many. Food prices are going up because of the blockade and inflation, so the poor can't buy anything more than basic rice or noodles. Medical supplies are becoming costly to secure. Miss Schwartz . . ." Papa paused. "We must use our privileged position to help others. You should always be asking yourself what you can do to help if you are in a position to do so."

"Like Herr Gruber helped us?"

"Precisely."

"And like you and Mutti at the St. Jean hospital?"

"Yes," said Papa, nodding. "Romy, sometimes when we are sad—when we are broken . . ." His voice started to crack and he took a deep breath. "When we feel that our grief will suffocate us and we simply don't know how to continue, we still have choices. We can choose to give up, or we can choose to fill our time helping others, even if that means you have to step outside the rules sometimes to do the right—the just—thing."

Papa looked Romy in the eye. "Do you understand what I'm saying, *Liebling*? You need to have something that drives you to *live*, not just exist. Don't take this good fortune for granted."

"Yes, Papa."

Papa was right, she knew. Romy *was* luckier than most, but luck felt heavy and complicated. When others said she was lucky, bile burned the back of her throat and made her lungs ache.

Chapter 27

SHANGHAI, JUNE 5, 2016

To: eugene.johns@ejlawyers.com.au
From: alexandra.laird@metbank.com
Subject: Adoption certificate for Sophia Shu Cohen

Dear Mr. Johns,

Thank you for your most recent email clarifying the final matters of probate.

I write today with some further questions regarding my mother's adoption. You may recall we discussed this at Oma's afternoon tea.

I used my mother's passport and Australian adoption certificate to search for her Chinese birth certificate and adoption record, but there are no records in China matching this name.

My research reveals that adoptions could be an oral agreement, and sometimes no adoption certificates were issued in China. Instead, a notarial certificate was issued with the birth parents' names, adoptive parents' names, and date of adoption. You will note my mother's certificate does not include the names of the natural parents. But the absence of a notarial certificate of abandonment from a police station suggests this was a mutually agreed adoption.

This is a rather sensitive matter and I do not wish to press my grandmother for details until I have further clarification, but I'm sure you will appreciate that the search for my mother's birth parents has become hugely important for me. I believe my mother was also beginning to research the circumstances of her adoption before she died.

I am just writing to ask if you can recall any mention by my grandparents of police records or if there is any document you may have overlooked.

Sincerely,

Alexandra Laird

Chapter 28

SHANGHAI, JUNE 20, 1940

Romy and her father caught the trolleybus from Frenchtown, switching to a different trolley in the International Settlement. Soon they reached the border of Hongkew at Garden Bridge where, on the opposite bank, Russian scythes flapped above the foreign consulate. Their trolleybus didn't stop for the Scottish soldiers standing sentry at the western end of the bridge; instead it braked for the Japanese soldiers standing to attention at the far end. Every Chinese passenger stood and bowed to the soldiers of the Imperial Japanese Army, fearful of receiving a beating or being hauled off and questioned. For the first time since she had arrived in Shanghai, Romy felt scared.

The windows were low and a warm breeze filled the trolley, bringing with it the fetid stink of sewage, garbage, and rotting animal corpses floating in the Soochow Creek below. Romy also caught a trace of boiled rice, frying fish, and vegetables as refugee Chinese families, huddled on the hundreds of sampans lining the creek between the two territories, prepared their meals.

With its thick steel trusses enclosing its top and sides, Garden Bridge felt like a cage. Romy took a step closer to her papa. Everyone trying to enter Hongkew on foot lined up to one side—Chinese and foreigners in one line, Japanese in another. Trucks and jeeps loaded with bags of rice and flour and bamboo baskets of pink dragon fruit, guava, and lychees drove past. There were often glassy-eyed workers in the back of the jeeps, squeezed between produce or sitting on jute bags, bobbing with every rev of the motor, smoking.

Romy and Papa waited for the Chinese to bow and show their papers to the Japanese guards. Romy squeezed her father's hand as they entered this new territory and joined the wave of people and rickshaws moving past the bombed-out terraces and *lilong* houses on Seward Road—the devastating legacy of Japan's invasion in 1937. Romy knew the Japanese had attacked Chungking in southwest China, and there was bombing in the north. Rumors swirled at her school that the Japanese would not settle for this little corner of Shanghai. Her heart started racing and her throat felt dry. *This* was what a war zone looked like. The *thwack* of hammers and repair work filled the dusty air; walls were being re-bricked, window frames knocked back into place.

Like many parents based in Frenchtown, Mutti insisted that Romy was never to enter the old city or Hongkew. She wanted her daughter close—and safe. Visits to the Bund and Nanking Road were permitted only with a parent. Nina came to visit the Bernfelds with Miss Schwartz every other week. On alternating weeks, Papa would visit Nina at the *Heime* with a care package. Papa's words had stung: *Don't take this good fortune for granted.* It was time for Romy to see the other side of Shanghai. To see how Nina was forced to live—despite the Bernfelds' constant pleas for the child to come and live with them.

Unlike Frenchtown, the footpaths were filthy, narrow, and crowded. Piles of rubble blocked roads and there was not a tree in sight. The smell of frying fish, garlic, and ginger lingered, along with manure and sweat. Romy resisted the urge to cover her mouth and nose with a handkerchief. Washing flapped on balconies overhead while the shopfronts below boasted neat signs:

DENTIST

E. WARSCHAUER

WIENER CAFÉ RESTAURANT
DELIKAT

Half the signs were in Chinese, the rest mostly in German. No wonder Nina called this area Little Vienna.

Romy stood at the gates of Nina's school with her father, watching as children in faded, shabby clothes poured onto the footpath. Papa had told her the school had been recently opened to cope with the hundreds of refugees arriving each week from all corners of Europe.

When some young boys took turns twirling a soccer ball on their index fingers, Romy's chest tightened. Daniel and Benjamin used to do that all the time, often in their apartment, until Mutti shooed them outside. Romy closed her eyes and remembered the deep laughs of her brothers.

She held up four fingers, one for each of the languages she recognized: English, Yiddish, Polish, and German.

Her father held up six. "You missed Lithuanian and Russian."

"Look, there's Miss Schwartz with Nina!" Romy waved her arms furiously at the pair. Nina was wearing the same blue-checked dress Romy's mother had given her aboard the *Conte Verde*, though now the hem sat well above her knee. Her stockings were spotty where they had been darned.

Romy wore a freshly laundered white shirt tucked into a navy skirt. She immediately regretted wearing her second-best outfit to Hongkew. She tried to swallow, but her guilt sat like a lump in her throat. At least she knew Papa had a present of a new dress for Nina tucked in his doctor's bag.

Miss Schwartz was wearing khakis, a military shirt, and a fuchsia bandanna. She reminded Romy of Greta Garbo—her lips were painted bright red and she was by far the sassiest woman Romy had ever met. She had no doubt the straight-shooting Miss Schwartz could lead an army. Romy wished she could be like Miss Schwartz. The older woman was so sure of herself.

"Hello," said Nina as she gave Romy a hug.

"Hi, Nina," replied Romy, trying to sound cheery.

Miss Schwartz shook Papa's hand, then turned to Romy. "I see you've come to take our girl out. Don't you look *well*, Romy." Miss Schwartz beamed.

Romy's guilt intensified.

"The principal says our Nina is top of her class in English, and an excellent dancer and gymnast." She winked at Nina as she ushered Papa a few steps away. "I'm sure you girls have plenty of catching up to do," Miss Schwartz said over her shoulder. "I'm just going to borrow Dr. Bernfeld for a few minutes to talk hospital business."

As the adults spoke in hushed voices Nina looked shyly at Romy, as if unsure who should speak first.

"We had an English test today," she said with a trace of an English accent.

"I bet you did well," said Romy as half a dozen Japanese soldiers marched past, rifles slung over their shoulders.

Nina froze and looked fearful. "They're everywhere . . ."

Romy reached out to take her friend's hand.

"Apparently, they help themselves to whatever they want at the markets. The old man at the bean stall complained last week and a whole troop came in, tipped over his table, shot the old man, and left him in the gutter." Nina shivered. "I was walking past and I could smell the burning from the gunpowder." Nina gulped, and Romy could tell she was trying not to cry. "Half his head was missing."

Romy squeezed her friend's hand tighter and tried not to think of Benjamin. "Go on," she said.

Nina said softly, "The old man—he used to slip me food on my way home to the *Heime* from school. Some pumpkin seeds, leftover beans, a couple of dumplings. He wore blue rags thinner than mine"—Nina flushed—"and he was so kind." She sniffed, then her voice hardened. "The same thing that happened at home is happening here, Romy. There's a war. We left home for nothing!"

Surely she couldn't be right. But Romy recalled how the Chinese had bowed to the Japanese soldiers while they inspected their paperwork at Garden Bridge, how fearful they had looked. And Li had told her about Chinese professors being dragged to Bridge House, at the rear of Shanghai's GPO, and stretched out on a rack and tortured. She'd thought her friend must be exaggerating—life in Frenchtown seemed the same as ever, with its endless social events, tennis matches, and coffee shops. Now she wasn't so sure. Romy's luck—her comfortable life—seemed undeserved. *This* was what Papa had been trying to tell her the other day in his study.

"We're safer here than at home, I promise you, Nina. This will all be over soon."

But was that true? On the footpath opposite sat an old man dressed in rags, a blue skullcap atop his head. Beside him were three small boys, the tiniest one curled up, asleep. In front of them was a white soup pot; they were begging for coins. They cowered as the soldiers walked past, and the old man raised his skullcap and gave the soldiers a respectful nod, then flinched as a Japanese boot landed hard in his gut.

Romy put a hand to her mouth to smother her gasp.

The sleeping toddler opened his eyes as the same Japanese soldier who had kicked the old man stopped and gently stroked the child's head. Perhaps he had left a child of his own at home? It was strange to see this tenderness coming from a man who had just acted with such brutality.

Papa and Miss Schwartz joined them. Papa's brow was furrowed with concern.

"Be careful, Dr. Bernfeld," Miss Schwartz warned.

"I will," he responded. "But it's your safety I worry about."

"Don't you worry about me." She pointed to a small two-story terrace farther up the road. "There are twenty people living in that house and the youngest couple is expecting a baby next month!" She shook her head. "They're the ones I worry about. We could do with some more doctors, nurses, and midwives. There are more refugees depending on us every day." She shook her head and smiled. "Enough of that. Have fun at Café Louis, girls. Eat some peach torte for me—and say hi to the divine Delma." With a wave, she strode over to her truck.

Nina and Romy walked with Papa past a row of shops—Romy noticed a Polish delicatessen with fat salamis dangling in the window, a kosher butcher, and a barbershop—toward the red-and-white-striped awning of Café Louis.

Three men were trying to urge a flock of goats across the road with long bamboo sticks, yelling and tapping at the animals' backs as cars beeped their horns and rickshaws tried to cycle around them.

On the corner, a newspaper vendor had piles of newspapers and magazines—*Shanghai Jewish Chronicle* and the *Jewish Voice, Die Gelbe Post, Shanghai Echo, Ta Mei Wan Pao*, and *North China Daily News*—organized into neat piles. Romy scanned the headlines for the past weeks:

NAZIS BOMB PARIS AIRFIELDS

ITALY DECLARES WAR ON FRANCE AND BRITAIN

NORWAY SURRENDERS

JAPANESE RAID CHINESE NEWSPAPER OFFICES AND ARREST
  DEPUTY EDITOR

Beside the papers was a metal bucket containing plump red peaches.

Papa handed over a copper coin and the vendor filled a paper bag with fruit. Papa gave it to Nina. "This bag should last a day, if Romy is anything to go by."

They pushed open the door of the café and walked over to a glass cabinet bursting with cakes and pastries. Romy caught her breath as she gazed at the rich chocolate Sacher torte. She remembered leaning over the glass counter in the café on Wipplingerstrasse, agonizing over what to choose after her Saturday piano lesson with Herr Bloch.

Nina had her finger pressed to her bottom lip as she deliberated over the pastries. "At night they have cabaret here," she told them. "Miette, who sleeps in the bed beside mine, sings here. Songs from *The Merry Widow.*"

Papa's smile froze and the muscle in his left cheek quivered as she named an opera Benjamin had sung in.

Romy said hastily, "My friend Li wants to be a cabaret singer or in the movies, like Ginger Rogers."

The distraction worked. Papa chuckled and said, "I'm sure Dr. Ho would have plenty to say about that."

"You don't think he'd approve?" Romy thought of the beautiful women draped in body-clinging silks and furs.

"Hanging around nightclubs with all those taipans and gangsters?" Nina shook her head.

Papa said carefully, "Shanghai has a bit of everything, girls. It's beautiful, to be sure, but I see plenty of people in my rooms . . . A town like this . . . can do a lot of damage."

"I don't think being a singer means you are definitely going to become addicted to opium, Papa," Romy argued.

Papa shook his head with his lips pulled tight. "This war. You girls already know about such things at fourteen?" He sighed and directed their attention back to the pastry display. "I say we get a few slices of the peach torte and some warm rolls." Papa winked at Romy behind Nina's back. "Nina, how about one of these famous hot chocolates?"

Nina's eyes shone. "Yes, please, Dr. Bernfeld."

"And a black coffee for me, please," he added to the tall, slim woman behind the counter.

"Good choice," she said. "We make the best peach torte in Shanghai."

"So I hear," said Papa. "Are you Delma? If so, our mutual friend Eva Schwartz sends her regards."

"Miss Schwartz?" The waitress blushed. "She works very hard. The *Heime* . . . we'd be lost without her." Delma glanced at Nina before she walked away to fix the orders and greet the stream of people coming in for their afternoon coffee.

"I recognize her," said Nina as they found seats at a table. "She comes to the *Heime* every evening, selling cheap coffee made from the used grounds. Sometimes she just gives it away."

"That's kind."

"My uncle doesn't get out much," said Nina with dismay. "She brings him coffee. Not just Uncle David. All the men who don't—" She bit her lip.

Her uncle was in the men's dormitory next door, Romy knew.

"Sometimes a tailor gives him a few silk ties to turn over and repair in exchange for cigarettes and a few cents."

As Nina gestured, Romy caught sight of her friend's hands. They were red, raw, and calloused at the fingertips.

"Nina, what happened to your hands?"

"Last night we had to drag the mattresses outside and scrub them with Lysol to get rid of the lice . . ." She paused awkwardly before rushing on, clearly made self-conscious by the horrified looks on Romy's and her father's faces. "It's probably the needlepoint lessons. They have sewing machines too. I hate sewing. I don't mind the cooking—we get to eat the fish and rice, and the occasional cake." She blushed. "The boys can choose from a barber school, carpentry, woodwork, leatherwork . . ."

"At least you have school," Romy said, trying to think of a way to console her friend.

Divine Delma delivered two hot chocolates, the cones of whipped cream on top piled so high they nearly toppled sideways when she put them down. "Best in town, girls."

"I believe you," said Nina as she spooned the cream into her mouth. Papa reached over and wiped the sprinkle of cinnamon from the tip of her nose.

"I'm sorry, I'm being greedy. It'll be soup tonight. If we're lucky, there's some floating gristle for flavor." Nina grimaced.

Romy pushed her unfinished hot chocolate away. There was that word again. *Lucky*. It always came laced with guilt. She thought of the feasts she'd described to Daniel and her regular trips with Mei to the market, where they bought all the food they needed as well as some they didn't.

They finished their afternoon treats and stepped out into the sunshine.

"Now we must do some shopping," Papa declared to an astonished Romy, who had never in her life seen her father shop. "Your mother gave me a list."

They walked to the Tongshan Elite Provision Store and purchased two loaves of bread, tins of white beans and sardines, a salami, and a small bag of white rice.

Laden with groceries, Papa and Romy walked Nina home along Chaoufong Road. Her *Heime* was as grand a building as any in Frenchtown, Romy was surprised to see, with arched windows and wide balconies. But washing hung from a rope fastened across the front of the building: everyone's faded and misshapen smalls were, along with sheets and dresses, on display. Romy peeked in one of the windows and counted twenty metal bunk beds lined up against the wall. Two girls lay sprawled on a rumpled bed, playing cards.

Outside on the footpath, men in singlets were sitting behind tables on which were arranged winter boots, heavy woolen coats, scarves, and felt hats, all for sale for only a few cents. What would they do when the bitter winds and rain came next year? Beside the clothes were an assortment of wire-rimmed spectacles, a pocket watch on a gold chain, and a harmonica. How were people getting by without their reading glasses?

They heard the rumble of a trolleybus and Romy leaned in to kiss Nina goodbye. As the trolley pulled to a stop, Papa pulled the dress from his bag and handed it to Nina along with the bags of groceries. "Tuck them in your suitcase. Ask Miss Schwartz for a can opener."

Waving away Nina's stammered thanks, he took Romy's arm and climbed into the trolley.

Romy looked back at Nina, standing on the footpath, the gutter filled with refuse. Romy waved and blew a kiss. "Bye, take care. I'll come again soon!" she shouted as the trolleybus moved away.

Chapter 29

Alexandra stood in the lobby of her apartment building, wondering if agreeing to go on a Saturday morning food tour with Zhang was really a good idea. She'd run into her neighbor here last night on her way in from work, frustrated and glum; her search for her mother's family had reached a dead end. Without any of the proper documents she had nothing to go on. She was possibly in the wrong city. Zhang had asked teasingly if she'd dared try any street food yet, and when she confessed she hadn't he offered to introduce her to the best stalls in the area.

She yawned. She'd been working late at the office all week and had managed to squeeze in only two of Barbara's suggested minimum of ten hours of Mandarin lessons per week. Who had time for that? She ran a team of fifty traders on her floor. She could really do with some sleep.

"Morning," said Zhang, coming down the stairs. He was wearing a crisp white shirt and loose ripped jeans, gray sneakers, and a pair of aviator sunglasses. His hair was disheveled and still a little damp, and he combed it out with his fingers.

"Sorry," he said. "Big night."

Alexandra had to stop herself from asking what he'd gotten up to. It was none of her business.

He rubbed his hands together. "Right. Street food, here we come. Then I'll take you to the nearest wet market."

Alexandra must have looked confused.

"So you can do your food shopping."

Alexandra didn't have the heart to tell him she had dinner delivered to her desk every evening. Most nights she got Sherpa's to deliver chicken wonton soup and added some extra chili; Romy would be proud. You could have anything delivered by scooter in Shanghai, she'd discovered. Joni, at the desk beside her, had an iced green tea and lemon juice delivered at eleven each morning. At two P.M. came fresh flat beef noodles or sticky Sichuan chicken and long beans.

"First stop, coffee—am I right?" Zhang said with a grin as they began to walk.

"What's that?" asked Alexandra as they passed a narrow alleyway crowded with people lining up behind bamboo steamers stacked like circular towers.

"That"—he pointed to a tiny hole-in-the-wall—"is breakfast."

Alexandra eyed the dozens of boiled eggs floating in a dark broth and recognized one of Romy's favorite dishes. At home, Romy would boil a dozen eggs, then crack them gently on the counter before dropping them into a crockpot filled with black tea. She'd add orange rind, cinnamon, star anise, five spice, cardamom, and soy sauce, and leave the eggs to soak overnight. Alexandra had loved the aromas of all the spices floating through the house, especially in winter. The next morning, Romy would scoop the eggs out with a slotted spoon and peel them to reveal a beautiful marbled pattern, each one in a slightly different hue. Romy would eat them for lunch in the garden. Tea eggs would be tucked into Alexandra's lunch box at primary school along with the usual carrot and celery sticks and a soft roll. Lunch was always a combination of European and Chinese—until the day in grade four when she'd shuffled into the kitchen after school and asked Romy to stop including tea eggs in her school lunches.

There was no need to tell Romy that she didn't want to be different. That Camilla and her posse had sneered at her "weird" food: "Eeew, that's disgusting. Stinky eggs! That must be why you're stinky too, Alexandra."

"Shut up!" Kate had shouted as she stood up beside Alexandra.

"You can't make us," Camilla had said with her chin jutting out and her hands on her hips.

"I'll stuff your boring sandwich in your stupid mouth—that should shut you up," Kate had retorted. "Now go eat somewhere else. I want this table to myself and Alexandra."

Kate was the captain of the basketball team and a champion tennis player. Everyone wanted to be on Kate's team. Or at Kate's table. Alexandra couldn't believe this feisty girl had just picked her over the other girls in the class. They had been best friends ever since.

Alexandra pulled her phone out of her pocket, snapped a picture of the eggs, and sent Kate a text: *Remember these?*

Kate's reply was instantaneous: *Those girls were witches. Probably driving brats to school in Land Rovers while husbands stay late at work to avoid them.*

Alexandra chuckled.

"Something funny about the eggs?" asked Zhang.

Alexandra blushed as she realized he'd been standing there watching her. "My grandmother's favorites," she replied.

Alexandra eyed the yellow corncobs grilling on a small barbecue, filling the air with a sweet aroma. But it was the fluffy white dumplings sitting in their steamers that were the center of the crowd's attention. People were buying two or three in plastic bags. "What're those buns?"

"That one"—Zhang pointed—"is *cai bao*. Shiitake mushroom and dried tofu."

"Perfect! I'll have one. I assume the other one is pork?"

"Among other things like garlic and spices, yes."

They joined the fast-moving queue, and when it was their turn Zhang spoke to the stall vendor, who put their buns in a plastic bag and handed it to Alexandra. She lifted out the first and took a bite, savoring the slightly bitter greens tempered with mushrooms and garlic as juice dribbled down her chin.

"Delicious!" she exclaimed.

They walked back out to Ruijin Lu, joining the throng of people on the footpath. The traffic was moving slowly, with rickshaws and tricycles loaded with sticks, rubbish bags, and piles of packaged clothes weaving between gleaming latest-model BMW and Audi SUVs.

Suddenly Zhang put his hand out to stop her from stepping into the gutter as a scooter whizzed past. Red lights were a suggestion, rather than a rule. The smart policeman in white gloves shrugged an apology at her before waving them across the road.

"C'mon," said Zhang, grabbing her hand. "Let's go to Tianzifang."

The narrow lanes of Tianzifang market were being hosed down as people prepared their stalls for the day. Overhead, lush vines threaded like tinsel between hanging terra-cotta pots cascading with plants. The first stall they came to had a series of hospital drip holders, with standard-issue saline drips (red cross still intact on the label) filled with sugared lime juice, pomegranate and cherry juice. A plastic storage tray on the table offered alternatives, complete with drip lines in garish blues, yellows, and oranges. The bin beside it was filled with equally colorful plastic baby bottles, and Alexandra wondered what adult would walk the streets sucking juice from a baby's bottle or hospital drip.

Next door was a frozen yogurt stall with a magnificent counter made from blue and yellow Moroccan tiles, offering chocolate, tea, cherry, and salted cheese varieties as hip-hop music blasted from a small speaker. The juice bar five steps along had a menu boasting cactus soda, apple oolong soda, mango sago, and an assortment of fruit-flavored jasmine and red teas. In a giant yellow starburst was the special: *Rock-salt cheese blended with jasmine tea.*

They stepped between the rivulets of water flowing down the alley as a team of tiny women in faded gray uniforms swept the footpaths with bamboo brooms.

"Hungry?" Zhang stopped in front of the most darling dumpling stand Alexandra had ever seen. Assorted bamboo steamers were filled with translucent white fish jellies, roses, artichokes, and leaves. Baskets brimmed with yellow rubber ducklings, or white pigs with pink ears and matching button snouts. There were purple rice balls with floral cake icing and neatly folded dumplings in a variety of pastel hues. Everywhere she turned the presentation was colorful and impeccable, even if she didn't always understand the flavor pairings.

Zhang led her through more alleys until they reached a sunny courtyard.

"This place has some of the best coffee around. Owned by Melbourne people."

"Naturally," said Alexandra, smiling as she lowered herself onto an uncomfortable-looking green milk crate.

As Zhang went to order the flat white she'd been dreaming about since she'd touched down in Shanghai, she examined the line of tiny kitchens with trestle tables and temporary cooktops opposite. A little round lady in a gingham shirt and apron was making crepes, pouring thin batter onto a circular hotplate. On went an egg, brown soybean paste, handfuls of coriander, spring onions, and pickles, plus a squirt of red chili sauce. A strip of deep-fried wonton wrapper was placed on top before the crepe was folded into a fan shape.

Alexandra couldn't resist. She got up and went to order one for herself, and when Zhang returned she was lost in a reverie of crunch and softness, the tang of the mustard tuber pickles and the sting of the chili.

"You like the *jianbing*?" Zhang grinned.

Too busy eating to speak, she nodded. As she finished the last of the crepe she wondered if it would be rude to get a second.

Zhang read her thoughts. "We're going to be trying a lot of stuff, so don't fill up too soon." He looked up as the waiter approached. "Here's your coffee."

Alexandra gratefully sipped from the cup. Zhang was right; it was good. "What are you drinking?" she asked.

"Oh, it's too hot for coffee. This is a Shanghai-style coffee tonic. It's an espresso with tonic water. Want to try?" He offered his glass.

She took a sip and raised her eyebrows. It was actually quite refreshing. Tart and zingy with enough traces of coffee to still get a kick.

"Nice. But I think I'll stick to my standard."

"You wait, we'll make a Shanghai girl out of you yet! C'mon, there's still lots to see."

They drained their cups and headed back into the lanes.

They walked deeper in the market as women wheeled out buckets of fresh lychees and coconuts, or armfuls of lilies, in front of stores brimming with cute handmade dresses and sunglasses. She made a note of a few stores in the labyrinth so she could come back and buy a cashmere scarf for Kate and some pretty cheongsams for her girls.

Zhang stopped and peered in the door of a homewares shop fitted out with blue industrial hanging lights and 1950s Scandinavian furniture. Shelves were filled with memorabilia: battered scooter helmets with red stars, handcrafted ceramics, peeling enamel cups stamped with SERVE THE PEOPLE, and neat rows of blue-and-white ginger jars.

Zhang picked up a small, asymmetrical bowl in a pale blue gray and gently ran his fingers around the edge. Under the lights, the gray finish looked soft and highlighted the bumps of the clay.

"It's perfect," he said.

"It's a bit uneven, isn't it?" said Alexandra critically.

"That's the beauty. You expect it to be glossy and perfect, and then there's this uneven edge." He tapped the edge of the bowl and put it down on the desk with both hands. "See how it doesn't wobble."

Alexandra tried to imagine Zhang's Hong Kong home. Was it all charcoal tones with carefully placed *objets* atop side tables he'd handcrafted? Did it feel like a gallery?

She thought about Hugo's apartment—her apartment too, for a while—with the harrowing Lucian Freud portrait in the entrance that made her feel cold, a stranger, every time she stepped in the front door. Perhaps it was just that she didn't know much about art . . .

Watching Zhang's response to a little bowl, the genuine warmth and wonder at the craftsmanship, she knew she'd made a mistake with Hugo. She needed to listen to her instincts. Alexandra had never dared to show her rough edges to anyone. Her fingers slid up to her neck and stroked her pendant. Perhaps it was time to stop filtering and polishing her response to everything in life.

As Zhang took the bowl to the counter and the saleswoman wrapped it in bubble wrap, Alexandra wandered back out the front door and stopped for a minute as a fleck of gold wallpaper in the window display caught her eye. She stepped into the alley to get a better look. Behind the mannequin, in a navy linen wrap dress, and brown handbags draped on a bamboo ladder was a wall covered with faded, peeling gold wallpaper with a pattern of loose dusty pink peonies on curved stems. But it was what lay on top of the wallpaper that had caught her eye.

Five sepia photographs in heavy wooden frames.

Alexandra stuck her head back in the door. The friendly proprietor was introducing herself and her partner and laughing at something Zhang had said as she started to tie some string around his package. Alexandra stepped inside the window display and pulled out her phone to get a close-up of the pictures.

The first was of a well-dressed man and woman standing on either side of a rickshaw. The man had a thick mustache and wore a three-piece suit and fob chain, bowler hat, and bow tie. The woman stood upright with her elbow on the handlebars and wore a black hat with two white angel wings that spanned the brim at the front. Despite the unorthodox pose, both wore somber expressions. Alexandra leaned in for a closer look at the rickshaw driver. The boy's bare feet were filthy and his eyes were half closed. Alexandra wasn't sure whether he was resting or wishing he were somewhere else.

The second picture was of a woman in a long skirt and dark jacket with oversized white cuffs and black gloves sitting in the back of a buggy.

The third and fourth were streetscapes. One was a photo of the Bund taken from the river, full of loaded sampans, a crowded dock in the background. The other was a street full of people in short sleeves and white shirts jumping on and off trolleybuses. Signs in Chinese characters and English promised a summer sale. The label read *Nanking Road, Shanghai, 1939.*

Romy had arrived in Shanghai in 1939. She wondered what her teenage grandmother had thought of this town. It must have seemed a long way from Vienna.

When she reached the last photo, Alexandra froze.

"Hey, there you are! I went outside to look for you, but I wasn't expecting you to be part of the window display. I'm pretty happy with my purchase." He waved his brown paper bag at her.

Alexandra fished her mother's diary out of her bag, slipped the photo of Romy and the pretty Chinese stranger from the back pocket, and held it up beside the bigger version. "It's—"

Zhang did a double take and leaned in closer. "No way! How do you have the same picture?"

Chapter 30

SHANGHAI, DECEMBER 8, 1941

Romy stood with her parents at the window of their apartment watching a handful of Annamese troops from Indochina, along with their French commanding officers, move in formation on Rue Bourgeat.

It was sleeting. Mud coated their black boots and clung to the legs of their khakis. The little canvas caps they usually wore had been replaced with gleaming helmets. Romy leaned out the window to see a convoy of jeeps and a camouflage tank forging through the traffic, using both lanes and causing the rickshaws and cars coming in the other direction to swerve into the gutter to allow them to pass.

"What are they doing, Oskar?" asked Mutti, her voice low.

"I don't know," said Papa.

Romy clenched her fists and dug her nails into her palms.

Bombs had struck the far side of Shanghai in the dark last night, like a heavy drumbeat. Romy had crept up the marble staircase and lain on the end of her parents' bed, rubbing her cheek on the silk and wrapping herself in her mother's cashmere throw until she drifted back to sleep. As the morning light streamed through the windows, they braced themselves for more thuds. Still wrapped in Mutti's shawl, Romy had trailed her and Papa downstairs to make sure Mei didn't go out to the markets at dawn.

The porcelain tea set rattled as trucks rumbled along the street below.

"What's happening? They—it's supposed to be safe here. What should we do, Oskar?" asked Mutti.

Papa rushed over to the radio and started twisting the dials as he listened for a signal.

The windowpanes rattled with the wind, echoing Romy's heartbeat.

"Look!" Romy pointed.

"That's Mrs. Kapov," her mother said. "I wonder why she's outside. It's not safe."

Romy's pulse quickened. A familiar figure—slim and dark—had stepped out from behind the newspaper stand and was gesturing for Mrs. Kapov to stop. There was nodding, the lifting of a camera, and a flash so quick it could be mistaken for the flick of a watch.

Another flash. A thud and a whistle on the far side of Shanghai—near the Whangpoo River.

Romy held her breath, praying the photographer stayed safe and the light from his flash did not attract the attention of the French police.

Mrs. Kapov waved down a rickshaw using a giant white feather. The oversized angel wings pinned to the front of her hat were starting to droop. She gestured for her husband to join her.

The Kapovs climbed into the rickshaw, pausing for just one more flash before she shooed the photographer away and urged the rickshaw driver on.

The photographer tucked his camera underneath his traditional cotton shirt and started to slip behind the newspaper stand, picking up a bouquet of pale yellow chrysanthemums to cover his face. Just before he slipped into the shadows, Jian looked up at Romy's window. Years later, she'd wonder if she'd imagined the slightest nod, a curl of the corner of his lips. As if he knew she was there, watching him, all along.

The room filled with abrasive static and then a radio announcement from a Russian-controlled radio station came on:

. . . We repeat, USS *Wake* has surrendered command to the Imperial Japanese Army. British gunboat HMS *Peterel* has been overtaken and sunk under fire by the Imperial Navy ships *Izumo* and *Toba*. The majority of the crew are not expected to have survived evacuating the boat, and it is estimated twelve British nationals have been taken prisoner.

Mutti and Papa stared at each other in silence as Papa started fiddling with the dial again.

More crackles of the radio.

The Imperial Japanese Army has taken control of the International Settlement and negotiations are under way with the Vichy government, who have promised to cooperate in the French Concession.

"Surely the Japanese are not going to take over all of Shanghai. They won't be allowed in here, will they?" asked Mutti.

"I don't know. The British and the U.S. are the enemy. That's why the Japanese have crossed the Garden Bridge into the rest of the

International Settlement, it seems. They've seized enemy territory," replied Papa.

Romy looked out the window at the cluster of soldiers moving slowly and deliberately through the street with their tank, as if they were merely out for a training exercise.

The hunched old woman on the opposite corner was dressed in a garbage bag to keep off the sleet while she unloaded silver buckets of white calla lilies from her wheelbarrow.

In minutes, the soldiers had disappeared and people poured into the streets.

Normal activities resumed on the footpaths, as men stepped out of the coffeehouses with their collars pulled up and hats pulled down. The sky was dark and low. Menacing. The street felt frozen, as if people were supposed to get on with their business for the day but weren't quite sure what to do.

Papa raised the volume on the wireless to listen to the announcer saying with a thick Russian accent:

And now we cross live to the president of the United States—

"What?" said Mutti.

"Shhh." Papa signaled for silence as he leaned closer and fiddled with the dials some more.

The booming voice of Franklin D. Roosevelt came over the radio:

Yesterday, December 7, 1941—a date which will live in infamy—the United States of America was suddenly and deliberately attacked by naval and air forces of the Empire of Japan.

The three of them sat on the sofa as a different voice cut in, speaking urgently. The reporter estimated that eighteen American navy ships had been sunk, perhaps as many as two thousand killed. America had joined the war and would ally itself with Britain against Germany and Japan.

Overnight, Shanghai had become the center of a war they had tried to avoid. China and Japan were already at war. Now America and its allies, like Britain and Australia, were at war with Japan too.

Romy slipped her hand into her mother's as her father switched between stations.

What would happen to her family now? They had nowhere else to go.

Chapter 31

SHANGHAI, JUNE 11, 2016

Alexandra walked back into the Tianzifang homewares store. Reaching into her back pocket, she pulled out the same photo that was framed in the shop window. The friendly owners nearly fell off their Eames stools.

"I don't believe it," said the slightly built woman as she pulled on a pair of thick tortoiseshell frames and leaned over the counter for a closer inspection. "I'm Cynthia, by the way." She smiled and held out a hand. "And this is Lu, my husband." She gestured toward a hipster in a faded Neil Young T-shirt who scratched his beard and nodded shyly.

Cynthia explained: "We found the photos at the bottom of a box containing Lalique sconces and an old sixteen-millimeter camera when we bought this place, didn't we, Lu?"

Alexandra tried to hide her disappointment that Cynthia and Lu didn't seem to know the exact origin of the photo. Instead she said, "Great place you've set up here," as she traced the lines of the teak cabinet acting as the shop counter and counted the neat sets of square drawers with brass handles. Twenty-six—four rows. One hundred and four drawers. It was an odd piece.

Following her gaze, Cynthia explained, "This is a traditional medicine cabinet. This shop was a deceased estate. The guy who owned it was a political prisoner for many years after the war. When he was released, he opened this shop." She pointed to a faded shingle with some Chinese characters and, below, CHINESE MEDICINE written in English, along with a name: DR. HO.

"When we renovated the shop, we were after a romantic Old Shanghai feel, so we thought, why not use the old photos we found on-site?" She turned to her husband. "There are some more photos at home, aren't there, Lu?"

"The Calendar Girls? All the photos have the same dreamy look with flowers or blossom trees in the background and an elegant woman posing in front. Just like the thirties and forties Shanghai advertisements for soaps, cigarettes, beer . . . I actually took them to the framer this week."

"Sure. But there are some streetscapes. A few more of this girl . . ." She tapped the Chinese girl's head. "She's cute enough here, but she grew up to be a real stunner."

Lu raised his eyebrows and nodded in agreement.

"Do you have a photo of her grown up?" asked Zhang. He turned to Alexandra. "I mean, if she knew your grandmother, maybe we could ask her about—" He stopped himself. "I'm sorry; it's not my business."

"That's fine." Alexandra found herself smiling at his interest. "I mean, if I can't find out through the formal channels, maybe this girl—woman—could point me in the right direction." She waved the photo in the air.

Cynthia shook her head. "I'm sorry, but she died a long time ago. Before her brother. There was a box of costumes, silk dresses, strands of pearls. Some newspaper articles and a stack of concert programs, plus paperwork like her identification pass and some family snaps. I couldn't believe someone would leave these vintage clothes and furs to be eaten by moths—let alone the pearls! They were just shoved in the cupboard, for years . . ."

She reached out and ran her hand over a battered wooden mannequin wearing a pale blue chiffon dress with a drop waist encrusted with crystals and a large silk bow tied at the back. She lifted the skirt so it looked like a translucent fan and waved it about to catch the light. "This is one of the dresses we've had cleaned and repaired."

"It's magnificent," said Alexandra, reaching out to stroke the crystal beads. "It must have cost a fortune."

"Well, she was the most famous cabaret singer in Shanghai: Yu Baihe. Li Ho." Cynthia hesitated. "Is there anything in particular you're looking for?"

"Do you know if the man who owned the shop or his sister had any relatives? Children? It's just they may have known my grandmother, if they were friends."

"I assume neither of them had any extended family. I mean, everything in this shop was sold as a job lot by the realtor. There were old receipts, the brother's photos, those books on Chinese medicine . . ." She pointed to some dusty books on a shelf. "It's a pity we don't have any of her stuff here. We're having a big launch party soon, you see, and we're having a lot of the original images scanned so we can make some big posters. It's dress-up, of course. Old Shanghai."

Zhang smiled and the corners of his eyes crinkled. Alexandra imagined how handsome he'd look in a white tuxedo with a silk scarf.

"You must come," Cynthia insisted. "It's in August. Here's the invitation." She handed over a card with a Calendar Girl in repose in front of a mountainscape, legs crossed and dressed in a maroon cheongsam with white peonies, shiny black hair pulled back into a bun with a red chrysanthemum tucked behind her ear. She had a demure smile.

"She's magic."

"She is. But you wait until you see *your* girl in the photo. The details are on the other side. Make sure you dress up!"

"Sounds like I'm off to the tailor," joked Zhang.

Alexandra felt a tingle of excitement. Zhang was supposed to be back in Hong Kong by August. Would he come back for the party?

"Thank you," replied Alexandra, handing her business card to Cynthia in return.

"I'll email if I find anything in the meantime," Cynthia promised. "Fingers crossed. I mean, what are the chances of you turning up with the same photo?"

Chances. As probabilities and numbers whirred in Alexandra's head, she felt different. Usually, her starting point for all research was to build in factors for a worst-case scenario. Instead, she felt something light. Hope.

Cynthia was reaching over the counter to hug her now. "It's a real-life mystery. See you at the party, if not before."

Lu waved at them and grinned. "Bye."

"Looking forward to it," said Zhang. "And now we have to finish Alexandra's tour." He pressed a hand to the small of her back, then removed it. Alexandra wished he'd let it linger there just a fraction longer.

Chapter 32

Mutti had quickly changed into her brown woolen suit and smart hat and instructed Romy to dress too.

"No school for you today, Romy. You can accompany me to the bank."

"I don't think it's such a good idea to go out," Papa said. "Why don't you leave it?"

"Frenchtown's safe—you said so yourself," Mutti reminded him as she walked to the coat cabinet in the entrance hall and pulled out a gray cashmere coat and fur stole, and a navy peacoat for Romy. "And there's been no mention of fighting or soldiers on the Bund."

"Still," Papa said, "it wouldn't be wise. Stay home until things settle down."

Mutti straightened her back and her voice cut like steel. "We have had no news of Daniel for over eighteen months. The Nazis won't renew our passports. We are *stateless*, Oskar. With all that's happening—" She paused, then took a deep breath to steady her voice. "Things may *never* settle down. We need to withdraw all our savings. No delays. Surely you understand that, Oskar? This may be our last chance to secure our freedom until this war is over. We might be able to find someone to pay—"

Pay for what? Romy stared at her mother, speechless. At fifteen, Romy had never known Mutti to break any rules. But you could buy almost anything on the black market in the dark alleys of Shanghai. Why not new passports? Even so, how would they leave? Shanghai was surrounded. Jews were not welcome anywhere else.

Mutti took a step toward Papa. "Oskar, look outside. There are very few soldiers on the street. It's not dangerous, like . . ."

The ghosts of Kristallnacht filled every corner of the dim room.

"Think of Daniel, of Romy . . ." Mutti whispered.

Papa sighed and reached for his own brown coat. "I'm sorry. I'm expected to supervise an urgent surgery at the hospital."

Mutti's voice softened and she reached for Papa's hand. "*Vergib mir*, you understand. Look out the window: the trolleybuses are still running, people are at the coffeehouses. The International Settlement will be the same, I'm sure of it." She looked at her husband pleadingly. "I need to do this," she said.

"I understand," Papa said, kissing her forehead. "But shouldn't Romy stay here with Mei?"

"No," Mutti replied firmly. "My child stays with me. I'll not risk losing another."

As soon as they alighted from the trolleybus on Nanking Road in the International Settlement, Romy realized they had made a mistake trying to get to the Bund at the end of the street.

Mutti grabbed her hand and together they pressed flat against the walls of another bank. Romy didn't need to be reminded of the rules this time. *Do not draw attention to yourself.*

Hundreds of Japanese soldiers marched in formation, navy helmets shining and bayonets pointed toward the sky. Despite the chill, the air was thick with smoke. When Romy took a breath the sour taste of metal and rubber filled her mouth. She gagged as Mutti passed her a silk handkerchief.

"Come. We'll try to get to the Cathay." Mutti tugged her arm and pointed at the green pyramid but was flung back against the wall as a man pulled up beside her. He smelled of sweat, rotten fish, and fear. Chest heaving with panic, the man reached out with spindly arms and yanked his rickshaw off the footpath, trying not to topple his load of newspapers tied up with brown string.

Romy glanced at yesterday's headlines.

The radio was what they needed now. Perhaps there would be one at the Cathay.

Romy craned her neck to look down the street. Brown and black furs pressed against faded blue cotton. People were trapped between the walls of the banks, shops, and insurance companies as if they formed a deep ravine. The doors to all the banks were locked. Nobody would be getting out money today.

Rickshaws lined the footpaths, creating space for the hundreds of trucks, tanks, and military vehicles that were moving down the street in double file, the Rising Sun flag waving proudly from each one. With or without permission, the Japanese were taking over the International Settlement.

Romy muttered under her breath, furious at herself for believing what had happened in Vienna couldn't happen here. "Mutti, what about Nina? Is she—"

"I don't know." Mutti looked helpless. "We can try to contact Miss Schwartz when we get home."

Home.

A truck changed gears, and the grinding echoed down the street as the truck behind honked impatiently. Hammering and yelling could be heard toward the top end of Nanking Road, where wooden barricades and sandbag walls were being erected by Japanese troops, cutting off the Bund. Romy found her mother's hand and squeezed. There would be no cash and no new passports. Perhaps ever.

Japanese civilians were streaming out of the cafés and shops to march alongside their compatriots, waving their armbands in the air. A soldier in blue webbing ran toward Mutti and Romy with a piece of paper and glued it onto the bank window beside Romy's head. PROPERTY OF THE IMPERIAL JAPANESE ARMY. The soldier smashed the window beside it to make his point and rushed back to join his fellows.

Romy closed her eyes, covered her face with both hands, and hunched low as she was showered in shards of glass.

"Romy!" yelled Mutti as she reached down to brush the broken glass from her daughter's clothes and hair.

"*Aya*," said a man, gesturing for Mutti to stand clear as he reached down and gently swept the glass from Romy's shoulders and feet. "Missee . . ." he said kindly as he tapped her on the shoulder to signal it was safe to stand.

"Thank you," said Romy, overwhelmed.

The man glanced at the Japanese parade, then returned his gaze to Romy. "*Tung yang ning*," he muttered under his breath.

Romy put a hand over her mouth to stifle a giggle and Mutti looked confused. "What did he say?" she asked.

The man smiled, revealing a single yellow tooth. His eyes were dancing as he nodded at Romy and curled his little finger.

"He's teasing the Japanese *Tung yang ning*," whispered Romy, feeling every bit the Shanghailander.

◇

At the Cathay, the doormen were waving the locals back behind the barricades.

"Mrs. Bernfeld, Miss Bernfeld, what are you doing out here?" asked Mr. Khaira as they squeezed to the front.

He shoved aside a pallet in the makeshift barrier and ushered them through to safety as his colleagues pushed back the Chinese in their rags. "Of all days to be on the street." He whisked them away from the sweat, screams, and smoke, through the revolving door and into the golden lobby of the Cathay. "Quick, come inside. It's safe here."

Romy glanced back at the sea of desperate faces outside and wondered what the kind rickshaw driver was doing now. Would he find a safe place?

Then she moved forward and was lost in the perfume of the lilies.

Mr. Khaira spoke to Mutti as Romy walked around the central table, staring at the flowers. "Should I book you a room? Is there someone you should call to let them know you're here?"

Before Mutti could respond a voice said, "Marta? Is that you?"

Wilma Ho, eyebrows creased with concern, was walking across the lobby with another woman. They both wore traditional loose-fitting cheongsams, one in ruby red, the other sky blue.

Mutti pulled a handkerchief from her bag and pressed it over her mouth as her shoulders shook and she started to sob.

"I've been such a fool—I put Romy in such danger—and she's . . . she's all I have left."

Wilma put her arms around Mutti and she brushed the hair back from her face. "Shush, my friend." She rubbed Mutti's back soothingly as the doorman walked quietly back to his post.

Romy's heart started to race with worry. Japanese soldiers were everywhere. What should they do?

As if she sensed Romy's anxiety, Mrs. Ho said firmly, "You'll come with us. I'll take care of you and we'll get you home safely. I promise. But first we have a meeting to attend." Her eyes darted sideways as she lowered her voice to a whisper: "We must find a way to resist. Our little theater group mustn't retreat . . . It's more important now than ever." As Wilma spoke the dimple on her left cheek quivered. She turned to the woman standing beside her. "This is my colleague Marjorie. Marjorie, I'd like you to meet my neighbors Romy and Marta Bernfeld. They will be joining us today."

All at once Li came flying around the table of lilies and flung her arms around Romy, standing on her toes to give her a kiss on the cheek.

"I am *so* glad you are here. I don't understand anything they talk about." She gave an exaggerated roll of her eyes and slipped her arm through Romy's. "I'm just here to sing later." She gestured to her cheongsam, which had a pink crane embroidered at the shoulder, and turned her head from side to side, lifting her hair to show off her pearl earrings and the dab of rouge on her cheeks. In her navy peacoat with a cashmere twinset underneath, Romy, as usual, felt drab beside her friend.

Romy waited for her mother to object, to insist they must return home at once, but instead she noticed the glimmer of something in Mutti's eyes. It was curiosity, intrigue, a fleeting trace of the mother who had taken her out on Sunday afternoons and run barefoot through Stadtpark with her skirts hitched up, laughing. The mother who collected fresh flowers every Thursday—creamy edelweiss, clumps of heather, pink carnations, or blue hyacinths—on her way home from work at the clinic.

This was the mother who saw delight in everything. The mother she remembered. That was worth taking a seat at the table.

She squeezed Li's slim hand and said, "Mutti, can we meet you inside the tearooms? There's something I want to show Li."

Chapter 33

Romy sat on the leather chesterfield in her secret wood-paneled dressing room at the Cathay, sipping her hot chocolate and watching Li twirl around the room, doing the jitterbug as if she didn't have a care in the world. Memories of Kristallnacht still churned in her gut. She'd wanted to come and sit awhile in this quiet place that took her back to her childhood but, as always, Li had other plans.

Her friend had changed into a blue chiffon gown that had been left on the rack, along with the peacock-blue feather boa Romy and Nina had found the first time they'd been here. There was a gramophone in the corner and the girls were listening to the high-pitched melodies of Li's favorite singer, Golden Voice. With each swirl and shimmy, the ruffles of Li's skirt took flight, and she kept turning and spinning in a frenzy as the song reached a crescendo.

As the final notes died away, Li collapsed breathless onto the sofa beside Romy.

"I can't believe you won't dance with me." She turned to look at Romy. "I know you think I'm silly, but I just love to sing and dance."

Romy looked into the big dark eyes of her best friend. With those two deep dimples, Li's smile was irresistible. But the beauty and fizz on the surface masked a faithful friend with a deep sense of honor.

Last week at school, Gretel Adalard had started to mutter, "*Heil Hitler*," under her breath every morning as the girls hung their satchels and coats on their hooks at school.

The teachers pretended not to hear.

Unbeknownst to Romy, Li had convinced Jian to help her purchase a burlap bag full of squirming black bullfrogs that she'd tipped into Gretel's bag on her way to French class. Gretel's screams echoed through the corridor and she immediately blamed Romy.

"It was the ugly Jew," she spat. But, of course, it couldn't have been, as Romy was already in class, going over her algebra homework with the teacher. Li had only let her in on the secret that afternoon after school.

Now Li rested her head on Romy's shoulder and stroked her pendant. "I really want to sing at the Opera House," she confided. "Then I want to sing in Paris."

"I'll come to the opening night, I promise."

"You could come to Paris with me. Jian will come and study photography and you can study medicine at the Sorbonne."

"Perhaps," said Romy. But even as she said it she knew she wouldn't go anywhere without her parents. How could she leave them after all they had been through?

"You *are* going to be a doctor?" Li persisted.

"I suppose so," said Romy. "It's the right thing to do. The wards are full of patients with typhoid and pneumonia since winter set in. Papa and Mutti . . ." Her voice trailed off.

"They work hard," agreed Li, finishing the sentence for her. "Have you ever thought of studying Chinese medicine? You are always watching Aba work—and I know you did the notes on the scroll for Jian so he could take some photographs of cicada shells instead."

Romy blushed.

Li lifted her chin and held Romy's gaze. "Sometimes I think you have more in common with my brother than with me," she said softly.

"That's not true." Romy felt a curious flutter in her belly.

Li started to hum the mournful opening bars of "J'attendrai" and then sang, so loudly that Romy feared she would be heard outside. Romy automatically started to translate:

I will wait night and day,
I will wait forever,
For you to come back . . .

Li was singing for Zhou, her lost brother. Romy lay on the couch, thinking of Benjamin and Daniel, her heart breaking for Mutti and Papa.

Li had tears in her eyes when she finished singing and Romy gave her a hug.

"That was beautiful. What will your stage name be?"

"Jade Lily," said Li instantly.

"Perfect. C'mon, change back into your own dress—we need to get back to the meeting."

As they stepped out of the secret door into the bright light of the lobby, a handsome man in a navy three-piece suit stood jiggling a gold pocket watch and speaking in low tones with three Japanese soldiers. The lobby was filling with Japanese troops and the energy had switched from calm to chaos. A soldier gave the man an affectionate pat on the shoulder, as if he was congratulating him.

Li did a double take. "That's Chang Wu. He was friends with my brother Zhou. They flew together up in Harbin. He came and took tea with my parents, after—" She paused. "But why is he smiling and shaking hands with Japanese soldiers?"

"Li, we need to go."

Out of the corner of her eye, Romy spotted some British, U.S., and Dutch consular officials with whom her parents often dined at Le Cercle Sportif Français being marched to the elevators by Japanese troops. Behind them was Miss Schwartz, and walking beside her was a woman addressing the Japanese soldiers in a firm American accent. Romy assumed this strong woman was Miss Schwartz's new boss from the JDC—Laura Margolis. From what Papa said, Miss Margolis had come with valuable American support from the Joint Distribution Committee to enlarge the operations of the soup kitchens and assist the growing population of refugees in Hongkew. Surely they weren't being arrested by the Japanese! Miss Schwartz, as if sensing Romy's gaze, turned. She narrowed her eyes and shook her head slightly—cautioning her to stay away.

What was going on? The Japanese were swarming in through the revolving doors and taking over the hotel. She felt as if she were trapped in a golden kaleidoscope. All the pieces were shifting and spinning.

Only Li stood still, a picture of grace in her cream cheongsam, suspended in a shaft of golden light.

Mr. Wu excused himself from the soldiers and approached the girls.

"Was that you singing? I heard a voice upstairs." He spoke warmly, meeting Li's eyes. He didn't notice Romy. "You're Li Ho, aren't you? Zhou's sister." He nodded without waiting for a reply. "You have the same eyes. He was a good man." He reached out to take Li's hand.

"I—" Li had lifted her chin a little and the strip of flesh above her cheongsam collar turned pink. Romy had never seen Li lost for words.

"I'm Chang Wu," he said as he held Li's hand for a beat longer than necessary.

"I remember," said Li as she demurely withdrew her hand. "Thank you. My brother was a good man," she agreed.

"Li . . ." Romy grabbed her friend's wrist and tried to tug her into the whirlpool of people. "We need to go. *Now!*"

"Forgive me, I've been rude." Chang Wu extended his hand to Romy and she reluctantly shook it. The grip was firm. Too firm.

"Romy Bernfeld."

Mr. Wu turned to gaze at Li. "You must come and sing here. In my club." Mr. Wu reached into his inside pocket for a silver box, opened it, and handed her a card. Li took it with both hands, nodding. "We have the best singers and orchestras in Shanghai," he boasted.

"I'm sure you do." Li giggled nervously. "I'd love to. But I'm not sure my parents would let me. They . . . I mean, I want to be a singer." She straightened her shoulders and lifted her chin a little higher. "I'm going to sing in Paris and Rome one day."

He chuckled. "I like your spirit." He leaned in close and Romy could smell the Brylcreem on his slicked-back hair, whisky on his breath. "It's a family trait."

Romy's skin prickled.

Mr. Wu's voice dropped in a warning. "Be careful, Li. That spirit could get you killed, if you're not careful." He raised his eyebrows and surveyed the sea of navy helmets, as if his words required no further explanation. "Please, I mean it. Contact me if you ever need anything. I promise there will always be a job for you at the Cathay, with that voice."

Romy tugged harder on Li's wrist and whispered, "We need to go. Now's not the time—"

Mr. Wu turned to Romy, appraising her, then said, "You should tell your friend to keep an open mind. Things are changing fast around here."

Chapter 34

SHANGHAI, JULY 1, 2016

Alexandra stepped into the humidity and weaved her way through crowds spilling out of office towers for lunch. The buildings in the center of Lujiazui were connected with walkways that threaded between skyscrapers and shopping malls like silver ribbons.

She rode the outdoor escalator, making a beeline for the little garden tucked between a silver high-rise, a giant TV screen, and the five-story curved golden wave of the Gucci store. Zhang mentioned he would try to meet her at this park today between meetings and she hurried so as not to miss him.

There were only three other people in the park when she reached it: a gardener sweeping leaves with a willow broom, a second gardener squatting on a square of raised lawn and plucking weeds from the turf with a tiny fork, and a man meditating on yellow river stones. Beyond the overpass was the shimmering pink disco ball of the Pearl Tower. A rustic stone wall blocked the chaos of the city. Avenues of trees were softened with lush dark ground cover, burgundy shrubs were pruned into perfect spheres. Loose grasses rippled with the wind.

The contrasting textures and explosion of flowers made her think of Oma. She took her phone out of her tote bag and sent a message and photo to Oma.

My local lunch spot.

Sitting in this strange garden, she realized that she'd come to value cities for their gardens, not their commodities exchanges. Perhaps she was more like her grandmother than she'd imagined.

Her phone pinged.

Glad you are enjoying the gardens. They tell me Suzhou gardens are very special. I never got the chance to visit. Perhaps you can.

Suzhou . . . Nearly ten years ago, some idiot at Oxford with too many lagers under his belt had ripped her pendant off her neck and she'd had to get the clasp repaired. The jeweler specialized in antiquities and he asked if he could keep the pendant for a few days. His verdict was that Alexandra's pendant was hundreds of years old. Early Qing dynasty. He thought it might have come from Suzhou.

She'd asked the jeweler about tracing its origin and he'd laughed. "People have been trading there for centuries. In a word: no chance, love." He must have sensed her disappointment. "If you're ever in that part of the world, there are some extraordinary gardens. Might be worth a look."

That's just what she was going to do.

◇

Zhang stepped off the escalator and walked toward her, smiling. With his briefcase slung over his shoulder, he was carrying a baguette and an apple juice. Alexandra had mentioned to Zhang on their food tour that she came to this park for twenty minutes over lunch. It was one he'd designed, so he'd arranged to meet her here today.

"Hello." He looked around the park. "Do you like it?" he asked as he sat on a grassy mound beside Alexandra.

"Love it," she responded as she broke off the end of his baguette and stuffed it into her mouth. As Alexandra chewed, she felt embarrassed, as if the breaking of someone else's baguette was an act of great intimacy.

"I don't get it, though. The park feels so contemporary, so simple and plain. But relaxing. Or at least I feel chilled out when I'm here." She broke off another piece of bread and studied the billowing grasses with seed heads that floated like clouds.

"Exactly what I had in mind," he said between mouthfuls. "I figured everyone's so busy over here in the financial zone, always thinking about the next deal. Where's the money coming from, and where's it going? How much did we make?"

Alexandra felt her ears burn at hearing her commodities deals described in such simple terms.

Zhang must have noticed, because he leaned forward and gently put a hand around her wrist. "Hey, I'm sorry. I didn't want to be glib about your job. It's not—that's not what I meant." He cocked his head to the side. He was frowning slightly with concern, and his dark eyes were apologetic.

Alexandra forced a smile and raised her eyebrows as she felt electricity run up her arm. It was unexpected, but comforting. His grip was strong, but tender. She studied his hand where it touched her skin; it was narrow and elegant, the nails manicured. The hands of a designer, or an artist, not the broad stumpy hands of a gardener, like her grandmother's.

Zhang caught her studying his hand and let go. "Sorry. I—I think you're amazing." He laughed and it felt like paper cranes lifting to the sky.

"So enough about my brilliant career," Alexandra said. "Tell me about this garden. Actually, now that I think about it, it does feel a bit like the one in my courtyard."

"Exactly. Are you religious?"

"I'm not. But my grandparents are Jewish. I mean, my grandfather *was*," she corrected herself. "But Oma is pretty much non-observant. Why? You're hitting all the big subjects today."

"Oh well, why not? We've known each other, what, five weeks? Shared noodles."

A shiver ran up Alexandra's back as she started to consider what else she might share with this kind man. He was so earnest, so free, compared with Hugo.

But it was way too soon. And she didn't have the strength to share her heart with anyone right now. Kate would tell her just to have a bit of fun and enjoy herself before he went back to Hong Kong for good. But she was too risk-averse to start something that she knew was doomed.

"It doesn't matter to me one way or another," Zhang said. "I'm not particularly religious. But there is something in Chinese philosophy I like to include in all my gardens. You can trace the lines in every garden in China, if you look closely enough. It's not religion, exactly, but it's definitely spiritual."

Alexandra's head shot up. She'd never heard a man talk about spirituality before. Or gardens. Especially over a baguette in a park.

"Speaking of gardens, I'm heading to Suzhou later this month," Alexandra told him. "I want to see some of the gardens. My grandmother loves gardening. She has a kind of Chinese garden at home. But she never got the chance to visit Suzhou."

"Shanghai was cut off from Suzhou by the Japanese during the war," Zhang explained. "But the gardens were preserved and I love a good excuse to visit . . ." He hesitated. "I'm sorry, I don't mean to invite myself. I just thought I might be able to help."

"No, that would be good," Alexandra said, feeling a bit breathless. She had to bite her tongue to stop herself from saying, "It's a date."

Chapter 35

Gong xi fa cai!

Tonight we celebrated Chinese New Year with the Ho family. Mei spent the day with Mutti and Mrs. Ho across in their apartment helping to prepare the feast. Mutti said it was the least she could do. Twice a week she goes with Mrs. Ho and her theater group to perform impromptu plays—huaju—in the streets in the International Settlement and Frenchtown. Papa and I went to watch her last week; we were sitting inside the window of a café with hot chocolates. Mutti didn't have a speaking role—she played a bird with a broken wing in a pretend cage. I giggled so hard I snorted some of the hot chocolate. But when I looked across at Papa his face looked sad. Now that I think of it, so did Mutti's. But she was acting, I think.

Mutti still misses Benjamin and Daniel—we all do—but thanks to Dr. Ho and Mei she is much better. I have asked Jian and Dr. Ho to teach me about the acupuncture points for the lungs and how to prepare some healing decoctions to keep her strong. Lately Mutti is busier than she's ever been, working at the hospital as a nurse alongside Papa, acting with Mrs. Ho, and she's also been helping other families get their documents in order to request releases from the work camps.

But back to the feast . . . When Papa and I arrived for dinner, I wished Li a happy New Year.

She laughed, kissed me on both cheeks, and presented me with a red envelope. Inside was a piece of sugarcane (for a sweet year) and the photo Jian took of Li and me in French Park three years ago, when we were just thirteen. We look far younger in our ponytails and pinafores. I promised I'd keep it forever.

We went into the drawing room, which had candles on the mantelpiece and the smell of cinnamon, cardamom, and master stock. Pomelos and tangelos were piled up in pyramids. Dr. Ho greeted us warmly and offered Papa the best chair. I barely said a word at all to Jian as Li kept squeezing my hands and tugging me away to point out the platters of dates, lotus seeds, and peanuts laid out for good luck. I ate way too many candied lychees and felt as if I was going to be sick before the dinner even started.

I feel like I've been gorging on luck since we left Vienna, and it sometimes leaves a sour taste in my mouth.

Li wore a golden cheongsam and treated us to a performance; Jian played the piano. I had to step outside onto the balcony for some fresh air while the table was being set, and when he'd finished accompanying Li, Jian came out to join me. Li kept on singing for everyone, asking each person to choose their favorite song. I had the strangest feeling she was prolonging her solos on purpose as she nodded slightly at Jian as he left the piano.

Jian glanced over his shoulder to see that no one was watching, then he pulled a small red envelope from his pocket and gave it to me. Inside was a thumb-sized piece of sugarcane, but underneath was the calligraphy symbol Fu.

"It means good fortune for the year ahead," he explained, and to my mortification I started to sob.

"I'm sorry," he said, bewildered. He stepped toward me and brushed a tear from my eye with his thumb. His hands smelled spicy and woody. He'd obviously been making moxa with Dr. Ho. Jian rested his hand on my cheek and for a moment I thought he was going to kiss me. I closed my eyes and tried to pretend our parents were not on the other side of the wall as my heart pounded.

But I must have been mistaken, because Jian removed his hand and stepped back inside without another word. I'd embarrassed him. I stayed on the balcony for another few minutes to make sure my cheeks were not red, and also because I didn't want to see Jian.

He'd been so kind to me lately, teaching me how to make a Sang Ju Yin formula with mulberry leaf and licorice. He'd even kept the illustration I made of the mulberry leaf and slipped me his recipe with amendments on a piece of parchment. It was silly for me to think that I'm anything more to him than his little sister's friend. But I'm sixteen now and I wonder if he's even noticed.

I keep thinking of those fine fingers, his hand against my cheek.

When I eventually went inside, everyone was preparing to sit down for dinner. Dr. Ho sat beside Mutti, Papa beside Mrs. Ho, and I sat between Li and Jian. There was a spare place at the table, and Mrs. Ho explained to us they always leave an empty chair if someone in the family cannot join them for the celebration. She reached across the table and squeezed both Mutti's and Papa's hands as she said it. Then it was Mutti's turn to sob. I looked at Papa—he looks so old now—and he gave a tired smile of thanks. Then we dined on dumplings, platters of fish and shrimp, and a bowl of clams (the clams open up like a new year, new horizons).

It was a dinner filled with food and laughter. There were so many different dishes they couldn't all fit on the table. It was very *messy. I was so nervous and jittery I tipped soy sauce all over the red tablecloth when I poured it, but I think I got away with it. I just wish Nina could have been there too. Papa assured me Delma and Miss Schwartz had arranged for Nina to have a special dinner with them at Café Louis, with David Damrosch. (I saw Papa slip the money to Miss Schwartz when she visited last week.)*

I miss Nina. I wonder what the New Year will bring for us all.

It's been two months since the bombs on the Whangpoo and the Japanese have taken over Shanghai. The Americans are in the war against Japan, but there's no sign of their troops in Shanghai. The French still hold Frenchtown, but everyone says that Japanese spies and troops are everywhere and that they pay no mind to the treaties. Even so, I hope this year is more settled, with no more bombs. Li and I must focus on our matriculation exams. I never imagined I'd be taking exams and applying for medical school in French!

Mostly, I hope the Year of the Horse brings Daniel back to us.

Chapter 36

SHANGHAI, JULY 13, 1942

Though it was summer break, Romy had spent the whole morning at the kitchen table studying chemistry and physics and completing mock exams. She sipped pomegranate juice and took comfort in the clatter of Mei's pans and the smell of star anise, garlic, and ginseng wafting across from the pot of master stock permanently simmering on the cooktop.

It had been seven months since the Pacific War had started with the Japanese attack on Pearl Harbor. America had well and truly joined the war against Japan—and Germany.

Papa was working at the hospital all hours, and one look at her parents' stooped shoulders and tired eyes told Romy there were simply not enough hands to help. She intended to study medicine at Aurora University when she matriculated in the autumn. This would be her *tzedakah*. She wondered what Nina was planning to do once she matriculated. Nina had topped her exams in English, Hebrew, German, and geography.

When Mei had finished mixing the cold noodles for lunch, she piled them into silver tins with a ladle. "Enough study. Your eyes will fall out of your head." She squeezed Romy's shoulders. "Time for swim. Take your mother with you. Chop-chop."

Romy closed her books, stood up, and stretched. As she grabbed the tins to take with her, she gave Mei a peck on the cheek. "Thank you. I never say it enough. I don't know what we'd do without you. Mutti—"

Mei's lips were pulled tight, but her cheeks were rosy and her eyes moist. "Go, child," she said, shooing Romy away with her bamboo lid.

The air outside was like warm molasses. Romy's yellow sundress stuck to her legs as she, Mutti, Wilma, Dr. Ho, Li, and Jian cycled to the YWCA pool for a dip. Mutti and Wilma had decided to hold one of their theater group meetings poolside that afternoon. To any outsider, the women draped nonchalantly around the pool in their bathing suits would have looked like a group of bored, mostly Shanghainese women, smoking and chattering as a cluster of amahs splashed and cooed over the younger children in the paddling pool.

Jian and Romy swam laps in the far lane, while Li stretched out like a cat on a towel nearby, reading Mutti's French *Vogue*s and humming to herself.

Romy enjoyed the cool water running through her fingers and across her back. She was a strong swimmer, though she preferred lakes. She was reminded of Daniel and Benjamin throwing her off the pontoon in Gänsehäufel with a big splash each July. She concentrated on her breathing, forcing herself to count and breathe so she didn't cry.

Today, Jian easily overtook her. As he swam past, she longed to reach out and touch the muscles rippling down his torso. Instead she stuck to the far side of the lane.

◇

After the swim, Dr. Ho, Li, Jian, and Romy walked along the footpath, thankful for the shade of the plane trees as they made their way to meet Dr. Ho's friends at Puyuan, the grand villa owned by the local bookseller.

After fifteen minutes listening to Li hum and skip her way through leafy Frenchtown, they eventually reached the villa. Romy eyed the brick archways smothered with jasmine stars and inhaled sweet sticky air as they clambered up the broad front steps and Dr. Ho knocked to gain entrance.

"Come, let's get inside out of this heat," he said as the heavy wooden door swung open.

Romy adored Puyuan—the dark walls, deep silk-covered sofas, vases filled with lilies, peonies, or branches of rose blossoms. Candles flickered on a dark sideboard, warming the marble bust of Sappho that was rumored to have been rescued from a pile of volcanic rubble in Pompeii. The scent of cloves and incense lingered in every room. Piles of the peeling leather-bound works of Baudelaire and slim volumes of Chinese poetry were stacked neatly on tables and on the floor.

In the corner was a grand piano—a Steinway. It made Romy think of her piano lessons with Herr Bloch and Saturday afternoon teas with Mutti. What she would give to have those music lessons back. To be teased by Daniel and Benjamin for her poor posture while she practiced her scales.

Luckily Jian would always be ready to distract her, laughing and playing the opening bars of Brahms, Mozart, or Mahler, or music she didn't recognize from a pile of musical scores bound in red snakeskin.

Sometimes he would ask Romy to sit on the stool beside him to turn the pages. As he played, Romy could feel the heat through his cotton shirt and the strength in his forearms as they stiffened and softened with the music. As he leaned toward the score at the end of each page, his fringe would fall across his eyebrows, casting a shadow across his cheekbones. How she longed to brush that fringe from his eyes. Instead, she concentrated on the closing bars of each page. Occasionally Li would sing, bringing the chatter to a halt and momentarily calming the anxious faces in the room.

Jian, Romy, and Li sat in the back library reading and staying cool under bamboo fans. Dr. Ho had bought them each a paperback copy of *Les Misérables*. Li was soon bored and took to scribbling tiny cartoon figures in the margins and writing secret messages between the lines, then silently passing her copy of the book to Romy. Sitting at a pair of sofas in the opposite corner, Dr. Ho and his friends sipped chrysanthemum tea and discussed Victor Hugo and Leconte de Lisle.

Help! I'm bored.

Can I unplait your hair outside? It looks so pretty when you show your curls.

What song should I sing?

Can you please help me finish my French assignment? (I already told Aba I'd done it so I could go to an extra singing lesson.)

Occasionally, Romy would look over the top of the book and wonder at Jian's intense expression: he was totally lost in Hugo's words. There was something so calm and self-assured about him. But she kept these thoughts to herself, turning to gaze at the *penjing* on the small table in front of her—a tiny pine tree, no taller than a meter, that had been clipped and shaped for over two centuries.

Dr. Ho walked across the room to join her. "We distill nature, Romy, to find its essence." Dr. Ho brushed his hand over the pine needles, releasing the sharp scent of the oil. "It *seems* like this tree has grown into this shape purely by chance. But"—he raised his eyebrows—"Confucius taught us to seek order and duty. Taoism seeks simplicity and restraint. This very place—Puyuan—means 'garden of simplicity.'"

Romy studied the *penjing* tree. How would she prune and clip her own life? She did arrive in Shanghai purely by chance. And yet she had a duty to the place—Papa had told her so. She needed to do more than survive. *Tzedakah.* She rolled the Hebrew word around on her tongue, as if it were a sticky date.

There was a thud as Li dropped her book on the floor and joined their conversation. "Papa," asked Li now as she lolled her head to one side. "Why do you bring us to these meetings?"

"Are you bored, little one?" He poked a dimple. "To starve to death is a very small matter; to lose one's integrity is a grave matter," said Dr. Ho. "We must stay loyal to Chinese customs, to speak the truth—even when the Japanese occupiers close our print houses and newspapers, or threaten imprisonment to any citizen who speaks out. Our country's rightful leaders have been exiled to Chungking."

Dr. Ho made eye contact with Jian, before turning to face the girls as his voice grew sad. "Wang Jingwei and his puppet government even want to stop the Chinese way of practicing medicine and focus on Western medicine. But we need both types. I like to look at the cause, the body, and the yin and yang, not just the treatment. There is plenty of room for both," he said softly, as if trying to convince himself. "You see, for every action we take in life with our body, what we consume, there are consequences . . ."

Jian noticed Romy's concern. "I don't think we should tell anyone at school we come to Puyuan." His voice dropped. "It's not safe. The Japanese military police are everywhere in Shanghai now."

Li and Romy looked shocked. "What? Why?" they asked in unison.

Jian shrugged and Dr. Ho shot him a warning look as he said, "Enough. It's time I delivered Romy home to her parents. Gather your things while I finish my tea."

Li groaned as they packed up their books and Jian stuffed his sheet music into his satchel. Li looked over her shoulder. "This means I'll have to finish my French assignment all by myself," she lamented. Dr. Ho politely chatted with a trio of gentlemen in the corner while they finished a pot of steaming tea.

As the last drops of tea were consumed, they bade polite farewells to everyone at the salon and wandered home to Grosvenor House, dodging rickshaws and peddlers kneeling on blankets selling shoes, gold necklaces, and peonies, as the dusk threw a golden hue across Shanghai.

Romy thought again of the tiny pine tree. She wondered what shape her life would take from here.

Chapter 37

SHANGHAI, JULY 7, 2016

After Alexandra's second Negroni at after-work drinks with her team she'd texted Zhang to join her. It turned out he was back at the shop in Tianzifang commissioning a larger pottery piece for his apartment, so she extended the invitation to Cynthia and Lu as well. Drinks turned into spicy prawns with lily bulbs and almonds and some jasmine-tea-smoked chicken.

Beyond black bamboo lattice walls and oversized red lanterns, tourist boats covered in fairy lights cruised the Huangpu River. On the opposite bank, the elegant skyscrapers of Pudong gave the sky a light purple haze. Music thumped in the background as waiters in miniskirts carried sizzling plates of food with spicy aromas.

Cynthia leaned in so she could be heard. "I'm sorry I haven't gotten back to you about the photos. The designers are scanning them to a higher resolution. I've asked them to make a set for you."

"That's very kind," Alexandra said, raising her voice to be heard over the music. "I'll pay you, of course."

"No need. Have you thought more about why you came to my shop that day? It must have been fate."

"I just assumed the photo was a random find. Dumb luck."

But even as she said it, she knew she didn't believe it. There was a pattern—a trajectory—for everything. Mathematicians didn't believe in luck.

Cynthia shook her head. "It's *yuanfen*," she said. "A fateful coincidence. Finding that matching photo was not about luck. Coincidence is about your fortune. Your future. The events of your life are linked to your history. Bad or good."

"Like karma?" Alexandra asked.

Cynthia shrugged. "Kind of. It means that your history has consequences. Your future—what we call fortune—is linked to your family's past."

"Fateful coincidence." Alexandra turned the phrase over in her mouth. She wasn't sure what to make of it. Both her grandparents had been forced to flee their country, and they were good people. To suggest otherwise was ludicrous. It was her *oma* and *opa* who had changed countries and given Alexandra her fortunate life. How could a Chinese family she'd never met shape her future? Or was she being far too literal?

She thought about the Google search she'd done on Li Ho at work that day. "I did some research on Li, the girl in the picture with my grandmother. There was only this one page."

She reached into her handbag and fished out a newspaper mention, dated June 21, 1945, she'd printed out. The headline read: TOP CATHAY HOTEL SINGER DISAPPEARS IN SUSPICIOUS CIRCUMSTANCES. Underneath was a single paragraph:

Li Ho, glamorous singer girl Yu Baihe, disappeared from her home in Frenchtown yesterday evening. The police are investigating the matter.

"I can't find any follow-up to the investigation. There's no mention of her in any newspaper or on the internet. No photos. It's as if she disappeared into thin air. It was so close to the end of the war. It must have been crazy here. I wonder what happened to her."

Cynthia shook her head. "We have all the paperwork. Jian Ho—the previous owner of the shop—kept *everything*. It took a month to sort through all the boxes. Mostly they were filled with old receipts. The only things worth keeping were the photos. There were no letters from his sister."

But as the gin, vermouth, and Campari from Alexandra's Negroni swirled in her belly, she considered the circumstances of finding this photo of her *oma* and a childhood friend in a city of millions. Also, didn't Opa mention a "Li" to Alexandra just before he died?

Li. You won't find her . . .

Alexandra shivered. What had Opa been trying to tell her?

In the darkened room, she could sense Zhang looking at her, feel his eyes on her bare shoulders as her heart beat with the crazy rhythm of the music. She looked up and met his eye. Zhang smiled shyly and then they both looked away.

Chapter 38

SHANGHAI, JULY 20, 1942

As Romy passed her father's office she started to push the heavy wooden door open, then stopped. Hearing voices, she glanced through the crack and saw Delma from Café Louis and Miss Schwartz. They must have arrived when Romy was cooking with Mei. There was no sign of Mutti. Romy presumed she was with Wilma Ho at one of her clandestine theater group meetings. The Japanese oppression of the Chinese had aroused her sense of justice. Whenever Romy begged her to be careful, Mutti smiled serenely and insisted she was an amateur "who was just trying a new skill to cheer up the locals" by performing *huaju*.

Delma was sitting quietly in the leather club chair as Miss Schwartz paced. It was the first time Romy had seen her since the day at the Cathay; Miss Schwartz and her boss, Laura Margolis, along with other international diplomats, had been detained there for two weeks.

"All our money and supplies from America have been cut off since we entered the war," she was saying now. "But Laura had already secured permission to borrow money."

"From whom?"

"Russians. Japanese. Anywhere we can get it. Some wealthy local families are helping with the schools. We have a letter saying once the Pacific War is over the JDC will repay this amount in full to anyone who lends it."

She handed Papa a sheet of paper. "This is what we need, Oskar. I'm still trying to chase medical supplies. But Laura needs me working full-time in the JDC kitchens. We're feeding over four thousand people lunch and dinner every day. Finding enough rice, flour, and millet is a huge challenge. And it's going to get worse—thousands of Jews and Chinese will starve to death. Laura wants us to be sure we have everything in place in case—"

"Eva thinks it's only a matter of time before the Americans and British are interned in camps," said Delma softly, wringing her hands.

Papa's voice was ever so slightly higher pitched than usual when he said, "But surely you both didn't need to risk coming here. Your boy could have passed on the medication list to Mei at the markets, as usual."

"There's something else." Miss Schwartz's voice had softened and she wiped her hands on her pants. "I need to talk to you about your neighbors."

"The Hos?" Papa sounded puzzled. "Miss Schwartz—Eva—I assure you the Hos are honorable people."

"I agree. But that's the problem: their outspoken loyalty to China."

There was a pause, and when Papa spoke again Romy could hear the quaver in his voice. "We owe them, Marta and I. His herbs, the decoctions and tinctures he made with Mei. The needling. I know the puppet government of Wang Jingwei is trying to outlaw traditional medicine. And I agree in part—it won't fix the typhoid, dysentery, and cholera that's flying around this damn city." He wiped his brow and his eyes moved from Miss Schwartz to Delma. "He gave me back my wife. Surely you understand? Besides, Romy and Li are inseparable. My wife and child have lost so much."

"I know." Miss Schwartz was speaking gently now. "So that's why I'm telling you. We know the Japanese are rounding up newspaper editors and torturing them at Bridge House. It's come to my attention that the Kempeitai—the Japanese military police—are working with Chinese collaborators and gangsters to make a list of intellectuals who may be, er, *resisting* the puppet Chinese government. People are being tortured on racks, Oskar. Toenails and fingernails ripped out . . . It's highly likely the Hos are on that list." She took a deep breath. "For Christ's sake, heads are being chopped off!"

Papa stared at her, his face pale, too shocked to speak.

"The Hos need to be careful," Miss Schwartz continued. "And so do you. If your family gets tangled up in this, we can kiss goodbye any more assistance. The Japanese turn a blind eye to us securing sulfa, ether, and insulin on the black market now that the pharmacy supplies are running low. And then there's the huge amount of food we need in order to feed thousands every week.

"The Japanese troops are helping us to rebuild Hongkew. Providing areas for Jewish refugees to live, giving our men work in factories. They may be Nazi allies, but as long as we are in Shanghai they are ours too. We cannot afford to make enemies of the Japanese or the Chinese government. Our job is to survive this war."

"I understand," said Papa quietly.

"It's a fine line. You could all be killed if they think you are part of the resistance." Miss Schwartz stopped pacing. "Do you hear what I'm saying, Oskar?"

"Eva . . ." Delma was standing beside Miss Schwartz now, touching her wrist. "It's not Oskar's fault."

"Oh, I know." Miss Schwartz rubbed her temples. "I'm sorry," she muttered to Papa.

"I keep telling Eva she must sleep more," said Delma apologetically. Her curly dark hair was knotted in a bun and her face was devoid of makeup. But with her aquiline nose, translucent skin, and high cheekbones, Delma was every bit as beautiful as she was kind.

Divine Delma.

"What are you doing?"

Romy jumped as Mei walked up behind her. "You should be upstairs doing your homework." Mei pulled the office door closed and Romy took the stairs two at a time. She couldn't wait to sneak across the corridor and tell Li what she'd just heard.

Her temples throbbed as she recalled Miss Schwartz's warning. She hoped now her parents would be sensible, follow the rules, and stop putting themselves in danger. They needed to stay together, and stay alive.

Chapter 39

SHANGHAI, JULY 30, 1942

30 July 1942
Grosvenor House
Mutti is very worried. Still no news from Daniel. Or Herr Gruber.
She has started taking to her bed in the afternoons again. Mutti and
Papa try not to talk about Daniel around me. But like everyone else
at school, I've heard some concentration camp leaders can be cruel,
the work grueling, and some inmates are taking ill. Daniel is strong.
I pray he keeps well until we can return and get him. Some days it
feels like that will never happen. But I mustn't allow myself to think
that way. Daniel would hate it.

When Papa and I met Nina last week at Café Louis, I heard
Miss Schwartz and Delma talking to Papa about someone from
the Gestapo—Colonel Josef Meisinger. He was sent to the East by the
Nazis to liaise with the Japanese and manage twenty thousand Jews
who have fled Europe to Shanghai. He was trying to source giant
barges to pull out to sea, or to secure sites for a camp. Delma called

Meisinger "Butcher" through gritted teeth, saying she's heard nothing of her family in Warsaw.

I'm petrified for Daniel, but ever so slightly relieved that he is in Dachau. It's far from the horror of Poland. In his last brief letter in March 1940, there was no mention of whether he has access to a piano, but I suspect not. I hope he is taking care of his hands.

The Japanese military is in charge here now, and Mutti and Papa—along with everyone else—call the Chinese administrators a puppet government. Japanese civilians wear bandannas with the Rising Sun symbol on their arms and get served first in every queue. But everyone says the Japanese take orders from the Führer and the Nazi Party. Except for Miss Schwartz. Her contacts tell her the Japanese push back against policies from the Third Reich, particularly the treatment of Jews.

School is going well. I am now fluent in Shanghainese and French, and most of my classes are in French. Math, chemistry, physics, and biology are my favorite subjects. I told Papa the other day that perhaps I'll be a doctor, like him. He hugged me tight when I said that. I felt more sad than proud.

On Saturdays, instead of piano lessons, I go to the YWCA swimming pool. There I practice my strokes, and they have a diving board. I don't seem to be able to get the bounce right (it's harder than it looks!).

Some of my friends from school, including Li, went to a diving competition against the girls over at the Catholic school and the British school. Li won the medal! She was as graceful as a swan and the dive that won was backward off the three-meter board. We all screamed so loudly when she won that when we got home Mrs. Ho made us drink tea with honey. Can you imagine?

Shanghai seems to be busier, and there are more Japanese soldiers in the streets. I saw them beat the man who sells boiled eggs last week.

Many locals are very poor. They eat snacks bought for a copper coin from street stalls selling hand-pulled noodles, soup, or egg crepes, and I often see them gathered outside the florist or butcher, sitting on a ragged square of fabric and begging with a tin used to boil soup. Sometimes they sleep on the footpath.

It's hot. Stifling. Mosquitoes and flies are everywhere. I have seen beggars lying dead on footpaths, hands curled like pigeon claws. No one pays them any attention, but the bodies are cleared daily. Some say the Japanese throw the bodies in the Whangpoo River. Babies and smaller children are bundled into straw mattresses and tied up with string and left on the footpath until the garbage truck comes around each morning. I cry every time I see one. So does Mutti. It's like those children don't matter.

Then, in Frenchtown, Mutti and Papa are going to dinners in the ballroom of the Cercle Sportif while Li, Jian, and I play lawn tennis as our amahs look on. (Jian is very good but he pretends to miss every now and again when I serve!)

Such a gloomy diary entry. It's hard to explain the different cities Shanghai can be.

I miss Daniel. I miss Nina. I pray they are safe. Amen.

Chapter 40

SUZHOU, JULY 22, 2016

Alexandra followed Zhang through a modest Moon Gate and along pebbled paths until they stood before an enormous lake filled with lily pads. The air was thick and sweet with the scent of Chinese star jasmine. They were at the less crowded end of the Humble Administrator's Garden, far from the schoolchildren lolling about when they were supposed to be sketching the shadows of the huge rock sculpture.

"This is my favorite part," said Zhang with a grin. "You know, this garden was created by a tax collector—or as we like to say, 'humble administrator.'"

"In his spare time?" Alexandra arched an eyebrow.

"Actually, it took decades. Thousands of hands. Every section has been meticulously planned. Every vista." He pointed to a wisteria-covered pagoda at the far end of the lake. He reached out and stroked a maple leaf.

"It looks like we've just arrived here by chance, but the paths have been guiding every step. Every tree—every single branch—has been carefully pruned and shaped."

He put out his hand and rubbed the bark on a maple tree and Alexandra copied him. They stood centimeters apart, rubbing the bark. His hands were smooth and strong. Alexandra shivered as she imagined those hands touching her face.

Alexandra picked up a yellow river stone as big as her hand. It was cool and smooth as she pressed it to her cheek. She preferred these simple stones to the towering jagged rocks of the Lion Grove Garden, which they'd visited earlier. It surprised Alexandra how such a grand space could feel so quiet and intimate. What would the humble administrator think of a commodities trader crouched beside his lake five hundred years later? Would he be proud he'd forced her to slow down and take in one view at a time?

Her *oma* would enjoy the simplicity and restraint of this garden. Oma's quiet thoughtfulness—and Puyuan—made sense to Alexandra as she eyed the wooden pavilion at the far end of the lake. She snapped photos on her phone for her grandmother—taking care to capture the texture of the pebbles, the pink lilies, and the shadows of the gnarly rocks. If the photos were any good Alexandra could print them onto a canvas for Oma when she was next home.

They wandered past the thin yellow stems of the bamboo forest swaying in the breeze. "Bamboo is everywhere in China," Zhang explained. "It's hardy, but it can move with the wind without breaking. Like a true gentleman does," he added.

Zhang strived with his work to create something special. Like the humble administrator. Alexandra specialized in a game that ripped commodities from the ground and left open cuts in the earth from Nepal to northern Australia. She had folders full of images from analysts on her desktop, so many they were all a blur. She'd lost track of when the jungles of Equatorial Guinea became indistinguishable from Brazil. It was a matter of which mine they could extend first. The only differences between countries were measured in pounds, dollars, or RMB. Where Zhang created something beautiful, she left a gaping wound.

She lifted her hand to her chest and stroked the pendant. What would be her legacy?

They wandered through a final Moon Gate into the exit courtyard and Zhang bought them each a bottle of water. An old man poured sheets of toffee and then smashed it up with a hammer. Nearby another stood with a bicycle loaded with baskets of pink and black cherries, prickly lychees, and mangosteens. They ordered half a kilo of lychees.

Alexandra sat beside Zhang on a low stone wall as they peeled their fruit before dropping the scraps back into the plastic bag, savoring the explosion of sour sweetness with every fleshy pink finger peeled away from the glossy black seed.

A couple of children ran past, blowing into gourds that screeched far higher than a recorder. Alexandra winced and covered her ears. Zhang laughed and the little boys started and ran back to hide behind their mother's skirt. The biggest of the two poked out his head with a shy smile and Zhang winked. Emboldened, the boy waved his gourd.

"Do you make friends with strangers everywhere you go?" teased Alexandra.

"Only the cute ones." The child's whistle started to screech. "Correction. Make that the talented ones." He had an easy lopsided smile and she longed to brush his fringe to one side to see his eyes.

They crinkled up at the edges when he smiled. The second button on his shirt had come undone, and when he swiveled she managed to catch a glimpse of his smooth chest and a hint of his musky scent.

To distract herself, she studied the table of trinkets beside her. There were silk and paper fans, calligraphy brushes with matching pots of black ink, red good-luck charms, and rows and rows of watery green pendants and a few white jade ones. Some had the daintiest carvings of pine trees, others had peonies, frogs, turtles, or Buddhas.

Her hand reached again for her own pendant.

"This area's famous for its jade carving," said Zhang, following her gaze. "Where's your necklace from? It's darker. Better quality than most."

Alexandra felt her heart beat a little faster as he eyed her clavicle.

"Jade's precious," he told her. "It's currency."

"Clearly," joked Alexandra as she waved at the table of trinkets for a few hundred RMB.

Zhang smiled and waited.

Alexandra instantly regretted being glib. She took a deep breath and spoke slowly. "This belonged to my mother. Before that, I've no idea. It was given to her when she was adopted from China." Alexandra gave him the abridged theory from her antiques specialist in Oxford.

He leaned in closer to look at her necklace. "May I?" His fingers brushed her skin as he tugged on the gold chain and held it up to catch the light. "Haven't you ever wondered about the riddle in this pendant?"

"Riddle?" asked Alexandra. "It's a lily. How can that be a riddle? I know the lily symbolizes pure love." Her voice wavered. "My *oma* filled her house with roses and lilies when Opa was dying. I had to explain to visitors that it was a Chinese thing!"

"Well, riddles are a Chinese thing too. We love a hidden meaning."

"Go on," said Alexandra.

He pointed to the table beside them. "See the pendant with the peony in a box? The white jade is called mutton-fat jade—"

Alexandra chuckled. "Sounds fetching."

"Well, that represents a peony being unlocked—the key to a happy marriage. The one beside it with two cats, that's for fidelity. The bat sitting on the left cat represents blessings."

He pointed to three fish surrounded by three rings. "That picture means: May you give birth to a son who can pass the civil exams.

"But this . . ." He stroked the lines of Alexandra's lily with his thumb. She could feel his breath on her face. "This pendant, this lily, is a play on words."

"A riddle."

"Exactly. *Baihe*—the word for *lily*—sounds like the proverb: *Bainian hao he.* Happy union for one hundred years . . . The gift of a lily ties you to that person forever."

Chapter 41

Recalling the sensation of Zhang's warm breath against her skin made Alexandra a little dizzy as they strolled beside the canal in Suzhou's old town. The banks were built up with clay bricks, and rows of medieval courtyard houses leaned against one another. The faded, whitewashed walls contrasted with the waves of black tiles on the rooftops. She'd read last night in her guidebook that the historic district of Pingjian was a thousand years old.

These lanes and alleyways had a pulse. She couldn't stop herself from peering over fences, staring at giggling toddlers in nappies sitting on the ground and eating rice straight from the bowl with their hands, or watching pairs of men navigating the narrow canal in wooden boats. The smell of frying fish floated from every alley, making her stomach grumble.

"That garden was massive, and we've done a lot of walking today," said Zhang. "Tomorrow we'll do the Master of Nets for the grand lake."

When Zhang had suggested they stay the night in Suzhou to visit more gardens on the Sunday, he'd offered to organize a driver and book them a room each in Suzhou. Alexandra was curious to see what kind of place he'd chosen—industrial chic, serene modern, or medieval charm? He'd be equally at home in all three.

Bikes and covered rickshaws flew past, dinging their bells to drum up business, weaving between the footpaths and the road.

"We'd better get you something to eat," said Zhang as they came to a row of street stalls built into a wall under a red awning. The first sold flavored rice milk in baby bottles, and the next had bamboo steamer trays loaded with sticky white fortune fish, smooth apple-green balls of glutinous rice, and sticky purple balls of grain.

"I'm not sure about the sweet treats. I adore them but I think I need something more substantial."

Zhang pointed to the next stall, which had trays of tawny chicken feet, duck tongues, feathery white shrimp, and cubes of chicken and fish on wooden sticks that were being grilled over hot coals. The cook twisted the wooden sticks between his thumb and forefinger over the dancing flame. He raised his shoulders and pointed at Alexandra—asking if she'd like one. She shook her head.

Zhang shrugged an apology to the man and gently took her hand, threading his fingers through hers. They were warm and strong.

"Come," he said softly. "I have somewhere special in mind."

He led her away from the stalls and back to the footpath, past two arched stone bridges where a stunning bride in a red embroidered cheongsam and another in a knockout white Vera Wang–style gown posed for photos with their grooms.

Zhang's project in Shanghai was finishing in August and he was heading back to Hong Kong. She'd sworn off relationships, yet here she was with her hand in his and she didn't want him to let go. Every time he brushed the small of her back, she shivered. She hardly even noticed the busy cyclists who chatted away on their mobile phones while they expertly weaved bikes loaded with cherries, pastries, or dumplings between throngs of tourists.

They were walking faster now, racing against the lowering hazy pink sky behind the houses. "Where are we going in such a hurry?" asked Alexandra.

But if she cared to admit it, she was happy to be led.

It was a balmy evening as they walked along cobblestones beside the main canal in the old part of Suzhou. They'd dined at a traditional noodle house with just three rickety tables on a terrace overlooking the canal. Alexandra had ordered the local *paopao* wonton soup for dinner and it was like eating balloons full of air, pork mince, prawns, mild pepper, and allspice. She could still feel the popping on her tongue. Zhang had sat opposite her, slurping up a bowl of fine noodles swimming in spicy chicken broth.

Zhang led her down a mysterious side street to a black bamboo lattice gate set in a whitewashed wall. They stepped into a courtyard lit with red paper lanterns and alternating patches of Chinese star jasmine and honeysuckle clinging to the walls. The ground was covered in raked white gravel with an expanse of moss on one side.

Alexandra looked at him. "You designed this place?"

He nodded. "It belongs to a client. It's a private home, but he only visits once a year. I got the driver to drop our bags off here and run a few errands after we went to the garden." He dropped her hand rather awkwardly and took a small step away from her as he cleared his throat.

"Your room is on the top floor, overlooking this garden."

Alexandra nodded and looked up to where he pointed, trying to stop herself from frowning and giving away her disappointment that her evening was about to end.

In one corner of the courtyard was a table and chairs with a silver ice bucket, a bottle of champagne, and two glasses. This must be one of the "errands" the driver had run, Alexandra realized.

"Shall we?" Zhang ushered her to a chair and poured them each a glass of champagne. "We have this place to ourselves for the night."

"Thank you," said Alexandra as they clinked glasses.

He leaned over, and she felt his breath on her cheek.

"So, this necklace of yours," he said. "Have you worked out the riddle?"

He was sitting close, their thighs almost touching. He twisted toward her and put out his hand and stroked the pendant, tracing the lines of the lily that almost formed part of Alexandra.

"Um . . ." Alexandra's voice was shaky. It was taking all her energy to concentrate as Zhang traced her lily and the circle of the pendant on her skin.

"It connects you to *your* mother. But who does it connect *your* mother to?"

"My grandmother always said it was the lucky charm that came with my mother. Or my mother was the lucky charm that came with the necklace!"

"Another riddle," he said. "You know, the thing about riddles is that the answer is often the most simple, obvious solution . . . It's not a riddle at all."

He drew a line from her chest to her lips, then leaned in and kissed her.

It wasn't the soft, tender kiss she'd imagined. It was deep. Ravenous.

She put her empty champagne glass on the table with a clatter and brushed his hair away from his eyes. He smelled of mint and the earth, and as he kissed her, she slid off her chair and onto his lap. She slowly ran her hands across his broad shoulders, savoring every muscle as he kissed her harder and deeper.

As she came up for air, he started to slowly unbutton her shirt and kissed the top of her breasts, brushing the pendant away. She pulled his T-shirt over his head and ran her flat palm across his chest and down to his hard belly.

In one swift move, Zhang stood and carried her across to the bed of moss, where he gently laid her down. He lay down beside her and Alexandra groaned and pulled him close, losing herself in a thick cloud of vanilla and moss. Losing herself in him . . .

Chapter 42

MELBOURNE, JULY 22, 2016

Nina lay propped up in bed with a pink shawl across her shoulders, her small studio filled with light. The afternoon sun streamed through her large window and bounced off all the piles of sequined cushions and shiny surfaces, making the room sparkle. Romy was certain it was the most colorful and glamorous apartment in the retirement village.

She pecked a very sleepy Nina on the forehead, then patted her hand before digging around in the kitchen for a vase.

"It's just a cold. No need for you to make this fuss," croaked Nina.

"Nonsense," said Romy as she filled the vase with yellow tulips and placed them on Nina's bedside table. "These will cheer you up."

"Thank you," replied Nina with an impish smile. "But a good whisky would do a better job. Don't suppose that's what you've brought in your bag there?"

Romy rolled her eyes, reached for Nina's wrist, and took her pulse. When she'd finished, she said, "Now show me your tongue."

Nina winced, but poked out her tongue and wriggled it like a naughty toddler.

266

Romy studied it for a minute before she said: "Just as I thought. You are worn out. I've got some yin tonic—*bai shao*—for the liver and circulation. It's made from dried peony roots."

"More gems from your garden. Lucky me," said Nina dryly.

Nina wriggled forward so Romy could plump her pillows, before collapsing back on the bed and sipping a warm cup of *bai shao* poured from Romy's old green thermos. Nina's lips puckered and brow creased as she spluttered and eventually drank the dark, bitter liquid.

"*Ach.*" She wiped her lips with the back of her hand. "That tastes like poison," she said, eyes twinkling. "I'll be back doing Zumba by the end of the week." She blinked at her friend, voice softening. "Worst one yet, *sturer Bock*!"

Romy had already pulled up the sheets to reveal Nina's swollen ankles and was poking them gently to see where to place her needles.

"You heard from Alexandra?"

"Ye-es," answered Romy, still prodding to find the right point on the outside of the left ankle. She slid a needle in without Nina noticing and looked up.

"And?" said Nina impatiently.

Romy shrugged. "She seems fine."

"Fine! That girl, she's been saying she's *fine* since she was a kid." She paused, imitating Alexandra. "'I'm *fine*, Aunt Nina,' she'd say with those big sad eyes. Like a little girl lost . . ." Nina closed her eyes, then opened them again. "You should tell her. What harm will it do now that Wilhelm has gone?"

Romy held another packet of needles up to the light and peeled away the plastic. She took a deep breath and slowly counted to ten. She'd believed all those years ago she'd made the right decision.

Nina shook her head, her eyelids closing again as she drifted toward sleep. "We're too old for secrets," she said.

Chapter 43

Dear Romy,
I've left this note with Delma at the café, hoping it will be delivered
to you soon.

I wanted to thank you for your parcel for my birthday. The jacket
and blue cashmere top were too generous. Your parents have always
been so kind. I can see where you get it from.

I shall wear my little pearl earrings and think of you every day.

I cannot stay at the Heime. *Food is running short and it is time*
for me to fend for myself since poor Uncle David died last week. There
is so much cholera and typhus now, at night it is nearly impossible
to sleep for the vomiting, hacking, and spluttering. If I stay, I'm sure to
be among the sick and fallen.

I have arranged for employment somewhere I'll be of use. I'm
luckier than most as I'll get bed and board in exchange for cleaning,
sewing, and lending a hand in a local boardinghouse.

I ask you to promise you won't come and try to find me. My decision is made and we must all get on in this war as best we can.

Promise me.

Your friend always,

Nina xx

Chapter 44

Alexandra lay wrapped in a sheet on a bed that overlooked the courtyard while Zhang dozed beside her. The main bedroom had floor-to-ceiling glass and she felt like she was floating just above the soft bed of moss, with the red leaves of a maple tree shimmering in the summer light. The ceramic roof tiles swept like a charcoal wave across the maze of old Suzhou.

She watched the steady rise and fall of Zhang's chest and thought about pulling back the sheet to rest her head on his skin. But she didn't want to wake him; he looked so peaceful. He approached life as if it were one of the gardens they had seen yesterday, she thought. Happy to follow the meandering paths wherever they took him, enjoying the beauty to be found in each new vista, no matter how humble or simple.

Reaching up to trace the lily on her pendant, she recalled him saying: *You know, the thing about riddles is that the answer is often the most simple, obvious solution . . . It's not a riddle at all.*

That was what she should focus on in the search for her mother's origins, she decided. Assemble all the facts, then look for the simple, obvious solution.

If only it were that easy . . .

Chapter 45

Romy stood huddled with Li at their school gate. They were both wearing coats, scarves, and berets. The clouds were low and dark, and the wind rattled every window in the street as it howled between the buildings. Footpaths were covered with brown slush from leftover snow. Girls streamed out of the gates, climbing into rickshaws to take them out of the bitter weather. The only cars on the street running on gas carried badges of the police, ambulance, or fire brigade. Some girls were wearing armbands marked with a red *A*, *B*, or *N*—indicating whether they were American, British, or Dutch citizens.

Romy pulled her coat close, letting the rabbit fur rub against her cheek. Mutti had taken her to Lane Crawford last week to purchase a new coat and be measured for some new dresses.

"I should have done it earlier, *Liebling*. But with the hospital . . ."

Romy didn't mind. Seeing her parents working so hard made her even more determined to help.

"Anyway," said Mutti, "you're seventeen. It's time you had a couple of *nice* things."

Romy felt a wave of shame at the thought that she should deserve nice things when others had so little—like Nina, for instance. There had been no word from Nina since her farewell letter, though Delma and Miss Schwartz assured Romy they were still looking. They had heard rumors that Nina was working in one of the less salubrious boardinghouses, but when they checked no one there had heard of her.

It was easy to disappear in Shanghai, according to Miss Schwartz. It was a city for chameleons. Reinvention. White Russian cleaners became glamorous cabaret singers and club owners, European bureaucrats ran healthy sidelines selling "information," Chinese country peasants grew fat selling opium—slipped to them under the table by the Japanese—to rickshaw drivers and laborers. It kept the men docile. For a girl to just disappear wasn't unusual in this swirling metropolis, where decadence and depravity skipped hand in hand and it seemed rules were meant to be broken.

"At last!" cried Li, breaking Romy's reverie. She looked up to see Jian approaching, hands plunged deep into his pockets and shoulders hunched against the cold.

The trio took a shortcut between some laneways to one of their favorite food stalls. As they sat down, the owner put a pot of steaming tea on the table. Romy took off her mittens and rubbed her hands together before wrapping them around her cup. Li and Jian ordered bowls of chicken broth with slivers of smoked eel, but Romy preferred the narrow noodles, served covered in a light coating of shallot oil. She ordered in Shanghainese, and the hunched man gave her a gap-toothed smile as he threw the noodles into the wok and gave them a shake over the blue flame before tipping them into a cracked white bowl. She added soy sauce, pink vinegar, and some fiery chili jam from a bowl on the table.

Jian watched Romy use chopsticks to stuff noodles into her mouth and laughed. "It's as if you were born using them," he said.

"Eat faster, Jian," his sister urged. "I want to go see Papa and sing him my latest song."

"Shh," said Jian, waving his chopsticks at Li. "We need to go straight home, remember? No stopping at Puyuan on the way past."

Romy lifted her bowl to slurp the last few salty noodles into her mouth and to hide her embarrassment.

Papa had forbidden Romy from visiting both Puyuan and Dr. Ho's clinic. Dr. Ho was most gracious about the new arrangements. He greeted Papa with the same beaming smile on the stairs every day and still gave Mei brown paper parcels of herbs to boil up for Mutti. On any given day, the kitchen was filled with the musky, spicy, and sometimes bitter steam of the Orient: peony tree root, star anise, and orange blossom.

When they'd finished eating they set off straight home to Grosvenor House. They were only a block away from Puyuan when Romy realized something was amiss. It was quiet. Too quiet. The usual hum of traffic had stopped, the endless shrieks of vendors and beggars silenced. Ahead of them people were blocking the footpath, watching something, but Romy couldn't see what they were looking at. When she glanced at Jian she saw that he looked apprehensive.

Romy shivered and reached for Li's hand. Beyond the wall of people were some muffled wails and a piercing cry, quickly whipped away by the wind.

Then through a gap Romy glimpsed Japanese soldiers tipping boxes of books onto the footpath. The smell of gasoline cut through the icy air. Above the eerie silence came the scratch of a match. The piles of books started to smolder, flames hungry for air.

A murmur swept through the crowd as people turned away, eyes wide with shock and fear.

Romy had seen such expressions before. She squeezed her eyes tight, trying to block out the memories of blood spattering her face, Benjamin's shattered forehead.

"We need to go!" said Romy as she grabbed her friends by their elbows and tried to pull them back through the crowd.

"Not until we see what's going on," said Jian, taking a step forward.

"Jian, maybe we should do as Romy says." Li turned to her friend, her pale face creased with uncertainty.

The crowd was moving in a panic now, current swirling like a whirlpool.

"We need to find Aba," said Jian. "He's here somewhere. We need to let him know we're safe."

A soldier lifted the butt of his rifle and smashed a nearby window. A baby started to cry, and a second window splintered. The sound of Kristallnacht rang in Romy's ears. They had to leave!

Romy's stomach churned as she shoved her way through the coats, remembering all those hips and shoulders knocking her head, the smell of gasoline, urine, and fear on Wipplingerstrasse.

Please! But she didn't know what to pray for. Worse, she wasn't sure she believed anyone was listening to her prayers.

Jian stuck out an elbow and cleared a path.

Romy took a deep breath, wanting to flee in the other direction, but knowing she must keep moving for her friends.

Li cried, *"Aba!"* People turned in horror as they saw Li screaming for her father.

Fear flickered in Jian's eyes and he yelled, "What is this?"

Two Japanese soldiers were standing to attention at either side of Puyuan's door, bayonets clasped tight to their sides. They were as rigid as the green topiary trees beside them. A cluster of glassy-eyed workmen stood nearby, hunched in thin blue rags.

Jian pushed his way through the crowd. When he reached the front of the throng, he dropped his head into his hands and howled.

Romy's throat went dry. She reached for Li's hand.

Jian turned and cried out, "Li, Romy—go back!" He started waving his hands at them to leave.

Li stared at Romy, eyes filled with tears. "What's happening? I don't understand—"

Suddenly Jian seemed to crumple. He dropped to his knees and let out a painful cry that ripped Romy's heart into pieces.

Li stood on her tiptoes to see what was happening and then she too let out a cry.

"No!" she screamed. Wrenching her hand from Romy's grip, she pushed through the crowd toward her brother.

When Romy saw what her friends had seen, the ground seemed to tilt beneath her.

Six bamboo stakes had been driven deep into the mud and they were dripping with crimson blood. On top of each stake was a severed head. In the middle was Dr. Ho, his brown eyes propped open with matchsticks. Beside him, Mrs. Ho's head waggled slightly to one side with the wind, warm sticky blood pooling at the bottom of her stake.

Nailed to a bamboo stake in front of the line of bodies was a piece of cardboard with a message scrawled in English:

LOOK! LOOK! THE RESULT OF ANTI-JAPANESE ELEMENTS.

Romy doubled over, placing her hands on her knees as she vomited onto the footpath. She accidentally knocked a clump of mustard greens and two purple cabbages from a willow basket clutched by the woman beside her. The kindly lady transferred her basket to the other arm, bent low, and held Romy tight, as if she were a child. Around them everyone had started to run, a mad stampede. But this tiny woman smelling of allspice held firm, rocking Romy and rubbing her back. A few paces in front, Li and Jian held each other.

Romy wiped her mouth with the back of her hand and, turning to thank the woman, saw that she was watching Li and Jian, eyes wide with fear. Was this woman afraid of the Hos—or afraid *for* them?

Romy knew she had to help Jian and Li escape from this crowd before they were spotted by the Japanese soldiers, who were pushing people on the far side with their backs turned. So many dark eyes were on her friends, but who could they trust?

Out of the corner of her eye, she recognized the profile of the handsome young man from the Cathay Hotel. He was standing serenely with his hands in his pockets, chewing a matchstick.

"Li, there's your brother's friend, Mr. Wu—he'll help us get away from here," said Romy, nodding in his direction.

Even as she said it, Chang Wu was already moving toward them.

Something about his calm demeanor made Romy hesitate. If he was friends with the Hos, how could he appear so unconcerned by the horrific sight of their two mutilated heads on stakes?

Romy stiffened and she started to back away, spreading her arms instinctively to shield Li and Jian.

"We need to go. *Now!* We can't trust anyone until we work out—" said Jian. He clenched his jaw and his cheeks tightened with anger and fury, but his eyes looked wild.

"But . . ." Li shifted her weight and straightened her shoulders. Her eyes flamed with fear and confusion, but she cocked her head and met the eyes of Chang Wu.

Romy looked between Chang and Li, confused. Could Mr. Wu have links with the Japanese? He seemed too calm, too still, as the crowd panicked and surged around him. He'd warned them that chaotic day in December 1941 at the Cathay as Japanese soldiers stormed the International Settlement. Romy had no idea if he would help now, but she agreed with Jian—they couldn't risk staying here any longer to find out.

Li stood frozen, looking from Chang Wu to the Japanese soldiers and back. She blinked several times, dazed and uncertain. She took an unsteady step backward.

The shadows of the afternoon were creeping along the gray bricks, the boughs of the plane trees looming over them. It was no longer clear who was friend and who was foe. Romy thought of their dear friend Herr Gruber, who'd risked his own life to help the Bernfelds escape Vienna. Now it was her turn.

Stepping between Chang Wu and her friends, she whispered, "We need to move quickly. You can't stay here. It isn't safe. Do not look up. Do not stop moving. Do not make eye contact with anyone." The rules poured from her mouth as if that dreadful day in Vienna were only yesterday and she hurried her friends away.

Chapter 46

Thunder rolled overhead as Romy and Jian walked along the footpath, their linked arms holding Li up between them. Li was sobbing as she pleaded with Romy and Jian to let her go back.

"We can't leave them like that!" she cried, struggling to break free.

"No," said Romy. "You must hide. They may come and take you away too." *Like Daniel.* "I'll take you to Papa—he'll know what to do. It's just a few blocks from here. We have to keep moving."

They stumbled past the familiar shop windows on Avenue Joffre, filled with mink coats and stylish dresses. The scent of baking bread and coffee swirled about in the freezing air.

Romy's mind flooded with images of crimson blood, bamboo stakes, Dr. Ho's dark eyes. Her throat went dry as she remembered Benjamin sprawled on the cobblestones with a hole in his head.

After fifteen minutes of brisk walking past shops, markets, and alleys and through parks, she led her friends into the back garden of the Shanghai Jewish Hospital. "Where are we?" asked Li in a daze. "Is this someone's house?"

"It's the hospital," Romy told her.

She took them in the back service entrance, wincing as the metal hinges squeaked. They moved quickly down the corridor until she spotted a white door labeled STOREROOM.

"In here, quickly." Romy flicked on the light and rearranged boxes of bandages and syringes into a sturdy pile on which her friends could sit. Spying a pile of blankets on a shelf, she took two and wrapped one each around Li and Jian. Li's teeth were chattering and Jian put his arm around her.

"I'll go make some tea. Then I'll fetch Papa."

She looked at her friends' drawn cheeks and hunched shoulders. They were both pale and listless, in deep shock. She didn't want to leave them alone for a second, but she needed help to organize a better hiding place for them. For now they were out of harm's way. Were the murderers of Dr. and Wilma Ho looking for Jian and Li too? She had a flash of fear for Mutti—she spent hours at street performances and rehearsals with Wilma. Would her name be linked with the Hos? Who had betrayed them? Romy remembered the hard gray eyes of Chang Wu appraising Li and felt the hair on the back of her neck prick—what was the strange, confused look that had passed between them?

She shook her head. Right now, she needed to focus on Jian and Li.

"Stay here," she said. "I'll be right back and we can figure out what to do. I promise I'll look after you."

As she slipped out the door, she hoped it was a promise she could keep.

Chapter 47

Romy sat at the enormous dining-room table and tried to remember when it had been last used. Not since the gathering after Wilhelm's funeral, she thought. She didn't have much call for it; when Nina visited they ate their meals in the kitchen. Eugene Johns had called to help her update her will. All the paperwork was lined up ready for her signature.

Eugene took a sip of his black tea and bit into a scone.

"There's another matter I wanted to discuss, Romy. Rather delicate."

Romy sighed and folded her hands. She had a feeling she knew what he was about to say.

"Alexandra has been in touch. She's asking about paperwork for her mother, but I don't have any records—only the death certificate. The official adoption certificate was issued in Australia, based on the landing permit. Was there any other documentation I'm not aware of?"

281

Romy forced herself to sip her tea as she closed her eyes and remembered that night in Hong Kong so many years ago. Dr. Adler had placed a hand on her wrist. "Romy, I know you're trying to get sponsored to go to Australia. The thing is, you can only enter if you are the relative of someone already there. Or someone with a business to assist you. The Australian government doesn't want to accept Jewish refugees, let alone Chinese." He'd glanced around the ballroom, the floor now covered with more than a hundred mattresses. "But I have someone here who might be able to help with the paperwork."

The notary adoption certificate was arranged by the kind Dr. Adler and hastily issued and signed by a police officer in the middle of the night. She'd used that piece of paper to arrange a ticket and landing permit for Sophia Shu to travel with her to Australia. The doctor had managed to convince the kind, but overwhelmed, immigration officials and JDC representatives that baby Sophia was the orphan of a fellow doctor and should be permitted safe passage and a landing permit to Australia with her adoptive mother, Romy, and carer, Nina. The JDC also made contact with Wilhelm Cohen in Australia and arranged for him to be Romy and Nina's sponsor. This paperwork—and a hot, screaming baby—was just enough to eventually convince weary immigration officials to authorize Nina, Sophia, and Romy a berth to Melbourne.

Romy opened her eyes. "I lost all the documents years ago, Eugene," she told the lawyer. "And we were never able to get replacements after the war." She scratched the inside of her wrist and glanced at the wall, willing her face not to color.

"Well"—Mr. Johns reached for a second scone—"I get the feeling Alexandra might be doing a bit of poking around in China. Perhaps you should have a word?"

Romy sipped her peppermint tea, her grief adding bitterness to the brew. She'd made so many missteps trying to protect the people she loved. All these years she'd tried to shelter Alexandra from trauma. To make a fresh new life in this country. But what if the shadow of sadness that had always seemed to cling to her granddaughter was tied to Romy's past?

Chapter 48

SHANGHAI, JANUARY 17, 1943

"Papa!" Romy burst in the door of her papa's office and found him leaning back in his chair, looking pale and tired. Mutti was standing beside him.

Romy ran around behind the desk and threw her arms around her father, sobbing on his shoulder as though she were still a child. Stuttering through her tears, she described the brutal murder of Dr. and Mrs. Ho.

"Where are Li and Jian now?" asked Mutti urgently.

"In the storeroom. The one near the back that you use for supplies for Miss Schwar—"

"Quickly!" Mutti was already out the door.

They hurried down the corridor and pushed open the door to the storeroom. The light had been switched off.

"Li, Jian," Mutti whispered. "Don't be frightened—it's us: Marta and Oskar."

Feeling on the wall for the switch, Romy turned on the light.

Her friends were gone.

Chapter 49

It had been four weeks since Li and Jian had disappeared from Shanghai Jewish Hospital. No one knew if they had been trailed and caught by the Kempeitai that day, or if her friends had snuck away to safety. Mutti, Papa, and Romy had searched the whole hospital but there'd been no sign of them. Returning home to Grosvenor House, Romy had kept watch on their front door, hoping that perhaps Jian and Li would return to their apartment to salvage some of their things.

Instead, there had been a steady stream of laborers carrying boxes in and out of the apartment with a Japanese captain barking instructions. Romy assumed most of the Hos' belongings were in the boxes being hauled down the steps. Dr. Ho's shop and rooms at the markets remained closed.

Soon it would be the Bernfelds' turn to move. The *Shanghai Herald* lay open on the mahogany coffee table in the drawing room as a cruel reminder:

*Due to military necessity, places of residence and businesses of
stateless refugees in the Shanghai area shall hereafter be restricted
to the undermentioned area in the International Settlement.*

The Bernfelds were to move to a ghetto in Hongkew by May.
Papa had already started to look for an apartment—but how would
Jian and Li find them if they came back to Grosvenor House? Her
heart yearned for her missing friends.

The day before, a different Japanese captain had moved into the
Hos' apartment. He'd removed his hat and bowed politely to Romy,
introducing himself as Captain Azuma. When he smiled, his eyes
creased at the sides.

"You must be Romy Bernfeld, daughter of Dr. Oskar and Marta
Bernfeld. You've just turned seventeen, I believe. Granted admission
to Aurora University to study medicine. Congratulations."

Romy's heart started racing and her stomach churned. What
else was in his dossier on her?

He reached out to shake her hand, and Romy felt trapped. The
Japanese had killed Dr. Ho and Wilma. Her dearest friends were
missing and she was petrified of the soldiers. And yet the man
standing in front of her was speaking so kindly, and his eyes were
clear and true.

"And your mother, she likes to watch theater occasionally?
Huaju?"

Romy's blood ran cold.

"I think when she gets to Hongkew she will not have time for
this hobby. She and your father work at the hospital. They have
saved many Japanese people. We are grateful. It's best if they focus
on their job. Do you understand, Miss Romy Bernfeld?"

Romy nodded slowly.

Captain Azuma stood there, still holding out his hand to Romy like a peace offering. He sighed. "I have a daughter your age—Junko." He shook his head and his voice sounded strained as he said softly, almost under his breath, "I haven't seen her for three years. She too is supposed to be continuing her study, but—" He paused. "She needs her mother." He shrugged as his face colored. He shook his head again. "This war . . ."

She instinctively liked Captain Azuma and it felt like a betrayal. Romy's throat was dry and she struggled to swallow. She wanted to ask where to find her friends, but instead she turned and went back into her apartment, pushing the heavy door closed behind her.

Romy sat on the edge of her chair in the living room opposite Mutti and Papa, who held hands on the sofa. Delma and Miss Schwartz sat on the other sofa as Mei poured black tea and passed each of them a cup.

Romy closed her eyes and inhaled the steam as she took her first sip. When she opened them, she caught Mutti wincing as she took a resigned sip. A lemon tea cake with glossy circles of caramelized lemon studded across the top sat untouched on the silver platter. No one had much of an appetite.

Delma gave Miss Schwartz an encouraging nod and said, "We've found Li, Romy."

Mutti covered her mouth with her hands, as if unsure whether to be relieved or frightened.

"Where?" Romy almost shouted. "Jian too?"

Papa shuffled to the edge of his seat. "Is she safe?"

Miss Schwartz took a deep breath. "As you know, I was held at the Cathay with Laura Margolis and some other American aid workers for a few weeks after the ships were bombed on the Whangpoo. I managed to make some contacts—"

"What's—" Romy tried to interrupt.

"Li is at the Cathay."

"Thank God," Mutti murmured. "She's alive."

"Is Jian there too?" Romy asked.

Miss Schwartz shook her head and shifted in her seat uncomfortably. Romy had an uneasy feeling she knew what Miss Schwartz was going to say next.

"Li's working as a singer. Her stage name is Yu Baihe. She's a star already."

"How can that be safe?" said Papa, his brow furrowed.

Miss Schwartz cleared her throat. "She is living with a gentleman at the hotel."

"What?" said Mutti angrily. "Who? She's just a child!" She turned to Romy and reached for her hand.

Romy didn't bother to correct her mother. Li was seventeen, almost a woman. She thought of the gold curve-hugging cheongsam Wilma had ordered six months ago to be beaded and fitted for Li's birthday, which had fallen last week. How had Li celebrated? Romy shook her head—desperate not to know, yet missing her friend dearly. She thought she might throw up.

"She's living with Chang Wu," Romy guessed flatly as everyone turned to her, stunned. "He gave her his card at the Cathay after the bombing. He was friends with their brother, Zhou. Li trusted him." Romy's tone expressed her doubt. "He was there that day—when Dr. and Mrs. Ho were killed." Her throat tightened.

"That's right," said Miss Schwartz. "I managed to see Li alone for a few minutes in the corridor at the Cathay and she explained everything. It seems the dashing Mr. Wu is a man with many connections. Close to the Japanese. Americans. British. Links to Chinese gangsters and racketeers. You name it."

"He's a gangster?" Mutti looked horrified. "But why would Li have anything to do with him? The Hos were people of *qijie*."

"Exactly. That integrity had them killed. They made no secret of their opposition to the Japanese occupation—at Puyuan, in Wilma's plays—and Dr. Ho persisted in practicing traditional medicine and speaking out against the puppet government."

Delma leaned forward in her seat. "The Japanese Kempeitai are everywhere—people whisper at Café Louis and in the lines for the soup kitchen that even the street sweepers are working for the Japanese."

She looked from Marta to Oskar. "You've seen the squalid conditions in which many Chinese families live. It's been a long, bitter winter. They're starving. Babies are being left at orphanages and police stations in the dead of night. Officials can't keep up. Is it any wonder Chinese hoodlums take money from the Kempeitai via fixers like Wu in exchange for 'favors' if it means they can keep their babies? They're just trying to stay alive." Delma pressed her thin hands together.

"Is Chang Wu looking after Li, or blackmailing her? Is he—" Mutti's face looked ghostly pale.

"I'm not sure . . ." Miss Schwartz seemed to be choosing her words carefully. "Marta, people wear a lot of different hats in Shanghai. I knew *of* him because he runs a sideline in, er, narcotics, tobacco, certain medications, munitions, and forging passports." She flushed. "He's a bit of a Mr. Fix-It—the kind who is very useful in wartime."

"But if he's close to the Japanese, why would Li go to him? Why didn't she come to us?" Mutti's voice started to break and Papa reached for her hand.

"Jian," said Romy softly. "She did it for her brother." Romy thought of all the times Li had stood up to her father about Jian's photography. The way she teased him, yet clearly doted on him.

Miss Schwartz said simply, "Yes."

For a moment the only noise in the room was a ticking clock.

"I had less than a minute with her," Miss Schwartz continued. "But she wanted me to let you know she's safe. She's made some kind of deal with Wu, and Jian has joined the Shanghai Municipal Police. In exchange for Li, Wu has promised protection for Jian."

Romy shivered as she recalled Wu eyeing Li as if she were some kind of prize. He wouldn't have betrayed the Hos in order to force Li into a corner, would he?

Her thoughts spun wildly. Jian might be working for the puppet government, but she refused to believe he was a collaborator. And could he ever be safe working so closely with the Japanese, considering the fate of his parents? Wu must be a formidable figure indeed. There was something about his careless charm that made her uneasy—but if he really was able to keep her friends safe, alive . . .

Her thoughts were interrupted by Miss Schwartz. "This is very important, Romy: Li insists that you don't make contact with her or Jian. And I agree—it's far too dangerous."

Romy wept for her friends and Mutti came to kneel beside her, wrapping her in her arms like she had back in Vienna. So many people they loved had been ripped from their lives.

"Nina?" Romy said hopefully.

"I'm so sorry," said Delma, shaking her head. "But I'll keep looking."

"I'm afraid I have more bad news," Miss Schwartz broke in. "I wanted to tell you in person. Laura Margolis and I—in fact all Britons, Dutch, and Americans—are being interned as enemy aliens. They're taking us to the Chapei camp tomorrow."

Mutti blanched and Papa groaned. Romy pictured Daniel being loaded onto a truck.

"But the important thing," Miss Schwartz continued, "is that Laura has arranged a committee to continue with the JDC's work. The two boilers that came via Sassoon's company—thanks to your connections, Oskar—allow us to cook more food using far less fuel. The Kitchen Fund will still be feeding over four thousand refugees lunch and dinner. The Japanese helped us requisition the boilers—they were worried about hunger riots in the ghetto. The night classes and schools will stay open. There will be medical supplies. You'll both start work at Ward Road Hospital, yes?"

"Of course," answered Mutti for them both.

"Laura has done a remarkable job," Miss Schwartz said.

"As have you, Eva," said Mutti.

Miss Schwartz looked out the window as her neck flushed red around the collar of her khaki shirt. "Delma will help at the kitchen when she can."

"We all will," said Romy.

"This is the way it has to be until this damn war is over," said Miss Schwartz. She reached across the table and rested her hand on Delma's. It was a simple, consoling gesture, but the gentle stroke of her little finger and the softening of Delma's eyes spoke volumes.

Romy smiled to herself. *Of course.* How had she missed *this*? She picked up her teacup and drained it.

Papa reached for Mutti's hand, and she smiled.

Delma continued. "Since Eva is leaving, I won't be able to come over to Frenchtown again before you move to Hongkew. Ghoya won't give me a pass out of the ghetto."

"Who's Ghoya?" Romy asked.

Delma and Miss Schwartz exchanged glances.

"You'll find out," Miss Schwartz said darkly.

Chapter 50

Alexandra and Zhang walked across the Garden Bridge to Hongkou. The beams were low and rusty, and it felt strange to be walking into a suburb where both the roads and footpaths were so clogged with vehicles. It was a far cry from the grand, leafy boulevards of the former French Concession. Scooters swarmed around them on the footpaths, loaded with bags of take-out noodles and curries. Cars and taxis honked and smoke spewed from their exhausts as they inched across the bridge.

The sky shimmered a dirty pink, and the tops of the Pudong skyscrapers disappeared into the smog. Low supply ships snaked up the Huangpu, and the walkway in the Bund was crowded with tourists, their selfie sticks extended so they could get a shot of themselves in front of the dazzling pink Oriental Pearl Tower.

As they crossed into Hongkou, the footpaths narrowed and the sound of jackhammers punctuated each step. New town houses and office towers were going up on every block and bamboo scaffolding arched over the footpath. It smelled of dust and concrete, yet when Alexandra glanced down the *longtang* lanes, she saw the curves of old redbrick buildings, faded wooden doors leading to mysterious courtyards, an orange T-shirt and pants fluttering like lanterns on a washing line threaded between buildings.

The next alley had a lemon duvet strung across the road, with a dozen scooters and bicycles parked underneath. Clusters of thick black wires and cables snaked from telephone poles on the street to the outside of each building, sometimes secured with only a piece of string or a coat hanger. Electricity cables weaved across streets and buildings, looking like a giant industrial cobweb.

"What if there's rain, or a gust of wind? These cables would blow all over the road and footpaths," said Alexandra as she studied the knot of black wires directly above her head.

Zhang shrugged. "They'd just reattach them."

In broad daylight, Hongkou felt cobbled together. This was a ramshackle face of Old Shanghai she'd yet to experience. Crumbling town houses with magnificent carved art deco doorframes and smashed windows crouched between anonymous shiny silver office buildings.

"Ready to meet my Shanghai family? You've already met Peta and Petra—who couldn't stop squealing when I said you were coming for dinner. My aunt will love you. My uncle is at work, sorry." He tilted his head and pulled a face. "Maybe a bit too much family? Brace yourself."

Alexandra just smiled.

Zhang knocked on a door with peeling paint and two bamboo mailboxes on which Chinese characters were written neatly in black felt pen. It was a red door, mottled like all the others studding the laneway, but as they stood and waited for it to open, Alexandra did a double take.

Set within the door panels was a rectangular frame. And within that frame was a simple star pattern made from steel scraps—the Star of David. Alexandra ran her fingers over the metal star, the rough steel scratching her finger as the warm aroma of garlic, ginger, and chicken soup floated over the wall from a nearby courtyard. She thought of her *oma*, home alone at Puyuan, and felt weak with guilt and longing.

Zhang pushed the door open and they stepped into a large concrete courtyard bordered by three brick town houses.

Half a dozen men sat in pajamas at a card table, smoking and arguing over mah-jongg, while a pair of poodles tussled under the table. A violin started to play from the top floor of the building farther along the laneway. Peta and Petra were sitting on two faded camping chairs, a ginger cat weaving between their legs. The girls had their heads down, earbuds in, absorbed in their phones.

Beside them, a wiry middle-aged lady was bent over a concrete sink as deep as a horse trough. Underneath sat neat stacks of colored plastic bowls and aluminum pots. A large wooden chopping board leaned against the wall.

When Zhang called out, she turned and hurried over to greet them. Zhang spoke in Mandarin as his aunt smoothed his shirt, squeezed his biceps, and pinched his cheeks. She turned to Alexandra with a broad smile, took both her hands, and squeezed them.

"Welcome," she said with a nod.

Zhang said something out of the corner of his mouth in a sharp tone to his cousins, who immediately jumped out of their chairs, tugged the buds from their ears, and hid their phones.

They both hugged Alexandra.

"Alexandra!" squealed Peta. "It's so good to see you."

"Don't forget me," said Petra, elbowing her sister out of the way.

Zhang fetched a beer for Alexandra while she sat on a milk crate, trying to imagine what a future with Zhang might look like. What life in Shanghai could be. It was a strange sensation of warmth and possibility, like the first delicate shoots of spring bulbs pushing through the soil. She studied the line of his square jaw and listened to his easy laugh as a child scrambled onto his shoulders.

Was she mixing up her feelings for Zhang with her fascination with Shanghai? This city, this house, the ghosts of the Hongkew Ghetto were filling the gaps she'd felt her whole life.

As if catching Alexandra's thoughts, Zhang looked up and smiled.

She flushed, feeling silly. Zhang was going back to Hong Kong tomorrow and she was too realistic to think a long-distance relationship would work. She couldn't make her last one thrive when she and Hugo had lived in the same apartment. Besides, would it be fair to start something serious with Zhang when she still felt so broken?

For a moment, she pictured Hugo's drawn face as he thrashed around in bed, dreaming of his dead brother. They'd each recognized a void in the other and it was this emptiness that had underpinned their pairing. It was time to recognize that loneliness was no basis for a relationship. She and Hugo were never meant to be. They both deserved more.

Chapter 51

SHANGHAI, MAY 3, 1943

Tiny pops of lime-colored leaves were unfurling at the tips of the plane trees. It was a magical day with clear skies and a light wind. Daffodils spilled haphazardly from window boxes, and servants swept the footpaths. The hum of automobiles, trolleybuses, and double-decker buses had all but disappeared.

Romy couldn't help but remember the day they'd pulled up in front of Grosvenor House in a shiny new Daimler, thanks to Mr. Sassoon. Today they were leaving this glorious apartment in a rickshaw with just a few suitcases. They had sold most of their clothes and goods because they would have no space for them in the tiny room they had managed to secure in a lane house in Hongkew. A local Chinese family of twelve—grandparents, parents, and six children—had agreed to rent their top room to the Bernfelds. Who knew how much more expensive their rent would get? Not to mention food. They would be trapped in the ghetto. They would need all the resources they could squirrel away.

Romy stood on the front steps of Grosvenor House, hugging Mei and sobbing.

"Where will you go?" she asked.

Mei shrugged, resigned. "Family. You take care now, Miss Romy. You too, Dr. Bernfeld." She reached out and took both of Mutti's hands, saying nothing but staring into her eyes.

Mutti nodded stiffly, lifted a hand to wipe the tears from her eyes, and then clasped Mei in a tight hug. "Thank you," she whispered. "You and Dr. Ho."

Mei pulled back and batted Mutti's thanks away, the tips of her ears pink, as she said to Romy in a sharp voice, "You use my knife properly. No floppy wrists. Stand straight. Yes?"

Romy looked at her suitcase. Mei's steel cleaver with the wooden handle was tucked inside with a scrawled recipe in her diary for Mei's master stock.

"Thank you." It wasn't nearly enough. Romy wiped her eyes with her thumbs.

Four years ago, Romy never imagined she'd be able to use the sweet pink lotus blossoms to wrap parcels of chicken for steaming. Or step out to the markets for Mei and order shrimp and tiny yellow saltwater fish to fry up in vinegar sauce to dissolve their tiny bones. Mei had taught her so much about patience, but most important of all, Mei and Dr. Ho had given her back her mother.

Mei climbed into a rickshaw and spoke to the driver, who took off down the street. Moments later, it had vanished around the corner.

Romy leaned against her father for a moment. She was so very tired of watching people she cherished disappear. Her bones ached and she felt seventy, not seventeen.

Mutti's jewels were once again sewn into the collar of Romy's coat. It wasn't quite cool enough to be wearing it, but they couldn't risk the jewels being confiscated or stolen. Romy climbed into the front rickshaw with the luggage, while Mutti and Papa sat in the one behind.

"Miss Bernfeld." Captain Azuma appeared beside her in his crisp white uniform. "I was hoping to catch you before you left. I understand you have an interest in Chinese medicine as well as the modern kind?"

His eyes met hers and she could sense her parents watching anxiously from behind. In his hand was a cream envelope. The corners were bent and filthy, and the seal ripped open. Captain Azuma had obviously checked the contents.

He leaned forward and his voice dropped almost to a whisper. "This is from Jian Ho. He asked—since I told him I was moving into his apartment—whether I could give it to you. It's unusual, but as you are studying to be a doctor . . ."

Romy sat and stared at Captain Azuma, wondering if this was a trick.

"He patrols under my command, mostly in Hongkew." The envelope slid from Romy's fingers onto the floor of the rickshaw.

The captain glanced over his shoulder and leaned in a fraction closer. "It is a list of herbs he wrote out for you in my office—an herbal tonic for you to make for your mother."

Romy shook her head. "I don't know—"

"She was unwell for a time, I believe?" he interrupted.

Romy nearly jumped off the rickshaw to hug him. Instead, she nodded demurely, trying to mask her racing heart. Captain Azuma gently picked up the envelope and wiped its front with his white sleeve. He pressed it into Romy's hands as he said, "Of course, it would be better for you all if you have no further contact."

He held her gaze for a beat without blinking. Then he stepped away from the rickshaw after giving it a tap to get it moving, like one might for a horse and cart. His voice was wistful, as if he were imagining he was somewhere else—that life, perhaps, was different.

"I saw his sister, Yu Baihe, sing at the Cathay. Her voice—it's really something. She should be singing in the Shanghai Opera."

◇

Riding in a rickshaw down Avenue Joffre for the last time, she barely noticed the boutiques and coffee shops as she opened the envelope.

In Jian's confident script was a recipe for *Sang Ju Yin* made from mulberry leaf and chrysanthemum. Suddenly she was back with Dr. Ho, Li, and Jian in his spice room, opening the jars and drawers, the scent of anise and licorice root filling her nostrils. Jian would be sketching or annotating the root of a lotus or peony. Li would be humming to herself, ignoring them both but sitting as close as possible all the same. How she missed her friends.

Romy tucked the letter in her coat pocket as other rickshaws pulled in beside her. They too were loaded with baggage and nervous passengers, and they all moved slowly toward the ghetto.

◇

As the Bernfelds approached the Garden Bridge, more rickshaws and pedicabs poured into the street. Some were carrying small children in dark stockings and dresses sitting atop trunks, antique chairs, and tables. Others were filled with piles of melons and bags of dried brown beans and rice.

Japanese army trucks and cars moved through the crowds, honking and gesturing for everyone to get out of the way. Gas was in short supply, and all cars had been handed over to—*requisitioned by*—the Imperial Japanese Army. Rickshaws and pedicabs were the only alternatives.

Soon the Bernfelds reached the checkpoint, where Japanese soldiers stood guard with their bayonets, Chinese soldiers alongside them. Each rickshaw was searched for cash, shortwave radios, or contraband tobacco.

Romy had tucked her note from Jian into a medical textbook. She peered closely at the faces of the Chinese soldiers, looking for Jian, but the soldiers stared straight ahead and ignored her. Eventually the Bernfelds climbed from the rickshaws, reached the front of the queue, and handed over their papers. A tiny man—not a thumb more than five feet tall—walked over in a smart suit and polished boots and sat behind the table to inspect them. This must be Ghoya. Delma and Eva had warned them not to attract the "arrogant, pint-sized" Japanese administrator's attention, as his mood changed with the wind.

There was a pause as Ghoya examined the documents. "Doctor? You will work at the hospital?" It wasn't a question. He nodded at Mutti, his gaze taking in her expensive brown suit. "And Mrs. Bernfeld?"

"That's correct," said Papa, bowing his head.

Ghoya narrowed his eyes, as if trying to work out if Papa's gesture was respectful or mocking. Romy eyed the guard with the bayonet behind Ghoya with a shudder.

"You—Miss Romy Bernfeld." He waved a letter in the air. "This letter requests a leave pass for you to go to university in Frenchtown. What are you studying?"

"Medicine," said Romy, wondering if she should bow her head like her father. But she pictured Dr. Ho's face on the stake and couldn't. Instead she looked the administrator dead in the eye.

"Unusual, for a woman." He stamped her paper. "But, you will see, there are not enough beds, not enough doctors and nurses at the hospital, they tell me. Always asking for more." He sighed, as if it were an unreasonable request. "You must work there with your father and mother. Help clean."

"Yes, sir."

"And if you are a good worker, I *may* give you an exit pass. For study."

Romy wanted to stamp on his shiny black boots with her heels and crush his feet, but instead she kept her eyes steady. "Thank you, sir."

Chapter 52

Romy sat at the window as the light faded, sifting through the rice she'd poured into her tin pot. She picked two squirming weevils out of the rice with her thumb and forefinger and flicked them out the window with disgust. Papa joked they should eat the weevils, as they were probably quite nutritious, but surely it hadn't come to that in just four months!

She could hear the three Lam children downstairs wrestling like puppies in the communal courtyard while their doting grandparents darned socks to earn an extra few cents. Just below her window, Mrs. Lam was chopping an onion and chives, preparing a thin soup from leftover fish bones at the makeshift wooden table.

Romy surveyed the tiny room that had become home for herself, Mutti, and Papa these past months. Two narrow mattresses were pushed up against the walls, and in the center of the room were a rickety table and chairs. If not for personal touches like the faded silk tablecloth and a handful of red roses in a jar, she'd swear she had been admitted to prison. She'd never had such a small bedroom in her life, and now, at seventeen, she had to share it with her parents. There was a limited number of houses in the ghetto, an area of about one square mile, and most were already full to the brim with poor Chinese families—over a hundred thousand people. Delma said they expected more than twenty thousand Jews to be living here by the month's end. Sharing was the only option.

"Well, it's not the Cathay, but it will have to do," joked Papa on the day they moved in. "Which side do you want?" He walked over to his bags. "I brought a blanket to divide our sleeping quarters. Don't want you keeping us up all night with your study!"

Romy swallowed and glanced around the room. The uneven floorboards were worn, but spotless. The sheets were clean. And there were two little windows looking out over the alley.

"Remember, Romy," Mutti had said as they walked away from the Garden Bridge on that first day, Ghoya's beady eyes boring into their backs. "We're the lucky ones. You heard what Ghoya said: you can still study."

Romy finished sifting the rice and placed a brick on the lid so the rats couldn't get at it while she went to the hospital with her parents to continue her unofficial surgical training.

The aroma of the soup downstairs was making her mouth water, but she couldn't face another bowl of rice or moldy millet. She took a coin from her carefully hoarded pocket money—there had been none since they arrived in the ghetto—and decided to splurge on some warm rolls for her parents, who had been on their feet at the hospital all day.

She left the laneway and walked past a cluster of Chinese and European children playing hopscotch in the street before entering the new bakery across the road.

A bell jingled as Romy opened the door and was greeted with the heady scent of baking bread. A few golden *Kaisersemmel* bread rolls sat on the counter—just big enough to cover her palm—with the five cuts curled like a pinwheel at the top. Below, in a clean window display, was a row of biscuits and cakes. Her mouth watered as she tried to select a treat.

"Can I help you?" She jumped, surprised by the deep voice. A young man with curly sandy-colored hair and dancing brown eyes was leaning on the counter.

"I haven't met you before," he said. "What do you make of our little ghetto?"

Romy pursed her lips as she thought of the full pot with the red lid she'd had to carry down the stairs this morning and tip into the square night soil cart. Her lips started to quiver and the man's demeanor changed as his eyes softened.

He stepped out from behind the counter and Romy saw he was wearing a smart white shirt and beige pants held up with suspenders. His shoes, however, looked ancient.

"I'm sorry," he said. "I've been a complete dummkopf. Let me try again. I don't get many pretty girls wandering in here alone."

A shiver went down Romy's spine when he smiled at her a second time. Romy looked at her own shoes, noticed a tiny hole in her stockings, and blushed. She hoped he hadn't noticed.

"I'm Wilhelm." The young man wiped his floury hands on his apron and extended one for her to shake.

"Romy." She smiled.

"Will you take coffee?" He glanced at his watch. "I was just about to have my afternoon break. Please, join me."

He ushered her to a small table in the corner, then went back behind the counter, returning minutes later with a silver coffeepot and two gold-lipped coffee cups. He placed them on the table with a clatter and went to the counter again, this time returning with a cake loaded with caramelized apricot halves. The scent of butter and honey wafted around them.

Romy rested her hands on the handle of the silver coffeepot, feeling the grooves. "It's beautiful," she said, too shy to look up. The back of her neck was hot.

"It . . . it belonged to my parents." He sighed. On his face was a familiar haunted look. "I lost them in Vienna. My sister too."

"I'm sorry." She shook her head and resisted the urge to reach out and touch his arm as he poured the coffee. Instead she said, "I'm from Vienna . . . Wipplingerstrasse," she said sadly as she pictured Benjamin, twisted and bloody on the cobblestones.

"My family were from the southern end of Stadtpark," he said. "I used to play football there with my sister, Louisa. She was brutal." He winced and blinked away tears.

The words *were* and *was* hung heavy in the air, along with the smell of damp yeast. The ghetto was filled with fractured families, dragged across borders and splintered. Whittled away. What would be left when this war was over?

He picked up a piece of cake and took a bite, blushing as crumbs spilled onto his chest. He brushed them onto the floor with a cheeky shrug.

Romy took a bite. "It's delicious. Tastes just like . . . home."

"It's getting harder to find the ingredients. Too expensive. I like to make the cakes to give away with the bread. I take it to the *Heime* every Wednesday. There's a woman called Delma—"

"I know Delma," Romy said quickly.

He laughed. "Of course." He raised his eyebrows. "Everyone around here knows Delma. Did you hear the news about Eva and Laura being sent back to the States? I mean, it's great for the Americans, but poor Delma . . ."

Over soup last night Papa and Mutti had told Romy the news of Miss Schwartz's sudden departure from the camp. The American government had agreed to a prisoner exchange with Japan, and several hundred American prisoners were escorted from China immediately. Romy should have been happy for Miss Schwartz, but right now she just felt even more rattled.

"Did Delma get to say goodbye?" Romy's voice trembled.

Wilhelm shook his head sadly. He checked the door and leaned in close. "But I managed to get a message to Eva." He tilted his head toward the high-top loaves. "While Eva was in prison, I was able to access the kitchens. I befriended a guard who was willing to carry verbal messages between us for an extra couple of kaiser rolls; I have a pass that allows me to leave the ghetto because I deliver bread all over Shanghai. The messages were Delma's idea. Sometimes a door would be 'accidentally' left open and I could speak to Eva . . ."

This handsome man was also brave. "You'd be killed if they found out," Romy exclaimed. "Ghoya—"

Wilhelm held up his hand. As he turned his head, Romy noticed the tension creases at the corners of his eyes.

They sat in silence for a minute, sipping thick coffee.

"I suppose it's better to be home and free than in a Shanghai prison," Wilhelm commented. "I'm sure Laura Margolis will tell her JDC superiors about what's really happening over here."

Romy blinked away her tears. "I didn't get to say goodbye. Miss Schwartz—"

"I know. We all feel the same. They've done so much for all of us."

Romy eyed the glossy apricot on her cake and wondered where this lovely man had managed to get such an expensive ingredient. She poked it with her fork, but her appetite had deserted her.

"They'd want you to eat the cake. Eva and Delma, I mean." He pointed at the cake and gave a weary smile.

Romy felt her chest flutter.

"It's the best in the ghetto. Now, where were you off to when I sidetracked you?"

"Ward Road Hospital."

His eyes looked at her thin blue dress and he nodded. "You're a nurse?"

"I'm actually studying medicine. My parents work at the hospital. Papa is a doctor, Mutti's a nurse. I'm on my way to help with the night shift." She glanced over at the display of cakes. "I wanted to get them something nice."

Wilhelm jumped up out of his chair so abruptly it nearly toppled over. "I know *exactly* who you are. You're Romy Bernfeld. Delma has told me all about you and your medical pedigree. She's very impressed by you."

Romy stared at her shoes, waiting for the flush to pass.

Wilhelm stepped behind the counter and loaded the kaiser rolls and a couple of baguettes into a bag and held them out. As she took it, she felt the warmth from the bag spread up her arms.

"That's too much, I only have this." She took the coin from her pocket and handed it to him.

"Not at all. Share it with someone who needs it at the hospital." He reached out to shake her hand as she thanked him for his generosity.

"The pleasure was all mine, Miss Bernfeld. And, please, come back tomorrow for another cup of coffee."

As the bell jangled behind her, Romy had an idea. Perhaps Wilhelm's bread delivery was the way to get a message to Li. She'd been trying to work out how she could contact her dear friend. Romy had already lost Nina and she didn't plan on letting another friend slip away so easily.

Chapter 53

Nina and Romy sat on opposite sides of the wooden island slurping chicken soup. Nina was feeling much better and was visiting for a game of mah-jongg. They had a masters competition coming up and Nina was determined to win. Romy wasn't worried about winning, but she was glad of Nina's company. She gave her broth a vigorous stir and watched the parsley swirl in the whirlpool in her bowl.

The steady stream of guests who had flowed through the door since Wilhelm's death all seemed to come with their own batch of chicken soup. Today they were eating her own version, the chicken fried in sesame oil, the broth infused with garlic and ginger and topped with greens from the herb garden outside the kitchen door. Nina reached over and added a few more drops of the rice wine.

"That will create too much heat in your liver," observed Romy.

"Why not?" Nina chuckled. "Might as well get it from somewhere." She used her finger to slide some fresh noodles onto her soup spoon.

Romy reached for the soy sauce and added another splash to her soup.

"You can take the girl out of Shanghai . . ." Nina said. "Speaking of which, how's our girl?"

"Fine."

Nina arched an eyebrow. "You two are so alike."

"Nonsense. Eat your soup—but no more rice wine." Romy snatched it and put it back in the cupboard. Before she sat down, she retrieved a creased padded envelope from the back of the cupboard.

"I've been keeping this in the clinic." She returned to her place at the island and opened the envelope. From inside she retrieved an old diary and the red envelope usually tucked in the back of her compendium.

She picked up the diary and ran her hand over the soft leather before opening the cover. A coffee-stained letter slipped onto the island and Romy picked it up and handed it to Nina.

"I kept it. We looked for you everywhere."

Nina studied the letter for a moment, before handing it back to Romy.

"I know." She bowed her head. "I was so ashamed . . ."

Romy put the diary aside on the island and reached over to grasp her friend's hand. They sat quietly for a moment, enjoying the soft winter sunshine streaming through the bay window, the sun warming Romy's back.

Eventually, Romy said, "I'm going to send my diary to Alexandra. She's been asking so many questions about our time in Shanghai . . . Remember what you said while I was giving you acupuncture last week? You were right—for once."

Nina looked bemused.

"We're far too old to keep burying our secrets," said Romy. "I think it's time she knew the truth, don't you?"

Chapter 54

"*Gong xi fa cai*," sang one of the smaller Lam girls, dressed in a red cheongsam and pigtails, as she went around the table and greeted all the guests.

Romy sat between her parents sipping her cup of tea at the round table the Lams had installed in their single room downstairs for Chinese New Year. Tonight, the room was filled with two dozen friends and members of the Lams' extended family. Children dressed in immaculate silk cheongsams climbed on and off the laps of their grinning grandparents. The windows were dripping with condensation as they all sat squeezed together, shoulder to shoulder. Two red silk lanterns had been brought out of storage and tied to the ceiling with some old rope. The lanterns cast a pink hue onto the peeling cement walls and made the room feel warm, though it was well below freezing outside.

Mrs. Lam had spent all day mopping and scrubbing the floors and walls with Lysol to sweep out misfortune and bring good fortune in the door for the New Year celebrations. Her hands were blistered and swollen, but her broad smile was contagious. Everyone wished each other good fortune without a hint of irony. Romy and her parents were enthralled by this explosion of goodwill.

Mutti reached over, took her daughter's hand, and gave it a kiss. "I remember when you were that adorable, *Liebling*," she said, gesturing to the pigtailed girl. She leaned in close and gave Romy a pinch on the cheek. "You still are. I'm so very proud of you." Mutti's eyes were shining and Romy rested her head on her mother's narrow shoulder and wished she could leave it there all night.

A bamboo basket of chive dumplings sat steaming on the table in front of them; chopsticks poking out the sides made the basket look like a star. Dumplings represented currency, which was lucky for everyone in the room as there were far more dumplings than coins to go around.

On the other side of the table Wilhelm leaned back in his chair and chatted with Delma about how he could source more flour. Last week Ghoya and his soldiers had requisitioned his sacks and loaded them into a rickshaw without payment.

Wilhelm was on the edge of his seat, waving his hands in the air to a captive audience as he described the soldiers tossing the bags over their shoulders and running from the shop like little worker ants. He got down on his knees mimicking Ghoya. The room roared with laughter, and toothless Great-Grandfather Lam snorted and slapped his wiry thigh.

A head of carp was placed in front of Great-Grandfather, who lifted a cheek with his chopsticks and ate it slowly, before shouting, "*Yu*," the Chinese word for *fish*. It was a pun, of course, as *fish* sounded like the word *abundance*. Romy watched everyone take a sliver of the carp as it was passed around the circle and felt lucky to be at this table, in a warm dry room with friends. The lucky *Fu* character hung upside down on a piece of faded red cloth above the door.

The guilt she carried alongside her luck was exhausting. But Shanghai had taught her good fortune was a mix of persevering through the bad, but also celebrating the good when you found it. And she knew she had a lot to be thankful for . . .

The week before, Romy had caught a rickshaw home from the hospital right on the stroke of curfew. Passing by a tavern, she had seen a tall Japanese sailor with his arm around the neck of a peroxide blond. Romy had shivered in distaste. Clearly the soldier had found himself a woman for the night. The blond's face was in shadow, but as she moved into a pool of light Romy almost gasped in shock as she recognized Nina. Her cheap blue nylon dress did little to disguise how thin she was; she seemed to be little more than skin and bones. With her sallow cheeks, orange-painted lips, and glassy eyes, she looked nothing like the pretty girl with the intense eyes from the *Conte Verde*.

As if sensing Romy's gaze, Nina looked over and caught sight of her friend.

The two stared at each other without blinking before the Japanese soldier checked to see what had distracted his date.

"Hey," he slurred. "You break curfew." He reached for his gun.

"Leave her," said Nina quickly, waving Romy away. "We have more important things to do." And she had pulled a key from her pocket, opened her front door, and led the sailor into the shadows inside . . .

With a sigh, Romy recalled her other absent friends, and the Chinese New Year celebration she had attended across the stairwell in the Hos' elegant apartment two years earlier. Jian had played piano and Li had sung. Side tables had been piled high with tangerines for success and pomelos for wealth.

She thought of Li and Jian, and her bones ached with guilt and longing. In September, she'd asked Wilhelm to find Li—or Yu Baihe—at the Cathay when he made his regular delivery there. She had wanted to know if Li was safe, how Romy could help her. Could Romy perhaps visit Li in secret? Wilhelm had made contact with Li just once in the service corridor—when she was on her way to the backstage area to perform and he was making his way from the kitchen. Li's return message to Romy was clear: *Yu Baihe is not receiving visitors at this time.*

The *Fu* sign dangled overhead and she blushed, thinking of the red envelopes—remembering how dreadfully she'd misread Jian's intentions on that balcony. She was just a girl, really. She'd seen him a couple of times in Hongkew, marching with his fellow soldiers, but the blank expression on his face as he marched told her everything. He had turned his dark, intense eyes away from hers. But how could she forget him? How she wanted to speak with him—but the thought of putting either him or his sister in danger was out of the question. Li had made it clear there was to be no contact. She had to respect their wishes. She knew how dire the consequences could be if she did otherwise.

Romy turned her gaze to Wilhelm—he never failed to make her smile. Her heart lifted whenever she saw him, and she had started scheduling her work and study around their afternoon coffee as well as his bread deliveries to the hospital. He listened patiently when she talked about her work; she'd been taking on more duties at the hospital. He hadn't flinched when she described how she'd had to drain a foot abscess with no ether or tried to relieve the howling pressure in a child's infected ears with acupuncture.

Wilhelm was standing up now, pretending to stagger with a burlap bag on his back, and the room roared with laughter.

A mandolin started to play in the corner and some children began to clap. Wilhelm collapsed back into his chair and Delma patted his arm like an affectionate aunt. He brushed a curl from his face and winked at Romy across the table.

She felt her face burn and looked at a child who was drawing a monkey with his fingertip on the window. Would the Year of the Monkey bring the end of the war?

After the dinner and music had finished, the round tabletop was rolled back out into the alley and Mutti, Papa, and Delma helped the Lams wash up in the freezing outdoor kitchen. Romy put six sleepy children to bed on the small straw mattress in the corner and covered them with the threadbare blanket. As the littlest child sucked his thumb and snuggled close to his brother, Romy stroked his hair and sang him her favorite German lullaby.

When all the children were asleep, she stood up to leave and saw Wilhelm leaning on the doorframe, his curls lit by the moon. "My mother used to sing that to me in Vienna when I was about his size." Wilhelm pointed at the little boy snuggled between his siblings.

"You're a natural with the kids," he said. "Your singing, however . . ."

". . . is terrible," she finished. "I know! That was my brother's gift." She smiled at him. "Are you leaving?"

"Yes. Thanks for including me. It's nice not to be an orphan for an evening."

Romy wanted to reach out and brush a curl from his cheek. Her blood ran hot and cold and she looked back at the children to hide her blushing cheeks.

It had been four months since she'd met Wilhelm. Her heart raced every time she saw the line of his broad shoulders above the crowd in the Chusan Road markets, or his lopsided smile when she walked into the bakery. She tried to find excuses to be near him—to hear his laugh or watch the way he folded the yeast and cardamom into the dough, pounding the rising mixture with his hands. He was funny, kind, and hardworking, and his generosity knew no limits. Every week there was always a "leftover" batch of kaiser rolls for the patients in the children's ward at the hospital, or a cinnamon bun to share between the nurses. After one of his mysterious contacts had delivered eggs and oranges to the bakery last week the scent of warm orange and poppyseed cake had filled the hospital.

"I'll walk you to the end of the alley," said Romy boldly.

"It's freezing. Your boots . . ." The soles of Romy's black boots were peeling away on one side and her feet would be sodden in the filthy snow.

"I like the fresh air," said Romy as she ushered him outside, past the clanging pots, gushing water, and excited chatter.

The smell of chicken stock and star anise escorted the pair down the narrow alley. Romy wanted to reach for Wilhelm's hand—to hold his palm against her cheek—but instead she thrust her hands deep into the pockets of her coat and gazed at the moon. She matched his stride through the slush. As they reached the corner, Romy leaned in and brushed his shoulder, turning to look up.

She held her breath as Wilhelm reached down and grasped a strand of her hair, rubbing it between his thumb and forefinger as if it were silk. She shivered.

"I'll find a way to get some bread to the hospital this week," he said. "It's the least I can do." He paused. "I don't think you realize, Romy, how strong you are. How you bring comfort to people."

He tucked her hair behind her ear and stepped in close so she could feel his warm breath on her cheek.

"Good night," he whispered.

Romy closed her eyes and tilted her face toward him—ready for the touch of his lips. Her heart slowed a fraction as she thought of Jian and that other New Year; could something have developed between them, given more time, different circumstances? But these last cruel months had taught her that time was precious. Tonight, with the glacial wind whipping around her legs and stinging her cheeks, she wanted to feel alive. Cherished. To feel Wilhelm's strong body connect with hers.

She felt his lips brush her cheek.

Impatient, excited, and determined not to be rejected, she reached up and, tucking her hands into his curls, brought his face down to hers. His lips were soft and salty, his neck warm under the collar.

Their kisses grew deeper and she pushed him up against a chilly wall, prizing his coat open so she could run her hands up his chest and across his shoulders.

A chicken in a cage by her feet began to cluck and the smell of broiled fish bones rose from the bin beside her.

Romy didn't care, kissing harder and inhaling the honey soap on his clean shirt. She moved her hips against his and felt Wilhelm's breath catch.

"Romy," he groaned. "We can't. Not here. You deserve so much more than this . . ." He looked despondently at the night soil bins and overflowing garbage.

The chatter from the alley had dried up as everyone finished their washing and rushed inside out of the bitter wind.

The heavy steps of patrolling Japanese soldiers nearby could be heard and two men slunk into the alley like stray cats, tipped over a bin, and stuffed stray noodles and fish bones into their mouths with trembling hands.

"Shhh." Wilhelm's heart was pounding and she rested her head against his chest. She wanted to peel these thin clothes from his sweaty skin. "We'll find a way . . ."

Chapter 55

SHANGHAI, AUGUST 8, 2016

The serene courtyard with its swaying bamboo beckoned as soon as Alexandra walked in the door to her apartment. Work had been all-consuming since her weekend away with Zhang. There were some problems with the contracts for the new buys she was proposing. She'd arranged a sweet joint venture deal out of the Hong Kong office—her company would be making a killing so everyone was happy. That was, until she'd asked her top analyst to check the environmental records for the mine proposals in central Africa and South America. She wanted to know how they rehabilitated the sites. She also had some misgivings about the relocation plans for a couple of local villages. Despite consultation at the community level, Alexandra had questioned her company's support for these developments in the team meeting this afternoon. Her boss, Bert, had gone ballistic, accusing her of stalling the deal.

"Alexandra, you've been doing these deals for years. It's what you *specialize* in, kiddo. Do I need to remind you of the fat bonus you took home last year? What's got into you? Don't get me wrong, it makes us look good if we can offer clean and green. But you know as well as I do that in the end it all comes down to the bottom line."

She'd walked out of Bert's office with balled fists. She wanted to call Zhang and . . . what? Cry? She wasn't sure *exactly*, but she did know she wanted to reach out and tell him how frustrated she was. She'd never even thought to unload with Hugo because coping with pressure and being busy had become almost a competitive sport between them. But now she'd started looking beyond the numbers and risk projections and wondering about the people, about their homes. When she closed her eyes at night, the bronze faces from the Jewish Refugees Museum stepped out of their sculpture and swirled through her dreams.

Without even pausing to change out of her work clothes, Alexandra took her phone from her bag and walked outside to Skype with Zhang. When his face appeared, she wanted to reach through the screen and touch him.

"Garden looking good?" he asked.

"Great!" She looked at the moss and flushed. She tilted the phone slightly upward so he couldn't see her face.

"Hey, where'd you go?" He laughed. "So listen, Alexandra, I'm so sorry, but—"

Alexandra held her breath, not wanting to hear it.

"—I'm not going to be able to come visit this weekend. I've got to speak at a landscape architecture conference. The keynote speaker from New York has had to cancel—his daughter's got appendicitis—so I'm it!"

She studied the shadows of the rock and tried to swallow her disappointment. They'd had a fling, nothing more. She'd been silly to forecast a solid future with Zhang when the location was a moving variable.

"That's *fine*," she said brightly. "I get it." And she did. This was the end of the line. Their relationship had combusted far sooner than she expected. There was no point in telling him she was planning an urgent trip to Hong Kong for work. She needed to finalize the contracts. Bert insisted.

Her doorbell chimed. "Oh, I've got to go. Dinner's here. Talk soon?"

"Alexandra—" Zhang frowned.

She ended the call.

◇

Alexandra sat outside on a wicker chair, poured herself a full glass of Californian chardonnay, and picked up her plate of *mapo doufu. Mapo* was her favorite detox dish—as comforting as hot chocolate. As a child, Alexandra would sit at the island going over her homework with Opa, while Oma diced the ginger and garlic and tossed them into a sizzling wok before she added a handful of pork mince, two dollops of Sichuan chili bean paste, and a splash of rice wine. Only at the end—when the pork was brown and the kitchen filled with sharp spices—would she add silky squares of tofu and swish it around quickly so it didn't get runny.

Alexandra devoured her dinner.

When she was done, she put her plate in the dishwasher and sat down to go through the parcel from her grandmother. This package was so special Alexandra had put it aside until she could focus on it without her phone constantly beeping about work. Alexandra ran her hand over the leather diary that had softened with age. She opened it and studied the girlish hand of her *oma.* The paper fluttered in her trembling fingers as she read the spidery letters.

Dearest Alexandra,
This is the diary my papa bought me.

I'm so sorry I haven't shared more about our time in Shanghai. I thought it was for the best. It's weighed on me heavily over the years. We were all so changed by the war. I know what it feels like to be an only child—and to lose people you love.

I wanted you to discover Shanghai and make your own future, free from our expectations and the traumas of the past.

I'm sure that's not really a good enough reason to have kept things from you. You'll have many questions and much to think about. I promise I'll answer all your questions when we see each other next.

I understand, now, our past and your future belong together like a master stock that changes over the years. Nina agrees that this diary belongs to you now. She and I both send our blessings and we look forward to seeing you for a visit after our hiking trip to the High Country.

With love,
Oma xxx

When she opened the back cover of the diary a red envelope, a coaster from the Peninsula Hotel in Hong Kong, and a letter from Nina to Romy slid out. She read Nina's goodbye letter to Romy and left the other scraps on her lap—poor Nina! It must have been so sad when her uncle died. But Alexandra wondered why Nina had been so determined that Romy not try to contact her when she started her new job. There were also two faded certificates: a landing permit for Australia and a document headed *Notice of Adoption*. The latter was marked with a stamp: HONG KONG.

She felt a rising sense of excitement. Could it be that the reason Alexandra hadn't been able to find any documents in China was because Romy had sailed to Australia from Hong Kong—maybe that's where the evidence was? Perhaps she could engage a Hong Kong–based adoption consultant to help her while she was there . . .

Finally, she flicked through her grandmother's diary. She read about Romy visiting Dr. Ho's treatment rooms, Chinese New Year gatherings, and prayers for Daniel. There was an American friend called Laura and another—Eva Schwartz—who had been deported back to America. Oma *had* been friends with both Li Ho and her brother Jian, but there was no mention of either after 1943. The newspaper article she had found said Li Ho disappeared in 1945. They must have lost contact when Oma was forced to move to the ghetto.

Alexandra was turning the pages, looking for more mentions of the Hos, when toward the back Nina's name caught her eye.

1 February 1944

Nina was waiting for me on the steps outside the hospital today when I finished work. I was elated to see her, but one look at her pale face, red-rimmed eyes, and the bruise on her cheek made me fearful. She wanted to thank me for the parcel of apple cake and kaiser rolls she'd received every day since the night I spotted her in the street, leading that Japanese sailor inside her front door.

Nina's wrists were like twigs. She hung her head and I could see her hair was charcoal at the roots though she had dyed it the color of corn. She begged me to forgive her, but I held her tight and told her there was nothing to forgive. I want Nina to give away her work and come and share our room. But Nina said she couldn't face Mutti and Papa. I'm sure they wouldn't have judged her, though; we see desperate women at the hospital every day, begging the gynecologists for vodka and quinine to hold off pregnancies.

This past winter has been bitter, with filthy snow choking the streets for weeks at a time. I worry Nina will fall ill, so I sent her away from the hospital with a small jar of honey that Delma had given me from Café Louis, two thumbs of fresh ginger, and a whole garlic bulb so she can boil up some ginger tea morning and night. Together with a small bowl of congee, this should help keep her lungs and spleen strong and the coughs away. I told her I add half a fresh red chili to mine along with the seeds, and she said, "What the hell?" then gave me a tight hug, spun on her stilettos, and walked away.

I agonize over the differences in circumstances between Nina and me, and it is only a thin veneer of luck that separates us. I don't deserve my life, my study, work, and family any more than Nina deserves her misfortune. She's grown so fierce, stubborn, and independent. She's one of the strongest people I know.

Alexandra's stomach churned for Nina. What had she endured? The diary explained Nina's tough exterior and Alexandra felt a strange mix of sadness and devotion. It didn't seem possible that she could love her grandparents and Nina more, but after reading this diary she did.

She took a sip of her wine and turned the page.

10 February 1944
My thoughts are mostly full of Wilhelm this past week. I close my eyes and smell the traces of spices and warm bread on his shirt. I long to hold him. I can hardly concentrate for all the dreaming—Papa asked if I was poorly!

Yesterday Wilhelm pressed me tight with my skirt pulled up against the counter in his mixing room, forearms flexed—but then we heard the jangle of the bell . . .

I need to find a way for Wilhelm and me to be together. Sometimes he seems hesitant—as if he doesn't want to hurt me. He tries to hide his gaunt face and haunted eyes with bright smiles, but I can sense his loneliness.

I know I sound like a besotted schoolgirl, but I think of his hands slowly working the dough, his warm breath on my cheek, whenever I'm alone. My skin twitches and burns when I try to sleep because I imagine him lying beside me, head on the pillow next to mine, brushing the curls from my face. His kind brown eyes staring into mine.

We've come close now so I'll have to think about precautions. Wilhelm is more conservative . . . respectful. We will be together long after we leave this ghetto, so there is no point waiting. I'm so tired of being cold, hungry, and poor. Of the weeks of unrelenting study and work. My head is so full of thoughts of disease and loss that the only time I forget is when I press my head to Wilhelm's chest and listen to the steady beat of his heart. We give each other strength and comfort. It feels selfish to ask for more.

Of one thing I am certain: it is better to face the future together than alone.

Alexandra dropped the diary onto her lap, embarrassed. It felt like peeking into her grandparents' bedroom. She traced her fingers over her grandmother's words. *We give each other strength and comfort.* What was it Opa had said to Alexandra as he was dying?

Your grandmother . . . was the strongest of us all. The three of us . . .

And it was true enough. It seemed Romy had shown Wilhelm not just how to survive the turmoil of the ghetto, but also how to live. She supported him right to the end. Perhaps Romy could never bear children of her own—was that why she'd apologized to her dying husband? Had she carried that guilt and grief all these years?

It certainly went some way to explaining why they might adopt a child from China. Or Hong Kong.

Romy had provided the scaffolding not just for Wilhelm, but also for Alexandra.

Alexandra flicked through the pages impatiently until she reached the hastily scratched recipe Oma had marked with a Post-it. It was stained gray from soy sauce, and if Alexandra were to lick the page she was sure it would still taste salty.

Mei's master stock
2 Leipzig jars of water
heavy pour soy sauce
heavy pour shao xing wine
handful yellow rock sugar, crushed
⅓ hand cup ginger, sliced
4 garlic cloves, crushed
green (spring) onions, washed and trimmed
spoon sesame oil
4 star anise
2 cassia bark
1 cinnamon stick
3 pieces dried mandarin rind or orange rind
handful of mixed mushrooms (dried better)
Sichuan pepper

This stock carried the scent of her childhood. At least once a week Oma would take her master stock out of the freezer and defrost it, before poaching chicken breasts, slicing them, and serving them over rice, or even putting a whole chicken in the broth to simmer with fresh greens tossed in before serving.

She smiled and shook her head—trust Romy to end her letter with food. It was as if her grandmother wanted to fortify her from afar as Alexandra read the diary.

Suddenly Alexandra didn't want to be alone.

She gulped down the rest of her chardonnay and called Zhang again.

"Alexandra!" His face beamed on the screen.

"If it's okay with you, I'm coming to Hong Kong on Thursday night for work! We can still spend the weekend together."

"Great! I was going to suggest that you fly here on Friday after work to join me when you hung up. Clearly you were just hungry! Anyway, the organizers had booked a suite at the Peninsula for this la-di-da speaker and they're offering it to me instead. Peta and Petra are staying in my apartment with my aunt to look at universities, so I was thinking we might as well take up the offer. What do you say?"

Alexandra eyed the faded coaster in her lap. "The Peninsula would be perfect."

Chapter 56

For four months Romy had not seen Wilhelm for more than snatched conversations. She'd fallen ill with pneumonia at the end of April just as the warmer spring winds started to blow through the lane houses. The summer typhoon season had been dreadful. As the winds and rains lashed the ghetto for days at a time, the drains became blocked and brown water spread ankle-deep on most streets. She was moved to the isolation hospital in the north of the ghetto and, after eight weeks of coughing and spluttering, Papa had declared her fit to come home.

But Mutti was adamant that Romy not be exposed to the dysentery, cholera, dengue fever, and typhoid swirling through the flooded city. She needed to rest and rebuild her strength. Romy had spent the long weeks in a strange solitary confinement on her lumpy mattress, reading textbooks, drinking tea, and eating congee with a slice of liver or tongue when Mutti could get it. Sometimes she read over Jian's notes, or placed fingertips on her arms and on her ankles, trying to remember acupuncture points. Nina didn't visit. Delma and Wilhelm were frantically busy trying to cope with all the thousands of extra mouths that needed feeding at the soup kitchens. Their visits were few and brief.

Today she was well enough to go back to work, so she decided to surprise Wilhelm at the bakery on the way to Ward Road Hospital. As she stepped inside, she noticed he was still wearing his armband stamped with FOREIGN PAO CHIA VIGILANCE CORPS. Like all Jewish men under forty-five, he was forced to patrol the boundaries of the ghetto, making sure that no one broke curfew, or came and went without a pass. Occasionally they were forced to punish their own, under the watchful eyes of the Japanese soldiers.

"Romy!" Wilhelm beamed. "You're out and about."

Romy smiled back, feeling a little shy.

"It's great to see you feeling better," he said as his ears turned pink.

"I'm on my way to work but I couldn't resist dropping by and . . ." Her voice faded. And what? "You were out last night?" Romy pointed awkwardly at his armband.

Wilhelm swallowed. "Yes." Swiftly changing the subject, he presented her with a warm freshly baked dense brown loaf. "What do you think of my *Brotgewürz*?" he asked.

This was more like Wilhelm. She'd smelled the fennel from the footpath. "What spices have you used?" she asked as she tore off a hunk and inhaled the spicy steam.

"Caraway, fennel, anise, and coriander seed."

Romy tore off a second piece before suggesting, "Why don't you try Chinese allspice, celery seed, and cardamom."

"Great idea." He gave her a crooked smile. "What would I do without you?"

They fell back into their old pattern of everyday banter about Wilhelm's plans for some new mixing equipment and his concern over whether Romy was strong enough to work full days at the hospital. She asked if he was still delivering bread to the Cathay. He said he was; the hotel was his biggest customer and Ghoya had approved another three-month pass for deliveries. "Ghoya can't resist my kaiser and *Brotgewürz* rolls, or my baguettes."

"Have you seen Li?" she asked hopefully.

"Her message is always the same," he answered.

Romy gave a small nod. She understood why her friend had cut her off, but it still hurt.

He gave a faraway look. "She's really something. I'm not much of one for music, but I could sit and listen to her all night."

"You've heard her perform?"

"The hotel always orders a second fresh delivery for the Japanese officers' late dinners on Thursdays, Fridays, and Saturdays. It was one of the kitchen hands who helped me find Li the first time so I could pass on your message. Sometimes, if I have a few minutes to spare before I have to be back on patrol, I'll duck through the doorway and listen. It's dark, so no one notices."

"I'd love to hear Li sing," said Romy, feeling wistful and a little jealous.

Wilhelm shifted uncomfortably and closed his eyes. She eyed his rumpled shirt and tousled hair. He was tired.

Checking that no one was walking past outside, Romy reached for his hand with both of hers and took a step closer. She was about to lift his hand to her neck, when she felt his arm stiffen. Wilhelm opened his eyes and took a step back.

"I'm sorry, Romy, it was a long patrol."

He paused, and they both stood facing each other as the bread mixer whirred in the background. A curl fell across his face and Romy resisted the temptation to push it aside.

He looked uncomfortable. "Look, Romy, there's something I need to—"

The shop bell jangled and two women walked in carrying a large basket between them.

"*Guten Morgen*," said the women, and Wilhelm smiled.

"I'd better go to work," said Romy as she brushed past the women and out the door without giving Wilhelm a chance to say goodbye.

Her months of illness had taken their toll on everyone.

Whatever they'd had between them before her illness and solitary recuperation seemed to have faded away.

With his kindness, his easygoing smile, Wilhelm had been a bright spot in this colorless world. They'd talked for hours, exchanging recipes, reminiscing about the places in Vienna they missed most. Sometimes they'd swapped stories of Louisa, Benjamin, and Daniel. Nights at the opera. The roar of the Danube in spring.

How she'd missed him these past four months.

Yearning and insecurity trickled through her body—what if Wilhelm had found someone less drab and studious? That's what he wanted to tell her, she was sure of it. Not in those words, of course. Instead, Wilhelm would look a little bewildered and upset as he broke the news. He still cared for her—he couldn't have been faking how pleased he was to see her when she'd walked into the bakery. But Romy could smell traces of guilt and uncertainty as clearly as the roasted fennel seed.

She didn't want to know. Not yet. Because she still had a small kernel of hope that they could find their way back to each other. She just needed to be patient.

Chapter 57

The weather had started to turn as autumn dawned, and by October it was growing cool in the evenings. Today, Romy had just emerged from the hospital after her double shift to find Wilhelm waiting at the bottom of the steps, his hands in the pockets of his threadbare blue coat.

He'd been avoiding her since she'd recovered in August—dashing out for deliveries no sooner than she arrived at the bakery, so she'd stopped visiting. Try as she might to be patient, Wilhelm's rejection stung.

She smiled and said hello as she tried to scoot down the steps without stopping. He reached gently for her elbow, but Romy had snatched it away.

"Please, Romy," Wilhelm had begged. "I need to talk to you alone. I want to explain—"

But Romy shrugged him off politely. "Wilhelm, it's all right. I understand." She was pleased to hear that her voice sounded far more reasonable than she felt.

She'd spent the afternoon on her knees sterilizing floors, cleaning up vomit and diarrhea, before scrubbing in and assisting a midwife with a difficult breech birth. There'd been a horrific amount of tearing that needed to be stitched without morphine or ether, and Romy was instructed to hold the woman's legs apart, knees up.

She felt too tired—too empty—to hear the truth. That it was over. That Wilhelm had perhaps found comfort elsewhere. And who could blame him, given her absence and then her increased workload?

"I can't stop, I'm afraid. I'm off to visit Nina, before she starts . . . work." Romy had taken to stopping in on her way home from the hospital for a cup of black tea. This was the comfort she craved now. She wanted to rest her head on Nina's lap as they perched on the edge of her lumpy mattress and listen to her tales of dancing in the glamorous nightclubs while Nina stroked her hair.

With a last wave to Wilhelm, she ran down the steps into the evening.

She no longer visited the bakery now. Besides, Romy had exams coming up, and Mutti and Papa were stretched thin at the hospital. Delma was feeding nearly ten thousand refugees each day at the kitchen and always needed an extra pair of hands. Romy decided to concentrate on where she could do some good. But a piece of her still longed for Wilhelm . . .

◇

It was Saturday evening, and Mutti and Papa were on the extended overnight shift. The sun had come out last week, and the streets were dry and filled with soccer matches, fruit peddlers, pedicabs, and rickshaws. Romy started to read *Les Misérables* for the third time, but was tempted to throw the book out the window. She was so bored and lonely. She wanted to do something. Anything.

She missed music, laughter, and joy. She missed Li. Perhaps she could find a way to go to the Cathay just to see for herself that her friend was well. She wasn't putting Li in any danger—her dear friend wouldn't even know Romy was in the audience. Besides, Romy had never stood out in crowds and she knew the hotel from her childhood. There was no way anyone in that heaving, dark, and smoky jazz bar could connect the two of them. She felt a frisson of excitement. Also, fear. She was breaking Papa's rules—or at least she would be if he'd ever considered she might want to visit a nightclub instead of studying. Or working. She could easily use her medical pass to get through the ghetto checkpoint to the Bund.

Jittery with nerves, Romy opened the wardrobe door. The only outfit not moth-bitten and ragged was a brown two-piece suit of Mutti's. She put it on and pinned it tight at the waist. Then she pulled her hair up in a bun and turned this way and that in front of the broken shard of mirror. She looked pale, hollow—and about fifty years old. She placed her identity card, hospital card, and refugee pass, showing she was a medical student in Frenchtown, into her jacket pocket. On impulse, she grabbed her infectious diseases textbook and tucked it into her satchel—just in case she was stopped and questioned—and took one last look at herself.

It would have to do.

Chapter 58

Romy walked nervously through the Cathay Hotel's golden atrium. Japanese soldiers were mingling with German, French, and Chinese couples, the men in white dinner jackets and the women with pastel feather boas threaded over their arms and diamond necklaces at their throats. These couples chatted with elegant Chinese ladies buttoned into embroidered cheongsams and low-backed lamé ball gowns. The women preened and smoothed their dresses as Romy overheard a smiling waiter say in English, "Ladies and gentlemen, if you'll follow me, the show is about to start. I'll escort you to your tables."

Taking care not to meet anyone's eye, Romy followed the scent of smoke and whisky through the heavy wooden door into the jazz bar. The room was all marble columns, gilded ceilings, and dark wood-paneled walls. Her eyes watered from the sting of smoke and cloying perfumes.

Romy sat at the dark bar, sipping the Coca-Cola slipped to her by the friendly barman. The sugar made her a little giddy and her heart raced in anticipation of seeing Li.

A group of Japanese soldiers was laughing and emptying a bottle of whisky at a far table. One man caught her eye and beckoned her over with his hand. Romy looked away, cheeks burning. She was a drab, bony woman with no money sitting at a bar . . . alone.

Romy sipped her cola and thought of Nina. Was this how she'd started? Every week Romy saw women come into the hospital with sick and lice-infested children dressed in clothes made from jute flour bags or old sheets. Men who'd had solid careers in Europe as lawyers, teachers, and accountants sat at the bottom of the hospital steps rattling tin cups in the hope of catching a coin from the staff. There was a rumor a couple of the doctors' wives worked the day shift at the brothel while their children were at school. It was a rare soul in the ghetto who was not hungry.

Yesterday, when she'd seen Nina, she was preparing for a night out with one of her regulars. Her friend had lightened her hair and lined her eyes with kohl to look like Greta Garbo; she blew Romy a kiss as she painted her lips.

"Don't look so sad, Romy," she said, swaying her hips to bring a smile to Romy's face as she slipped a pink silk cheongsam over her head and buttoned it up. Nina's hips were rounded now and her breasts filled the dress nicely. She was taking care of herself and was healthier and more robust than most women in the ghetto. Nina had drifted from scrubbing floors in her boardinghouse—and almost starving to death—to relationships of convenience with a few lonely Japanese soldiers in exchange for bread, cheese, fresh fruit, a new coat, and enough money to share around among the younger girls from the *Heime* so they didn't have to do the same. Romy and her parents both wished Nina would come and live with them so they could share what little they had with her, but Nina insisted on her independence. Nina had become the queen of chameleons. Of survivors.

Romy closed her eyes, sipped her drink, and allowed the fizz to fill her stomach. She let the music wash over her and ignored the Japanese soldiers and businessmen cutting into slabs of sizzling steaks at the table beside her as the lights dimmed and Yu Baihe was introduced to the stage.

The band started to play and Li stepped into the spotlight. She wore a long midnight-blue lamé gown that was scooped low at the back. The crowd cheered and whistled as a trumpet started to blast. Li put one hand demurely on the microphone and started to sing "I've Got You Under My Skin" in a low, husky voice.

The room fell silent. A service door built into the wood paneling to one side of the stage opened a little. From her position at the bar in the far corner of the room, Romy could see past the shadows to the profile of a man holding a jute bag filled with baguettes; an open basket of kaiser rolls sat at his feet. Wilhelm. He leaned on the doorframe, smiling to himself.

Romy's heart skipped a beat.

She tried to catch his eye, but he was too far away.

Li wiggled her hips and winked at the front table of Japanese soldiers before her face turned serious and she lifted her jaw to focus on someone else in the room. Li started to sing the finale with pure raw emotion; her throat sounded like it was burning.

Romy's eyes started to water as she felt Li's yearning with each word of "I've Got You Under My Skin" above the strings.

Romy looked from Wilhelm to the stage and back again. Li was singing to Wilhelm, her red lips parted, eyes shining with adoration. One of the Japanese soldiers narrowed his eyes, beckoned a waiter over, and whispered something in his ear. Then the soldier stuffed a piece of paper in the waiter's pocket and shooed him from the table as his eyes flicked briefly between Li and the tall deliveryman standing just inside the half-open service door.

◇

Romy had been so shocked by the look that passed between Wilhelm and Li she'd put her hands over her face and tried to collect herself. Whatever was going on with Wilhelm, Romy felt ready to talk about it without dissolving into tears and making a fool of herself. Perhaps she'd gotten it all wrong; perhaps he really was just exhausted from working so hard, along with his Pao Chia patrols. He never stopped—and when he did, he was all alone. Should she leave her quiet spot at the bar and try to find him?

But when she looked up, Wilhelm was gone. She walked casually from the bar, through the atrium to the service passage she used to roam as a child. She tiptoed along the threadbare corridor into the hotel's main kitchen, but there was no sign of him.

Romy returned to the atrium and stood there, motionless, as Japanese soldiers and wealthy couples streamed around her, dripping with furs and jewelry. The centerpiece flowers had gone, she saw, but people were still coming to the Cathay for a little magic. And Li—Yu Baihe—was part of that. It was her job to enthrall the crowds and make them fall in love with her. Wilhelm was no exception—just another man in a besotted audience. Li had always been a performer. It was how she'd survived. Romy felt churlish for imagining anything else.

Still, her stomach curdled with a strange mix of longing and jealousy. Li had always had the knack of standing out in the crowd. But Wilhelm hadn't even noticed Romy at the bar. When she had spotted Wilhelm standing in the doorway Romy had let herself imagine that his eyes would find hers across the hazy room and widen with delight. She picked at a stray thread on her brown suit. She looked so drab she was invisible.

Romy brushed aside her disappointment about Wilhelm and remembered the reason she'd come to the Cathay tonight: Li.

Now that she'd seen her, it wasn't enough to leave without speaking with her. Hugging her. She wanted to be sure Chang Wu was taking care of her.

She looked up at the glass pieces of the atrium ceiling and tried to think of a way to speak with Li—without placing her in danger. An elegant Chinese couple came out of the jazz bar and, as the woman pulled on her fur coat beside Romy, she said, "Yu Baihe is the best. I'm too tired to stay for the next girl."

Where would she find Li now that she'd left the stage?

The atrium was filling up, and Romy found herself knocked into a corner as people swarmed nonstop in and out of the jazz bar and restaurants. Greetings and farewells in many dialects filled the lobby. Romy looked up to see old Mr. Khaira standing by the entrance to the hallway that led to the secret dressing room—as though he'd been stationed there. His sideburns had turned silver and his face looked somber. Romy swallowed her joy at seeing his familiar face, remembering she had to be anonymous.

Mr. Khaira's eyes widened with recognition and he tried to suppress a smile before his brow became furrowed. As she pointed past the doorway Romy leaned in to whisper, "Li?"

His eyes scanned the crowd and his legs twitched, before he nodded and ushered Romy quickly into the hidden passage and closed the door behind her, leaving her to climb the dim stairs alone.

As she took the stairs two at a time, her stomach settled. She was just nervous and excited, that was all. She and Li hadn't seen each other in a long time.

Romy stood outside the door to the dressing room, running her fingers over the letters she'd etched all those years ago: *RB 1939*.

How naive she'd been, thinking this strange city, Shanghai, was a safe haven for her family, that it would last forever . . .

From the other side of the door came a wild cry.

Someone was hurting Li!

Romy pressed open the door a fraction. Li was sitting on the old table, the blue lamé dress pulled from her shoulders and scrunched around her waist, a pearl necklace draped over one bare breast and her jade lily pendant at her throat.

Li's head was thrown back in ecstasy, her lips open and wet. Her long slim legs were wrapped around the waist of a man who was standing with his back to Romy, thrusting and groaning. His sandy curls fell across his collar, his shirt stretched across his muscular shoulders.

Romy's breath caught as the couple groaned in unison.

She was unable to move her feet.

The same strong hand that had wiped away Romy's tears many months ago—smelling of yeast and covered with flour—was resting at the nape of Li's neck. The full lips she imagined might kiss her own brushed one of Li's nipples.

The music from the gramophone was so loud—and they were so caught up in their own rapture—they didn't notice Romy in the doorway.

She tugged the door closed and raced down the corridor. When she reached Mr. Khaira, she stopped and begged him not to tell anyone she'd been there.

She was about to run through the lobby when Chang Wu stormed past them into the bar, shouting over his shoulder at the waiter, "Well, if she's not in her room, find her!"

Romy froze. Her eyes were full of tears, but when she blinked all she saw was dark blood. Looking over her shoulder to make sure no one was watching, she stole back past a suddenly white-faced

Mr. Khaira into the secret passage. Romy marched up the stairs and knocked on the dressing-room door to sound a warning, before quickly running downstairs again to avoid being seen.

"Please make sure they don't get caught," she begged Mr. Khaira, who was now doing his best to blend into the wallpaper. Then, looking as casual as she could manage, Romy strolled with a group of departing guests across the mosaic floor into the night.

Chapter 59

25 November 1944

After all the mad ramblings during my illness, I realize I've been remiss about updating this diary ever since.

I am back at the university after missing the semester and will have to work extra hard to catch up so I can graduate.

Papa is one of the directors at the hospital now. This means no extra pay, of course, but more hours and paperwork. Mutti helps him as best she can, as do I.

I haven't seen Wilhelm for a month. He's called for me at the hospital occasionally and sent some bread, but I always manage to avoid him. Truth be told, I can't bear to see his earnest face. I love him dearly, of course—that will never change.

I have not seen Li, but from time to time Nina and I have coffee with Delma, who keeps us updated with the news from the Heime and kitchens. Occasionally I see Jian on patrol with Captain Azuma, but he continues to pretend I do not exist.

27 November 1944

The Japanese are as hungry and desperate as we are. They patrol with gaunt cheeks and hollow stomachs. Hunger has turned some soldiers into savages.

As I walked home from work last night I spotted a Chinese woman squatting in the gutter and rocking back and forth rubbing her belly, eyes squeezed tight. She was giving birth. But three Japanese soldiers were yelling at her, prodding the woman in the back with their bayonets. They were trying to get her to move.

"Curfew," they hissed. "You go now."

Ignoring the soldiers, I placed my cheek on the ground. I said, "The head is crowning. This baby is coming right now." With some tugging and a gush of blood, the baby slid out with the blue umbilical cord dangling like a string of sausages. I held the baby out to check the chest and comforted the sobbing woman.

Then I asked one of the Japanese soldiers to cut the cord with his bayonet.

The soldier looked equal parts bemused and repulsed.

He speared the baby through the heart. The baby convulsed and flopped backward in my arms and the mother collapsed into the gutter with a wail that echoed deep and low along the dark alley.

It's unclear what happened next. I know I went crazy and screamed at them, pounding at one soldier with my fists. I think one soldier smacked me across the cheek with the back of his hand and knocked me to the ground. They kicked the woman once, before tossing the dead baby into the gutter and walking down the alley, laughing and passing a packet of cigarettes between them.

I went to Garden Bridge today to find Captain Azuma and tell him of this incident. I had not spoken with him since the day we left Frenchtown, but I felt he would never approve of this barbarity. He was appalled and promised to catch the culprits.

He sighed and said we had to be careful this war didn't make monsters of us all. Then he offered to help find some rare sulfa drugs for Ward Road Hospital. He is a good man.

Chapter 60

Alexandra sat sipping a peppermint tea in the lobby of the Peninsula Hotel as she waited for Mary Chu, her adoption consultant, to arrive. Tourists wandered about the vast space, photographing every detail of the soaring ceilings, gold cornices, marble columns, and giant potted palms. Despite the grandeur, it didn't feel too overwrought. It felt special, magical. She wondered what Oma had thought of it.

Alexandra really wanted a gin and tonic to settle her nerves, but it was probably best to wait until her appointment was over. Instead, she ordered the high tea—a three-tiered silver stand loaded with cucumber sandwiches, delicate French pastries, and cupcakes with thick layers of icing. She hoped Mary Chu was hungry.

Her phone beeped and she checked the text.

Get it done. That's why we sent you to HK. No excuses.

Her boss was livid she hadn't yet closed the deal she'd flown over for this morning. But if she was honest, it wasn't her priority for this trip. The office wanted her to attend a meeting this afternoon.

345

The Hong Kong office had also gotten wind of her concerns. They wanted a briefing on how local populations would be resettled. Guidelines. She was used to complicated, but this was a mess.

She sent a reply: *I'll be there.*

"Alexandra Laird?" Standing in front of her was a birdlike woman with a briefcase. "The concierge directed me over. I'm Mary Chu."

They shook hands and Alexandra ordered more tea.

Mary pulled a folder from her briefcase and placed it on the table. Alexandra had to stop herself from grabbing it greedily.

"Your grandmother sent you some of these papers that you couriered to me?"

"Correct. With this diary." She touched the diary in the same way she had touched her comfort blanket as a child.

Mary peered at the diary curiously. "She doesn't say anything in it about the adoption?"

"No. It only goes through September 1945. But she sounds a little . . . detached by 1944."

"Yes, I understand. That last year was particularly grueling for everyone in Shanghai—the Chinese, Jews, *and* the Japanese."

"What did you find?"

"Well"—Mary opened the folder and pushed back the glasses that kept slipping down the bridge of her nose—"every case has its quirks. Yours has a couple."

Alexandra wiped her sweaty hands on her skirt.

"I picked up where you left off. The Jewish Refugees Museum in Shanghai confirmed that Romy Bernfeld did travel to Hong Kong; she was booked as a pair with a Miss Nina Milch."

Alexandra smiled at the mention of Nina.

"But there's no record of a child's passage from Shanghai."

"What about that other Chinese name I gave you—Li Ho?" Alexandra plucked the original photo from the diary and gave it to Mary. "It's the only photo Oma kept from Shanghai, so they must have been close. They were obviously school friends."

"That's circumstantial evidence, I'm afraid. They may well have known each other, but there is no proof they were in touch. You say there is nothing in the diary after 1945. Add in a war—"

"So, did you find *anything* on Li?" For once, Alexandra didn't trust the facts.

"No. Only your original article. Li Ho disappeared. No death—or birth of a baby—was ever recorded."

Alexandra slumped back in her chair, deflated. So far she had paid a hefty fee for nothing.

"But this is interesting." Mary slid the creased Hong Kong notarial adoption certificate across the table. "You said this came from your grandmother. Are you sure?"

"Yes."

"Well, this certificate is a forgery. See down at the bottom here—the police station referred to never actually existed. Whoever signed it made sure this certificate couldn't be traced. Now, I'm taking a bit of a leap here, but I'd say this adoption note was issued in a hurry to get a baby a landing certificate for Australia. No certificate, no passage.

"Now, there is something I want to show you."

Mary had brought Alexandra upstairs to the Rose Ballroom. Alexandra gazed at the black-and-white photograph in Mary's hand, then looked around her in astonishment. The photo was of this very ballroom at the Peninsula—she recognized the enormous windows draped with silk—but where there were lines of elegant white tables set for ten, Mary's photo showed lines of camp beds and racks of clothing tucked in corners. A woman reclined on a stretcher, reading under a paper umbrella, and it occurred to Alexandra that that was perhaps her only privacy.

"Your grandmother and Nina Milch lived like this for six months after the war ended," Mary Chu explained. "The current owners of the Peninsula, the Kadoorie family, provided shelter and immigration assistance for hundreds of Jewish refugees who were hoping to get to Australia, Israel, Britain, America . . ."

"That's so generous—"

"Very. More than can be said for your government at the time, I'm afraid." She shook her head. "The Australian government redeployed the ships they had promised to use to collect some refugees for war brides and troops. They were under pressure to reject Jewish refugees, and they certainly wouldn't have accepted Asian immigrants." She paused before carefully articulating each word. "It was tough to get to Australia. Particularly without the correct immigration paperwork."

Alexandra looked at the giant crystal chandelier and shook her head, confused. Oma and Nina lived in this ballroom for at least half a year. They sailed with an Asian baby and fake paperwork to a country that was reluctant to receive them. Why take such an enormous risk?

"I'm sorry I don't have the answers you need. It would have been expensive and difficult to get a forgery, but it was a war, so not impossible—all kinds of lines were blurred." Mary's voice softened. "Your grandmother must have been determined to get to Australia, and take that baby—your mother—with her."

Chapter 61

Romy sat in the back of the rickshaw racing down Avenue Joffre wringing her hands. Usually she loved Frenchtown's wide avenues, elegant villas, and soaring trees, but today the streetscape felt menacing. Japanese soldiers disappeared around the opposite corner. The branches of the plane trees swooped and overlapped, blocking the searing heat and casting ghostly shadows on the footpath.

These past two weeks she'd spent many sticky nights with a cool damp cloth on her neck, huddled around Mr. Lam's secret shortwave radio with Mutti and Papa. They crowded under the stairs at night after work—sipping tea or perhaps a mug of vegetable stock with some chunks of turnip or soggy millet. Sometimes Romy bounced one of the Lam toddlers on her knee, hugging the squishy little body tight. The German government had surrendered in May—just a little over a week after the Führer committed suicide with his younger lover. The Allies were negotiating how to carve up the territories. But the *real* reason they listened was to catch the whispers of liberation of the northern European concentration camps. Some prisoners were walking free, but still there were mutterings . . . Chatter in the laneways, at the Chusan Road markets, and at the hospital was always an unreliable mixture of conjecture, Russian propaganda, and exaggeration. The Japanese, of course, never confirmed or denied the rumors.

It was difficult to get mail into Shanghai, as Japan still controlled the supply lines. But the Americans were bombing Tokyo, so perhaps they would have news of Daniel soon. If the bombs loosened the Japanese stranglehold on China, surely there might be some gaps in the blockades where news and supplies could be smuggled through. Delma knew someone who'd received a letter from family in Europe. Romy wasn't giving up hope.

The war may have ended in Europe, but the Japanese were digging their claws into Shanghai. Even if Daniel were free to travel now, it would be impossible for him to find a ship permitted to enter the port.

As soon as she'd arrived at Ward Road Hospital that morning, a man with dull eyes had leaped in front of her and handed her a paperback copy of *Les Misérables*.

"Missee Romy?"

"Yes."

"This is for you. You must come now." Then he'd leaned in close enough for her to smell his sour breath and whispered, "Chop-chop. I have rickshaw. Come."

Romy knew the heavy book was from Li. It was a newer edition than the one from their days at Puyuan, and she flipped through the crisp pages, softening at the sight of Li's doodles. When she reached a page with a folded corner, somewhere in the middle of the back third, she squinted at the faintest lettering in lead pencil between the lines of thick serif text. So faint that, unless you were looking for it, it seemed like merely a scratch on the page.

Romy, please help. Come now. Bring your medical bag.

Now Romy clutched the bag beside her as the rickshaw pulled up outside a Spanish villa covered with creeping Chinese star jasmine.

Jumping out of the rickshaw with a breathless thanks to the driver, she ran to the front door.

The heavy oak door was opened before she had a chance to knock. The housekeeper glanced at the medical kit Romy was carrying and said, "She's been waiting for you."

The small woman ushered Romy into a grand sitting room lined with black Chinoiserie wallpaper painted with turquoise peonies and kingfishers. Plush Persian carpets covered the black marble floor. A glossy grand piano stood in the far corner. This opulence made Romy queasy—as if she had gorged on a whole steamer basket of pork dumplings after a long fast.

She took a deep breath.

At the end of the room was an enormous photograph of Li in a heavy gold frame. Though it was softened and blurred at the edges to look like a painting of a Calendar Girl, the plunging crystal ball gown shimmered in the light. Li wore a striking beaded headband. Romy sighed—she still had Jian's photo from when they were girls tucked into her diary.

In this recent picture, Li's black hair was trimmed to a sleek bob, her chin was raised, and those mesmerizing dark eyes stared defiantly at the camera.

"Li?" Romy said, striding toward the shadow standing beneath the photo. "What's wrong? Are you hurt?"

"You came," said Li with relief. "Thank you, dear Romy." She sounded a little out of breath. Li waved at the photo overhead. "Jian took this, of course. Chang insisted on having some photographs of his new cabaret singer, and I begged him to let my brother take them."

There was a pause, and when Li spoke again, her voice was low and broken. "What is the point of all this"—she waved her arm around to indicate the luxurious surroundings—"if I can't help to save the ones I love?"

She clasped her pendant.

"I did all this to save Jian. They were going to kill him, you know. Kill us both if we refused to collaborate."

Romy swallowed and nodded. The Hos' faces visited her in her sleep sometimes. Benjamin's and Daniel's sunny faces merged with the decapitated Hos as her dreams turned to terror.

"I agreed to sing for Chang Wu at the Cathay if he spared my brother. But he wanted . . ." Her voice trailed off.

Romy nodded her understanding.

"He insisted Jian work for the police. Told him I would be killed if he didn't. He said the Kempeitai wanted to make an example of Jian because his parents openly resisted the occupation. They wanted a living reminder just a hair away from the scythe. So you see, we were trapped." She sighed. "I wish some days I'd chosen death. Do you think we are cowards, Romy?"

Romy froze. She didn't know what to think.

"I thought *you* would understand. You aren't welcome in your own country, and we are treated like dogs in ours. My parents refused to collaborate, and now they are dead. I do not wish this for my brother."

Li flicked on a golden lamp, then turned to Romy with mournful eyes. There was no mistaking the ripe belly beneath her yellow silk kimono. Li was with child. In her last trimester, certainly. Her best friend was going to be a mother.

She hesitated, then enveloped Li in a hug. "A baby! And you didn't tell me?" Romy was crying now. Her tears were a salty mix of resentment and jealousy mixed with fresh fear and excitement for her friend. *A baby!*

"How could I? I tried to send Jian to tell you, but he said it was better for you if you didn't know. This is our burden, not yours."

"You're never a burden," said Romy, feeling uncharitable as her blood pumped with rejection. She was furious with Li for not responding to the messages she sent via Wilhelm. Hurt that Wilhelm had chosen Li over Romy. The tears stung her cheeks as she struggled to focus.

Li needed her help. Romy wiped her cheeks with the back of her hand as she worked out what to do next. She eyed Li's stomach and stepped a little closer.

"I'm here now." Romy placed her hands on Li's protruding belly and felt the taut skin and movements of elbows and legs stretching the skin. Li looked tired, but she had a natural rosiness to her cheeks.

Romy felt the contraction and looked up. "You're in labor."

"Yes." Li's voice quavered. "I'm sorry." She started to sob. "I didn't want to involve you—but I *need* you. This baby . . . I still have"—she looked at her housekeeper, who held up her fingers—"four weeks left."

Li wiped away her tears as Romy felt the tightening in Li's belly.

"I haven't worked for months. Chang has moved on to fresher flowers, of course. Though he keeps watch. This baby is his sweet prize, after all, from his best cabaret singer. Everything is a game he has to win. Jian brings me food: rice, a sliver of duck breast. And Wilhelm sends bread." She flushed as she met Romy's eyes before looking sad. "That night at the Cathay when we were almost caught by Chang, Mr. Khaira said it was you who warned us. We realized it was too dangerous. I haven't seen Wilhelm since."

Romy nodded.

"I'm sorry I didn't tell you. But"—she smiled sadly—"we couldn't help it."

Romy tried to smile her understanding but her lungs felt tight with jealousy. She couldn't help but love Wilhelm too. His easy smile, the way his fingers shaped the dough, the permanent smattering of flour in his hair and on the tip of his nose. Wilhelm had a quiet strength. Romy missed their friendship.

"I tried to protect you from this mess. Wu made it clear that any friend I tried to contact would be killed—and Jian would be killed too." Li's voice was raw. "He has spies everywhere: Kempeitai, White Russians—he even has spies in the Jewish ghetto. Chang Wu works for the highest bidder." Her voice dripped with contempt. She ran her finger across the black wallpaper and traced the petals of a peony. "He sneaks through this war like a filthy rat, living off the scraps from all sides."

Romy thought of Dr. Ho standing in the living room at Puyuan in his white cotton shirt reciting, "*To starve to death is a very small matter; to lose one's integrity is a grave matter.*" She closed her eyes, willing away the image of Benjamin's bloody face and twisted body. Benjamin, Dr. Ho, and Wilma all spoke out and they were all dead. Li was doing what was necessary to protect her brother. To save her baby . . .

"Sometimes Wu arranges deals for weapons and tobacco. He doesn't care who for—Chinese or Japanese. Whoever pays the most." Li sighed. "When I met Wilhelm at the Cathay, he'd already started to notice the movements of the Japanese munitions trucks from the Hongkew factories during his weekly Pao Chia patrols. He wanted to find some way to stop them."

Suddenly, as a contraction hit, Li doubled over and clutched the edge of the velvet sofa. The housekeeper rubbed her back, murmuring in a low voice as Li rocked her hips from side to side for almost a minute.

"You should let me check how dilated you are," said Romy, frowning. Her main concern was Li and this baby. Explanations could wait.

Li batted Romy's hand away and gritted her teeth. "I—I asked Wilhelm to take some messages to Jian for me. To let Jian know I was okay, but also"—she gasped for air and rocked again, groaning with pain—"to let Jian know about the deals. The weapons . . ."

"Shh," said Romy softly, brushing the damp hair from Li's forehead. "Let me feel your stomach properly." She reached inside the kimono and felt the contraction.

Li looked up and placed both hands on Romy's cheeks as she sobbed. "I miss you. I never got to thank you for trying to protect us. But I think about you every day. You and Jian."

She reached up and grabbed one of Romy's curls, winding it around her finger before letting it spring back into place. "Fancy you being nearly a doctor. My clever friend." She sighed and rested her forehead against Romy's for a beat.

As Li winced and squeezed her eyes shut with pain again, Romy inhaled the shame of her own resentment. Li had lost none of her *qijie*.

But this baby was coming right now, far too early. Romy needed to focus.

"Can you please fetch some towels and hot water?" Romy asked the housekeeper as she ushered Li onto the Persian carpet so she could check how dilated she was and get a proper feel of the baby's position. Romy's hands shook—she'd only assisted at births at Ward Road when there were midwives present.

"Did anyone see you arrive?" Li asked urgently.

"I've no idea. Why?"

"I'm being watched by Japanese soldiers. Even though Wu doesn't want me himself, I am forbidden to leave the house or receive visitors. He doesn't know about Wilhelm, but there were times when he couldn't exactly place where I was at the Cathay—that was enough for him to grow suspicious. Especially as I became less . . . convincing in my responses to him. This is my prison."

Li sighed and cupped her belly. "Wu thinks this baby is his. That's the only reason I'm allowed to stay here."

"Is it?"

"It's Wilhelm's." She rubbed her belly. "I can feel her—the rolling, the strength. This is a happy child, not a poisoned one."

She yelped out as water gushed from between her legs onto the Persian carpet.

Romy knelt between Li's shaking legs, coaxing out the baby's head. The baby had taken less than an hour to crown once Li's water broke.

"Just one more push, Li."

Li screamed and groaned in agony as she clenched her housekeeper's hands and pushed the baby out.

As she entered the world, the baby screwed up her pink little face and started to squall.

The housekeeper rolled the baby over, rotated the hips, and administered two swift thumps between the shoulder blades before opening Li's kimono and placing the naked baby on her chest to suckle. The baby's hair was not quite black, and she had curls. She was clearly Wilhelm's daughter.

Li lay back on silk cushions, cooing at her baby even though her face was pale and scrunched up with pain. Romy was busy with one hand in Li's uterus, trying to stem a postpartum bleed—but still the blood gushed and pooled around her knees on the carpet. She prodded Li's stomach with her other hand as she continued to probe internally for the piece of retained placenta. Li was bleeding out, sweat beading on her brow and upper lip as she fought to remain conscious. Her grip on her child loosened.

The housekeeper grabbed a sheet and swaddled the baby tight.

Romy kissed her dear friend on the forehead.

There was a knock at the door and some shouting.

Li sank deeper into the pillow, struggling to speak. Her voice was barely a whisper. "It's them. Chang Wu and his men. The soldiers must have seen you arrive and reported it to him. He'll know this isn't his baby. Look . . ." She reached out to stroke the child's lighter curls as her housekeeper held the child. "They'll kill you, Romy. You have to leave."

Romy shook her head and begged the housekeeper, "Help me! Help me move her."

"Quickly," Li moaned. "There's no time. Take my housekeeper and Shu."

The housekeeper stood and shook her head as she held the baby out.

Romy took the wriggling bundle and pulled it to her chest.

"You must go," begged Li. "I had a dead bolt put on the door because Wu has a key. But it won't hold out for long . . ."

There was more furious beating at the door and yelling. It sounded like there was a screaming mob gathered outside on the doorstep.

Li grabbed Romy's hand. "Leave now through the kitchen into the back alley. Take her to Wilhelm." She ripped the jade pendant from her neck and held it out for Romy. "And give Shu this. Tell her I love her."

"I promise."

"Tell Jian—" But all at once she subsided, too weak to continue.

Hot tears were streaming down Romy's cheeks as she tried to quell her panic. Her lungs were so heavy with shock she wasn't sure if she could run.

She pressed her wet cheek to the pale, clammy cheek of her friend. "I'm so sorry, Li," she choked out. Why had she wasted a minute being angry or jealous of her dear friend? After all they'd been through.

"Go. Save my daughter," Li begged in a whisper. "Give her this"— she ripped her jade necklace from her neck—"but wait until she is safe. That necklace will link her to me . . . if Chang Wu or his men recognize it, they will kill Shu. I'm sure of it."

"I'll take care of her. I'll take her to Wilhelm, I promise. And I'll find Jian . . ."

Romy took one last glance at her friend slipping into unconsciousness and felt her heart break. Then holding the baby close, she ran toward the kitchen.

She was just slipping through the side gate when she heard two shots.

Chapter 62

Romy stood in the queue at the ghetto checkpoint, jiggling Li's newborn baby, swaddled tight under a woolen coat she had purchased for a couple of dollars from a sallow man sitting at a trestle table. Sweat dripped down her neck in rivulets and she flapped the coat to let fresh air circulate inside. She drew stagnant air deep into her aching lungs.

Just as she stepped over the line the baby started to squirm and gave a weak cry like a kitten. She wrapped both arms around her bundle and pulled it snug against her belly. Her sweat was sour. If Chang Wu somehow found out Romy had been at the house with Li, she couldn't risk him finding out that she had entered the ghetto with a Chinese baby. They would both be killed once he realized the little girl was not his child.

She coughed and stepped forward with her chin slightly raised, showing more bravado than she felt.

"Pass," snapped a Chinese guard. He turned to look at Romy, and the dark eyes were unmistakable as he held out his hand.

Jian.

He held his bayonet in front of his chest and with a shake of his head signaled to Romy to get moving, as if she were merely another prisoner he had to follow on this hot day.

"You are a student. Special pass," he said loudly as he quietly gestured that she should show her pass while he shielded her body from the Japanese soldiers.

Romy peeled back one side of the coat to reveal the swaddled baby as adrenaline pumped through her veins.

When they were out of earshot, Romy couldn't stifle her tears any longer. "I'm sorry. She's—she's . . ." Romy couldn't bear to say Li's name.

"What?" Jian held her gaze and shook his head in disbelief. Blood drained from his face. "Li . . ." His voice broke with anguish.

Romy's grief switched to a burning fury. "You knew she was pregnant and you didn't help her?" Romy spat out the words in disgust and stepped into the filthy gutter away from Jian.

Other soldiers started to approach Romy, leering and pulling coins from their pockets. Jian waved them away quickly, as if to indicate he was escorting her to a back alley for his own pleasure.

"She didn't tell *me* she was in labor." He touched her elbow, imploring her to look at him. "Please, we need to keep walking." He glanced left and right. "People will be watching us if we don't move away quickly."

As they started to walk toward the hospital, the baby's crying changed gears and Romy started to shake with fury.

"We had people watching her house. Protecting her." His voice quivered with shock as he covered his face with his hands.

"Well, they failed," she hissed. "How could you let this happen? Your own sister!" Romy felt so tired, so bereft, she could lie down in the filthy gutter and never get up again.

Jian removed his hands and his face was pale. When he looked at Romy, his eyes brimmed with tears and she regretted her outburst. Jian blamed himself. His breath had shortened and each step was agony.

Romy understood Jian's pain. To live, when those you love are dead, is a cruel, bitter luck.

"She knew the risks, Romy," he whispered softly. "You were there when our parents were killed. Did you know they also had stakes prepared for Li and me?"

Romy shivered, despite the rivulets of sweat running down her back.

"We've been living on borrowed time—"

"No." Romy shook her head, not wanting to think about losing Jian too.

Jian touched her arm gently. "That night in the storeroom, we made a pact that we would do whatever it took to see that the Japanese don't win this war."

Romy shook her head. "Your parents would have wanted you to survive."

"My parents taught us to do our duty. To do what is right. You *know* this, Romy."

"Why did you let Li go to Chang Wu?" she sobbed, clutching the baby.

"No one else would help us—everyone else was too scared after they killed our parents. I still don't know why your mother was spared. If we'd stayed with you and your parents, they would have killed you too. Do you think we would risk that? It was Li's idea to go to Chang Wu. I disagreed at first. Why should we put our trust in a gangster? And he was there when our parents—" Jian's voice started to crack. "But he offered protection, and we agreed that it was better to *appear* to collaborate. To stay close to our enemies. The best revenge in war is victory, no?"

Romy let that sink in, before she asked, "You said *we*, before. *We had people watching the house.* Who's *we*?" Romy inhaled sharply. "I never thought you were a collaborator. I just—"

Jian stepped closer to her now, and once more she was sixteen years old on the balcony at Grosvenor House. Jian's voice cracked. "It wouldn't be the first time you've misunderstood me, Romy."

Romy wanted to reach out and hold Jian, but she couldn't risk being spotted. Instead, she pressed her face against the bricks to cool her cheek and jiggled the baby.

Jian explained: "Li was passing messages about Chang Wu's shady business agreements with the Japanese. Wilhelm started to track when an order was fulfilled by a Hongkew factory. He discovered that Jewish- and Chinese-owned plants were forced to produce unmarked grenades for the Japanese army—on the hush-hush, of course."

Romy shook her head, struggling to keep up.

"Wilhelm arranged for his Jewish contacts working at the factory to shorten the fuses, so the grenades wouldn't explode. My part was to let resisters know about the munitions factories and when orders were made. All thanks to Li." Jian's voice was a sad whisper.

"*Wilhelm* is a spy? Li too?" Romy gasped and shook her head. "You're *all* in the resistance?"

"Call it what you want, but really we were just cobbling together information when we could get it, then feeding it to the right people. It's no different from what your father has been doing for years to secure anesthetics, insulin, and equipment on the black market." Jian looked tired as he shrugged. "Doing the right thing sometimes means breaking rules."

Romy clutched the baby and thought of Papa's words in his study when she was fourteen and complaining about him breaking the law to treat people and secure drugs. *It's worth the risk.* She remembered the young Jian she'd loved and her chest tightened with loss and confusion.

"Please . . ." He stopped and looked into her eyes. His were flooded with tears and he swallowed as he tried to speak. "I can't talk about it here. It's too dangerous." He tugged on her elbow, pulling her closer to him; to anyone observing it would look like a threat, but Romy knew the gesture was meant to be a small comfort.

As they walked, Jian asked, "Did you get my recipe from Captain Azuma? I was trying to tell you to stay strong. Not that you need it—you've always been strong." He looked up at the inky swirls in the sky.

The baby wriggled and coughed, and Romy rubbed her back to ease the congestion that came with being born too early. She stopped and leaned against a wall to catch her breath. Jian wiped away a piece of hair, sticky with sweat, from her face. Romy closed her eyes and tried to digest the enormity of Li and Jian's sacrifice as she felt the baby burrow into her chest.

The smell of frying noodles and shallot oil filled Romy's nostrils, and her stomach lurched. When had she last eaten? Romy opened her eyes and stared at the old lady standing behind a pile of stacked bamboo baskets, the smell of steamed pork and mushroom dumplings making her mouth water. She wished they were not so expensive.

"You're too thin, Romy," said Jian, eyeing the coat hanging loose around her waist.

"No thinner than anyone else," she snapped, embarrassed, as they weaved through the crowds, the baby's head tucked under her chin as they turned into the crowd at the Chusan Road markets. The buildings on either side of the street were grand, with high arched windows, but paint peeled from the facades and washing hung from every balcony. Jewish men walked around in singlets, wet towels draped around their necks, while Chinese women held umbrellas to protect them from the glare of the sun.

The end stall had a motley collection of jars filled with cinnamon sticks, star anise, peach stones, and several different types of dried green leaves.

"Wait, let me get you some herbs."

"I'm fine. We need to get to the hospital."

"You need to stay well if you are to care for this baby," Jian said firmly, before talking rapidly to the woman tending the stall. She nodded and scooped tea leaves, herbs, and spices into a burlap bag for him. She waved Romy over and indicated that she should poke out her tongue.

Romy obeyed and the woman leaned in close with a nod and a "humph," then added some sweet brown powder to the mixture.

As she hugged Li's baby and took the scent of the spice mix deep into her lungs, Romy remembered all the times she'd laughed with Jian over mah-jongg in French Park as Li twirled around them through the peach blossoms. The acupuncture lessons at Dr. Ho's clinic, how Dr. Ho had nurtured Mutti and Wilma had given her back her spark. Their families overlapped so tightly . . . She loved them. She looked at Jian's sad eyes and mourned what could never be—she gulped at the realization of just how alone he'd been, what he'd had to endure. Still had to endure.

She understood why Li and Jian had cut her off, but it still hurt.

He reached out and placed his palm over her heart. "I know you loved her. And now you are mother to her child. Your heart is broken, when it needs to be strong." He peeled his palm away, leaving a burning sensation on her chest in its place. "You're angry. Frightened." He nodded. "Your heart *shen*, your spirit, they are not at peace." His voice softened as he gestured at the baby. "For you. And for the baby."

He lifted the tablecloth and pointed at a sack hidden under the table; it was filled with glittering mother-of-pearl dust. "*Zhen zhu mu*," he said to the woman, and she nodded, her thin hands adding angelica and foxglove—*dang gui* and *shu di huang*. She mixed the spices in a metal cup and added some boiling water, then handed it to Romy.

The brown liquid was salty and sour, and the grit clung to her teeth like coffee grinds.

"This is revolting," Romy said with a grimace as she swallowed the lot in two gulps. The baby clucked and grizzled against her chest. "I need to get this baby to the hospital," she fretted. "She needs fluids. It's so hot, she's in real danger."

As they passed into the shadows, Romy pulled Li's pendant from her pocket and offered it to Jian. It swung in the air between them, back and forth, offering forgiveness and understanding.

They were both too exhausted to speak.

Jian sighed and a tear slid down his cheek. He wiped it away with the back of his hand, then said, "Keep it. Give it to Wilhelm. For—"

"Shu. Her name is Shu."

"Warmhearted," he said as he met Romy's eyes. "Li named her for you." He placed his hands over hers before continuing. "She was trying to protect you."

Romy's ears burned with shame and regret. She had to focus on the future. Here she was, holding Li's baby. A baby she would do anything to protect.

Romy was sitting in a rocking chair in the hospital nursery trying to coax Shu's mouth open with a rubber teat on a bottle of rice milk when Wilhelm appeared. He reached out and put one hand on her forearm; the other stroked Shu's head.

He traced the baby's nose and gently tapped her chin. When he looked at Romy, his eyes were filled with concern and regret.

"She's tiny. Is she . . . okay?"

"She's about four pounds. I can't be sure of dates." Romy blushed before rushing on. "She's much smaller than a full-term newborn." Romy was uncertain of what to say to reassure a new father. "But so many in these wards are—" She stopped herself. There was no need to scare the man by explaining the poor diet.

Wilhelm said, "She's perfect." He looked at Romy and added, "She looks like her mother," then dropped his head and sobbed for a full minute.

Romy felt his anguish and her eyes filled with tears. Li was gone. As Wilhelm sat, touching her arm, her grief felt tainted by the faintest hint of something sour—jealousy. She was still wounded by Wilhelm, but he'd always been kind to her.

Seeing Wilhelm stroke Li's baby was bittersweet. Hiding her own heartbreak, she pasted a smile on her face.

"Yes," she agreed. "She does look like Li—especially these." Romy gently poked one of her dimples.

Wilhelm smiled too, though his eyes were empty. She would have to go back to the old herbalist in the corner of the market for a brew for him. Her body felt heavy with sorrow. She had missed Li for so long. They shared that much, at least.

"I'm sorry, Wilhelm. I know you loved her."

Wilhelm looked Romy in the eye and put his arm around her bony shoulders. "We both did."

Romy pulled the bottle out of Shu's lips and burped the baby over her shoulder.

"Here. You nurse her." She gently showed him how to hold his daughter. He jiggled her awkwardly and her neck flopped sideways. He grimaced and looked at Romy for help.

"Am I doing it right? I've never held a baby."

The frosted door was closed, but through the glass panel she could see a familiar peaked cap. Jian. He was keeping watch.

The door opened and Jian entered, closing it behind him.

"Wilhelm. We need to leave."

Romy looked from one man to the other, confused. Her heart started to race.

"I—" Wilhelm looked at his feet as if they were about to offer an explanation. His brown leather boots were cracked, the shoelaces mismatched string, and the sole on his left boot had peeled away at the toe.

"We've arranged for his escape tonight."

"How?" asked Romy in disbelief. The Japanese controlled Rangoon and Hong Kong. There was no way out of Shanghai.

"He'll go with my Chinese contacts up into the hinterland of Chungking and over the mountains to Calcutta." Jian looked at Wilhelm before speaking directly to Romy. "Chang Wu has put a bounty on Wilhelm's head. He needs to disappear; Shu stays."

Of course, Romy realized; the baby was far too fragile to travel.

"But how does Wu even know about Wilhelm? Li said you hadn't seen her since—"

Wilhelm pressed his cheek to Shu's head and closed his eyes. When he opened his eyes again and turned to Romy, his face looked haunted.

"It's true, I didn't see Li. But Wu traced the bread deliveries I made weekly to her house in Frenchtown. There were no notes, of course. Just bread—kaiser rolls and bread with *Brotgewürz*."

The baby squirmed as Wilhelm awkwardly adjusted her against his chest. "But he'd already been suspicious after Japanese soldiers reported seeing us together at the Cathay—even though we were careful. He had lost face. That's why I stopped taking the deliveries myself."

Romy thought about the look the pair had exchanged at the Cathay when Li was onstage. If Romy had spotted it, who was to say others hadn't?

Wilhelm continued. "But when Wu learned of the faulty grenades, he had a private meeting with the manager. That factory manager was fished out of the Whangpoo River last week."

Bile burned the back of Romy's throat.

Jian added, "When I was on patrol last night I heard that the manager had been tortured. He volunteered Wilhelm's name. And then when the baby went missing . . ."

"Wu just connected all the dots," Romy whispered. "They all led to Wilhelm." Romy looked at Jian, fearful. "What about you? Li was only with Wu to protect you. Now she's gone . . ."

"I'll stay and continue to work as usual. I need to prove I knew nothing of the link between Li and Wilhelm," said Jian. He took a deep breath and went on. "People will be suspicious, watching me—and I will be watching them, trying to identify the traitors."

Romy's head started to spin as she tried to take it all in. "Where will you go?" she asked Wilhelm as he returned the baby to her arms.

"I'll try for Britain or Australia," he said.

Romy shuddered. So far? "I'll look after Shu and bring her to you," Romy blurted. "When she's well enough to travel."

Wilhelm raised his eyebrows and shook his head. "Romy, that's too—"

"I'll hide her from Chang Wu here at the hospital. We have so many orphans it will be easy. As soon as she's well enough." Romy picked up the bottle, gave it a swirl to dislodge the bits at the bottom, and started feeding her again.

She glanced sideways at Jian, who was studying her face with an inscrutable expression. Would he come too? But how could she ask him to leave China when his family had died fighting for it? He'd have to decide between his country and his niece.

Romy raised her eyes to the heavens. She'd long ago stopped believing in God, but she could do with some help if she was to keep this audacious promise. She'd do it for Wilhelm, because she loved him unconditionally. And for Li and the Hos, whom she carried deep in her soul.

Wilhelm choked back his tears as he smothered Romy and the baby in a hug. Romy could smell yeast, flour, and cardamom on his skin and she held her breath. She'd yearned for his touch, yet now it felt like a scalpel against her cheek.

"Romy," he said with a tremor in his voice as he stroked her back.

As her heart broke all over again, Romy thought: *This is enough. This love is enough.*

Chapter 63

HONG KONG, AUGUST 12, 2016

Alexandra was two hours late. Her deal was done but she'd missed dinner with Zhang and his colleagues. She sprinted in her heels down some stairs lined on one side with hundreds of cute gold cat charms with waving paws set in neat lines against a rough concrete wall. Each cat was to bring luck and food fortune—just like the ones that sat on shop countertops across China. Then she passed a peacock mural and descended into a dark basement. As her eyes adjusted to the light—and her ears to the thumping music—she scanned the packed restaurant for Zhang.

He was sitting at the end booth alone, sipping a beer. Empty plates were scattered on the table.

Alexandra winced. "I'm so sorry, Zhang. The meeting took twice as long as I expected. I couldn't leave until it was signed off. Then they wanted to discuss all this other stuff . . ." She leaned over and kissed him on the lips, but he didn't return the kiss. She sat down beside him.

"That's okay," said Zhang, taking a deep breath as he called the waiter over for a drink. "Are we celebrating?" he asked in a flat voice.

"I said I was sorry," said Alexandra, exhausted. Zhang was disappointed in her. She was disappointed too—she'd wanted to meet his colleagues. She ordered a dry martini and a beer for Zhang, a plate of the pork and cabbage dumplings, noodles, and some "drunken clams."

"The deal went well?" said Zhang.

"Oh, fine. It's just—"

"What?"

"Since I've been in Shanghai the past couple of months, I haven't really had the rush I usually get when I make a deal."

Zhang put his hand over Alexandra's. "That's understandable. You're still grieving."

She nodded. She wasn't sure this grief would ever pass.

"Do you ever think, maybe, of making a change? I mean, just because you loved it in London doesn't mean you have to love it in Shanghai."

She shrugged. "What else would I do?"

"Anything. Your grasp of numbers is brilliant, you can manage a team. Your work ethic is clearly insane." He raised his eyebrows pointedly. "You could do anything."

"Thanks," said Alexandra. "It's something I've been considering." Alexandra didn't say that with Hugo the workload hadn't mattered because it was what united them. But since she'd been with Zhang, she wanted more time for herself—for *them*.

"What was the 'other stuff' you had to stay back for?" Zhang looked concerned.

"Oh." Alexandra felt the martini burn a little in her stomach. "We just had to go over some guidelines for new projections."

"In English, please." He smiled.

"I raised some questions about benchmarks for reforestation and the occasional relocation of local villages."

"Okay," Zhang said slowly. "I get the revegetation, but relocation? You mean forcing people to leave their homes?"

"They are definitely *not* forced. There's strict consultation and protocols—"

"Sounds like semantics to me. No wonder you're having second thoughts."

Zhang was right: the world was hungry for the commodities she traded, but at what cost? At least her Hong Kong superiors had had the grace to look contrite when she left the office tonight. That was a start.

She took a sip of her martini, before turning to Zhang. "You're right. I'm having second thoughts about this job. But I don't want to throw the baby out with the bathwater. I meet a lot of interesting people—the real decision-makers. What if I can get them to make *different* decisions? I need to think about this more on my own, tease it out." She shrugged. "I also need to be sure my career rethink is for the right reasons, not just because a gorgeous full-time landscape architect and part-time philosopher is sitting in front of me."

Zhang smiled and nodded. "I get that."

And it was true. When she was with Hugo she'd become the player, not the dispassionate bystander mathematician she'd assured her Oxford lecturer she'd remain. She'd lost her boundaries somewhere in the city of London.

Romy never said anything, but Alexandra had always wondered if she wished her granddaughter was more like Sophia. Her mother's work helped countless families find answers to why their baby was born with an inherited trait.

Alexandra thought about those formulas in the back of her mother's old diary—they were early workings in algebra that led to her Ph.D., she was sure of it. She'd compared the workings with her mother's Oxford thesis. Was it any surprise that the teenage Sophia grew up to have a fascination with genetic algebra?

But lately, I've been wondering if my new body shape, if my eyes, if my math skills, come from my real mother and father.

"Do you think this search for your heritage—"

"Maybe," she cut him off as the food filled the booth with the scent of lemongrass and basil. Alexandra tasted the noodles. "These are *so* good." As Alexandra ate she told him about her meeting with the consultant that afternoon and about the forged certificate.

"So what are you going to do?"

"Don't know," she said as she finished a dumpling and licked her fingers. "I'll go back to Shanghai and start again. I want to know more about the Ho family, so maybe I'll look around the shop. Cynthia said I was welcome any time."

Zhang ate a dumpling.

"Speaking of Cynthia," said Alexandra, suddenly feeling shy, "are you still planning to come back to Shanghai for the party?"

Zhang looked her in the eye. "Do you mean am I coming to the party, or am I coming for you?"

"Both," she said, and took a sip of her martini as her cheeks started to warm.

"I'm coming for you," said Zhang as he slid closer to her on the banquette. His thigh was pressing against hers now and she rested her head on his shoulder. "I want to do this, Alexandra. Us. Properly. I know it's early and you've got so much going on, but I want to find a way for us to be together."

She sat back up and turned to face him. "I do too. It's just . . ."

"What?"

"It's just that with my work hours and the travel and living in different cities . . ."

Zhang put his hand on her cheek and leaned in for a slow kiss. Alexandra was grateful for their hidden corner booth and the dim lighting as she kissed him back. She wanted to be with him, but she didn't know how to make it work. But she *did* know that she wanted whatever this was with Zhang to work. She adored this poised, calm man.

Zhang stood up and reached for her hand. "Let's go back to the hotel. I don't want to miss a minute with you."

Chapter 64

SHANGHAI, JUNE 30, 1945

Romy followed her father out of the operating room, pulling her bandanna from her hair, desperate to change out of her scrubs and wash. She wiggled her toes, a trick Papa had taught her in surgery to help her concentrate, and noticed the sole of her shoe peeling away. Papa had sutured the edges last month, joking he'd stitched the legs of tougher patients lately.

That morning Delma had rushed in an eight-year-old girl from the *Heime* who'd woken during the night with a boil on her shoulder.

"Look," said Delma as she tugged away a shawl to reveal an angry red shoulder.

"What's your name?" asked Romy as she gently probed the child's taut, burning skin.

"Rachel," the child replied, wincing.

"Will she be okay?" Rachel's mother asked anxiously. "We hoped it would just go down by itself. We didn't have—we don't—"

"Don't blame yourself," said Delma gently as she looked around at the peeling walls of the hospital and staff crossing the corridors

375

in all directions. "The important thing is to make Rachel well again, and Dr. Bernfeld is just the person to do that." She tickled the girl under the chin and gave her a reassuring smile.

Papa pulled up his mask and leaned toward the girl. Her shoulder was so red and swollen they couldn't see the line of it, and Papa worried she may end up with blood poisoning and lose the arm, or worse. That week they'd already had to amputate the infected thumb of the local mushroom seller and the gangrenous foot of a carpenter. The carpenter hadn't made it through the night.

Both Romy and her mother had assisted Papa in this surgery, holding Rachel down by both arms under the lights so he could lance the boil, scrape away the rotten flesh with a sterilized spoon, and clean the wound. The hospital was out of anesthetic and low on equipment, so they'd just had to make do. As the child writhed and thrashed her head from side to side, Romy tried to soothe her. Finally the child went limp, and Papa was able to pack the wound with gauze—but Romy found herself wiping away her own silent tears with the back of her sleeve.

Perhaps she would consult Jian's notes and go to the spice stall at the market to see if they could recommend a decoction. It was just a tiny stall selling chilies and spices, but the woman served anyone who needed more traditional treatments. Last week the old lady helped Romy treat a child recovering from stomach cramps with an acrid blend of dandelion, peach seed, red peony root, and rhubarb. The child had gone home yesterday.

After the boil surgery, Romy and her parents had had to go straight into delivering twins. The mother's blood pressure had crept up, and Romy thought of Nina, standing on the deck of the *Conte Verde* all those years ago, watching the bodies of her mother and baby sister, wrapped in bedsheets, being dropped into the ocean. The passengers standing shoulder to shoulder, reciting the Kaddish.

May there be abundant peace from Heaven.

Romy sighed. Dear Nina. Her red lips and makeup couldn't hide the sad brown eyes of the child who had lost her mother.

When she had finished cleaning up, Romy would hurry across to the nursery to spend some time with little Shu—singing to her, feeding her a bottle, or just tracing her fine fingers and kissing each fragile joint one by one—as she did on every break. She was trying to fill this tiny baby with enough love for Li and Wilhelm. And Jian. Given her premature birth, it was remarkable how Shu had thrived. Papa called her their tiny miracle. Each day Shu looked a little pinker and a little stronger. Yesterday, she had gripped Romy's index finger and opened her eyes—Romy was unprepared for the jolt of love this minuscule gesture sent right through her body.

◇

Papa and Mutti had just finished delivering the twins and walked outside to sit beside Romy under the big sash windows for some fresh air and a break. All three had been lost in their own thoughts, stretching their legs, when Delma came down the long corridor toward them, pulling an envelope marked DACHAU from her pocket.

"I've been meaning to give you this, but there hasn't been a quiet moment this morning."

"It must be from Daniel!" said Mutti, sitting up straight, eyes filled with tears. "At last!" They'd heard nothing for almost five years.

Papa took the envelope, a smile forming on his lips as he tore it open, removed a sheet of paper, and began to read aloud.

May 7, 1945
116 Evacuation Hospital
Dachau
Germany

Dr. Bernfeld,
I was asked to personally oversee the posting of the enclosed letter by my patient Daniel Bernfeld.

I am a surgeon with the 116 Evacuation Hospital at Dachau. We have been moved in to help care for the people liberated from this concentration camp.

It is with great regret that I must inform you Daniel passed away this morning from a combination of typhus and extreme malnutrition.

Though it may be of little comfort to you, we were able to make his last hours bearable, and the rabbi sat with him throughout the evening, reciting the Kaddish and holding his hand to provide some small human solace.

I am most sorry for your loss. Daniel was buried this morning in a shroud, in accordance with the requests made by the team of rabbis working with us in the camp.

I'm most upset to confess our unit was unprepared for the devastation at Dachau. This letter is not the place to dwell on the horror and squalor I have encountered here. It is true, however, the atrocities committed by the Nazis defy comprehension. It is testimony to your son's fortitude and endurance that he was able to survive such trying conditions for years. I will remember Daniel and his fellow prisoners for the rest of my life.

As one medical practitioner to another, and as a father even more so, if I can offer any consolation it is that Daniel's passing was peaceful and without pain.

Before he lost consciousness, he asked me to transcribe the following few lines for you.

Herewith find the final words of Daniel. His love and thoughts were with his family until the end.

Sincerely,

Dr. James Webber

Dear Mutti, Papa, and Romy,

I may not be making my passage to Shanghai, Mutti. Your unwavering love has kept me focused and strong.

When there was only stale bread and gruel, I would fill myself with the words in your early letters. Even in the darkest times, it is possible to feed oneself with hope.

When this war is finished I hope that the three of you find a safe place to call home. I wonder: Will Vienna open its arms to you once more? Or perhaps you will travel to America.

I've not had much thought for God lately. In Dachau, He seemed so absent. But then I look into the kind souls of the men in my gang, the ones who gave me their shoes when I had to walk extra miles, those who shared their portion of bread and soup when I was ailing to give me strength, and I see His goodness.

My hands are calloused and scarred from lifting rocks and using a pick for almost seven years. They are far stronger than the fine fingers of the pianist who left you and I'm not sure you would recognize them. I barely feel they belong to me, so long is it since I played. But the Nazis cannot take the music from me. At night, as it rains outside, I lie on my bunk and drift to sleep listening to the jazz of Django Reinhardt in my head.

I sing for my roommates.

Sometimes, when I am too tired to move my jaw, my body sunk deep in the mattress, they sing to me. Music soothes, takes us beyond these walls and prepares me for the next day. This has been my unexpected gift in the camp.

Pray for me, but do not weep for me, Mutti.

Papa, you were the most tender father, a great leader. In all my time here, I strived to make you and Mutti proud. To make the best of my circumstances. Every day I asked myself: What would Papa do? It helped on the most bitter of days when my bones ached and my stomach screamed for a decent meal.

And to dear Romy—your descriptions of life in Shanghai have brought me such joy. I see from your letters you have lost none of your sparkle, nor your kindness. I wish you all the best with your studies. I am so proud of what you have become in the most difficult time. I can be sure that you will make your life happy. Remember what I said in my last letter.

It is up to you, Romy, to carry our legacy. To meet evil with kindness.

That is what I wish for you all: peace and happiness.

My love and blessing to you always,

Your Daniel

Papa hunched over. He rocked, eyes wide and mouth open as if to scream—but instead his body shuddered, betraying him with silence. It was almost too much to bear.

Mutti dropped her head into her hands and sobbed. "If only I'd managed to get his papers to exit the work camp sooner. This is my fault."

Romy wrapped one arm around her father to soothe his shaking and felt the corrugations of his ribs. He dropped his head into both hands and moaned. They sat in a wounded circle Romy never wanted to break.

Chapter 65

SHANGHAI, JULY 17, 1945

American bomber planes had been flying overhead for over a week and the *rat-tat-tat* and *boom* of Japanese antiaircraft guns were as regular as clockwork. The Americans flew mostly at midday, but the warning sirens set up by the Japanese would continue to wail well after the thrum of engines could be heard across the city. Bombs were being dropped on Japanese airfields and warehouses on the outskirts of Shanghai and along the Yangtze. It was comforting to know the Americans were close and that they were safe in Hongkew. Everyone knew the Americans wouldn't bomb the ghetto.

Romy's dress clung to her back as she made her way to the checkpoint. It had been easier for her to get her monthly pass since Ghoya's redeployment.

She touched the pocket in her jacket where she carried Li's pendant and thought about Daniel's letter. Mutti kept it wrapped in a handkerchief with his other letters. They were her most treasured possessions.

In all my time here, I strived to make you and Mutti proud. To make the best of my circumstances. Every day I asked myself: What would Papa do? It helped on the most bitter of days . . .

She rubbed her raw red hands together, lamenting she could not hide them with gloves despite the heat. Romy hoped whoever was wearing her old soft kid gloves from Paris was enjoying them. She smiled at the thought of a small child, fists balled inside the gloves. If they kept that child healthy, clean, and off her wards . . .

There was nothing left of value to steal. Romy had sold their candlesticks in Frenchtown last week to buy some insulin on the black market for Gretel, a little girl on the children's ward who was going to die. A brooch of Mutti's had bought a month of ether and sulfa from some surly gangsters. But Mutti didn't mind. Mutti's head was full of little Shu—she insisted on the baby coming home from the hospital to live with the Bernfelds. "Shu is *family*, Romy. Li's baby, *Liebling.*"

"It's safer," Romy agreed. There had been two suspicious Chinese officials in suits who had requested a list of orphans in the nursery with their dates of admittance and notary certificates. It was rumored hospitals and police stations all over Shanghai were being met with the same strange request. Romy couldn't be sure, but she had a feeling these "inspectors" could be connected with Chang Wu. There had been no such requests before. Either way, it wasn't worth the risk. Romy had inked out Shu's record from the hospital files and brought her home that very night.

Mutti blew a raspberry on Shu's cheek. "She belongs with us."

A very excited Mrs. Lam found a drawer for the baby to sleep in and a mosquito net to drape over her, and insisted on getting up every two hours through the night to feed her with a bottle. "You must sleep," she told the Bernfelds. "So you can work at the hospital. Besides"—she poked Romy in the chest—"you need to study. Otherwise you'll be crazy with study fever next year too." She snorted at her own joke before turning serious. "I worry about these black rings." She touched Romy's cheeks before nudging her out into the lane.

Mutti had shown Romy how to massage Shu's tummy to release bubbles of gas, how to change nappies and swaddle her tight like an Egyptian mummy so she would sleep through the night. When Mutti was home, she tied the baby onto her front with a sheet like Mrs. Lam had shown her. And when Romy finished studying each night, she took the clean, fed Shu and lay with her on the mattress, mesmerized by this tiny creature who had nuzzled and snuffled her way into all their hearts. She could pass hours just stroking her cheeks, tracing the line of her nose, smelling the sweet musk at the top of her scalp . . .

Today, like every day, she had to go to the university, leaving Shu at home with Mutti. When Mrs. Lam had to work and Mutti and Papa were both needed at the hospital, Shu sometimes went too and spent the day hidden in an isolation room—away from patients—to the delight of the nurses on duty in that room, who took turns to sing and to squeeze her thin little legs.

A fighter plane passed overhead and the sky boomed.

"Americans," someone whispered. The crowd sighed with relief. The Yanks were flying their B-29s nonstop these last months and it felt like an Allied victory was imminent. Mr. Lam had a black-and-white map tacked on the back of the front door; there were pins for every spot the Allies advanced in the Pacific. He added new pins every week.

The humming grew louder. An air-raid siren screeched out of speakers on the lampposts but it was too late to seek cover.

The air whistled as a bomb headed toward them. Everyone dropped to the ground and a thud rumbled through the earth as windows shattered. Suddenly, Romy was twelve again and reaching for Mutti's hand.

"They're bombing us! They're bombing the ghetto!" someone cried.

"They wouldn't—"

Bodies dropped to the ground and screams filled the air. Romy pressed her flushed cheek to the scorching concrete as a spray of bullets flew overhead. She felt a hand on her head and a wiry body covered hers.

"Keep your head down," a familiar voice whispered in her ear.

"But Mutti, Papa, and Shu are at home. We must go and help them."

"You're no use to anyone dead," Jian said.

When the bombing had ceased, he took her hand and pulled her to her feet. "Quickly!" he urged.

They ran through the streets toward the *longtang* lanes where the Bernfelds lived.

Buildings had been razed, piles of bamboo and wood smoldered, and flames flickered out of windows. Bodies lay strewn at all angles, crushed under collapsed brick walls, pinned under window frames.

Japanese soldiers ran among the bodies with first-aid kits, removing debris and loading the injured onto stretchers with the help of native workers. Everywhere she looked, Chinese, Jewish, and Japanese people were working frantically together to free or resuscitate victims.

All at once Romy caught sight of Nina, crouched beside a Chinese boy who was trapped under a concrete boulder. She was ripping her petticoat into strips to make bandages. She wore a blue dress, though her hair, face, and neck were white and red—she was covered in dust and blood.

"Nina!" Romy squeezed Nina's arm, then grabbed the big boulder with Jian, and together they heaved it away from the boy. Nina poured water from her flagon and started to wipe his crying face. She leaned down close and whispered something to the child before brushing the hair off his forehead and giving him a kiss.

"Where are his parents?"

They were interrupted by a shriek as a woman ran over and scooped the boy up in her arms. She looked at Nina—her gaze taking in the silken dress, the messy brassy-blond hair, and the kohl-rimmed eyes—and mouthed a silent "thank you."

Nina stood dazed, looking at the bodies around them. Then she focused on her friend. "Romy!" The two young women hugged each other fiercely and they were thirteen again. "I'm so glad you're okay. But you need to find your family. Go, let us deal with all this."

Romy stared at her friend, reluctant to leave her side.

Jian crouched down to help a man dig through a pile of bricks and rubble with his bare hands to reach a whimpering woman underneath. They grabbed her arms and pulled her out. Her cheongsam was shredded and blood ran in rivulets down her legs. Nina directed the men to lay the woman down gently, then, murmuring soothingly, started to clean her legs with a rag.

She turned to see Romy still standing there. "Go!" she shouted.

Chinese men and women from nearby laneways ran between the bodies, lugging lumpy mattresses from their own houses, carrying sheets for the injured. Others carried pots of steaming water and bowls of soup.

When Jian and Romy reached her lane it was a tall pile of smoldering rubble and blocked off by the police.

Romy froze. Japanese soldiers had been marshaled into a line and were marching out of an office building with machinery on their shoulders, hurrying it to another location.

"They're moving their radio and signals station in case the bombers come back," said Jian in disbelief.

"That's what the Americans must have been aiming for," said a man as he marched past with a pile of sheets. "They wouldn't deliberately hit this ghetto, would they?" Uncertainty and shock hung in the air.

About thirty bodies were lined up on the footpath, and nurses and doctors who had rushed to the scene moved along the row checking for pulses, doing their best to stem the flow of blood and treat injuries with the scant resources they had in hand. The man with the sheets walked behind, quickly covering dead bodies.

Romy ran up and down the line, searching for her parents and Shu. People crowded around the fallen, looking for their loved ones. Her gut twisted with relief when she reached the end of the line and there was no sign of her family. Or the Lams. Mutti and Papa were both scheduled at Ward Road Hospital this morning. If they hadn't already left for work when the bombs hit, they would have gone with Shu immediately, knowing they'd be needed. The Lams must be helping somewhere. Romy craned her head to look for her neighbors and double-check her parents weren't nearby. She was relieved they were not here among the smoke and debris. Little Shu's lungs would struggle to cope with this much dust.

Sirens wailed in the background as people all around them shouted and screamed for help.

Romy's feet were cemented to the footpath.

Medics ran between patients with bags of fluids and syringes. Japanese troops followed, bearing stretchers and medical kits. Romy had to get to work. She needed to help. It was as if she had to switch on a different engine—her body felt so numb. *This* was her duty.

Romy kneeled beside the young man closest to her and started to make a tourniquet for his arm. She glanced at the body of a young woman next to him—his wife, perhaps, or sister—and waved to a Japanese soldier for some morphine . . .

Romy was tapping the arm of an old man, trying to find a vein, when Jian appeared beside her.

He said, "The baby . . . Where is Shu?"

"I can't find them, so perhaps she is with my parents at the hospital. I'm trying to get to the Lams'. Can you please help find them? Tell them I'll be there as soon as possible. I'll come but I just—" She gestured at the old man she was treating. She couldn't just leave him. Jian ran off toward the Lams' house. Romy administered an injection, then gently placed the man's arm on the ground. "Your pain will be gone in a minute. Keep your eyes open."

She gestured to a Chinese woman who was walking between the patients, looking for someone to help.

"Could you please sit here for a minute and hold this man's hand?" She took the man's giant hand and placed it in the woman's tiny one. "I'll be just over there . . ."

Romy stood up and brushed rubble from her knees, then walked around the corner past two police officers who were lifting the seriously injured into rickshaws and pedicabs that would take them to the hospital.

Romy slowly stepped around the rubble and edged past the collapsed houses in her lane. Her eyes stung. With each step, she was pushed back by shouting police officers putting up barricades and Japanese soldiers carrying stretchers. She tried to pick her way around deep craters that pockmarked the road and coughed from all the smoke. Hair stuck to her sweaty face. Her parents were not among the line of dead bodies assembled at the end of *this* lane. But rescuers were still clearing the rubble, finding bodies under mountains of bricks—she couldn't be certain.

Her chest tightened and she started to wheeze when she saw a familiar form through the dust.

Jian was standing with a fellow policeman right where the Lams' house used to be. The policeman was shaking his head and pointing at the rubble—gesturing at something Romy couldn't see. Romy ran a few steps to get a better look at her house, and Jian reached for her hand.

"I'm so sorry," the policeman was saying. "The top floor of this house—plus the one next door—just collapsed. It was so fast and we were halfway through removing people." He gestured toward a row of bodies covered in filthy dust and ash lying on the footpath. Romy's Chinese neighbors were rolled on their sides, coughing or clutching an injured limb with loud cries. Others lay motionless.

Romy ran up and down the line of writhing bodies on the footpath, comforting three small Lam boys. She covered the round faces of Mr. and Mrs. Lam with a sheet so their children couldn't see the blood. She was trying to calculate who was alive and who might be inside. Did her parents go to the hospital? She kept having to restart her counting as other neighbors, nurses, and policemen crowded in to help. Bodies were lined up, wrapped, and bundled away.

"I'm sorry, Romy," said a red-eyed nurse she recognized from Ward Road Hospital as she rushed past holding a bleeding Lam toddler.

Romy continued along the line, sobbing for the dear Lam family who had opened their home and their hearts to the Bernfelds.

Romy stopped walking.

She was looking at a familiar pair of black shoes. Handmade by the finest bootmaker in Vienna, now worn thin with holes in the soles.

She stared at the feet for a moment, before finally daring to look at his face. There was a slight gash to the forehead. Papa looked peaceful, as if he were merely sleeping. But when she checked for the telltale rise of his chest, there was none.

Beside Papa, in a white uniform now stained red across the middle, was Mutti. She must have been getting ready to go to work.

Nine of the twelve members of the Lam family were laid out neatly in a row beside the Bernfelds. Several people from their laneway were crouched over the bloody, crushed, and contorted bodies, crying and waving fists at the sky.

Romy knelt down, placed her hands on her parents' foreheads, and closed her eyes. She tried to swallow, then sob, but her throat was dry. She rocked forward and placed her forehead on the ground and shuddered. With her next breath, she howled into the earth for so long she felt empty and her lungs ached. When she sat up, she looked to the sky and sobbed, *"Baruch dayan ha'emet."*

Jian looked at her and she repeated it for him in English: "Blessed is the true judge."

She looked around in a frenzy. Shu? Where was Shu?

She staggered to her feet, wiping her eyes with the hem of her dress. Spying a second row of bodies shrouded in sheets, Romy ran toward them and started peeling back the coverings one by one until she reached the end of the line. Hands trembling, she pulled back a small shroud and saw the tiniest baby with cherry lips, still sucking her thumb. Pale skinny legs, bent slightly at the knees. There was not a scratch or a mark. Shu looked like a sleeping angel.

Romy's knees collapsed beneath her and everything went black.

Chapter 66

SHANGHAI, JULY 18, 1945

When Romy awoke, she was lying on a lumpy mattress in a dim room. She tried to swallow, but her throat felt tight and raw.

"Here, have some water," said a familiar voice beside her as a hand slid under her neck to support her head. A metal cup touched her lips.

"Jian," she said.

The water soothed her throat, but almost immediately her stomach started to churn and she covered her mouth with her hand as she tasted bile.

Mutti, Papa. Shu. *Wilhelm.*

The tiny bird of a baby nestled in the crook of Wilhelm's arm.

It hurt to remember.

"Where am I?" she asked.

"You're safe," Jian reassured her. "My men checked to make sure that no one followed us. This is an apartment we keep for hiding people who need to disappear for a while." His arm was damp with sweat; traces of bitter gunpowder mingled with the sweeter allspice on his skin. She squeezed her eyes shut. The air was thick and steamy and each breath made her body ache.

"Tea?" he asked softly as she heard him pad to the corner of the room. "I just boiled some."

He came back and sat on the edge of the bed as she struggled to sit up.

He passed her a chipped blue china cup. "Careful, it's hot." He sipped his own tea from what looked like a glass jar.

"What happened?" Romy held her tea with both hands.

"You fainted," he explained. "You collapsed in front of Shu's body, but I caught you and laid you safely on the ground before I picked up Shu. I'm not sure how long I stood clutching her little broken body before Wu's men stepped out of the shadows and started asking questions." He paused and his cheeks reddened. "I'd been sobbing so much I hadn't noticed anyone approach." Jian paused.

"The Japanese Kempeitai had been watching me for weeks— alongside two of Chang Wu's men—thinking I would eventually lead them to Chang Wu's missing baby. Li's baby." Jian grimaced. "I didn't know any of this—though I suspected. Why else wouldn't they just kill me? Luckily they didn't know you were the one at the villa that day helping Li, otherwise . . ." He closed his eyes.

Romy's skin felt numb, her body hollow. She no longer feared death. With so many loved ones gone, it seemed futile to contemplate a future.

He opened his eyes and held Romy's gaze. "That's why I haven't been to see you."

"What happened next?" Romy croaked.

"Chang Wu's men wanted to know who the baby I was holding belonged to. The nurse beside us was flustered—annoyed at being pulled away from treating the injured—and snapped at Wu's men. The entire neighborhood was swarming on the footpath. Screaming . . . tripping over bodies . . . falling in holes.

"The hoodlums didn't even notice you on the ground, lying among the debris and the fallen. The nurse pressed them into service, instructing them to find a rickshaw and take three howling children—one with blood streaming down his forehead—straight to Ward Road Hospital. I think they were too surprised to object.

"The second they disappeared around the corner, I promised the nurse I'd take care of you and carried you away over my shoulder before anyone else came looking."

Romy wiped her tears away with the sleeve of her shirt, too distraught to speak. She thought of her parents' faces covered with soot and white plaster dust. Mutti's red lips. The worn soles of Papa's boots. The lines of broken, bloody bodies in the laneways.

"I'm sorry about Marta and Oskar," Jian said softly. "They were fine people."

Romy nodded as hot tears slid down her cheeks.

Jian took a sip of his tea. "Chang Wu had become fixated on Wilhelm—his connection to Li. My comrades told me he was furious. The *diulian*."

"Loss of face," said Romy, shaking her head.

Romy's head thrummed because she had lost face too. She'd offered her heart to Wilhelm, and he'd chosen another. She closed her eyes and remembered the catch in Wilhelm's breath as he'd pressed her against the worktable in the bakery and she'd wrapped her legs around him, the quiver in his hands as he slid them up her skirt. The yearning in his eyes outside her *lilong* that icy Chinese New Year.

Despite everything, she loved Wilhelm and wanted him to survive.

"Where's Wilhelm now?" she asked.

"Chungking." Nine hundred miles west of Shanghai, in the heart of China. "Probably on his way over the mountains to Calcutta. From there, we have military contacts who may be able to get him to Australia."

Romy squeezed her eyes shut. How could she tell him she'd failed him? She'd lost his beloved daughter.

Jian's voice softened. "You love him." It wasn't a question. "You were prepared to sacrifice yourself for this man, for his baby. For Li . . ." He sighed.

Romy touched her scalp. Her head was throbbing, or perhaps it was the sound of bombs falling nearby. The pounding in her ears was relentless.

"Do you have a headache?" he asked. "I put some camphor oil on it. And I have my needles." He reached beside the mattress and unrolled the leather pouch with his needles and the manuscript he was always working on at Dr. Ho's treatment rooms.

She reached out and ran her fingers over the script, admiring the fine calligraphy and accompanying ink sketches of cardamom buds and lotus roots.

"You kept it."

"It's my blood, my story," he said, looking wistful. "It's like Li's pendant. These are the things that connect us to those who came before." He bit his lip. "I'll never forgive myself for not saving Li. Why didn't she tell me the baby was coming that morning?"

"She wanted to protect you. She always did." Romy thought back to the dreamy boy with a camera, prodding and poking cockleshells, being lectured about duty by his father. "That's why she had you take her portrait, so you had enough money to survive."

He sighed. "She tried to keep me as far away from Chang Wu as possible." Tears dampened his eyes.

"She put all her energy into saving you, protecting Wilhelm, and saving her baby."

"I didn't do enough. I failed my duty."

"No," said Romy, looking Jian in the eyes. "That was her gift to you."

They sat in heavy silence.

"But you, Romy"—he gently reached for her chin and tilted her head so he was looking directly into her eyes—"you always had enough." He tapped his chest. "You always had enough in here. You absorb the energy of others around you. Your mother, the patients at the hospital . . . You're beautiful."

Romy snorted. Men didn't blink when she walked into a room.

His fingers stroked her cheek. "So much pain for you, Romy. I always watched you as a girl, sitting slightly to one side. You carried the weight of the world on your shoulders. You always have."

And when she looked up she saw admiration in those dark eyes.

Jian blushed, and she remembered the bashful boy with the long eyelashes and rosy cheeks among the peach blossoms all those years ago.

She put her head on his broad shoulder, nestling into his neck as though her head had always fit there. Her cheek rubbed against his sticky skin. Jian took the cup from her hand and placed it on the floor as they lay back on the thin mattress. She fell asleep to the rhythm of his chest rising and falling and thought, *This is all I have left in the world.*

Chapter 67

Alexandra stood in the middle of her sitting area and sank her bare feet into the blue Persian rug. She savored the air-conditioned calm of her sleek apartment while the hot, smoggy peak-hour traffic on Xinle Lu crawled past outside. As she'd walked along her street on her way home this evening, black luxury cars had honked and beeped in frustration at bicycles loaded with newspapers and burlap sacks, while rickshaws and pedestrians weaved nonchalantly among the traffic. Blue tarpaulins laid out on street corners were piled with lychees, mangosteens, and pomelos, while men on tricycles sold drinking coconuts straight from coolers.

Despite the cloying heat and chaos, Alexandra adored Shanghai. The majestic limbs of the old plane trees stretched across both sides of the street, green leaves casting a dappled light onto the store windows.

Since she'd left Zhang in Hong Kong, Alexandra had been counting the minutes till she saw him again. They were off to Cynthia and Lu's party tonight and her stomach buzzed with excitement. He had texted to say he was coming straight from the airport.

She pursed her lips and checked her red lipstick in the mirror one last time, running her hands over the bodice that hugged her curves until just below her hips, giving way to an ivory bias-cut silk skirt that fell to the floor. She adjusted the shoulder straps so her new art deco brooch sat just above her cleavage.

She turned sideways and snapped a photo, sending it to Kate.

Her phone pinged instantly with a reply. It was a photo of a pair of red rubber boots beside a metal bucket collecting drips that looked like they were coming from the ceiling. Kitchen cabinets in plastic wrapping were behind the boots—a little person had scrawled all over the wrapping with black marker. Kate's message read: *Wanna swap?*

Despite the chaos and cold, they both knew Kate wouldn't trade places for a second. She loved her job, was still mad about her husband, and adored her kids. She cherished their ramshackle bungalow so much she was nursing it back to life one leaky room at a time.

Alexandra felt the tentacles of envy seep into her bones and banished them just as quickly, embarrassed.

For so long Alexandra had *chosen* to be alone. Sure, she'd been with Hugo, but that was based on the thrill of the deal and the certainty that neither of them wanted to put down roots. They were both too haunted by family ghosts.

Zhang was completely different. Open, engaging, and decidedly untroubled.

She missed him. Life was richer yet less complicated when he was around. Could her future really be that simple if she stopped trying to analyze every risk?

When she'd tried on this dress in the vintage store yesterday, the sales assistant had clapped her hands and squealed.

"That's the one. It's perfect. Turn around and let me see the pearl cobweb across your back. They're real by the way"—her voice dropped—"as I guess you must have figured by the price tag!"

Alexandra had chuckled as she held the skirt up and watched it shimmer under the chandelier.

"It's from the thirties. The label here says *Old Hollywood*, but it's way too divine. It's art deco meets Miss Shanghai. When's the date?"

"Tomorrow night."

The shop assistant's eyes nearly popped out of her head. "You're kidding! You're buying your wedding dress the night before?"

Alexandra laughed so hard she thought she'd split the seams.

The shop assistant looked askance. "Did I say something?"

"No." Alexandra waved her hand. "It's just—it's not a wedding dress. As a matter of fact, it's for an Old Shanghai party over near Tianzifang."

"Well, it's perfect. Are you going with a boyfriend? Because trust me, when he sees you in this dress . . ."

"I'll take it," Alexandra had said quickly.

The doorbell rang, and she opened it to find Zhang holding a lush bouquet of white lilies, peonies, and roses interspersed with native grasses and bamboo and maple leaves. He was dressed in a white tuxedo, and his hair was slicked back with a part to one side.

She gasped and reached for the flowers as his eyes devoured her neckline.

Zhang whistled. "Well, this was worth flying over for." He pulled a lily out and tucked it behind her ear and then stepped close and kissed her. She pressed herself against his body, feeling his warmth. He smelled of citrus peel, cedar, and the earth, and she ran her hand inside his jacket, tracing his muscles through his shirt.

He stepped back to take another look at her, head cocked to one side. She slipped on her shoes and did a little twirl, feeling very silly and giddy. As she turned, he traced the lines of pearls on her back and she shivered.

"Mmm. I've missed you." He leaned in for another lingering kiss, holding the flowers above her head. "I'd better get these in some water and grab a cab. If I kiss you again that glamorous art deco number will be a goner."

"Plenty of time for that," she promised, but even as she said it, she felt a pang of regret. He'd be back on the plane to Hong Kong tomorrow afternoon. She wanted more time.

"There's a vase on the top shelf." She picked up the jade necklace she had left on the hallway table and fastened it around her neck. She'd removed it because she'd thought it might be too much with the crystal brooch, but she felt adrift without it.

Zhang was back beside her within the minute, acknowledging the pendant with a wink. "Let's go."

Chapter 68

SHANGHAI, JULY 25, 1945

Romy rubbed her cheek on a scratchy pillow. She drifted in and out of sleep, listening to voices outside her window. Russian, Polish, German, Japanese, and Shanghainese accents came and went, and she tried not to think about the mounds of rubble outside. She knew she should go and help. But every time she thought of Papa's face—his gray cheeks and crushed limbs—or Shu's rosebud lips, she found herself unable to move.

Shadows crept across the ceiling as the sun came and went.

Plates were left beside her bed. A thin soup—water with small cubes of turnip. Later, pot stickers and a few drops of drippings. A warm kaiser roll remained untouched because it reminded her of Wilhelm.

How many cups of tea had she sipped these last few days?

She sat up, and by the rusty glow on the ceiling she could tell it was dusk. The smell of fish stock and chrysanthemum tea drifted in the window and her stomach rumbled.

"How long have I been here?"

"A week. It's the shock." His voice was kind. It was the voice of his father.

"I'm sorry, I was cruel. I didn't realize . . ." Her voice faded. She didn't realize he had been looking out for his sister. For Shu and Romy. His sense of duty was as strong as ever.

She felt tears slide down her cheeks, and he reached out and put his palm against her face, wiping away her tears with his thumb. "Shhh, Romy," he said as he wrapped her in a hug. "To tell you I used my position with the police to get close to the Kempeitai would have placed you all in danger. We couldn't be sure of who supported the resistance. I didn't trust Wilhelm. I didn't trust anyone . . . only Li." Jian's voice was sad.

Romy swallowed.

"But Wilhelm's a good man. The father of my sister's baby—my family. I had to help him flee. Chang Wu suspects I was connected to Wilhelm. He's put a bounty on my head too." Jian sighed. "I'll be leaving for Chungking at first light tomorrow. I won't be able to come back to Shanghai. Not under the Japanese occupation."

"You can't leave!"

"It's all arranged. I depart tomorrow before dawn."

Romy pictured Dr. Ho's severed head on a spike in Frenchtown and fell back on the bed.

"If they find out what you've done, they'll kill you too," Romy said softly to the ceiling.

"Come with me," Jian urged.

Romy shook her head. "I can't. I can't leave Nina now. Besides, they need me at the hospital—there's so much illness and malnourishment. I have to help."

Jian nodded, understanding at once.

They lay on the pillow together, breathing in sync.

Jian was shirtless and Romy longed to press her cheek against his smooth chest and trail her fingers along the faint line of hair disappearing beneath his cotton trousers.

Her body was filled with yearning and confusion. For so long she'd dreamed of being with Wilhelm. She loved him still. Perhaps, if she hadn't been so cautious, so keen to be with him the right way, to find the right space—if she'd lived more in the moment and worried less about rules. If she'd been more like Li . . .

She'd dreamed of kissing Jian when she was younger.

But what she felt now was far more primal, more powerful. Any residual doubt and confusion she'd had about Jian's role in Li's death had vanished. Wilhelm had been gone for weeks. Romy was overtaken by a desire to feel alive. To feel something other than loss.

She lay staring at the ceiling in the stifling room, listening to every breath.

Out of the corner of her eye, she noticed Jian start to doze. How many hours had he lain awake watching over her, waiting to protect her from an intruder?

She tentatively rested her head on his chest and went back to sleep.

When she awoke, Romy rolled over and moved close to Jian, gently tucking her head under his neck so her chin rested on his chest. He took a breath and wrapped his arm around her. It was sticky and dripping with sweat.

She traced a line down the center of Jian's rib cage. His eyes remained closed, but his chest twitched. Something shifted beneath his pants. He sighed, and she felt his hot breath exhale into her hair.

She kept exploring his sticky torso with her hands, tracing the lines of his abdominal muscles, running her fingers over his dark nipples and watching them harden. Something was stirring in her stomach and lower in her groin, and she wanted to press against him. Feel connected. Blot out her loneliness and loss.

She took a deep breath and rolled on top of Jian, straddling him and sliding her dress above her thighs so she could feel him through her cotton underwear. She moved as if she were in a half dream, not daring to believe she would do this if she were awake.

He groaned and opened his eyes, putting his hands on her shoulders.

"Romy," he said, dark eyes locked on hers. "We can't. You're hurt. This is shock."

She moved above him with a shy grin, and he dropped his head back on the pillow as he wrapped his arms around her and pulled her close for a hug. His hands lingered at her shoulders, as if trying to make a decision.

They both took deep breaths, rocking gently against each other.

Giving in to his instinct, Jian ran his hands down the length of her back and rested them at the base of her spine. He pressed her downward against him, before bringing one hand back up to brush her damp hair away. Jian stretched up for a lingering kiss.

He tasted of black tea. The kiss was gentle. Soft, but thirsty. She kissed him deeper and harder as they pressed against each other, clinging for comfort.

Slowly, she reached down and untied the knot of his pants, then slid them off, after which he gently, reverently, slid the dress over her head as she held her arms in the air.

She shivered with nerves.

"Romy," he whispered as he buried his head in her breasts and unfastened her bra at the back. She wriggled out of her sagging gray underpants.

They rocked together, finding a natural rhythm.

Jian brushed the hair off her face, paused, and asked: "Are you sure?"

Romy nodded. She loved Jian. She wanted him—she always had.

He looked deep into Romy's eyes as he threw his head back and groaned, never breaking her gaze. "Romy, I love you—I always have," he said as the moonlight rippled across the ceiling.

Chapter 69

SHANGHAI, AUGUST 27, 2016

As they stepped from the cab into the steaming night, Zhang placed his hand on the small of her back and said, "Your dress is perfect for the party. Very Old Shanghai." A sea of people wandered around the raised promenade along the Bund, their gazes moving between the line of grand old European-style buildings on one side of the Huangpu River and the dazzling skyscrapers disappearing into clouds on the other. Everyone was taking selfies. A sizzling barrel of plump *sheng jian bao*—crispy on the bottom and pillowy soft on top—filled the street with the scent of caramelized pork and fennel seed. Alexandra's mouth watered, but she didn't dare buy a dumpling for fear the soup inside would drip onto her dress.

Alexandra and Zhang walked through revolving doors into the cool gold and marble-domed lobby of the Fairmont Peace Hotel. The room was bathed in golden light and filled with the fruity aroma of hundreds of dusky pink lotus flowers piled into vases on the central table.

"This dome matches your dress," Zhang said, laughing.

Alexandra studied the ceiling. "My grandmother stayed here once. She used to rave about the food. Lots of ladies who lunched here in the glory days, apparently. Champagne from six—in the morning!"

"I can't ever see you doing that!"

"Oh, I don't know. I'm thinking I might have a bit more time . . . Maybe I'll get a new job!"

"Really?" He wrinkled his nose. "I hope it's not because of what I said. I didn't mean . . ." Zhang paused. "What I mean is, I think you are wonderful just the way you are."

Alexandra's cheeks burned as she said, "Thank you."

He plucked a tight bud that seemed painted with soft pink at the tip and placed it in his top pocket, beside his lapel. As they stepped into the elevator he adjusted the lotus bloom and leaned toward her. "I never get tired of that sweetness. You know, lotus for me means summer. Also, purity. It's a miracle that something so perfect grows from the mud." Zhang laced his fingers with hers and squeezed. The hair on Alexandra's arms stood on end. She looked up at Zhang, who gave her a wink—as if he could read her mind.

They stepped out of the elevator onto a packed rooftop terrace with the shimmering lights of the Bund as the backdrop. The party was in full swing. A jazz band played on a small stage in the far corner, and a stunning woman in a gold cheongsam sang in a low husky voice as her finger trailed up the stem of the microphone. Waitresses dressed as showgirls swirled around the room.

A champagne fountain flowed, filling coupe glasses on a central table. Decadent chandeliers and vases of lotus flowers added sparkle and magic.

"*There* you are," said Cynthia as she gathered them both in a tight hug. "I'm so pleased you made it."

Lu kissed Alexandra. "Wow!" He raised his eyebrows as she twisted to show him the web of pearls at the back before he shook Zhang's hand.

"Here, try these." Cynthia grabbed two pink drinks from a waitress. "Lychee and ginger martinis."

"*Ganbei!*" They clinked glasses.

Cynthia looked stunning in a figure-hugging black chiffon dress with a thigh-high split. Her nails were black with gold half-moons, and her hair was set in tight curls. While most of the women wore extravagant feather hats and fur shrugs, Cynthia kept it simple with a crystal-beaded headpiece.

As they sipped cocktails, Lu started to laugh as he tried to keep his fake mustache stuck on. "Oh, just lose it," Cynthia said, smiling. She ripped it off and gave him a kiss on the lips as she raised her glass. "To Shanghai. Old and new."

"To Shanghai." They clinked glasses again and Zhang stepped closer to Alexandra, wrapping an arm around her waist.

"Come inside," said Cynthia. "I want to show you the poster of our girl all grown up."

They stepped inside as the singer switched to a broody jazz tune that suited the dark wood-paneled room. More oversized chandeliers dripped and sparkled from the ceiling, and towers of flushing lilies, roses, orchids, and lotus flowers stopped Alexandra in her tracks.

"This room!" she gasped. "It's magnificent."

"Thanks to Zhang. He organized the flowers from the markets— *then* sent someone to arrange them for us."

Zhang ducked his head modestly. Alexandra ran her fingers over a piece of red silk embroidered with gold calligraphy that was wrapped around the central vase.

"These banners are traditionally used for Chinese New Year," explained Cynthia.

Zhang stepped closer to the calligraphy. "It's another riddle. That's an upside-down character. So an upside-down *Fu* means that the sender hopes good luck will arrive on your doorstep. Good fortune."

"Very thoughtful. Let's hope it brings some prosperity too." Cynthia reached for Lu's hand. "I already have the good fortune."

Lu beamed and took another sip of his drink.

Between the flowers were seven life-sized colored posters designed to look like Calendar Girls.

"These are the seven great singers in Shanghai of the thirties and forties."

The first was a soft-focus close-up of an oval porcelain face, wavy hair pinned back just like Cynthia's, diamond earrings falling onto the silver collar of a cheongsam.

"White Rainbow," said Lu. "Her hit single was 'He Is Like the Spring Wind.'"

"Indeed," said Zhang as they stepped to the next photo.

A sassy woman stood sideways with her hair pulled tight off her face in a ponytail, cascades of curls streaming down her back. Her ebony eyes dared you to blink first.

"Golden Voice," said Lu. "She was a feisty one too." He looked at Cynthia fondly and she stood on her toes and gave her husband a peck on the cheek.

The third photo was of a woman in a yellow cheongsam embroidered with blue roses, reclining on a large wicker chair and exposing a large part of her upper thigh. She held a mandolin on her lap, and an orchard of cherry blossoms flowed into the distance behind her.

"They called her Queen of the Nasal Voice," said Cynthia, and Alexandra chuckled.

"It was a thing, back in the day," explained Lu. "More nasal, more dough. Now, this is your girl from the blossom photo. Li Ho."

The photo's focus was softened at the edges, so it looked like a painting. The subject was a beautiful woman with a high forehead and regal nose wearing a plunging V-neck dress dotted with crystals. Layers of ruffled sleeves poured from the shoulders and three rows of pearls were slung lazily across her modest chest. Her hair was pinned in a bob, and she wore a dazzling pearl-and-crystal headband, like a beaded chain, across her forehead. She was staring directly at the camera. Proud. Sitting in a high-backed peacock cane chair, lips slightly parted. An open fan sat demurely just under her chin and she was smiling, two deep dimples giving her an impish charm.

There was no mistaking the jade pendant—etched with a lily—sitting at the base of her throat. It was Alexandra's pendant.

"Yu Baihe—she's my favorite," said Cynthia.

"The Jade Lily," said Lu. "Some say she was a Japanese collaborator, but I'm not so sure."

Alexandra was too shocked to speak. Instead, she stepped toward the photo and touched the pendant.

"Those eyes look pretty haunted to me . . ."

"That deep brown—they're your eyes," said Zhang softly as he turned to face Alexandra.

Everyone stared between the photo and Alexandra as the music changed to a swing.

Alexandra was a little dizzy and confused. "I need to go—" She was about to say "home," but it struck her that she was no longer sure where home was. She'd been in Shanghai only a short time and it was supposed to be a limited placement. She looked from Cynthia and Lu to Zhang and felt for the first time in ages that she wasn't alone. She wanted to stay.

But first, she needed closure. For her mother, but also for herself. She wanted to understand her history. The truth would eliminate the well of uncertainty and grief she'd carried since Opa's death, she was sure of it.

"I need to go to Melbourne. I need to tell Oma I found my other grandmother." Oma must have been given the child for safekeeping, surely. But, then, what did she really know of Oma's life in Shanghai?

Zhang put his arm around her shoulders and she nestled against him. Alexandra looked up at Zhang and knew what she had to do.

"Will you come home with me? Please . . ." She reached for his hand. "I don't want to do this alone."

Chapter 70

Something was afoot in Hongkew.

The ghetto was almost silent. People were pouring from their tiny *lilongs* onto the streets, faces creased with anxiety. The Japanese soldiers were nowhere to be seen.

Romy pulled her coat collar close around her neck. The sky was charcoal and a few dirty brown leaves were stuck to the sidewalk. Refuse choked the gutters. Her stomach churned and she put her hand to her mouth to stop herself from throwing up. She'd had black tea this morning, not daring to take the extra minutes to go downstairs and outside into the frost to prepare congee. Even the smell of soy sauce and noodles made her retch.

It had been seven painful weeks since the Lams' *lilong* had been bombed—since Wilhelm, and then Jian, had disappeared. The thud of bombs and gunfire had been constant in that time.

Romy spent her days just putting one foot in front of the other, working at the hospital, tending to the surviving Lam children along with all the others injured in the July bombings. Jian had left for Chungking, but there was no news, of course.

Bereft, Romy had run to her childhood friend and fallen into her arms. Nina had insisted Romy move into her room. Romy wanted to pay for everything and take care of Nina so she wouldn't have to go out at night, but Nina wouldn't have it.

"You have no idea how much I eat, young lady." She'd winked, pushed up her ample breasts, and poked Romy's hips. "I'll bring you some cheese and meat."

The two girls shared a mattress but each had her own blanket. Nina was out most nights and Romy worked all day, so they slept in shifts in the bed. On the nights they were both home, they curled together like two kittens, each soothed by the other's company. Nina kept her word—there was always a tin of hard white cheese and delicious salamis. Occasionally she brought home smoked duck. Romy felt guilty eating it, but Nina insisted.

"Would you like to sit and watch me eat, *sturer Bock*?"

Romy had to laugh at being called a stubborn goat.

She immersed herself in the rhythm of her days, rising at dawn to boil them both a bowl of thin congee, working at the hospital cleaning and nursing, then tossing and turning through the night on their musty straw mattress, trying to flee from her ghosts.

Sometimes she'd awake drenched in sweat, dreaming she'd been in Jian's and Wilhelm's arms. Their bodies and faces merged with alarming regularity.

Romy filled her days with hard, meaningful work so at night she could collapse into bed exhausted. Yet her mind wouldn't rest. She'd bury her head in a pillow to block the scent of gasoline and blood. In these dreams, she cut her feet and knees as she crawled over glass.

Sometimes, Benjamin or Daniel would step forward from the mist, their hollow faces covered in blood. Mutti and Papa stood behind her brothers, arms linked with the Hos. Desperate. Always, there were Wilhelm and Jian, one's broad shoulders merging with the other's slim hips and delicate wrists, a jumble of melting figures tearing at her clothes and haunting her until she woke . . .

When she wasn't working at the hospital or helping Delma at the soup kitchen, she'd hide under the stairwell at Nina's with her textbooks and a few pumpkin seeds—sometimes with a ginger cat warming her feet for company.

Men sat on cartons, playing cards and rolling dice while their rickshaws sat idle nearby. As Romy walked past a narrow lane, a handful of Chinese and Jewish children jostled one another with their elbows and shins as they played a game of soccer. The ball shot out in front of her.

"Sorry, missee," said a round-faced Chinese child, his face streaked with dirt.

Romy smiled, took a running start, and kicked the ball back to him, just like Daniel had taught her.

She quickened her pace—careful to avoid footpaths pitted with the rough dugouts the Chinese locals had been forced to dig as bomb shelters. Not that they did much good, she thought bitterly. In the weeks since Jian had disappeared, she'd worked through the night at Ward Road Hospital, resetting legs, arms, and collarbones for men, women, and children who'd accidentally stumbled into the bunkers in the dark.

There was such a limited amount of ether that she'd taken Jian's medicine kit to work. For the past two days she had been treating a girl's torn knee ligament with needles around her elbow to get the blood circulating. She'd used the same acupuncture technique for a Polish man whose ankles were so swollen they had completely disappeared. And a young woman laboring with twins insisted the two curled needles in each earlobe helped ease the intensity of her contractions.

For the wards filled with malaria patients, Romy had boiled up a decoction of sweet wormwood for them to sip. She also kept tall pots of boiling water in each room for the patients writhing with cholera and dysentery. Fluids were all she could offer.

The Japanese were struggling to hold their position. The Americans had cut off all the main trade routes to China. Eggs and bread could cost the best part of a day's wages. There was no fuel, so cars lay abandoned wherever they stopped. Reports of a new type of bomb used by the Americans in Japan had been in the newspapers for weeks. She and Delma had discussed the bombs at length as the reported injuries were horrific.

"The Japanese are calling it *pikadon*. Giant bombs exploded in the air like lightning." Delma had leaned in over her coffee in their corner booth at Café Louis as she spoke in a low voice. "One in Hiroshima. Another in Nagasaki."

Romy prayed Shanghai would not be next. Everyone did.

Delma shifted in her seat and smoothed her already neat hair back into her bun. Then she picked up her spoon and stirred her coffee—even though she had not been able to afford sugar for months. The *ting-ting* of the tap of her spoon against the lip of the cup rang between them. She put the spoon down, leaned back in the chair, and let out an exhausted sigh.

Romy picked up her coffee and drained the cup of lukewarm grit. She spluttered and puckered her mouth.

"Sorry," said Delma. "We have to make the grounds last the whole week."

"I think we'll have the tea next time," Romy murmured.

"I have news of the liberation in Poland and Germany." Delma's somber tone suggested it was anything but good. "I've still heard nothing of my brothers in Auschwitz . . ."

Romy reached for her friend's hand.

"What about Wilhelm?" she asked. "I haven't heard anything. Did he—?"

"Wilhelm crossed into India," Delma replied. "He was shot, but he's fine. Scraped his shin. More lives than a cat, that one." She shook her head with a half laugh. "He may travel from there to England or Australia in a special envoy military plane."

"And Jian?"

A pause. "We haven't heard anything, Romy. I'm sorry."

◇

People were starting to shout and gather in the streets, knocking her shoulders as they ran past or jumped for joy on the spot. Above the nervous chatter she heard a woman shout: "Ceasefire!" A hunched old rabbi scratched his beard and straightened his jacket as he shot Romy a bewildered look.

"Are we . . . free?"

Romy caught her breath and replied, "I'm not sure."

The crowd of soccer players scooted past on the footpath, almost bowling her over as they ran screaming into the courtyard apartments where their parents squatted over boiling pots of stock and rice. "Mama, Papa, have you heard—"

Romy pulled her bag close to her hip, protecting her body from stray knocks. "What's going on?" she asked.

"The *Tung yang ning* have gone! The war is over!" shouted a young boy in rags and bare feet as his much larger friend shimmied up a wooden telegraph pole and tore down the sign reading: STATELESS REFUGEES ARE NOT ALLOWED TO PASS.

Before he jumped down, the larger boy glanced around to check he wasn't going to get a beating, then the two boys scurried off into the jubilant crowd.

People were pouring out of doors and alleyways now, hugging, dancing, and crying. Chinese mothers jiggled babies on their hips and hugged their Jewish neighbors. A piano accordion and a mandolin started to play at the far end of the street.

"Hey, there's no one at the police station!" yelled a man above the crowd.

"They're really gone!" whooped another.

Romy allowed herself to be swept up in the jubilation, dancing a few steps to a violin waltz before stopping.

Where was she going? After all this time, her luck had held and she had made it through the war.

Her stomach fluttered and churned with loss and sadness as people cheered and stomped and clapped each other on the back. Hats were tossed into the air.

A stunning woman emerged from a side doorway, head down and coiffed red hair spilling over her face as she tied a white silk kimono around her body. She stepped into the street in little silk slippers and glanced around in surprise as if she'd just woken up and couldn't believe the Japanese had left.

Then she flipped her hair off her face and her brown eyes met Romy's. Her lips curled into a smile.

"It's over!" Romy cried as she took Nina's hand and they danced around as they had all those years ago at the Cathay.

"The war is over?" Nina's eyes looked like they were about to pop out of her head.

"Come. We need to find Delma. We need to celebrate. Besides," she added, "I have some news of my own."

Chapter 71

Alexandra poured boiling water from the kettle into a teapot stuffed with a handful of fresh mint and took a moment to breathe in the steam and calm herself. She leaned against the worn wooden island and counted to sixty.

Though it was Romy who was lying on the sofa needing care, she'd sent her granddaughter into the kitchen for tea with instructions to inhale the steam for a minute. Satisfied she'd followed Oma's instructions, Alexandra took one last deep breath and loaded up the tray with the croissants and the raspberry jam in a silver pot with matching spoon, then carried it into Puyuan's sitting room.

She poured tea into green Chinoiserie teacups and passed a cup to Nina before taking another across to the window seat, where she collapsed into the cushions. Romy dozed on the sofa, a navy woolen blanket pulled up under her chin.

"I don't want to wake her," said Alexandra, longing to stroke Romy's translucent papery skin.

Her *oma* looked peaceful—the tightness that normally lingered across her brow had eased.

Nina walked over with her tea to stand beside Alexandra on the window seat. "You weren't to know your grandmother would have a fall. None of us were." She raised her eyebrows and shrugged. "And we'd just paid for our next hiking trip up in the High Country." She rocked back and forth with her hands on her hips—she needed to stretch.

Alexandra couldn't help but smile at the prospect of the two of them trailing a buff mountain guide, shuffling up the hill, side-stepping when it got too steep, and using the walking poles to help them along.

Romy stirred and eyed the warm croissants. "Breakfast. You are spoiling me, Alexandra."

Nina had already prepared a plate with a thumbnail-sized piece of soft cheese, a sliver of prosciutto, and half a slice of rye bread.

Romy and Alexandra eyed each other. Alexandra waited for Oma to speak.

"So, why this rush from Shanghai?" Romy paused, eyes dancing. "I didn't tell you about my ankle, but it's fine." She shot Nina an accusing look. "Nina and I have the mah-jongg competition tomorrow. I suspect your sudden return is not due to an urge to score?"

Alexandra glanced through the window at Zhang, who was down on his knees weeding in the garden. The winter kale curled in a dark and luscious dance above his head.

Smiling, she turned back to Romy.

"You love him," said Romy.

"How could she not?" said Nina, chuckling as she watched Zhang roll up the sleeves of his shirt.

But before she could face her own future, and the family she dared to hope for, Alexandra needed some questions answered. The same ones her mother had asked.

But mostly I wonder: Did they love me?

Because if they did, then why did they give me away?

No more secrets.

Alexandra took a deep breath and pulled out the faded Calendar Girl photo of Li Ho that Cynthia had kindly given her. She placed it on the old oak coffee table and ran her hands over it to flatten the corners.

Nina and Oma exchanged a look.

Alexandra tapped Li's neck. "Oma, that's my necklace." She touched a hand to the pendant around her throat. "Isn't it?"

Romy ran her fingers over the photograph, her eyes filling with tears. Nina passed her a tissue. A guttural, animal noise burst from Romy's lips, startling Alexandra.

Not quite a groan, the noise sat somewhere between relief and anguish. Her thin shoulders hunched.

Alexandra regretted bringing the photo. She held her breath.

Her grandmother leaned over and began to sob so hard Alexandra thought she might break in half.

Alexandra walked over to the sofa and wrapped her grandmother in a hug.

"Oma, what is it?"

A beat.

Romy wiped her nose, collecting herself. Nina moved across the room to stand behind the sofa and placed a hand on Romy's shoulder.

"It's time, Romy. Wilhelm's gone—bless his soul." Nina looked at the ceiling. "What good can come of this secret now?" Her voice was coaxing, encouraging.

Romy blew her nose and nodded. "You're right." And she reached out to touch the pendant, before stroking Alexandra's cheek. "You are so like her," she whispered.

"You knew her." Alexandra produced the photo of the two girls standing by the trees. "This was with Mum's stuff."

Romy raised an eyebrow. "I thought I'd gone mad. Your mother must have taken it." She shook her head. "Li Ho was my neighbor and dear, dear friend." She sighed. "She was beautiful. A light brighter than the rest of us put together."

Nina coughed, rolled her eyes, sat on the sofa beside Alexandra, and straightened her kaftan as she shifted in her seat.

"What happened?"

"She was killed. Shot. There was no escape. I—I tried . . ."

Alexandra felt herself go perfectly still.

"She lived with a gangster—to keep her brother alive," Romy continued softly. "I delivered her baby. She was bleeding out, the soldiers were breaking the door down. She begged me to take her daughter. I promised I'd look after her. Take her to her real father and hide her from the horrid man she lived with."

Romy's voice was raspy, her hands shaking as she lifted her tea for a sip.

Alexandra's hand moved to her pendant and she gave it a stroke. "And the necklace?" she whispered, fearful of the answer.

"She ripped it from her neck and bade me to give it to her daughter at a time when it could not be traced back to her."

Alexandra was just about to ask when she'd given the daughter the necklace when Romy turned to face her and clasped both her hands.

"There's something I should have shown you a long time ago. Nina, can you get me the box, please?"

Nina looked from Romy to Alexandra and said, "I *told* you . . ."

"Nina—" Romy's voice was a mix of exasperation and defeat. She shook her head. "Please?"

Nina left Romy and Alexandra snuggling deeper into the sofa and shuffled into the kitchen. When she returned, she was holding a brown mahogany box. She placed two envelopes on Alexandra's lap.

Alexandra opened the first envelope. Inside was a birth certificate issued by the Jewish Hospital, Ward Road, Hongkew.

Mother: Li Ho
Father: Wilhelm Cohen

Alexandra gasped. Wilhelm had had a baby girl during the war. Her mum wasn't adopted at all. Opa was her real grandfather. That explained her special connection with him. All those hours studying. It was like she always knew . . . Her face flushed with pleasure.

"Yes. He was the father of Li's child. Even as a mewling newborn, she had the same magnetic focus as her mother. Unmistakable." Romy paused and closed her eyes, as if summoning the strength to keep talking. She tapped the second envelope gently with her finger but didn't open it.

"But that baby died in 1945 when the Americans bombed the ghetto. I was going to my lesson, and the chaos . . ." She paused. "There were soldiers everywhere. So much blood. I tried to save—" Her voice broke and she took a deep breath and gathered herself. "There were so many . . ."

"Was this the same bombing in which your parents were killed?" Alexandra remembered Romy telling her that story many years ago.

"Yes. Li and Wilhelm's baby, Shu, was also killed." She gave an anguished cry and covered her face with her hands. "I promised to keep her safe, but I failed—"

"*Ach*," comforted Nina. "Your family cherished that baby, Romy. You *know* this. She was loved." It was clear from Nina's voice that they had discussed this many times over the years.

Alexandra gasped. "You were there, Nina?"

Nina nodded. "Your grandmother didn't stop moving that day. Working alongside the Japanese soldiers, slinging patients over her shoulders, holding their hands and easing their pain as they—" She stopped.

When she spoke again, her tone was far softer. "You can't imagine the chaos. The carnage. We were still in danger, but Romy . . . They say war brings out the worst in humans. In your grandmother, I saw only the best."

Romy looked at Alexandra, the hurt so fresh in her brown eyes. "I wasn't prepared for a child. I was just nineteen myself. There was so little food. The Lams fed her rice milk." She hesitated. "I thought it was for the best. Papa signed her birth certificate. For Li. He adored her—we all did. And Wilhelm, well, you know what a good man he was."

She covered her face with her hands and started sobbing again.

"What is it, Oma? What is it you're not telling me?"

"My biggest regret. I lied to Wilhelm. I had a baby too. Nina and I were on our way to Australia and we were held up in Hong Kong. We stayed at the Peninsula for just over ten months." She reached for Nina's hand. "Nina helped me deliver the baby. And a doctor . . ." She paused, as if to add something, then decided against it. She exhaled. "The father—your grandfather—was Jian Ho. Li's brother."

"Jian Ho?" Alexandra echoed. She told Oma of the old treatment rooms in Tianzifang, and Cynthia's discovery that Dr. Jian Ho had been a political prisoner for four decades in Chongqing. He'd been caught trying to escape Shanghai and, after the war ended, he was convicted of being a Japanese collaborator.

The three women sat on the sofa, holding hands as long-guarded secrets and memories both happy and sad tumbled out and filled the room. Sometimes Oma's voice would waver and Alexandra worried it was too hard on her grandmother to relive such sorrow. But then Nina would interrupt, describing the apricot torte at Café Louis in Hongkew and the American soldiers she'd danced with at the Cathay until all three women were hoarse from laughing as well as crying.

Alexandra looked at the flickering candle on the mantelpiece. A candle had been burning there for as long as she could remember. A burning light for Romy's loved ones. Another child lost to war.

Alexandra held Oma's gaze, trying to digest all her grandmother had just revealed. So many secrets.

"I read your diary, Oma. I keep reading it. You both lost your families and witnessed such terrible things." Alexandra shook her head. She looked at the two women. She understood now why they never spoke about the war and the hardships of life in Shanghai. "How did you . . ." She paused, not quite sure how to phrase her question.

"You want to know how we stay so *fabelhaft*?" Nina shimmied in her seat. She was wearing a fuchsia kaftan and hooped earrings. Even at eleven in the morning she was dressed for cocktails.

Romy snorted. "Speak for yourself. I'm more dummkopf!" She gestured at her injured ankle. "It's like our friend Delma wrote to us back in 1948. Can you pass me her letter, please, Nina?"

Her friend rummaged in the box and handed over a brownish letter as thin as tissue paper.

Romy lifted the half-moon glasses that hung on a cord around her neck and started to read. "This was not long after Delma settled in America and had started working for the Red Cross."

I remember my time in Shanghai—Little Vienna—with gratitude. While our people were destitute, I think of what my family had to endure in those German and Polish death camps. The hollow faces and lines of bodies I see in the newspapers haunt me. I have stopped reading the stories, but I cannot look away from the images. People knee-deep in excrement as if they were cattle lining up for slaughter. Enough!

I have no news of my brother, or my parents. I don't know if I shall ever find out what became of them but I shall keep trying. I have found answers for others and it is always bittersweet.

I try to honor those left behind by taking new steps in this country. I will stay strong and healthy. Eva and I are happy enough with our new life in Chicago. We are lucky.

"You see, *Liebling*. We made so many mistakes—"

Nina tutted and smoothed her kaftan out across her legs. "Speak for yourself!"

"Stop interrupting!" Romy scolded. "We can't choose what happens to us. But we can choose how we respond."

Alexandra embraced both women. *She* was the lucky one.

She tapped on the window to attract Zhang's attention. He stood and brushed the dirt off the front of his pants, tilting his head to one side. She beckoned him to come in.

A few minutes later he joined them in the sitting room. "Everything all right?"

Romy picked up the red envelope and pulled out the page with the painted calligraphy symbol. *Fu.* It was a message sending good luck and good fortune. It had arrived mysteriously in the post about twenty years after Romy had migrated to Australia.

"He knew," said Alexandra.

"Yes," said Romy. "Jian was a wonderful, wonderful man."

Chapter 72

MELBOURNE, FEBRUARY 11, 1947

Romy pressed against Nina's shoulder as they lined up at the gangplank to disembark from the *Hwa Lien*. White seagulls swooped and cawed overhead, gliding on a whiff of breeze through the flat blue sky. One swooped low and nipped a cracker clean out of a little girl's hand as she reached out to her mother. Her tiny mouth made a surprised O, before her brown eyes spilled over with tears.

The crowd crammed on the foredeck shuffled and murmured in sympathy as they baked in the midmorning sun.

Romy squeezed Nina's hand, remembering the last time they'd done this—when they were really just girls. They hadn't known then, of course, that when the time came for them to set sail from the brown waters of the Yangtze they'd cry for the rice terraces and bombed-out factories along the shore. That just as they'd left loved ones in Austria, pieces of their heart would forever be scattered in Shanghai.

Romy shifted Sophia to her other hip—she was heavy for just ten months, and her ruddy face and broad torso made her look like a toddler. She reached down and squeezed her daughter's calf before tickling her all the way up to the back of her knee. Sophia threw her head back and giggled, revealing deep dimples on both cheeks. Romy's stomach flipped. Sophia was the spitting image of her aunt.

The giggles petered out and the child tilted her head and squinted as her eyes tried to adjust to the harsh light beating down on the foredeck. She rubbed her eyes with both fists and snuggled her head between Romy's breasts. Romy placed a protective hand over Sophia's head to shade her. The future was in her hands. Australia would be a fresh start for them all. She was twenty-one.

Nina pulled a silk fan from her handbag and started to flutter it like a madwoman, tutting and cursing as she brushed sweaty strands of hair from Sophia's red cheeks. Nina's mascara was smudged down one cheek and her rouge had melted.

Romy watched the sailors start to usher passengers down the gangplank.

"Careful now, bit of a step there, ma'am."

"Over that way to customs, sir."

"No English? I see. Take this form."

An official pointed toward a sign: IMMIGRATION.

Romy watched rows of shoulders square themselves and move ashore. Passengers dressed for the occasion wore smart jackets and their best shirts, dark patches of sweat on the backs, circles under the arms. Melbourne lacked the humidity of the tropics; instead the day hummed with a dry heat and warm wind, even though it was not yet midday.

On the dock stood a handful of officials holding up signs alongside Anzacs with slouch hats. She slowly scanned the crowd, swatting flies from Sophia's face, when she suddenly stopped.

Romy gasped.

"What?" said Nina, perplexed, as she turned her head to shore.

Romy felt her heart quicken as Nina said, "Oh, Romy . . ."

Wilhelm was standing on the dock in smart blue pants and a crisp white shirt with the sleeves rolled up, waving both hands above his head to catch their attention. Even from this distance, Romy could see his lopsided smile. The line of his broad shoulders.

Her lungs tightened, seared with this strange hot air and guilt. She *promised* to deliver his daughter. His future. And she'd failed him, just like she'd failed Li.

She clutched Sophia tight to her chest; the heat had made the baby drowsy.

As they stepped off the gangplank, Romy and Nina ignored the Australian officials speaking English with strange vowels flattened by the heat. With polite nods they accepted multiple flyers in German instructing them on how to register, offering English lessons, hostels, and boardinghouses. Nina opened the clasp of her handbag and stuffed them inside before closing it with a click.

Romy struggled to maintain eye contact with Wilhelm over the bobbing heads of the crowd.

The joy in his eyes made Romy's heart flutter all over again, but she admonished herself for daring to hope. She had her child and that was enough. She mustn't be greedy.

She looked at the hollow faces in the queues around her—all skeletons in faded suits who were unprepared for this harsh sunlight and wide blue sky. The air was clear. Fresh. Not a trace of the dusty smog and gas they'd left behind. No hint of frying fish or sweet spices either.

Romy inhaled through her nose and took another deep breath. There were traces of something cutting. Lemon rind and menthol. A blossom perhaps. Sharper. Maybe it was this strange eucalyptus she'd heard people speak of during the voyage. She closed her eyes and took this sharp scent deep into her lungs along with the salt and seaweed.

Wherever she was safe with Sophia would be home. Family was home.

Beyond the fence, a handful of protesters were waving placards.

GO HOME REFOS

WE WANT A WHITE AUSTRALIA

DON'T LET CROOKS TAKE OUR JOBS

She handed their landing permits to the customs official and held her breath as he peered at Sophia with a grim expression.

"This one here is Sophia Shu Cohen?"

"Yes, sir," said Romy, not trusting herself to say more.

Sophia cooed and tried to rip off the bonnet Romy had jammed tight and low on her head to mask the mass of black hair.

"And it says you have all been granted special refugee passage. You know someone with a business in Australia who sponsored you, eh? You're lucky."

Romy politely ignored the rabble with their signs shouting louder. "That's correct. There he is." She pointed to where Wilhelm was standing with a handful of paperwork beside an immigration officer on the other side of the gates.

The queue behind them was also getting noisy as people grew restless in the heat.

"Well, we'd better not keep the little one in this heat, had we?" He pinched Sophia's sweaty cheek and she smiled from under the deep brim of her hat.

As he stamped the landing permits Romy thought her legs might give way.

"Welcome to Australia, ladies." He eyed Nina up and down. "You *may* be able to apply for Australian citizenship in five years—if you are eligible."

Nina squeezed Romy's hand as they stepped through the gate into their new home.

Wilhelm had pushed through the crowd so he was standing right behind the large black customs gates marking entry to Australia. His shoulders looked broader and his face was tanned. He took off his gray felt hat and waved it above the crowds.

"Romy! Over here! Romy Bernfeld!"

She walked toward the gates with Nina following close behind. Wilhelm rushed over and enclosed both her and Sophia in a giant hug, and Romy felt herself blushing. After a minute's rocking in silence, he pulled back and stroked the child's cheek. Sophia looked at him quizzically, pulling her blanket up and sucking the corner before burying her head in her mother's chest.

"My child," he said. And then: "She's tiny." He took one of Sophia's little hands in his own.

Romy felt bile burning the back of her throat. Had he said, *My child*? "Did you get a private letter from the Red Cross last year?" she asked.

Nina drew a sharp breath through her nose and shot Romy a pained look.

Wilhelm lifted his head and his brown eyes met hers. He slowly shook his head and scratched it. "No. No letter. Just your telegram three months ago from the JDC at the Peninsula with the ship details. Were you really at the Peninsula for nearly a year?" His face creased with confusion.

Romy's shoulders sank and her heart started beating double time. *He doesn't know.*

Wilhelm cocked his head to one side, a lock of hair falling across his brow as he narrowed his eyes. "You look different. Your cheeks are glowing. You look older."

"*Danke*," said Romy, too tired to be irritated.

Wilhelm reached out and tucked a curl behind her ear. "You're beautiful, Romy."

A snort erupted from her shoulder. Sophia had fallen asleep with her thumb in her mouth. Her little sausage legs dangled down and Romy curled her hand around a swinging ankle. She took a deep breath as she felt heat creeping up from her neck to her ears.

She thought this long year had erased how she felt about Wilhelm. But now that he was standing here in a white shirt, head tilted to the side and grinning from ear to ear, Romy's heart melted all over again.

Love felt different now. Fierce. All the nights in Hong Kong she'd lain on her mattress in the corner of the ballroom that had been converted to a dormitory for over a hundred women and children, praying for Sophia to make it through the night as she shuddered and shook through tropical fevers and monsoons. She had forgone her own portion of rice and mashed it so Sophia could have another. Caressed her chubby red cheeks with a thumb as the child slept. Or just lay awake beside her, feeling her tiny rib cage contract, enjoying the snorts and occasional kicks. There was no better feeling in the world than a warm sleepy child pressing against you for comfort, the little body curled perfectly against yours.

Romy had spent so many nights crying for Li and her lost child. Mother and child had disappeared into the dark chasm of loss brought by the war. First Benjamin, then Daniel. The Hos. Mutti and Papa. Li . . . Jian.

Romy stared into her daughter's dark eyes and saw them all. Where was Jian now? she wondered.

He'd tried to protect her in the ghetto. Then he'd disappeared. She stroked Sophia's feathery dark hair and tucked the little head back under her chin. She flushed a little and wiped some sweat from her brow as she remembered pressing her cheek to Jian's smooth chest as he consoled her. The steady rhythm of his breath.

How could she have doubted him? She'd always love him. Her heart felt broken.

Romy owed it to Jian to give their daughter a good life. To keep Sophia safe. It was a vow she'd made every morning as she took great strides along the deck while Nina gave Sophia her morning bottle of rice milk and crusts with honey, followed by some shaky toddles on the foredeck.

As Romy walked around the ship, she recalled Dr. Ho's lessons at Puyuan about order and duty, simplicity and restraint. The scent of chrysanthemum tea and sweet dates.

Romy had been given another chance. Another life. She was determined to build a new life for her child. It was the only way to honor Jian.

Romy would suck salty air deep into her lungs and enjoy the soft spray of ocean mist across her cheeks. She wasn't much for praying—how could He have permitted so much horror? When she closed her eyes she saw Jian being dragged away, or ghostlike bodies at Dachau stacked up like old newspapers. Bloodied babies in the gutters of Hongkew. With every step she railed against the God who seemed to have abandoned not only her people, but also the Chinese. And yet . . .

Each morning, as she rounded the deck on her second lap, she soothed herself with the Kaddish, hoping the words would sweeten the bitterness that threatened to flood her veins.

May there be abundant peace from Heaven. Amen.

Now Romy looked from her sleepy child to Wilhelm. After so much loss, the pain of her unrequited love for Wilhelm surprised her, beating loudly in her ears.

But she had Sophia now and that was all that mattered.

"I've been thinking about you nonstop since I got the telegram," said Wilhelm softly.

Romy stared at her feet, unsure how to read the affection in his tone. She'd made a mistake once before.

"I've started work in a bakery here. Bread mostly. It may be possible for me to take on a partnership one day. And I've rented a little house. A bungalow not far from here." She looked up and his eyes met hers. "It has three bedrooms." He blushed.

Romy could see Nina out of the corner of her eye, sitting on her brown suitcase. The red bandanna around her neck was flapping in the breeze. Her head was thrown back and her gravelly laugh could be heard across the docks as she shared a cigarette with two sailors in their pressed white suits. The young men were enthralled.

Romy repressed a smile. Nina was going to be just fine in this new land.

Wilhelm followed Romy's gaze to Nina, who stubbed out her cigarette under the sole of her brown pump and extended her hand for another.

"I take it that's our responsible guardian, Nina."

Romy smiled and nodded, her heart swelling with love for her dear friend.

Looking from Nina to Romy, Wilhelm cleared his throat and said, "I'd like you to move in with me. That is, unless you have already made other plans . . . But I just thought, as you seem to have such a bond with—"

"Sophia," Romy told him, with a sideways look to make sure no customs officials were nearby. "It means 'wise.' In Hong Kong they said Australia only accepted white refugees, so I thought this would be a good name." She paused, not trusting herself to say more.

"Sophia." Wilhelm smiled and repeated the name to himself. "A good strong name for a new Australian." He wiped his brow, revealing sweat stains under his arms. "Sounds strong—Sophia Shu." His smile dropped and his face turned serious. "Romy, I mean it: I'd like you to come live with me. With my daughter." He paused.

Romy felt dizzy. It was true: he thought Sophia was his child. She looked around, desperate for some water. She needed to tell him the truth immediately. Sort all this out as soon as they got away from customs. With this heat and her thirst it was impossible to think.

A man walked past and shoved a flyer into her hand. Not wanting to make eye contact with Wilhelm—how could she?—she began to read it.

Suggestions for your new country:
Try to minimise speaking German in public (i.e., on trams, out in shops, in school).

Nina already had the flyer and she waved it at the shocked sailors. "Dummkopfs," she snorted.

Romy shook her head and screwed the flyer up with one hand, too tired to read any more.

Wilhelm stepped closer, whispering to Romy with real urgency, "Of course, your friend is welcome to live with us too, if that's what you'd prefer."

He embraced her again and she could smell traces of sweat and sweet yeast on his skin. He stepped back and put his hands on Romy's shoulders before tilting her chin gently so she could look directly into his eyes.

"Romy, let's raise Sophia together. Start afresh."

Romy felt the blood rush from her face and she wrapped her arms around Sophia. Wilhelm was all she had ever wanted, and yet . . .

She coughed, willing some words to form so she could tell him his beautiful girl was dead, but her throat was too tight.

Sophia snuggled against Romy, pressing the jade pendant against her skin. Romy savored the cool of the stone and thought of Li and Jian.

Happy union for one hundred years.

With a rush of blood to the head, the words from Dr. Ho at Puyuan came back.

Order and duty, simplicity and restraint.

"Sometimes, Romy, the answer is simple," Dr. Ho would say. "The answer lies in front of us. *Wheresoever you go, go with all your heart.*"

Romy had been given another chance.

"What's going on over here?" said Nina as she sauntered over to where Romy and Wilhelm were standing. She shamelessly looked the handsome man up and down, then put her hand out and said, "Don't tell me, this is Wilhelm. Quite the hero, I hear."

Romy blushed.

"I'm Nina." She smiled as she shook his hand. "You were right, Romy. He is *ein gutaussehender Mann*."

Romy was so embarrassed she wanted to sink into the ocean.

Nina patted Sophia's head affectionately. "And what do you think of the little one?"

"She's perfect. We have a lot to catch up on. Too much."

As if on cue, Sophia coughed and twisted her head, switched sides, and nuzzled into Romy's neck.

"Can I—can I hold her?" he asked.

Feeling miserable, Romy lifted the sleeping baby and handed her to Wilhelm, who clumsily tucked her onto his shoulder. "She's heavier than she looks," he joked. "Must be her mother."

Nina shot Romy an indignant look, as if to say: *Are you going to let a man say that about you?*

"Sophia," he cooed. "How I've longed for this moment, to hold you in my arms like this. I promise, I'll take care of you, *meine Tochter.*"

My daughter.

As realization dawned, Nina's eyes narrowed and she looked from Wilhelm to Romy. She glared at Romy, brown eyes on fire, and Romy knew what she was thinking. *You have to tell him.*

But as Romy watched Wilhelm cradle the back of Sophia's head and whisper to her in German, his voice full of love, she felt her heart fill and sing. She'd made a promise to the people she loved most, and she'd let them all down. She couldn't shatter this moment. Break his heart.

Not again.

Too many lives had been destroyed by this war. She fingered her pendant and took a deep breath. It was time to make amends.

As Sophia started to stir, she rubbed her eyes and she looked up at the face of the strange man holding her. Instead of crying, her brown eyes widened and she reached up and grabbed his nose. Wilhelm laughed.

It was a fresh chance for all of them. Wasn't that what she'd been searching for since the train rolled out of Brenner Pass a lifetime ago?

She couldn't alter the past, but she could make things right for her daughter.

"Let's take Sophia home," said Romy as she squeezed Nina's forearm with force.

Nina nodded quietly, refusing to look at Romy as she leaned down for her bag.

Wilhelm gazed at Sophia in rapture as the toddler giggled, her nose scrunched up and her eyes wide. She looked just like Li.

Romy felt his loss. She recalled Li laughing among the peach blossoms in French Park, back when the girls were thirteen and Jian fifteen and he had taken a picture of them. It was the only photo she had, buried deep in her suitcase with Sophia's original birth certificate, her diary, and the Chinese medicine notes Jian had thrust into her hands at their last meeting.

Romy closed her eyes.

When she opened them again, Wilhelm was holding out his arm to wrap around Romy's shoulders while jiggling a shy Sophia on his other hip. His eyes were filled with gratitude, warmth, and kindness. For Romy, it was enough.

"Let's go home," he said.

Chapter 73

MELBOURNE, AUGUST 31, 2016

Zhang stood in the living room beside the bay window, one side of his face lit by the sun. Alexandra could see beyond him into the winter garden. The bare branches of the maple trees stretched into the blue sky. Dewdrops shimmered on long grasses rippling like waves with the wind. Alexandra felt peaceful. Content. She touched her pendant and trusted in fate.

Zhang walked over to the old mahogany sideboard and picked up the faded wedding photo of Wilhelm and Romy, taken on the steps of Melbourne's town hall. Opa had gotten down on one knee and proposed just six weeks after Romy had landed in Melbourne.

Alexandra didn't need to see the picture—she knew it by heart. Wilhelm wore a dark suit and tie, Romy an elegant wool crepe suit with a scalloped hem at the knee. She held her felt pillbox hat to stop it from blowing away as strands of curly hair whipped around her face. Their eyes were locked. A modern photographer would probably be fired: unfortunately, in the background to one side,

Nina was blowing her nose, her cheeks puffy and eyes bulging behind the handkerchief like a *Tatzelwurm* monster.

"I guess they *were* the real deal," said Zhang.

"In all my searching, that was the one fact I *never* doubted." She went to stand beside Zhang, using her sleeve to wipe the dust from the glass.

As she stared at the photo, Alexandra was suddenly five, on her first day of school. Her uniform was too stiff and it scratched the back of her neck. She longed to be in her swimsuit, running through the sprinkler on the front lawn, her feet bare on the scratchy brown grass. But she was curious about school and new friends. She planned to learn how to read that very first day! She'd told Opa and Oma so, and they'd chuckled.

Oma was tightening Alexandra's pigtails, retying navy bows, hitching up her socks, and twirling her around for a last inspection.

"Now you have your lunch box in your bag. You have a cheese and pickle sandwich for lunch and a banana for morning tea—"

"*Ach*, thank goodness. I missed the tram and thought I was too late." Nina jogged up the front footpath with her skirt hitched above her knees, round cheeks glowing like red apples and dripping with sweat. "I'm here for the photo."

They all busied themselves taking turns to be in a photo with Alexandra on the front steps. Nina insisted on coming and meeting Alexandra's teacher (*to check a dummkopf is not teaching our little genius*). Just before it was time to get in the car, Opa held up his hand.

"Wait." He ducked behind the front seat. "I got these on the way home from the bakery this morning." He pulled out a bouquet of white and green lilies bigger than Alexandra's head. They smelled like honey and cinnamon, and the happy look Opa gave Oma made

Alexandra buzz in her tummy and her arms in ways she couldn't quite explain.

Oma's eyes started to fill with tears. Alexandra frowned, puzzled.

"*Baihe hua*," said Wilhelm so softly Alexandra almost missed it. Oma touched his arm and he embraced her so tightly Alexandra thought he might crush her.

Alexandra understood now what it was to feel an energy so ferocious it sometimes hurt. And yet, when she was with Zhang she felt nothing but calm.

"You'll stay here, with your *oma*."

"Of course, but we can—"

Zhang smiled. "Well, the dahlias could do with a prune, and the grasses need chopping back. I might look at transplanting the peonies in the spring."

Alexandra stood on her toes and kissed him.

He pulled her close and tucked Alexandra's head under his chin. He smelled like the earth. Safe and solid. "I thought I'd stay for a bit—if your *oma* doesn't mind."

"I think she'd love it. I've been telling her for years she needs a gardener!"

Zhang laughed. "Well, I have drawn up a few more plans for the garden. Also, I figure you'll have some kind of plan of your own. If anyone can juggle three countries it will be you. We'll just take it as it comes."

Alexandra smiled and felt the sun warm her back as she reached for his hand and pressed it to her cheek. She was willing to take the risk.

Chapter 74

In the rearview mirror, Wilhelm watched Sophia in the back seat of his new Ford Customline, curling her legs so her thighs wouldn't stick to the olive-colored vinyl. It would be nearly ninety-five degrees outside, and the sky shimmered in the steamy haze.

"We promised Sophia an ice cream," said Romy as she shifted in her seat and flicked her shoulder strap back onto her smooth shoulder, where it refused to stay.

Wilhelm glanced across at his wife, admiring her strong shoulders and proud square jaw. He reached out with his spare hand and traced the line of her neck with his thumb, allowing it to rest on her sweaty collarbone for a beat. He felt her shiver, and a flicker of desire shot down his spine.

"Good idea. Why don't we *all* have one?" He pulled over to the curb so Romy and Sophia could jump out. They ran into the deli while he looked for somewhere to park.

Five minutes later he slipped into the narrow corridor that was Hans Deli. Romy was standing at the glass counter laughing with Hans, deliberating over the selection of hard cheeses and sampling a new type of fat green olive. She picked one off the counter and held it up as the strap of her yellow sundress slipped from her shoulder again. She blushed and ordered the tub of olives.

A diagonal shaft of light streamed through the window, bathing Romy in a warm glow and making her dress look golden. Her hair—usually so curly—was tugged back into a tight ponytail but threatened to unfurl with the humidity.

Wilhelm stood beside Sophia at the ice-cream counter. His daughter had her forehead pressed to the glass and was trying to choose between chocolate, strawberry, pistachio, and lemon sorbet.

"I wish I could have *three* flavors," she pleaded.

"There's not enough room in your tummy," said Wilhelm, ruffling her hair.

"I have a special place for ice cream. A second stomach." The little girl looked up and smiled, revealing a dark gap where both her front teeth should have been. She'd lost them almost a year later than her classmates. He'd had to pull the second one out for her just last night. Later, when she was asleep, he'd left a shilling under her pillow. He was spoiling her. Romy always teased him about it.

An elderly man who had been finishing a cup of coffee in the back corner shuffled past with a baguette under his arm.

"Romy? Romy Bernfeld? Is that you? I don't believe it. You made it to Melbourne!"

Sophia had her ice cream in hand—chocolate and strawberry—and slinked up beside her mother, leaning her head against her waist. "Look, Mama." She held the ice cream up before she noticed the man staring at her. "Excuse me." She lowered her cone and took a shy lick.

Romy's face was frozen, brow furrowed.

The child looked from the strange man to her mother, wrinkling her tiny nose in confusion.

The man with thin strands of feathery white hair stared at Sophia's pendant for a moment, before blinking twice.

No one spoke.

"Sophia, hop outside, near the car. Quickly! Before the ice cream starts melting all over Hans's tiles. Quick sticks."

It wasn't like Romy to be so brusque, and her slang felt awkward.

"Oh, Mama, no," whined Sophia, who clearly did not want to go back outside. Wilhelm didn't blame her. It was much nicer here in the air-conditioned deli.

"Oh, so this is your little one. Hello, S—!"

"Quickly, Sophia, I said go!" There was an urgency to Romy's voice. Not danger so much as fear.

"Listen to your mother, *Liebling*. Off you go." Wilhelm came to the rescue of his wife. Something about this man was troubling her and no doubt she would tell him all about it when they were back in the car.

He wiped his finger down the side of Sophia's cone to stop the melted ice cream from dripping onto the floor. He licked the chocolate off his finger and Sophia giggled. It was one of his favorite sounds.

He turned back to the old man. "Forgive my manners. I'm Wilhelm Cohen. Romy's husband."

"Hello." The gentleman beamed and shook Wilhelm's hand. "I'm Peter Adler. And I'm mighty pleased to see Romy and the little one doing so well." He scratched his head in amazement. "Was touch and go for a while there in Hong Kong."

Romy snapped out of her trance. "Yes, sorry! Lovely to see you, Dr. Adler, but I'm afraid we're in rather a hurry . . ." Beads of sweat were gathering at her temples and along the top of her lip. Her sundress hung lank against her body. It was as if Romy had started melting, along with the ice cream.

Sensing Romy's discomfort, Dr. Adler glanced at Wilhelm, then his wife. "We've settled in Perth, but I'm in Melbourne to visit an old friend for the weekend."

Wilhelm tried to steady himself by watching Sophia's ponytail swing back and forth as she skipped outside between the cracks on the footpath. She was playing an imaginary game of hopscotch. Ice cream spattered in brown and pink dots on the concrete.

The bags of bread, salami, and olives were hanging heavily from Romy's hands. "I'd better get these in the car," she said, staring at her feet as her chest flushed red. When she looked up, her eyes were locked in a silent plea with Peter Adler's.

What was the matter with her?

Dr. Adler opened his mouth as if to say something, then closed it. As Romy hurried out of the deli, a look of resignation crossed his face.

Wilhelm took another lick of his ice cream, pondering his wife's strange behavior.

Seconds later, Sophia ran back into the deli.

"Papa, are you coming? Mama's already in the car." She pulled a strand of hair away from her face and tucked it behind her ear.

Exactly as her mother did.

Her brown eyes were twinkling. "Or I could get another scoop?" Her voice was teasing. Hopeful.

Romy was always telling him Sophia was a proper daddy's girl. "Could wind you around her finger, that slip of a thing," she'd say, chuckling with pride.

"Not a chance, my girl." He made as if to tickle her tummy and she grinned, a deep dimple in each cheek. He gently poked her left dimple and turned back to the stranger.

"Lovely to meet you, Dr. Adler. I'd, ah, better go help my wife."

"I understand. Very nice to meet you, Mr. Cohen."

Wilhelm said, "You go on to the car. Tell Mama I'm just confirming next week's bread order with Hans—he wants a little extra."

"Okay, but don't take *too* long. It's so sticky in the car."

"You're the sticky one. Look, that ice cream is dripping onto your wrist." He grinned and shooed Sophia out of the shop.

When he turned back to Dr. Adler, the older man was putting on his hat. He was about to leave. Catching Wilhelm's eye, he muttered, "I'm sorry." He shrugged and suddenly looked tired. "It must be this heat. I'm too old now."

Wilhelm smiled and touched the man's sleeve. "This heat, this country . . . it's all new. My daughter—she loves it." He grinned. "She loves to swim, does Sophia. Lap after lap. Hates it when the winter rains set in." He was chattering nervously, trying to smooth over Romy's abrupt departure. Then he stopped smiling, before leaning toward the old man and speaking so low only they could hear: "You knew Romy well in Hong Kong?"

Dr. Adler looked down at his spotless black patent leather shoes and shrugged his shoulders. "I . . . ah . . . I treated her."

Wilhelm took a moment to work out how to ask his question. "By treated, Doctor, might you mean you delivered our Sophia?"

The doctor's head shot up and the two men eyed each other.

Hans's big belly laugh could be heard down at the far end of the deli, as he plucked a couple of salamis from hooks overhead. Two stout women were bickering affectionately in Polish at the glass counter as they patted their foreheads with hankies.

Wilhelm waited for the doctor to answer.

Eventually, Dr. Adler lifted his brows and nodded in silence. Apologetic. He shifted his weight uneasily between both feet.

"It was a difficult birth?" Wilhelm was suddenly desperate to know the truth. Romy's pregnancies slipped away no sooner than they began. He'd wanted to give her a child of her own.

A slow nod. "So much blood—a hemorrhage," he whispered. "But your wife, Romy—she was so strong. Brave. Insisted I save the child ahead of herself." He looked at Wilhelm and something shifted. "Romy said she'd already lost one child in the hospital bombing in Shanghai. This child was of the same blood, apparently. She was hallucinating, though. We very nearly lost her . . ."

The two men stood there for a minute in the hum of the air-conditioning as Hans wrapped up the salamis in white butcher paper, whistling.

"She had a friend—"

"Nina?" said Wilhelm.

The old doctor's head shot up with surprise. "Yes. That's her. I couldn't have saved them both without her. There was a terrible typhoon, you see. We had to make do in a bathroom."

Wilhelm tilted his head to the side and considered the doctor for a minute as he took a long lick of his ice cream.

So *this* was why Romy had insisted they tell Sophia she was adopted. She'd shielded him from further pain and trauma by not revealing Shu's death. Wilhelm's family was dead. Li was dead. Shu had died, but death no longer shocked him. He thought of the tiny baby smelling of rice milk snuggled along his forearm and was grateful he'd been given the chance to hold her. To smell her. The war sprawling across continents had taught him to treasure these pockets of bliss.

Romy understood Wilhelm's grief and guilt because hers ran just as deep. She'd always said her luck was bittersweet as she survived when her brothers didn't. It was the same for little Shu. But in letting Wilhelm believe Sophia was his blood, Romy had forfeited any claim to Sophia as her own. She'd chosen to protect his heart—to forget her own needs—to give him the family he so desperately wanted.

He pictured Li's lily hanging around Sophia's neck.

Eventually, Wilhelm smiled. "That's Romy for you." He didn't think it was possible to love her any more, but this secret, this gift . . .

The doctor patted Wilhelm's shoulder. In a low voice, he murmured, "I understand . . ."

"The war . . ." Wilhelm's voice started to break as his eyes filled with tears.

Dr. Adler's eyes were watering too, and he pulled out a hankie to wipe them.

Wilhelm finished his ice cream before he reached out and squeezed the man's arm. The doctor had saved his family. Without Romy and Sophia, his life would be empty. He was lucky.

"Thank you," said Wilhelm. Every bit of his heart felt full.

The old man nodded as a ripple of understanding passed between them.

Wilhelm gestured toward the door with a flick of his head. "I'd better go join my girls."

Dr. Adler smiled and tilted his hat. "*Mazel tov.*"

When Wilhelm opened the car door, Romy was shifting about in her seat, adjusting the circular skirt of her dress. Her legs were jittery. She spoke a little too quickly, glancing sideways at Wilhelm as if she were afraid to look him in the eye. "What took you so long?" she asked, before softening. "Sorry, I just had to get the food in the car—I don't want it to spoil in this heat." Her voice was light, but she was wringing her hands in her lap.

"Oh," he said casually, "Hans just wanted to order a bit more bread for Monday. He's selling more of the bread with *Brotgewürz* and the rye than he expected."

"Well," Romy said, a little too brightly, "that *is* good news."

Wilhelm reached over and grabbed Romy's hand, lifting it to his lips for a kiss. It smelled of peppermint. He held her hand against his cheek for a beat.

"Oh, Wilhelm, what's got into you?"

"Nothing! Just giving my beautiful wife a kiss. Do I need a reason?"

Romy turned to face him, her eyes narrowed. She gnawed on her bottom lip, as if expecting him to say something else.

"Did you . . . did Dr. Adler—"

"Want to know where to get the best whisky sour in town?"

"Are you teasing?"

"Never. The good doctor said he developed quite a taste for them at the Peninsula. Bit of a rogue, that one!"

Sophia giggled in the back seat and he caught her eye in the rearview mirror.

Wilhelm leaned over and straightened one of Romy's lovely curls, just like he had that first Chinese New Year together in the ghetto. He kissed her softly on the lips as Sophia exploded with more giggles and covered her eyes with her hands.

"I promise it was nothing worth worrying about. Hans wants to double his order—that's a good thing, right? The least I can do is have a bit of a chat and say thank you. He's been a great supporter."

Romy sat back in her seat and exhaled, tugging that stray piece of hair behind her ear, clearly relieved.

"Now let's get you home out of this heat. Can't have you melting. We might put the sprinkler on so Sophia can run through it a bit later."

Wilhelm pulled into the driveway of Puyuan, where dusty pink roses and Chinese star jasmine spilled over the fence and wafts of vanilla drifted in through the car window. After he finished mowing the front lawn, he was looking forward to stretching out on the daybed on the wide veranda to read the paper. Romy would take advantage of the quiet and spread out her anatomy books on the kitchen table to study her herbs, scribbling away at the old manuscript and tweaking her treatments. He was home with his girls and there was no place he'd rather be.

Insights,
Interviews
& More...

Meet Kirsty Manning

Tommy Devy

KIRSTY MANNING grew up in northern New South Wales. She has degrees in literature and communications and worked as an editor and publishing manager in book publishing for over a decade. Her first novel, *The Midsummer Garden*, was published in 2017.

A country girl with wanderlust, her travels and studies have taken her through most of Europe, the east and west coasts of the United States, and pockets of Asia. Kirsty's journalism and photography specializing in lifestyle and travel regularly appear in magazines and newspapers and online.

In 2007, Kirsty and her husband, with two toddlers and a baby in tow, built a house in an old chestnut grove in the Macedon Ranges. Together, they planted an orchard and veggie patch, created large herbal "walks" brimming with sage and rosemary, wove borders from chestnut branches, and constructed far too many stone walls by hand.

With husband Alex Wilcox, Kirsty is a partner in the award-winning Melbourne wine bar Bellota and the Prince Wine Store in Sydney and Melbourne. ∾

Author's Note

Ideas for *The Song of the Jade Lily* began on a family holiday in Shanghai. Like Alexandra's, my first visit there led to an explosive love affair. The city captivated me with its lights, spices, laneways full of sizzling dumplings and noodles with chili oil, markets, tables of writhing fish, and grand buildings.

But, always, the warmth of the local people pulled me back. During subsequent trips, I visited parks and gardens in Shanghai, then was wooed by the waterways and historic gardens of Suzhou. I've sampled the delights of acupuncture and downed many decoctions in the making of this book.

In Hongkou, I noticed a rusted Star of David inset into a doorway. What was this symbol doing in the middle of an old *longtang* laneway?

A visit to the nearby Shanghai Jewish Refugees Museum revealed that Shanghai had opened its doors to more than twenty thousand refugees fleeing Europe, at a time when no other country—including my own— would. How had I missed this crucial snippet of history?

I also discovered that before 1940 it was possible to be released from a concentration camp if you had a valid passport, visa, permit to take up residency in another country, and proof of transport. Such release was always subject to the prisoner leaving Germany within a limited time. The time frame and the documents needed varied from case to case. A Chinese visa did not guarantee passage to Asia. If you failed to leave within the stipulated time, you were taken back to the concentration camp.

And so ideas for *The Song of the Jade Lily* started to bloom. I started to think about friendship and loyalties, the price of love and the power of war. How hardship and courage can shape us. The unexpected bargains that are made when we make our own rules.

How do we shape our own identity? What does it mean to be generous as a person? And as a country? What is our duty?

While I was writing a story about refugees and how China opened their doors and hearts to the Jews, Australia was locking up refugees who attempted to come here via boat. Why haven't the lessons of history taught us to treat people better?

THE INTERPLAY OF history and fiction is a moveable feast. I made every endeavor to capture the feel of the era, but in some cases I took some liberties with time lines and the historical record, shifting some events and compressing others to serve the story.

For example, the letters to and from Daniel at Dachau are far longer than were permitted, and it was unlikely a letter from Germany would have been received in Shanghai as early as July 1945. Ships carrying European refugees from Hong Kong mostly arrived in Sydney, and the refugees stayed a little longer at the Peninsula.

Finally, there is no secret passageway off the foyer of the Fairmont Peace Hotel (the former Catnay), so please leave the wood paneling alone should you happen to visit.

What is both true and extraordinary is the courage, generosity, and fortitude shown by the following real-life people: Dr. Feng Shan Ho (no relation to my fictional Hos); Laura Margolis of the Jewish Distribution Committee, who saved thousands of lives in the ghetto with her food program; the remarkable Kadoorie family of the Peninsula Hotel; and Sir Victor Ellis Sassoon. ▶

Author's Note *(continued)*

There are mixed reports about the Japanese administrator, Ghoya.

The rest of my characters are fictional and I've tried to capture the era without crossing too deeply into any single person's experience.

I've tried to show how people can be shaped by circumstance. That very few people, or "sides" are wholly bad or good. There are a lot of grey areas in life.

There are differences in the usage of words, to reflect the time eras; Honkew/Hongkou, Soochow/Sozhou, Whangpoo/Huangpu.

In Chinese cultures traditionally the family name (or married name) comes first, before the given names. That order has been transposed in English translation for this novel.

In all cases I have tried to use the correct Chinese dialect and anglicized version. Shanghai in the 1930s was a melting pot of languages: Ningpoo, Gompo, Shanghainese, and successful merchants would have spoken Mandarin or Cantonese. I have made every endeavor to check the usage, but in the end referred to the professional translation agency LOTE Marketing to correct any Chinese terms. They translate many official documents into the Chinese languages for profits and not-for-profits.

The Song of the Jade Lily was read (and cross-checked!) by Horst Eisfelder, author of *Chinese Exile: My Years in Shanghai and Nanking*, and Sam Moshinsky, author of *Goodbye Shanghai*, both of whom lived in Shanghai during the Occupation and migrated to Australia afterward.

Both missed a second career opportunity as book editors, so keen was their eye for detail. I am greatly honored that they took time to read an early draft and answer endless questions about their respective time in the Hongkew Ghetto and French Concession.

Both gentlemen were enormously generous and patient as I tried to walk in another person's shoes and capture a small part of this Shanghai era. They took time to make me understand what it meant to be a refugee, to lose both your country and your family. I'm inspired by the lessons these gentlemen taught me about how to navigate life in a new country; how to be resilient, positive, and gracious. They are both very special men indeed.

Sydney academic and author Andrew Jakubowicz was incredibly helpful as I sounded out the historical plausibility of my novel.

From Shanghai, Jamie Barys of UnTour read the manuscript and checked my food and Chinese language references. I'm dreaming of when I can go back and redo what is possibly one of the best food tours in the world!

Chinese doctor (and dear friend) Sandie Griffiths read the manuscript and checked all things traditional Chinese medicine (TCM). TCM doctor Peter Gigante gave me a splendid tour of his Chinese herb garden where I discovered a love of the blue monkshood, and he also read a draft of the book to ensure my herb lore and Shanghai history was on track. I'm indebted to both TCM specialists for their expertise.

Any mistakes or misrepresentations in *The Song of the Jade Lily* are entirely my responsibility.

My sister, Prudence Hannon, accompanied me to Shanghai for my research visit. She proved to be a thoughtful, engaged, and fun traveling companion and I can't wait to hit Shanghai again soon.

A book comes to life only when there are readers. Writing is a solitary business and I'm ▶

Author's Note *(continued)*

grateful for a handful of honest and intuitive beta readers and editors. Thanks to Sue Peacock, Kate Daniel, Kate O'Donnell, Sara James Butcher, and Carolyn Manning for their generous and astute feedback. Annette Barlow and the Allen & Unwin Australia publishing team have been rocks—a joy to work with.

I'm most grateful for my agent Clare Forster of Curtis Brown Australia, and her lovely colleagues Kate Cooper and Lucy Morris of Curtis Brown UK and Stacy Testa of Writers House for their ongoing support.

A most sincere thanks to Tessa Woodward, Elle Keck, and the William Morrow team for their wisdom and enthusiasm, and the extraordinary US and UK cover for *The Song of the Jade Lily*.

A huge shout-out to my readers, who have been so kind with their feedback about this little-known pocket of Jewish history in Shanghai. You all seem to love food, travel, history, and gardens as much as I do! Thank you.

Finally, love and gratitude to my family: Alex, Henry, Jemima and Charlie—I'd cross every ocean for you.

THIS A WORK OF FICTION, and I am very respectful of all those whose lives have been touched by the periods and circumstances I write about. My thoughts are always with those people and their families. ❧

Reading Group Guide

1. Before reading *The Song of the Jade Lily*, were you aware of this particular era of Jewish history in Shanghai? What intrigued you most about this story?

2. This is a story about refugees and how China opened their ports and their hearts to the Jewish refugees fleeing Europe. Today, thousands of people around the world are seeking refuge, freedom, and a safe home and country for their families who may spend years in transit or stranded in isolated refugee camps. Why haven't the lessons of history taught us to treat people better? Did *The Song of the Jade Lily* make you stop and think about what it would feel like to be a refugee? What does it mean to be generous as a person? And as a country?

3. In Chapter 37, Cynthia talks about coincidence: "It's *yuanfen*," she said. "A fateful coincidence. Finding that matching photo was not about luck. Coincidence is about your fortune. Your future. The events of your life are linked to your history. Bad or good." Is it impossible to separate coincidence from the path of history, as we can only see the coincidence in hindsight? Do you believe in "fateful coincidence"?

4. The mystery of Alexandra's maternal grandparents provides the story's driving search. Did the answer surprise you? How did Alexandra learn and change during this search? ▶

5. Female friendship is a constant theme in *The Song of the Jade Lily.* Li and Romy are firm friends from the start, as are Kate and Alexandra and the wonderful Nina. How does each friendship grow and change over the course of the book? Is the bond between two female friends as important as that between family or lovers?

6. The theme of duty and generosity arises throughout the narrative. Nina feels a duty to protect younger girls in the Heim, the Ho parents feel a strong duty toward their country and pay a heavy price for it. Jian has a duty to carry on as a Chinese doctor, but also later in the novel he feels a strong duty to revenge his parents and fight for his country, as does his sister Li. Laura Margolis, Miss Schwartz, and "Divine Delma" all work altruistically for others, as do both of Romy's parents. How is Romy's sense of duty shaped by those around her? Is that sense of duty passed down through the generations, to Alexandra? If so, how?

7. Romy's family is forced to leave Vienna with just a suitcase and ten Reichsmarks. They took some clothes and medical books and equipment. What would you pack if you were forced to flee your home overnight and could take only one suitcase?

8. Alexandra's mother, Sophia, was always told she was adopted. It turned out that Wilhelm knew the truth all along, and understood that Romy's secret was her gift to him—and loved her all the more for the sacrifice. "So *this* was why Romy had insisted

they tell Sophia she was adopted.
She'd shielded him from further pain
and trauma by not revealing Shu's death. . . .
But in letting Wilhelm believe Sophia was
his blood, she'd forfeited any claim to
Sophia as her own." Do you agree with
Romy's decision to spare Wilhelm more
heartbreak and trauma? Should we make
allowances for decisions made during the
hardship of war?

9. Alexandra meets the landscape designer
Zhang Wei and he leads her not only to
nightclubs, noodle bars, and wet markets,
but also to the historic gardens where he
teaches her the Chinese principles of order
and duty, simplicity, and restraint. The Ho
family teaches Romy about traditional
Chinese medicine. Shanghai is a mix of
so many cultures, old and new. Did you
learn about Shanghai and come to love the
city as you would a character? How did
Shanghai seem to change across the two
eras? How did it stay the same?

10. How did hardship and courage shape all
the characters in the book? Alexandra did
not live through the war, and so her trauma
was more personal in the loss of her parents
and her search for identity. Even so, how was
Alexandra's life shaped by the trauma of her
grandparents?

11. In Chapter 19, Dr Ho talks about yin and
yang: "It's the energy in everything. At its
most basic, good and evil. We all have both
these energies in us. We just get to choose
which one we use more." Do you think ▶

that is true for all the characters in *The Song of the Jade Lily*? Was there any character that was wholly good, or evil?

12. Romy loves both Jian and Wilhelm, for different reasons. What were the differences between the men, and in her relationships with them? Were there any similarities? How did Romy's feelings for Jian affect her relationship with Wilhelm? Did that change over the course of her lifetime?

13. How did the theme of the lily—pure, unfiltered love—span across the different families, friendships, and generations?

14. Alexandra works as a commodities trader in Shanghai. So much of what we consume is manufactured in China, and so many of our natural resources go to China to be manufactured. How does *The Song of the Jade Lily* capture that intense energy that comes the growth of a large economy like China's? How does Alexandra highlight the issues associated with that growth?

15. There are a lot of food and recipes featured in *The Song of the Jade Lily*. Do you have a favorite dish from the novel? Would you try cooking any of them at home? ❧

Further Reading

The complete list of sources consulted in the writing of *The Song of the Jade Lily* is too long to detail here. Below is a list of essential resources.

TOURS
In Shanghai, I took a walking tour that included the former Hongkew Ghetto and Shanghai Jewish Refugees Museum with Dvir Bar-Gal of Shanghai Jewish Tours (www.shanghai-jews .com), who provided an astounding overview of the Jewish history in Shanghai.

I also undertook two walking tours of art deco buildings and the former French Concession with history enthusiast and longtime Shanghai resident Patrick Cranley and the Shanghai Art Deco team (www.shanghaiartdeco.net).

I spent a mouthwatering morning with Jamie Barys of UnTour exploring traditional and new Shanghai cuisine in the former French Concession (untourfoodtours.com).

With all these tours and interviews, any mistakes or misinterpretations are entirely my own.

BOOKS
Shanghai: China's Gateway to Modernity, Marie Clare Bergère (Stanford, CA: Stanford University Press, 2009); *Tales of Old Shanghai*, Graham Earnshaw (Hong Kong: Earnshaw Books, 2008); *Women Warriors and Wartime Spies of China*, Louise Edwards (Cambridge: Cambridge University Press, 2016); *The Diary of a Young Girl*, Anne Frank (Garden City, NY: Doubleday, 1952); *Passivity, Resistance, and Collaboration: Intellectual Choices in Occupied Shanghai, 1937–1945*, Poshek Fu (Stanford, CA: Stanford ▶

Further Reading *(continued)*

University Press, 1993); *Once Upon a Time in Shanghai: A Jewish Woman's Journey Through the 20th Century China*, Rena Krasno (Beijing: China Intercontinental Press, 2008); *Shanghai Modern: The Flowering of a New Urban Culture in China, 1930–1945*, Leo Ou-Fan Lee (Cambridge, MA: Harvard University Press, 1999); *Growing Up in Shanghai*, Dan Moalem (Sydney: Sydney Jewish Museum, 2007); *Goodbye Shanghai: A Memoir*, Sam Moshinsky (Armadale, Australia: Mind and Film Publishing, 2009); *The Chinese Medicine Bible: The Definitive Guide to Holistic Healing*, Penelope Ody (Alresford, UK: Godsfield, 2010); *Eternal Memories: The Jews in Shanghai*, Ren Panguang (Shanghai: Brilliant Publishing House, 2015); *Shanghai Policeman*, E. W. Peters (London: Rich & Cowan, 1937); *All Under Heaven: Recipes from the 35 Cuisines of China*, Carolyn Phillips (Berkeley, CA: Ten Speed Press, 2016); *Port of Last Resort: The Diaspora Communities of Shanghai*, Marcia Reynders Ristaino (Stanford, CA: Stanford University Press, 2001); *Escape to Shanghai: A Jewish Community in China*, James R. Ross (New York: Free Press, 1994); *Culture and Imperialism*, Edward W. Said (New York: Knopf, 1993); *Street of Eternal Happiness: Big City Dreams Along a Shanghai Road*, Rob Schmitz (New York: Crown Publishers, 2016); *Culinary Nostalgia: Regional Food Culture and the Urban Experience in Shanghai*, Mark Swislocki (Stanford, CA: Stanford University Press, 2008); *Policing Shanghai, 1927–1937*, Frederic Wakeman Jr. (Berkeley, CA: University of California Press, 1995); *The Complete Illustrated Guide to Chinese Medicine: A Comprehensive Guide to Health and Fitness*, Tom Williams (London: Thorsons, 2003); *Shanghai Splendor: Economic Sentiments and the Making of Modern China, 1943–1949*,

Wen-Hsin Yeh (Berkeley, CA: University of
California Press, 2007); *Man's Search for
Meaning*, Victor E. Frankl (London: Hodder &
Stoughton, 1964).

Various articles and documents, such as the letter
written by an American soldier to his parents
after the liberation of Dachau: www.slate.com/
blogs/the_vault/2014/05/02/holocaust_
liberation_letter_from_american_soldier_
at_dachau.html

MUSEUMS
Shanghai Jewish Refugees Museum
Jewish Holocaust Centre, Melbourne
Sydney Jewish Museum
Immigration Museum, Melbourne

Snippets plucked from original sources include:
The following words/ideas/extracts from
   *Passivity, Resistance, and Collaboration:
   Intellectual Choices in Occupied Shanghai,
   1937–1945*, Poshek Fu, op. cit.
Chapter 16: *Zhe Buguo Shi Chuntian* (*It's Only
   Spring*) (p. 72), original play by Li Jianwu.
Chapter 35: For details of patriotism through
   street performances, *huaju* (p. 71) was a term
   coined in the 1020s by Tian Han.
Chapter 36: The Neo-Confucian phrase "To
   starve to death is a very small matter; to lose
   one's integrity is a grave matter" (p. 57) is a
   famous quote from Song philosopher Zhu Xi
   (1130–1200). Also "Puyuan" is a figment of
   my imagination, but the original Puyuan
   (garden of simplicity) was a home owned
   by Zhu Pu, which, together with Zhou
   Lian's Spanish-style villa, became a site of
   "elegant gatherings" and salons where they
   discussed music, theater, and art; studied
   rare manuscripts; and dined on fine food
   and wine (p. 139). ▶

Further Reading *(continued)*

Chapter 45: Stories of beheadings and the phrase "Look! Look! The result of anti-Japanese elements" (p. 36) were originally referenced in Tao Juyin, *My Experience in the Solitary Island, Shanghai, 1979*, pp. 30–32. See also Zhu Meguhua, "The Brutality of Japanese Militarists in Shanghai," *Shanghai Difang Shi Zilao*, 1982, pp. 152–54.

Chapter 49: Neo-Confucian concept of *qijie* (p. 54) as interpreted by Wang Tongzhao in "Remembering Old Gentleman Tongxuan" in *Qui lai jin*, pp. 40–46.

Other original sources:

Chapter 13: The recipe names *basi pingguo*, *lü dagun* (Rolling Donkeys), Laughing Doughnut Holes, and Too Soft a Heart come from *All Under Heaven: Recipes from the 35 Cuisines of China*, Carolyn Phillips, op. cit.

Chapter 17: The pidgin lexicon is from *Tales of Old Shanghai*, Graham Earnshaw, op. cit., p. 38.

Chapter 24: The quote "Documents like this were often used as proof of emigration to secure the release of Jews imprisoned after Kristallnacht" is on the wall signage at the Shanghai Jewish Refugees Museum.

Chapter 26: Park Regulations, 1917 extract from *Tales of Old Shanghai*, Graham Earnshaw, op. cit., p. 136.

Chapter 28: Name of dentist and café on Chusan Road taken from image in *Eternal Memories: The Jews in Shanghai*, Ren Panguang, op. cit., p. 43.

Chapter 30: Excerpt from speech by U.S. president Franklin D. Roosevelt, December 8, 1941.

Chapter 40: Historical jade carving descriptions referenced in the article "Unraveling the Ancient Riddles of Chinese Jewelry," Ben Marks (www.collectorsweekly.com/articles

/unraveling-the-ancient-riddles-of-chinese
-jewelry).

Chapter 49: The proclamation issued by
Japanese authorities on February 18, 1943,
was published in most Shanghai newspapers.
Reproduced in *Eternal Memories: The Jews in
Shanghai*, Ren Panguang, op. cit. Full text also
reproduced at https://encyclopedia.ushmm
.org/content/en/document/proclamation-of-
restricted-zone-in-shanghai-for-refugees.

Chapter 62: The story of the sabotage to hand
grenades is fictional, but inspired by a true
account at the Shanghai Jewish Refugees
Museum.

Chapter 69: Singers' names, such as Golden
Voice, were sourced from https://en.wikipedia
.org/wiki/Seven_Great_Singing_Stars. ∾